The

PARIS

NETWORK

SIOBHAN
CURHAM

GRAND
CENTRAL

New York   Boston

Copyright © 2022 by Siobhan Curham
Reading group guide copyright © 2024 by Siobhan Curham and Hachette Book Group, Inc.

Cover design by Shreya Gupta
Cover images: Woman portrait © Jeff Cottenden Photography; Paris scene by Andrey Anisimov / Alamy Stock Photo; Airplanes © Shutterstock.com; Bookshelf © Getty Images
Cover copyright © 2024 by Hachette Book Group, Inc.

Grand Central Publishing
Hachette Book Group
1290 Avenue of the Americas, New York, NY 10104
grandcentralpublishing.com
twitter.com/grandcentralpub

Originally published in 2022 by Bookouture
First U.S. Edition: March 2024

Grand Central Publishing is a division of Hachette Book Group, Inc. The Grand Central Publishing name and logo is a trademark of Hachette Book Group, Inc.

The publisher is not responsible for websites (or their content) that are not owned by the publisher.

The Hachette Speakers Bureau provides a wide range of authors for speaking events. To find out more, go to hachettespeakersbureau.com or email HachetteSpeakers@hbgusa.com.

Grand Central Publishing books may be purchased in bulk for business, educational, or promotional use. For information, please contact your local bookseller or the Hachette Book Group Special Markets Department at special.markets@hbgusa.com.

Library of Congress Cataloging-in-Publication Data
Names: Curham, Siobhan, author.
Title: The Paris network / Siobhan Curham.
Description: First U.S. edition. | New York : Grand Central, 2024.
Identifiers: LCCN 2023041003 | ISBN 9781538759257 (trade paperback)
Subjects: LCSH: World War, 1939–1945—France—Fiction. | LCGFT: Historical fiction. | Novels.
Classification: LCC PR6053.U63 P37 2024
LC record available at https://lccn.loc.gov/2023041003

ISBN: 9781538759257 (trade paperback)

Printed in the United States of America

LSC

Printing 1, 2024

This book is dedicated to the memory of Tony Leonard. Your generous and loving spirit will never stop inspiring me.

I am not afraid. I was born to do this.
Joan of Arc

PROLOGUE

The novelist Gustave Flaubert once wrote that there is not a particle of life that does not bear poetry within it. As I sit huddled in the corner of the room that has become my prison, I try desperately to find something—*anything*—that could be construed as poetic. Somewhere in the building high above me, I hear the bark of German voices and the sharp clip of footsteps echoing along the corridors. But these sounds aren't poetic, they're torturous. I press Maman's tiny Nénette doll to my stinging lips and pray that the lucky charm is somehow able to work a miracle. She kept Wendell safe, didn't she? Perhaps she'll save my life too. But when I take the doll from my lips, I see that the white yarn of her face is now stained with my blood.

"Oh, Maman, what have I done?" I moan softly as I rock back and forth, every movement sending a sharp spike of pain through my body. People could die because of me. Innocent women and children. An image of their haunted faces staring out at me from the church looms into my mind. "I was only trying to do the right thing," I sob. "I was only trying to win liberty for France. I was only trying to win freedom for my daughter." I picture her cherub-like face giggling up at me, and then a montage of memories of her father tumble and twirl before my eyes like the glass beads in a kaleidoscope. His plane landing in the clearing, his feet pressed into the small of my back, his words the last time I saw him, in that soft American drawl: "I love you. I haven't stopped thinking about you. And when this is all over, I'm coming to get you. Both of you."

I take a deep breath and close my swollen eyes, and finally I am able to find the poetry.

1

LAURENCE—SEPTEMBER 1939

Once upon a time, my darling *maman* told me that we humans need stories more than we need food. I was seven years old and we were engaged in an epic battle of wills over pain au chocolat and school homework. Madame Bonheur, who owned the boulangerie next to Maman's dress shop, had just baked a fresh batch of the chocolate pastries and their scent was wafting through the open door on the breeze. How was I supposed to concentrate on my homework—writing a story about what I had done at the weekend—when the tantalizing aroma was sending my taste buds into such a frenzy? But Maman would not be budged. "We need stories more than we need food," she said again, twisting my long hair into a plait and handing me a pencil.

The story of my weekend is very sad! I wrote at the top of the page. *Now I know how Cinderella felt when her evil stepmother told her she could not go to the ball.*

But I was to learn the truth of Maman's statement just a few months later, when the demons that had plagued my papa for so long caused him to take his own life. Terrified of a world capable of delivering such a shocking and painful plot twist, I spent the rest of my childhood seeking refuge in books, befriending their characters and taking comfort in their neat and tidy happy endings.

I think of Maman now, as I look around her store. *My* store. When she died last year, I had half a mind to sell up and join my *bouquiniste* friend, Michel, in Paris, selling books on the banks of the River Seine. But there's something magical about my home town, La Vallée du Cerf, with its ancient forest and crooked stone buildings and winding cobbled streets. It's like a kindly grandpa of a place, and I could hear it whispering to me, through the breeze in the trees and the soft thud of the deer's hooves in the forest. *Stay, stay, and be a dispenser of words . . .*

"What do you think, Maman?" I whisper, gazing up into the old wooden beams lining the ceiling. "Do you like what I've done with the place?"

Turning my mother's dress shop into a bookstore named The Book Dispensary felt like the best possible plot twist after her death from pneumonia. Not only was it an opportunity to keep our family store, but it would finally enable me to turn my cherished hobby into a profession. You see, ever since I discovered my love of the written word, I have passed that love on, through prescriptions of books, short stories and poems, for any friend or neighbor in need. Over the years, as my book collection grew, I turned it into an informal lending library, issuing each prescription with a handwritten note: instructions on how the patient ought to take their remedy. Things like: *"Lose yourself in the kiss on page 27"* for the lovesick, or *"re-read the stanza about the ocean ten times before sleep,"* to calm those afflicted by night horrors.

But now I no longer have stacks of second-hand books to lend; I have shelves of books for people to buy and treasure forever. I look around the store. Every nook and cranny is lined with shelves made from the same dark oak as the beams in the ceiling. I go over to the poetry section at the back of the shop, close my eyes and take a volume from the shelf. It's a collection of poems by the writer Rainer Maria Rilke. I turn to a random page, praying for the prescription I need. The book opens on one of my favorite poems, "Go to the Limits of your Longing." My eyes are drawn to the fifth stanza where Rilke talks about letting everything happen to you, terror as well as beauty, because no feeling lasts forever.

I give a sad smile. As always, it's exactly what I needed to read. *Let everything happen to you,* I tell myself as I sit in one of the armchairs by the hearth. The fire I lit earlier is now crackling away, sending amber sparks shooting up the chimney. It's still early September, but there's already a chill in the air and the nights are drawing in, a fact I take great pleasure from, as surely there's no greater delight than curling up with a good book in front of a roaring fire. Madame Bonheur thinks it's a mistake to have armchairs in a bookstore. "You'll never get rid of your customers, Laurence!" she cried as soon as she saw them. "You are making it far too cozy." But she doesn't understand; she sells bread, not books. Her customers don't need to linger, trying to decipher which baguette is the perfect fit for their personality or their mood; every batch Madame Bonheur bakes is the same— and equally delicious, I might add. But buying a book is like choosing a friend or, if I may be so bold in spite of having tragically little experience, a lover. They're all so different. You have to be certain it's the right match before you take it home.

The bell above the door lets out its cheery tinkle and Luc walks in wearing his crisp new army uniform. It's a sight that makes my stomach clench. *"Let it happen to you ... it won't last forever ..."* Rilke whispers to me from the book in my lap and I try to calm my breathing. When Luc was first issued with his uniform after being called up last week, I made him put it on for me and he marched up and down, saluting merrily. It felt as if we were kids again, playing at dress-up. It didn't feel real, maybe because Luc is the most unlikely soldier. He's a bookkeeper by trade, and by personality, it has to be said. He likes life to be arranged into neat rows and columns, whereas I, well, I prefer life to dance and flow like the most lyrical of poems.

"I should have known I'd find you reading the stock," he says with a laugh. But he's tense, I can tell. Lifelong friends are as easy to read as well-loved books. I've seen his jaw clench like that many times in the twenty years we've known each other. Luc's no longer playing dress-up. He's about to leave on the train for the Maginot Line, to help guard France against the Germans, who recently invaded Poland.

I leap out of the chair and run over to give him a hug.

"I noticed that your window display is uneven," he murmurs into my hair.

"What?" I pull back and frown at him.

"You have a stack of ten books to the right of the mannequin but only six to the left."

Why do you always have to be so sensible? I want to say, but I manage to bite my tongue. Luc's need for order never used to bother me; in fact, I used to appreciate the way it grounded me. He was the perfect balance for my frequent flights of fantasy. But that was before we started courting. It's funny how things that seem endearing in a friendship can become infuriating once seen through the prism of romantic love. *He's about to go away and possibly have to fight the Germans,* I remind myself, and instantly my frustration melts.

"I meant for it to be like that," I reply. "The mannequin is supposed to be in the throes of a reading frenzy. She wouldn't give a fig how many books are placed where."

He looks at me as if I'm crazy, and I can't help wondering if the things he used to like about me when we were just friends have also now become annoying.

Outside, the cobbled street echoes with the sound of people walking by. I peer through the window and see more newly conscripted soldiers on their way to the station. Soon there won't be any young men left in the valley.

"I should go," Luc says quietly, and I have to fight the urge to pull him into the kitchen and lock him in the pantry.

He isn't going to die, I tell myself. *The Maginot Line is impenetrable.* And anyway, surely the Germans will have too much on their hands dealing with Austria and Poland.

"I'll walk you to the station." I fetch my coat from the chair behind my desk.

"Before we go . . ." he says.

I turn and see that he's holding a small box. The kind of box that normally contains jewelry. The *size* of box that would normally contain a ring.

"Oh no!" This time I'm unable to censor my thoughts and they burst from my mouth, seeming to echo again and again in the silence. *Oh no! Oh no! Oh no!*

"What?" He frowns.

None of my favorite proposal scenes in novels have been anything like this. The woman has never yelped, "Oh no!" She's either cried tears of joy or—in the case of one page-turner of an American romance—she's yelled, "Yes! Yes! Yes! Yes times infinity!"

"I don't—I'm not sure—I don't think we're ready . . ." I stammer, staring at the floor, too embarrassed to look at him. We've known each other since we were three; if we're not ready to get engaged now, then surely there's no hope for us.

"It's all right," he says softly. "It isn't a ring."

"It isn't?" Now I'm unable to disguise my relief.

I glance at him and see that he's smiling. But his eyes don't look happy; they look as if they're holding back tears. I walk over and place my hand on his arm.

"It's something I found when I was in Paris recently. I

thought you might like it." He hands the box to me. "I thought it might be of some comfort, while I'm away."

Now I know that I haven't been plunged into an unwanted marriage proposal, reality hits me once more like a punch to the stomach. My best friend in the world is leaving to go to war and I don't know when I will see him again.

I open the box with trembling fingers. Inside, on a bed of dark blue velvet, lies a silver pendant. A figure has been etched onto the silver, holding a sword aloft.

"It's your hero, Jeanne of Arc," Luc says with a smile.

When we were kids and our friend Genevieve still lived in the valley, we used to play battles in the forest with the children from a neighboring village. I would cast those poor children as the invading English army and we would be the loyal Burgundians, fighting for the freedom of France. As I had invented the game, I always cast myself as the fearless Maid of Orléans, leading us to victory, with a sword I'd fashioned from a stick. "It's been a long time since I played Jeanne," I laugh, touched that he's remembered my childhood hero.

"Yes, well, I thought you might need to call upon her strength, what with the store opening—and everything else..." He trails off.

"Thank you so much, it's the perfect gift. I have something for you too." I go over to the desk and take a pair of tiny dolls made from blue, white and red yarn from the top drawer. "It's my parents' Nénette and Rintintin dolls," I explain, handing Luc the male doll. "Maman gave my papa this Rintintin when he went to fight in the Great War. They were meant to bring soldiers good fortune. I shall keep Nénette and that way you are bound to stay safe, because the dolls have to be reunited."

"Thank you." He tucks Rintintin into his breast pocket and I wonder if he is looking so despondent because of my reaction to the jewelry box or because he thinks the doll is silly.

I have a moment of inspiration and hurry over to the armchair and pick up the collection of Rilke poems. "And I have another gift." I go back to my desk and take one of the small creamy sheets of paper I use for my prescriptions from the top drawer. I place the paper into my brand new Royal Quiet Deluxe typewriter, rumored to be the very same model Hemingway uses, wind it into place and type:

READ THE FIFTH STANZA ON PAGE 59 WHENEVER YOU'RE IN NEED OF FORTIFICATION.

I pop the prescription into the book by the poem. "Here," I say, handing it to him.

"Thank you." He smiles weakly.

Outside, the town hall clock begins striking seven.

"I have to go."

I nod, unable to speak.

We step outside and I lock the door. A horrible silence has fallen over us, laden with anxiety.

As we walk through the town square, past the memorial statue to the previous war—a soldier leaning on his rifle, head bowed—Luc stuffs his hands in his pockets and clears his throat. "I've only ever wanted you to be happy," he says quietly. And, because I've known him forever, I'm instantly able to read between the lines.

"I know," I reply, linking my arm through his. "And I've only ever wanted that for you too."

"I would never ask you to do something you didn't want to," he continues, gazing straight ahead.

I have no idea what to say to this. Part of me wants to lie, to try to convince him that my reaction to the jewelry box was just a moment of silliness and that of course I want to marry him one day. But I love him too much to lie. "Thank you," I murmur, wishing that none of this had ever happened. I don't want him taking this awkwardness with him like an unwanted gift.

We turn the corner and start walking down the hill. The air above the station is filled with the billowing cloud from a waiting locomotive. I feel sick as I think of where the train is going to take Luc. None of this feels real.

When we reach the station, the platform is crowded with other couples—the men in their uniforms, the women crying.

"I'm sorry," I say, standing in front of Luc and gazing up at him.

"Don't be." He puts down his suitcase and places his hands on my shoulders. "I'm going to miss you, Laurence."

In an instant, my anxieties disappear and all I see in front of me is my beloved childhood friend. "I'm going to miss you too, Monsieur Potato Face." Luc banned me from using my childhood nickname for him when he turned thirteen, but now he doesn't seem to mind. He smiles down at me, his eyes shiny with tears. "But I'm sure you'll be back soon."

He nods, but because I've known him forever, I can see the fear and uncertainty in his gaze.

The train whistle blows, but I don't want to let him go. *What if he doesn't come back soon? What if he doesn't come back at all?* I swallow hard. The last thing he needs is me falling apart.

I plant a kiss on his cheek. "Make sure you write to me."

"Of course." He picks up his case and goes over to the nearest train door.

"And don't forget the book. I've written you a prescription inside."

Now his smile reaches his eyes. "Thank you."

I watch as he gets on the train. The guard blows his whistle as he marches alongside the train, slamming the doors.

The Germans wouldn't dare attack France, I tell myself

as I force my mouth into a cheery grin. *The Maginot Line is impenetrable.*

I wave at Luc through the window in the door. The train starts chugging out of the station, and it feels as if it's taking part of my heart with it.

2

JEANNE—1993

Jeanne stared at the casket by the altar in front of her, overwhelmed by a choking sense of loss. But unlike the other mourners in the church, she wasn't just grieving for the loss of her mother, she was grieving for a lost opportunity. Now she would never have the chance to get close to Lorilee; she would never be able to chip through the invisible barrier that had always existed between them.

She looked at the lilies spilling over the polished beech wood and the wreath of pink and white carnations made to spell MOM—Danny's idea of course. On the pew beside her, her father, Wendell, gripped his walking cane, his fingers trembling slightly. A hush fell over the church as the priest stepped up into the pulpit and cleared his throat. How many funerals must he have had to officiate? Jeanne wondered. Did it all become mundane after a while, like a cubicle worker changing the ink in the fax machine, going through the motions of a dreary routine? She focused in on his face. Judging by his purple-tinged mottled skin, he had a fondness for more than just the communion wine. The way he was shuffling his papers gave the impression that he was nervous too—like a suspect with something to hide. She sighed; once a detective, always a detective. But she was no longer a detective, she reminded herself, and anger began burning through her sorrow as she remembered her last day in the job and that godawful meeting with Captain Fitzpatrick.

"I think maybe it's time you took early retirement, Jensen," he'd told her, although there was no "maybe" about the way he said it. "You've done thirty years. Have some fun. Buy a condo in Florida. Take up golf." As if moving to God's waiting room and endlessly hitting a ball at a hole would somehow compensate for the crap she'd had to endure over the past thirty years. There was no mention of the multiple times she'd risked her life, the multiple promotions she should have gotten, and let's face it, would have gotten, if she had a penis.

She focused back on the priest.

"Lorilee was a much-loved member of our community," he was saying. "She always had time for anyone in need."

Jeanne's pain grew with every gushing adjective. "Kind . . . loving . . . upstanding . . ." *No . . . no . . . no . . .* she wanted to cry. That wasn't what she was like at all. But of course it was—to everyone apart from her own daughter. She heard Danny sniffing on the other side of their father. Perhaps it was because Danny was the baby, or the boy, but Lorilee had never had a problem demonstrating her love for her "Dan-Dan" as she called him. There was no such fond nickname for Jeanne.

Stop it! she berated herself. *This is her funeral, for Christ's sake.*

The priest began telling the story of how Lorilee once rallied the community in their Chicago suburb to raise funds to help fix the church's leaky roof. "Her plum jelly raised hundreds of dollars alone," he chuckled.

Was this why her mom had been so distant with her, Jeanne mused, because she didn't share in her love of homemaking? But surely you don't have to be identical to a parent for them to love you. Danny and her dad were the perfect case in point.

Academic Danny had just accepted a position at Michigan University as a professor in art history, whereas their father had spent most of his working life building his landscape gardening business. But their differences seemed to bring them closer rather than force them apart, both of them always so eager to hear what the other was doing.

Perhaps Jeanne's career had made Lorilee resentful—she'd never seemed remotely interested in it and certainly didn't share in her father's obvious pride. At Jeanne's graduation ceremony, Lorilee had seemed more concerned with the weather, complaining endlessly about having to stand outside in the heat during the parade. And when Jeanne had been commended for her bravery in the line of duty—a huge achievement for a woman in the 1980s—Lorilee had adopted the shrill, slightly labored tone she usually reserved for shop assistants or people with special educational needs, saying, "That's *awesome*, honey," before immediately changing the subject to talk about how well her azaleas were doing.

Jeanne desperately tried to ignore the hurt now consuming her, but she'd plunged down the rabbit hole and seemingly there was no way back. It wasn't as if Lorilee had been cruel to her—or at least not overtly, not like some of the cases she'd seen over the years, where children had been starved or locked in cupboards or even had cigarettes stubbed out on them by their parents. Lorilee had been the model parent on the surface. As a kid, Jeanne had always had delicious, home-cooked meals, clean, smartly pressed clothes, and enough toys to open a store. She was never neglected physically. But emotionally . . .

Geez, pull yourself together, you're not a kid any more, you're almost fifty. Jeanne shifted in her seat. Perhaps it was the timing of events that was making her feel so vulnerable. Her mom dying just two weeks after her being crowbarred out of her job and into early retirement was certainly what you could deem a life crisis—or two life crises, in fact. And, to top it all, her fiftieth birthday was now looming like a searchlight sweeping her life for mistakes and regrets.

"And now Wendell is going to say a few words about his beloved wife," the minister said, snapping Jeanne back into the present.

"Are you OK, Pops? Do you need any help?" she whispered as she got up to let him out. Glancing down the aisle, she saw that the church was full to the rafters.

"I should be all right, honey," Wendell replied.

She sat back down and watched as he slowly made his way to the pulpit. He'd been walking with a cane for a few years now, although he'd confessed to Jeanne that he only used it at first to get priority treatment in restaurants and stores. "Holding this thing is like having a VIP pass," he told her with his customary boyish grin. "Folks treat me like royalty."

Now, though, Wendell's arthritis meant that he was leaning on the stick for real. Jeanne held her breath as he went up the pulpit steps. Thankfully, he made it in one piece.

"Well, hello," he said, his voice cracking slightly. "Thank you all so much for coming." He clenched his hands into fists, clearly nervous at speaking in front of so many people. "A lot of you know that Lorilee and I have known each other—sorry, *knew* each other—since childhood, but what you might not know . . ." He paused. ". . . is how she saved my life after the war."

Jeanne sat up straight. Wendell never talked about the war. She knew he'd been in the air force and stationed in Britain, but that was about it. She'd learned long ago not to push the subject.

"Most of us who were involved in the war don't like to talk about it," Wendell continued, "but I'll say this—the war changed me—and not for the better. But Lorilee didn't mind, or at least she never let on that she did. She loved me warts and all and she never stopped loving me, in spite of some huge challenges." He looked at the casket and wiped his eyes. "Thank you, sweetheart, for putting up with me."

Jeanne watched, mesmerized. She'd always had her Pops down as the tolerant, unconditionally loving one in her parents' marriage.

"And now I'd like to read a poem," he continued.

Jeanne shot a sideways glance at Danny. He was clearly thinking the exact same thing, judging by his raised eyebrows. Jeanne couldn't recall Wendell ever saying the word poem before, let alone reading one.

He fumbled in his suit pocket and pulled out a scrap of paper—scrap being the operative word, it looked ancient. "This a poem by someone called Anne Brontë," he said. "It's called, 'Farewell.'"

Once the service was over, a party of close friends and family returned to Jeanne's parents' home in Clarendon Hills. Thankfully, it was a warm spring day so they were able to gather in the beautiful backyard. Jeanne drank in the bright splashes of color in the flower beds, the bluebells and tulips and the last of the daffodils, all framed by the dark green wall of pine trees bordering the property. This was the one thing Jeanne missed about living outside of the city—how the wide open spaces and fresh clean air helped her to breathe, mentally as well as physically. She stood for a moment drinking it all in, zoning out the chatter of the mourners and focusing on the sweet song of a bird perched in one of the apple trees.

"Hi, Jeanne." The nasal voice of her aunt Shirl broke her from her reverie, causing her heart to sink. Shirl was a thin streak of a woman, as sour as vinegar and tighter than Midas's fist. Jeanne took a deep breath and forced herself to smile.

"Hey, Shirl. How you doing?"

"Hmm, as well as can be expected." As Shirl eyed her up and down, Jeanne could practically read her thoughts: *I'm not sure that a trouser suit and boots are appropriate attire for your mother's funeral. And why is your hair so short?* "I hear from your father that you've taken early retirement."

"Uh-huh."

"It's all right for some." She sniffed, her thin lips pursed.

"I'm actually not that thrilled about it."

Shirl stared at her. "Why not?"

Jeanne sighed. Why had she told her she wasn't happy? Why hadn't she just lied? There was no way she wanted Shirl knowing the real reason for her early retirement; there was no way she'd understand the crushing disappointment she was currently feeling. "I just don't know what I'm going to do with my days," she joked, trying to save the situation.

Shirl gave one of her intensely annoying sarcastic snorts. "Some people are never satisfied. I remember your mom telling me . . ." She broke off and stared at the glass of wine in her hand.

"What?" Jeanne's hackles began to rise.

"It doesn't matter."

"It does. It matters to me what my mom said about me."

The tips of Shirl's pale cheeks began to flush. "She just said that you—you could be very ungrateful."

The thought of Lorilee and her sourpuss sister sitting around sniping about her hurt way more than Jeanne wanted to admit.

"Well, maybe if she'd been a little kinder to me things would have been different," she muttered.

Shirl's pale cheeks flushed red. "If *she'd* been kinder to *you*?" she echoed indignantly. "I think she was more than kind to you, given the circumstances."

"What circumstances?" Jeanne watched as Shirl glanced up the garden to Wendell, who was chatting away to Danny and his wife and kids. The sunshine was causing his silver hair to glow against his weather-beaten skin.

"It's not my place to say any more," Shirl replied with a smugness that made Jeanne want to scream.

"It's a bit late for that now, don't you think?"

"You need to ask your father," Shirl replied before scurrying off up the garden, clutching her purse and drink in her claw-like hands.

Jeanne stood watching her, trying to process what had just happened. What did Shirl mean, saying Lorilee had been more than kind to her given the circumstances? What circumstances? And why did she need to ask her dad about it? She looked back at Wendell, who was now entertaining Danny's youngest boy with his infamous disappearing dime trick. Should she tell him what Shirl had said? Should she ask him what she'd meant? She decided to wait for an appropriate moment, when they were alone.

After what felt like an endless round of polite conversations and that exhausting forced jollity unique to funerals, the last of the mourners departed. Although it had been a warm day, there was a definite chill in the air now the night was drawing in.

"Shall I light a fire?" Jeanne asked as she and Wendell made their way into the living room.

"That would be great," Wendell replied, slowly easing himself into his armchair. There was a time when the large, leather-bound chair had been a perfect fit for Wendell, back when he was landscaping all day. But now that his once broad shoulders had begun curving inwards, the chair seemed to dwarf him. It was a sight that brought a lump to Jeanne's throat.

She took some logs from the basket by the hearth and started building a fire.

"It's the funniest thing..." Wendell said as she added some balled-up sheets of newspaper as kindling.

"What is?"

"Watching you do that."

"Lighting the fire?" She turned and looked at him. "What's funny about it?"

"You look so like . . ." His eyes clouded over and he looked away.

"Like what?"

"A ghost," he murmured.

Jeanne felt a prickle of concern, trying to remember the warning signs of dementia. Hopefully he'd just had one too many drinks at the wake. She lit the kindling and went and sat in the armchair facing his. "How are you feeling, Pops?"

"All right I guess. It's been quite a day." He gave a sad smile. "But I think we did your mom proud, don't you?"

She nodded; perhaps now would be an opportunity to mention her conversation with Shirl. "Can I ask you something?"

"Of course."

"Did Mom ever say anything to you about me . . . about me being difficult?"

He frowned. "What do you mean?"

"Did she ever complain that I was never satisfied?"

His frown deepened. "I don't understand. Why are you asking this?"

"It was just something Shirl said to me this afternoon."

He shifted upright. "What did she say?"

"She said that Mom complained to her that I was always ungrateful. And then I might have said something that made things worse . . ."

"No!" He raised his eyebrows in mock surprise, as if he couldn't believe she'd be capable of any kind of hot-headedness.

" 'Fraid so. I said that maybe if Mom had been kinder to me, I would have been less difficult."

"If Mom had been kinder to you?" He gave Jeanne a concerned look. "She was kind to you, wasn't she?"

Jeanne bit her lip. The day of Lorilee's funeral was hardly the time to unleash her years of bottled-up hurt upon her dad.

Besides, she had her newly booked therapist for that. "Let's just say that Mom and I had our issues," she said diplomatically. "Anyways, Shirl had a hissy fit and told me that Mom had been very kind to me, given the circumstances. But when I asked her what circumstances, she clammed up and said I should ask you."

"Oh." Wendell stared into the fire. A piece of wood cracked, sending sparks spiraling like fireflies up the chimney.

Jeanne watched him and waited, trying to analyze what his "oh" could have meant. Was it an "oh" of recognition or confusion? "I'm sorry, Pops, I don't mean to get all heavy, especially today, it's just that I can't stop thinking about what she said."

"Yeah, and I bet that old misery guts fully intended to say it," he replied bitterly.

Jeanne stared at him, surprised. She'd never heard Wendell talk badly of Shirl before. "What do you mean?"

"I mean, I don't think it's any coincidence that she let it slip today."

"Let what slip? What's going on, Pops?"

He sighed, then nodded to the drinks cabinet in the corner. "I think we're both going to need a stiff drink."

"OK." Jeanne went over and poured shots of brandy into two crystal tumblers, then added another splash in each for luck. She took the drinks over to him, then, rather than go back to her chair, she sat on the rug by his feet. It was something she always used to do as a kid, usually with her nose in one of her favorite Nancy Drew books.

"There's something you need to know, honey, but there's no easy way for me to say it," he began.

"OK." She turned and looked at the fire, hoping that a lack of eye contact would make it easier for him to open up.

"Your mom . . ."

"Yes . . ."

"Well, she wasn't your biological mother."

"What?" Jeanne turned and stared at him in shock.

"She loved you as her own but—"

"Whoa, hang on? Am I adopted?"

"No."

"Then how is she—was she—not my mom?"

"Someone else was your mom."

"And who is my dad?"

"I am, of course."

"Pops, given what you've just told me, I don't think there's any 'of course' about this." She shook her head in disbelief.

"You're right, I'm sorry." He cleared his throat and took a sip of his drink. "I'm your father, but your mother—your birth mother—was someone else."

"Wait—what? Did you and Lorilee use a surrogate? Was that even a thing in the 1940s?"

"No."

Jeanne wracked her brain for another possible explanation. "Did you . . . did you cheat on Lorilee?"

"No! She and I—we didn't get married until after you were born."

"But I . . . I thought you were childhood sweethearts."

He shook his head. "We were childhood friends."

Jeanne took a moment to process this information. "So, you were with someone else and you got her pregnant, but then you and I ended up with Lorilee?"

"Yes."

"But that doesn't make sense. What happened to my real mom?" It felt as if Jeanne's world as she knew it was being shaken like a pair of dice and she had no idea how things were going to land.

He looked down into his brandy and she noticed that his hand was shaking. "She . . . I . . ."

It hurt her heart to see him looking so upset, but surely she was entitled to know the full story. She looked back at the fire and took a sip of her drink. The heat from the flames and warmth of the brandy was making her face burn and her brain foggy. "Why didn't you tell me Lorilee wasn't my real mom?"

"It was part of her conditions."

"Her conditions?" She stared at him blankly. It was as if he was talking double Dutch.

He nodded. "For marrying me and taking us both on. She wanted to bring you up as her own. That's why we moved from Missouri to Chicago after the war, so we could have a fresh start."

But why would her birth mother have allowed this? A terrible thought occurred to her. Maybe her birth mother hadn't wanted her. "How long were you with my real mom for?"

His face flushed and he looked down into his lap. "Uh—two nights."

Jeanne almost spluttered her mouthful of brandy all over the rug. "Two nights?"

"We met during the war."

"Right." So she'd been the product of a two-night stand, a quick liaison during a blackout, probably, and that's why her birth mom hadn't wanted her. Great. She'd been weirdly excited to discover that she wasn't genetically related to Lorilee, but now all she felt was crushing disappointment.

"Are you all right, honey?" he asked.

"Not really. I can't believe you guys didn't tell me."

"I had to respect Lorilee's wishes."

Jeanne thought back to his eulogy. What was it he'd said about Lorilee loving him? "In spite of some huge challenges." That would have been her then, the huge challenge of being another woman's kid. No wonder Lorilee had always been so strained with her.

She stumbled to her feet. "I think I'm going to hit the hay. It's been a long day."

"Don't go, honey. Please." He grabbed hold of her wrist. His grip which had once been so strong now felt as feeble as a child's. Everything suddenly felt so heartbreakingly sad. "You must have some more questions."

"Not really." She pulled away and headed for the door. "I think I've figured it out. I was the product of a one-night, no, sorry, *two*-night stand during the war, and your dirty secret, but Saint Lorilee saved the day by taking on the huge challenge of pretending to be my mom." Try as she might, there was no way she could keep her bitterness from oozing out.

"There was nothing shameful about the way you were conceived," Wendell said, so forcefully it made her stop in her tracks.

"What do you mean?"

He took another sip from his drink. "Your mom—your real mom—was a wonderful woman. She was a hero."

"Steady on, Pops," Jeanne quipped, trying to lighten the mood.

"She was . . ." His voice wavered and she saw that his eyes had filled with tears . . . "She was the bravest person I ever met."

Jeanne noted his use of the word "was." But was he using the past tense because her real mom was dead or because Wendell no longer knew her? She went back over to the rug. "All right, I have some more questions . . ."

3

LAURENCE—MARCH 1940

On the first day of March 1940, I wake to find an icicle dangling from the top of my bedroom window—on the inside. I get out of bed and get dressed as quickly as my trembling fingers will allow. Then I reach for my papa's old greatcoat, hanging on the back of the door, and put it on over my dress. It's been one of the longest, bitterest winters I can remember, and I've taken to wearing Papa's coat as a kind of housecoat. I dread to think what it must be like for Luc and the rest of the town's young men, all freezing in their camps and forts along the Maginot Line. Luc downplays the weather in his letters, but I know how much he hates the cold.

I hurry down the steep narrow stairs and light a fresh fire in the store. Then I go into the kitchen and put the kettle on the stove. I feel in the pocket of Papa's coat for Luc's most recent letter, nestled next to my Nénette doll, and read it again while I wait for the water to boil.

Dear Laurence,

I'm happy to report that my English is now almost as good as yours, thanks to the British soldiers I've been billeted with. They're actually really nice—I only hope the ghost of Jeanne of Arc doesn't read this!

The village nearest to our post has been evacuated. It's a very strange sensation, walking around the streets. It's like a ghost town. I keep thinking of when you, Genevieve and I were children. Oh the adventures we would have had here! Speaking of which, yesterday, when I was taking a stroll through the village, I heard a sudden burst of music. It sounded strangely familiar and yet wonderfully bizarre all at the same time. I followed the sound until I reached the village church. By that time I had worked out that the tune was "Moonlight Serenade" by Glenn Miller, but it was being played on a church organ, making it sound more like a hymn! I crept up the steps and peered inside the church, to find two of the English soldiers I'm stationed with playing the organ! They were having a great time, I can tell you! And I have to admit, so was I, as I sat on the steps and listened. It was wonderful to hear a church being filled with joyful music again. For a moment I was able to forget why I am here.

In other news, I've been spending most of my spare time creating puzzles for the men to try to solve. I have to say, it's nice having something to tax my brain, and the men seem to enjoy them too.

I hope The Book Dispensary is doing well. I can't think of a better gift than to receive one of your prescriptions. I'm still loving the Rilke book, and I read my poem every time I hear gunfire in the distance, to remind myself that nothing lasts forever—not even a seemingly endless phoney war.

Very much looking forward to your next letter and your latest update about the Valley Players—I love how there's always more drama backstage than onstage in our amateur dramatics society!

Love always,

Luc

At the thought of the Valley Players, I groan. Violeta Dupont, the company treasurer and town busybody, is insistent that our next production be an abridged version of *Romeo and Juliet*. How she could think that a tale of two lovers ending in tragedy is appropriate at a time when most the town's young men are away at war is beyond me. But Violeta will not be budged, and as she holds the purse strings—and indeed fills the purse from the over-flowing coffers of her inherited estate—we have no choice but to go along with it.

This evening, the Valley Players committee, of which I am a reluctant conscript, is meeting to discuss the casting. Given that most of the remaining men in the town are over sixty, I dread to think who will end up playing Romeo. Still, my account of the meeting should provide an entertaining dispatch for Luc, and for that reason alone it will be worth it.

I make a cup of coffee and go and sit in front of the fire. It's been six months since Luc left, six months since I opened The Book Dispensary. I look around the place and feel the tension in me ease. With Genevieve and Luc both now gone, I'd worried I'd be lonely, but this place has become a sanctuary—and not just for me. I spend most of my days prescribing love poems for the wives of soldiers, and adventure stories for the men too old to go and fight, but who are chomping at the bit for some action nevertheless. It's not quite how I'd imagined life in The Book Dispensary to be, but who could have imagined France becoming caught up in a phoney war, waiting, waiting, waiting, for something to happen.

All of this early-morning philosophizing has made me hungry and I'm about to go next door for one of Madame Bonheur's freshly baked croissants when there's a hammering on the front door. I look over and see Charlotte Martel standing outside. Charlotte Martel is the type of character who appears in a novel as the feisty heroine's nice but slightly less interesting friend. The perfect calm and kindly foil for the heroine's faults and foibles. But as I go over to unlock the door, I see that there's nothing calm about Charlotte today. Tears are streaming down her face and her light brown hair, which is normally pulled back into a neat bun, is hanging loose in disheveled tendrils.

"Charlotte, what on earth's happened?" I say as I open the door.

"It's Jacques," she gasps, a shiny trail of snot coming from her nose. "He's dead."

"What? No! Come in." I pull her inside and sit her down by the fire. "What's happened?" I ask, crouching in front of her.

"His unit was bombed, by the Germans," she sobs.

My heart skips a beat as I try to recall where Jacques was posted. Was he stationed with Luc? Has Luc been bombed too? Then I remember that Jacques had been sent further east and I'm ashamed at the relief I feel. "Oh, my dear, I'm so sorry." I grab her hands and squeeze them tightly.

"I thought . . . I thought . . . it was just a phoney war. I didn't think the Germans would start killing the French. I didn't . . ." She starts sobbing again.

"I don't think any of us did. Oh, Charlotte. Here, have a drink." I pass her my cup of coffee.

"Thank you. I had to come and see you. You've been such a help to me since he's been gone."

As she takes a sip of the drink, I wrack my brains trying to think of something suitable to say, but my words appear to have scrambled themselves into a dull and pathetic mess, incapable of meeting such a challenge. I need the help of a far finer wordsmith.

"Wait here," I say, "I have something for you."

I go over to the poetry section, tucked into the nook at the back of the store, and fetch a collection of Anne Brontë's poems from the shelf. Then I go over to my desk, put a piece of paper in the typewriter and type Charlotte her prescription.

IN TIMES OF DESPAIR, READ THE POEM "FAREWELL" AND LET THE FIRST FOUR LINES BE A BALM TO YOUR ACHING HEART. YOU WILL NEVER BE PARTED FROM YOUR MEMORIES OF JACQUES. MAY THEY ALWAYS BE A COMFORT TO YOU.

LAURENCE

I tuck the prescription inside the book beside "Farewell," and take it over to Charlotte. "Here's your remedy—I hope it helps."

"Thank you." She clutches the book to her chest. "I . . . I can't imagine Jacques being dead—he was so full of life."

I nod as a memory of Jacques sitting at the hotel bar comes back to me. He's holding a glass of beer, his face as shiny and red as one of the apples from his orchard, and he's snorting with laughter at a joke he just cracked. He always laughed the loudest at his own jokes, but that only made them seem funnier. My eyes sting with tears. He was so strong and full of spirit, but even that isn't a match for a German bomb. A chill passes through me and I pick up the poker and stoke the fire.

"I should go and see the priest," Charlotte says, wiping her tears.

"Yes, do. Père Rambert will pray with you." Another memory enters my mind, of the Père praying with me when both Papa and then Maman died. Père Rambert isn't just a Father in title; he is like a loving papa to the whole town. If anyone can comfort Charlotte now it will be him.

I see Charlotte out, hugging her tightly before she leaves, and gaze after her into the square. The memorial soldier in the center of the square is shining rosy gold in the rays of the rising sun. Will we need another memorial by the time this new war is over? A vision forms in my mind of Luc's name being chiseled into a pale stone plinth . . .

Stop it! I tell myself crossly. There's no way the Germans would be stupid enough to take on the might of the French and British armies. The bombings that have happened recently are just skirmishes, Nazi posturing. Life will soon return to normal, and I must carry on as normal.

I turn the sign on the shop door to OPEN.

For the rest of the day, all talk in the store is of Jacques, and I end up prescribing numerous copies of Jane Austen novels to try to provide some light relief for the town's women, now even more anxious about the safety of their men. By the time I turn the sign to CLOSED again, I have a pounding headache. The last thing I feel like doing is going to the Valley Players casting meeting, but I don't want to get on the wrong side of Violeta as she has the sharpest tongue in the valley and has been known to destroy a person's reputation on just the strength of her adjectives.

After a quick supper of chicken and tarragon broth and one of Madame Bonheur's baguettes, I make my way across the square to the Hotel Belle Vue. As its name implies, the hotel boasts one of the best views in town, looking out over the square and across the valley, to the lush green forest that surrounds us. But just like the rest of town, the hotel seems to be a stiller, quieter version of itself since the men left. It's as if the entire valley is holding its breath, waiting to see what will happen.

Down at the station, the shriek of a train's whistle pierces the silence. I hurry up the hotel steps and into the bar. Before France entered the war, there would always be a jazz band playing in the evenings and the townsfolk would gather to chat and laugh and dance the cares of the day away. Now, the only musician left is an aged trumpet player named Tomas. At first, he carried on playing solo in the evenings, but it wasn't the same. For a start, his fingers are so swollen with rheumatism it's a rare thing if he hits the right note and he's always a beat or two behind. This didn't matter when he had the rest of the band to drown him out, but, left to his own devices, well, let's just say he had everyone wincing rather than dancing. Thankfully, Madame Bonheur had a discreet word with him, telling him that, as much as we loved his playing, it felt disrespectful to the other members of the band to enjoy music while they were away. Mercifully, Tomas agreed to stop playing; the basket of pastries Madame Bonheur offered as a consolation no doubt helped soften the blow.

I arrive in the bar to find the Valley Players committee sitting at the small round tables rearranged in a semicircle, talking in hushed tones.

"Ah, Laurence, there you are," Madame Bonheur calls, gesturing at me to join her. When we were kids, Luc, Genevieve and I used to joke that, due to her generous rolls of soft pale flesh, Madame Bonheur was made from the same dough she baked her bread from. If anything, she's become larger over the years, but I love her softness and the way she always smells of sugar and cinnamon—she's the closest thing I have to a mother these days. "Come, sit down," she says, tapping the empty chair beside her. "We were just talking about poor dear Jacques and Charlotte."

"Such a terrible loss," Père Rambert says from his stool at the bar. As always, he's wearing his long black cassock and white collar, his untamable graying hair springing from his head in all directions. Ever since I was a child, Père Rambert has had the power to instantly make me feel calmer. There's something so constant and solid about his tall broad frame clad all in black—a pillar of strength in any storm.

"It really is an awful loss." Violeta sniffs from her seat at the head of the semicircle. Her hair is set in its usual helmet of tight dark waves and her thin lips are tightly pursed. "I'd been so hoping she'd play Juliet."

"I was talking about the loss of Jacques," Père Rambert mutters before taking a sip of his red wine.

"I was looking forward to playing her Romeo," Leon the blacksmith says with one of his lecherous, toothless grins.

"You are playing Romeo?" I ask, astounded. A lifetime of drinking and smoking has not been kind to Leon and has added at least ten years to his appearance. Given that he's in his sixties, this definitely does not make him leading man material.

"Do you have any other suggestions?" Violeta peers at me like a hawk over the top of her round, wire-framed glasses.

I look around the bar. Aside from Père Rambert, the only other men present are Tomas the trumpet player, who is sitting in the corner puffing away on one of his potent cigarettes, and the owner of the hotel, Monsieur Tissier, who is standing behind the bar, absentmindedly picking at the hairs sprouting from his ears. I picture William Shakespeare spinning in his grave.

"What about Raul?" I ask, in a moment of inspiration. "Do you think we could persuade him to join us?" Raul works on Charlotte and Jacques' farm. He was unable to enlist for the war as a case of double pneumonia as a child left his lungs too weak. He's quite a surly and monosyllabic character, but at least he's under thirty.

"Don't be so foolish." Violeta sniffs. "The man is illiterate. We'd never be able to get him to read a script, let alone memorize it."

I feel my temper rising. Père Rambert, who knows all about my hot-headedness as it has been the subject of many a regretful outpouring in the confessional, glances my way and raises his bushy eyebrows. I am fluent in the language of the Père's eyebrows so I know that they are saying, *Cool it, Laurence!* But how can I stay cool in the face of such snobbery? This whole play is a farce.

"Maybe we should just cancel the play?" I suggest as the door to the bar opens.

"Cancel a play?" a woman's voice calls, sweet and high as a lark. "How can you suggest such sacrilege? Oops, sorry, Père Rambert!" She giggles.

I freeze for a moment. Surely it can't be ... but I turn and see that it is.

My beloved childhood friend Genevieve, who I haven't seen in five years, is standing in the doorway. Or rather, a very glamorous version of my childhood friend is standing in the doorway. With her immaculately coiled blonde hair, high cheekbones and pink rosebud lips, she looks as perfect as a porcelain doll. A well-traveled trunk covered in stickers sits next to her feet.

"Ooh la la!" Madame Bonheur cries.

"Genevieve!" I exclaim, leaping up.

"Actually, I go by Gigi now," she says.

"Oh, yes, of course." I was aware that Gigi is her stage name—how could I not be, given her rise to fame on the Paris stage—but I'd always assumed that she'd still refer to herself privately as Genevieve. "What are you doing here?" I hurry over and give her a hug. Is it my imagination or does she feel slightly stiff in my embrace?

"Is that any way to welcome a girl home?" she murmurs into my shoulder.

I let go and take a step back. "I didn't mean that I wasn't pleased to see you, it's just that it's been so long. I thought you might never be able to drag yourself away from the bright lights of Gay Paree."

Her smile fades and now that I'm up close I can see dark shadows beneath her eyes that her makeup hasn't quite been able to conceal. "Let's just say the bright lights of Paris might have started to dim." She looks me up and down. "You haven't changed at all."

There are certain contexts where this statement would be classed as a compliment—if, for example, I had been diagnosed with a hideous flesh-eating illness—but I can't help feeling that this is not one of them. The last time Genevieve saw me I was a gangly girl of eighteen, Hans Christian Andersen's ugly duckling in human form. Since then, I have miraculously developed what can almost certainly be described as breasts and my previously mud-colored hair has deepened to a much richer shade of chestnut. I have definitely changed since she last saw me, so my preferred response from her would have been something along the lines of, "*Laurence, what a wonderful specimen of womanhood you have become!*"

"You look wonderful," I say magnanimously.

"Thank you," she says with a hearty nod, as if she couldn't agree more.

"*Zut alors*, but you are so thin!" Madame Bonheur exclaims as Genevieve takes off her fur coat to reveal a perfectly fitted scarlet dress, clinging to the curves of her hourglass figure.

Genevieve stares at her blankly for a moment and then her bright blue eyes show a flicker of recognition. "Madame Bonheur, is that you?"

"Of course it is, who else would I be?" Madame Bonheur retorts.

"Gigi, my dear," Violeta exclaims. "It is so wonderful to see you. I have been following your career with such interest all these years."

I frown. Violeta is actually smiling, although this gives her the unfortunate appearance of a terrier baring its teeth. What on earth has prompted this sudden and uncharacteristic display of charm?

"Thank you, Violeta," Genevieve replies.

"She remembers me." Violeta clasps her knobbly hands to her chest.

"Of course I do." Genevieve treats her to a dazzling smile. Clearly she can't remember our resident busybody all that well.

"Well, I have to say this is a moment of divine timing," Violeta says.

Père Rambert grunts and takes another sip of his drink.

"Oh really, how so?" Genevieve asks, with a sideways glance at me.

"The Valley Players are putting on a production of *Romeo and Juliet* and sadly we just lost our leading lady," Violeta explains. "But then you walk in—a professional actress, a star of the Paris stage no less, like a guardian angel sent to save us." I stare at her open-mouthed, half expecting her to prostrate herself on the floor in front of our surprise visitor.

A look of horror falls upon Genevieve's face. "The Valley Players—they are still going?" she finally stammers.

"Of course we are. And we refuse to be thwarted by this hideous war." Violeta looks at me pointedly.

"I'm Romeo," Leon calls across to Gigi, followed by a poorly disguised belch.

The urge to laugh swells inside of me. I bite down hard on my bottom lip.

"Romeo, but he's supposed to be . . ." Genevieve breaks off.

I try to guess at how she might have ended her sentence. *Handsome? Heroic? Under sixty.* And suddenly it's as if Genevieve and I are children again and I feel the urge for mischief.

"I think you would make the perfect coupling," I say drolly.

Genevieve's eyes widen, made even bigger by her false eyelashes. "But ..."

I'm no longer able to hide my grin.

Her eyes narrow. She's on to me.

"Oh, do you now?" She pauses for a moment as if to think of her next move, then she turns to Violeta. "I would love to play Juliet, but on one condition. I need a Romeo who is in my age group."

"You'll be lucky," Madame Bonheur says, with a shake of her head. "All of our young men have been dispatched to the front."

"Hmm." Genevieve purses her rosebud lips and looks at me. "In that case, I nominate Laurence to play opposite me."

"Laurence! But she's a woman," Violeta cries.

"So?" Genevieve smirks. "In Shakespeare's day, women weren't allowed on stage, so all the roles had to be played by men. Having Romeo played by a woman will give our production a certain *je ne sais quoi*, don't you think? And Laurence will so easily pass as a man."

Ouch! I stare at her, confused. Genevieve and I always liked to spark off each other, but there was something barbed about her last remark that I can't help but take personally. Anyone would think I was the one who left and didn't come back for five years, and who didn't even bother to write for the last two.

"Hmm, it certainly would get people's attention," Violeta says thoughtfully. "And you're right. Laurence does have the figure of a young boy."

The others all look at me and start nodding, as if examining a chicken in the market.

I look at Leon hopefully. Surely he won't give up the chance to play opposite Genevieve without a fight.

"Would they have to kiss each other?" he asks lecherously, the froth from his beer spilling from his mouth like drool.

"It would only be a stage kiss," Violeta replies haughtily.

Leon licks his lips.

"Yes, I'm sure it will create a splash," Violeta continues. "And to have a professional actress in the lead role too!"

"In *one* of the lead roles," I interject.

"Yes well, beggars can't be choosers." Violeta sniffs.

"Swell!" Genevieve exclaims as if she's American.

A lesson from our childhood battles in the forest rushes back to greet me: never let your adversary know that you're smarting from their victory. And besides, didn't my childhood hero, Jeanne of Arc, dress and live like a man?

"Yes," I say with a nod. "I very much look forward to playing the hero. After all, it's a far more exciting role than that balcony-wailing female, Juliet."

4

LAURENCE—MARCH 1940

"*Voilà!*" I say as I unlock the door and usher Gigi into the store. I watch as she stands for a moment and gazes around. I'd left the lamp on my desk lit and the remains of a fire is still glowing in the hearth, giving the store a magical feel. I wait for Gigi's gasp of awe. But she remains silent.

"It is so different from before," she eventually says.

I wait for her to add some gushing adjectives, like "magical," "cozy" or "beautiful," as most of my customers say the first time they see it, but she doesn't elaborate.

"Well, yes," I say to break the silence. "A bookstore is going to look quite different to a dressmaker's shop. I kept one of Maman's dummies, though." I nod at the mannequin sitting reading in the window, expecting Gigi to giggle, but there's still no response.

"I discovered the most exquisite bookstore in Paris by the bank of the Seine," Gigi says. "It's owned by an American and all of the books are in English. It's called Shakespeare and Company."

Even though I'm familiar with the store and fluent in English due to my love of British and American writers and my desire to read their work in their mother tongue, I feel anger rising inside of me.

"*Cool it, Laurence, turn the other cheek,*" I imagine Père Rambert saying. I take a deep breath and count to three.

"I'm aware of Shakespeare and Company," I reply. "But I prefer to visit the *bouquinistes* on the Seine whenever I'm in Paris."

"You go to Paris regularly?" she asks.

I nod. "I have a friend there, Michel, one of the *bouquinistes*, who keeps me up to date with all of the latest books that are published."

An awkward silence falls, caused no doubt by the fact that I've been to Paris and not met up with her. But this is hardly my fault. As far as I'm concerned, she made it perfectly clear that she didn't want to maintain contact when she stopped replying to my letters.

"Talking of Shakespeare," I say, to break the silence, "I'm so pleased you're going to be playing Juliet."

"I can't believe the Valley Players are still going." She goes over to the fire and sits in one of the armchairs, crossing her perfect legs. Her nylon stockings shimmer in the glow of the flames. "What does that mean?" She points to the sign next to my typewriter saying, *Book prescriptions here.*

"It's just a little something I offer my customers." I decide not to tell her any more as I can't face another of her putdowns. There are only so many cheeks I'm able to turn after all. "So, what made you come back here?"

"I needed to get away for a while, and besides, Paris won't be safe when the Germans invade," she replies matter-of-factly.

"You can't seriously think they're going to invade?" I stare at her.

"Why not? Look at what they've done to Austria and Poland." She takes a gold cigarette case from her purse.

"Yes, but they haven't come up against our army. And we have the British fighting alongside us."

"Hmm." She gives me a patronizing smile as if I am some ignorant little country mouse, poorly educated in world affairs. It's hard to imagine that our conversation used to flow so effortlessly, so much so that Maman likened us to wrens chattering.

"Luc tells me it's all quiet on the Maginot Line," I say, pressing on.

"Luc is in the army?"

"Of course. All of the men in town have been called up. Well, those young enough and able."

"I can't imagine Luc as a soldier." Finally, her façade slips a little and I see warmth in her eyes.

"I try not to think of him having to fight." I come and sit in the armchair opposite hers. "He and I, we've . . . we've been courting this past year."

Her eyes widen and her perfectly painted mouth falls open in shock. "You and Luc? You're . . . you're an item?"

"Yes."

"But you are so . . ."

"What?"

She pauses and looks me up and down. "Different."

"Opposites can attract, you know."

"I know, but still. Smoke?" She offers me a cigarette.

I shake my head, hoping that she'll take the hint and refrain, but she shrugs and lights one anyway.

"At least enlisting has got him out of this place for a while," she says, wisps of smoke trailing from her mouth on every word. "I can't believe neither of you ever left."

"Why would I leave? It's beautiful here," I say, my hackles rising again.

"Hmm, if you're a child maybe," she murmurs. "Or elderly."

My face flushes. I pick up the poker and start prodding the fire. "I do hope it won't be too boring for you," I say sarcastically.

"Yes, well, I've had more than my fair share of excitement," she replies, clearly too busy trying to be enigmatic to detect my sarcasm. "It'll do me good to do nothing for a while."

"I'm actually very tired," I say, feigning a yawn.

"Oh, OK." She takes another drag on her cigarette before standing. "I need to go anyway. I have to get to the chateau before my parents go to sleep." Genevieve's parents live in Chateau Blanc, an imposing country house on the hill overlooking the town. With its turrets and beautifully manicured gardens, it made the perfect castle for our childhood games. She flicks her cigarette into the fire. "Well, it's been nice seeing you again."

I feel like shaking her by the shoulders and yelling, *What have you done to my friend?* but I nod instead. "You too."

I see her to the door and half expect her to go marching off without another word, but she turns and looks at me. It's hard to tell in the dark, but her eyes look shiny, as if she might be fighting back tears. "Hopefully I will see you again soon?"

"Yes, of course," I reply automatically.

I watch as she sashays off through the square, holding her suitcase, her high heels clicking on the cobbles. Something is wrong with Gigi. Even after all these years, I can still tell.

The town hall clock chimes the half-hour and somewhere in the distance an owl hoots. I breathe in the sweet smell of woodsmoke coiling from the chimneys in the valley. Gigi might think this place is boring, but there's no place I'd rather be.

I turn back into the store and lock the door, then head straight to my desk for a fresh sheet of paper.

Dear Luc,

Well, today the strangest thing happened. A ghost from the past wafted back into town in the form of our Genevieve. Only she isn't at all how she used to be. For a start, she now insists on being called her stage name, Gigi. I remember you saying once that you were worried her fame might go to her head. I'm sorry to inform you that you appear to have been correct. She now seems to take great pleasure in looking down her nose at me, and the rest of the town too. She says she's come back because she needs to "do nothing" for a while. Apparently she's had too much excitement in Paris.

Seeing her again only made me miss you more; it's sparked so many memories of the games we used to play together in the forest.

In other news, but not entirely unrelated, I am to play Romeo in the latest Valley Players production. And yes, you read that correctly. "Gigi" suggested I play the role due to the shortage of young men in the village and the fact that I would pass so easily as a man! I am happy to report that I managed to maintain my cool and now that I've had more time to think about it, I am actually relishing the chance to play a more substantial role!

I miss you.

Laurence

The next morning, I wake bright and early to discover that the icicle in my bedroom has melted. I open the window and breathe in the air. For the first time in what feels like forever, I can smell the warm floral scent of spring. The sky is a richer shade of blue too, making the cream stone of the buildings appear cleaner and brighter.

Across the square, Abram Dabrowski is arranging the seats

in a row outside his café. I decide to treat myself to one of his crêpes for breakfast to celebrate the return of spring. As I get dressed, I stare at my reflection in the mirror on the wardrobe door. I long ago came to the realization that I will never be traditionally beautiful like Gigi, or any of the other women adorning the pages of magazines, but it has never bothered me. Maman did such a good job of convincing me that I was "striking" rather than beautiful and that this was a far more interesting thing. "Your nose is as majestic as a Roman's," she would tell me. "Your cheekbones are as sharp as a panther's." How could I not feel content with my appearance, hearing this every day? But since seeing Gigi it's as if my old childhood insecurities have been nibbling away at me like hungry mice while I sleep. Am I too flat-chested? Do I look too masculine?

Stop being so pathetic, I tell myself and I put on my favorite emerald-green dress, which Maman made for me, and the nylons I'd been saving for a special occasion. After all, there's no more special occasion than the return of spring.

I make my way across the square and take a seat at one of the tables outside Belle Vie café. When Abram named his café Belle Vie, he and Monsieur Tissier almost came to blows. Monsieur Tissier was incensed that the name was so similar to that of his Hotel Belle Vue. Thankfully, I was on hand to calm things down, providing both men with a lecture on how their disagreement was in fact an excellent example of the power of the written word and how just one letter can make a world of difference. "And besides," I concluded with a knowing smile in Monsieur Tissier's direction, "without such a beautiful view, we could not have such a beautiful life." Content that the café's name could not exist without that of the hotel's, Monsieur Tissier gave a brisk nod and the two men patched things up over a cup of Abram's delicious coffee.

"Laurence!" Abram cries in greeting as he comes out holding his order pad and pencil, although why he would need to write down my order, I don't know. I have the same thing for breakfast every time I come here. It's lovely to see him looking so cheery, though. As a Jew originally from Poland, Abram has looked wracked with worry ever since France joined the war.

"Good morning," I reply. "Isn't the weather beautiful?"

We both take a moment to gaze appreciatively at the square. High above us in the bright blue sky, a handful of fluffy white clouds drift by like giant blossom.

"It certainly is," Abram replies. "Thank God winter is over. What can I get for you?"

"Do you really need to ask?"

He chuckles. "You never know, maybe one day you will tire of my crêpes and whipped cream."

"Well, that day is not this day," I say with a grin.

"And your usual coffee?" He tucks his notepad into the pocket in his apron.

"But of course."

As he goes back inside, I allow myself to feel the slightest sense of hope. Maybe the change in the weather will also signify a change in France's fortunes. Maybe Luc will soon be back home, sitting at one of these tables with me. My reverie is interrupted by the sound of heels on the cobbled pavement and I turn to see Gigi walking toward me.

"Good morning," I call gaily. Writing to Luc about her return helped me get my hurt feelings off my woefully flat chest and I'm determined to try to overcome the awkwardness of last night.

"Good morning," she mutters as she reaches the café. She's wearing a pinstripe trouser suit that's so well cut it only makes her look more feminine, and a black fedora hat is perched on top of her perfectly set hair. Her eyelashes are extra-long and black and her lips are painted ruby red. She looks like the femme fatale from a gangster movie and my emerald dress instantly seems to fade in her light. She pulls out the chair next to mine and sits down.

"How are your parents?" I ask in an attempt to avoid an awkward silence, but I almost instantly regret it, as Gigi's parents were never her favorite subject.

"The same as ever," she mutters, looking out over the square.

I know that this time she isn't making a dig. Her parents are indeed completely unchanged. Grayer in the hair department perhaps, but in terms of their personalities, her father is still as stiff as a poker and her insipid mother still clings to him like a shadow.

"Are you sure you should have come back here?" I blurt out.

She gives a dry little laugh. "Thanks!"

"No, I mean for your own sake. It just doesn't seem like there's a lot for you to like here."

"*You're* here," she says and I feel a bud of hope. Maybe she still likes me after all. Maybe last night she was crotchety from traveling. "And as I said last night, right now *anywhere* would be better—and safer—than Paris."

"Do you really think the Germans will invade?" I last went to Paris about a month ago, to buy some new books for the store from Michel. There had seemed to be a sense of foreboding in the air, but I'd put that down to the austere winter, stripping the pavements of people and the people of joy.

She nods. "Who knows, maybe it wouldn't be such a bad thing."

"What on earth do you mean?" I ask, taken aback.

She shrugs and looks away.

"How can you say that after what they've done in Austria and Poland? What they've done to their own people—the way they're treating the Jews."

"Hmm." She purses her rosebud lips. "I don't see why we should care about the Jews."

"You can't be serious?" I glance around, anxiously checking

Abram isn't within earshot and see him coming back outside with my coffee. When he spots Gigi, he gives her a warm smile of recognition.

"Genevieve?" he calls cheerily.

I hold my breath, hoping she won't make her new-found indifference to the Jewish obvious. Thankfully, she smiles and it's like a switch inside her has been flicked, removing all trace of her previous bitterness. But as she and Abram exchange greetings, I feel a chill run up my spine. What on earth has happened to my childhood friend?

5

JEANNE—1993

"Your mother and I met during the war, in France," Wendell said, as Jeanne sat back down on the rug in front of him.

"You were in France?" Jeanne wracked her brains trying to remember what she'd learned about the Second World War in her high-school history lessons. She was pretty sure France was one of the countries that had been occupied by the Nazis.

"Uh-huh."

"But I thought you were stationed in the UK."

"I was, but I'd often fly missions into France."

The thought of her sweet-natured landscape gardener of a dad "flying missions" into Nazi-occupied territory was like something out of a movie and almost impossible for Jeanne to comprehend. "So how did you guys meet?"

"When I did my first drop-off in France. But I really got to know her after I crash-landed another night and she rescued me."

The identikit image Jeanne had been mentally building of her real mom morphed from a chick who had a two-night stand in a blackout to the kind of kick-ass broad who rescued downed pilots.

"So she was French then?"

"Uh-huh."

"What was her name?"

"Laurence," he replied, with a French intonation, making it sound like Laur-*on*-ce.

"Laurence? Isn't that a guy's name?"

"Not in France." Wendell took a handkerchief from his trouser pocket and blew his nose.

"Pops, are you OK?"

"I just . . . It's been quite a day." His voice was wavering again, like it had when he delivered his eulogy, what now seemed like a whole lifetime ago. "I'm so sorry I didn't tell you, honey. I was only doing what I thought was best. I wanted to give you a family."

Jeanne leaned forward and placed her hand on his leg. "Hey, it's OK. It's just a lot to process."

"I can imagine. Maybe we could talk about it some more tomorrow? I'm dead beat."

Jeanne swallowed down her disappointment, along with the hundreds of questions that were forming in her mind. "Sure."

Wendell stood up slowly and leaned on the back of the chair. "Was she really unkind to you, your mom?"

"She was definitely . . ." Jeanne paused. ". . . difficult. And distant. But now it's starting to make sense."

He nodded. "I'm sorry."

Jeanne sprang up and gave him a hug. "It's OK."

"I'll see you in the morning then. And we can talk some more."

Jeanne nodded and watched him leave, then she went and sat in front of the fire, gazing into the flames. "Laurence," she whispered.

. . .

The next morning, Jeanne woke to the smell of bacon cooking. It was a smell guaranteed to get her out of a bed in an instant and, like a sniffer dog, she followed her nose to the kitchen. Wendell was standing at the stove clad in his trademark plaid shirt and faded jeans, tending to a sizzling frying pan. The radio in the corner was playing his favorite rock music.

"Morning, Pops."

"Hey there, honey," he called over the sizzling. She was relieved to see that he was much more his relaxed, cheery self. "How did you sleep?"

"Hmm, could have been better."

"I guess I dropped a bit of a bombshell on you last night," he said with a sheepish grin.

"You sure did." She went over and planted a kiss on the back of his head. "Bacon smells awesome."

"Take a seat, honey, it's almost done."

She went and sat at the table in the bay window overlooking the backyard. The early-morning sun was starting to filter through the pine trees in thin shafts of pale gold. The table had been laid with a jug of orange juice, a pot of coffee, plates of sliced tomato and watermelon and a bowl of shiny bagels. Her stomach growled in appreciation.

Wendell came over with a plate of crispy bacon and sat down. "So I'm guessing you might have a few questions . . ."

"Uh, yes, just a few!"

"All righty then, go ahead." He poured them both a glass of juice.

"What did my real mom—Laurence—do for a living?"

"She owned a bookstore—and she was a member of the French Resistance. That's how I got to meet her."

A balaclava and shotgun instantly appeared on Jeanne's mental identikit of her mom. "The Resistance?"

"Uh-huh." Wendell began buttering an onion bagel. "A lot of folks think that the French rolled over and gave in to the Nazis, but it wasn't true. Their government might have capitulated, but there were thousands of brave people who risked everything to try to win freedom for France. And your mom was one of them."

Jeanne sat back in her seat, a lump forming in her throat. Learning that she was descended from someone like this already seemed to be achieving way more than her recent excruciating foray into therapy. But why hadn't Laurence wanted to keep Jeanne? How had she ended up in America with someone else pretending to be her mom? She took a paper napkin from the pile on the table and blew her nose.

"You OK, honey?" Wendell asked, looking concerned.

"Yes...I...She sounds amazing."

"She was." He put down his bagel and gazed out of the window.

"So, was I born in France during the war?"

"You were indeed."

"Wow." With every question he answered, a fresh cluster appeared. "How long was I there? How did I get out of there? What happened to Laurence?"

"Whoa, slow down..." Wendell poured them both a cup of coffee and again Jeanne noticed that his hand was trembling. "I came to get you. It was the most important mission I ever flew."

"What happened to Laurence?" she asked again.

"I—uh—I made a terrible mistake," he muttered.

What was that supposed to mean? She stared across the table at him. He bowed his head, clearly distressed, and she noticed a tear roll from his face onto his plate. She decided to put the interrogation on hold for now, let him tell her what happened to Laurence when he was ready. She reached across the table and took hold of his hand. "It's OK, Pops."

He looked at her and smiled weakly, his eyes brimming with tears.

. . .

After breakfast, Wendell unlocked the back door. "Follow me," he said, "I have something to show you."

He led Jeanne to the copse of pine trees at the bottom of the yard, and the large shed where he kept his gardening tools. Or, at least, that was how Jeanne remembered the shed as a kid. But as he opened the door and let her in, she couldn't help gasping in surprise.

"Geez, nice bachelor pad." She laughed, taking in the poster of Homer Simpson eating a doughnut above the La-Z-Boy reclining armchair, which was perfectly positioned in front of a huge TV and shelves full of videos. There was even a small fridge in the corner, and not a gardening tool in sight.

"Yeah well, I like it down here, amongst the trees." Wendell grinned. "It's peaceful."

Jeanne couldn't help wondering if he'd come down here to escape from Lorilee and her constant nagging about keeping the house pristine. After all, that was what had driven Jeanne to getting her own place at the ripe old age of eighteen. "So what was it you wanted me to see?"

He went over to a cupboard in the corner and pulled out a pile of gardening magazines. Then he reached in and brought out an old tin box. He handed it to her and went over to the fridge.

"It's locked, Pops," Jeanne said, trying to lift the lid.

"I know, hold your horses." Wendell opened the icebox, reached into the back and took out a key.

"This is all a bit cloak-and-dagger, isn't it?" Jeanne said, raising her eyebrows.

"Yeah, well, I didn't want..." He broke off, but Jeanne could guess what he'd been going to say. He didn't want Lorilee seeing whatever was inside.

Her skin erupted in goosebumps as he passed her the key. As Jeanne unlocked the box, Wendell perched on the edge of his recliner, running his hand through his hair anxiously.

"I feel like that Pandora dame," Jeanne quipped. "Was that her name? The one who opened the box and let all the bad shit out?"

Wendell just shrugged.

As Jeanne opened the box, she couldn't help feeling a slight sense of anticlimax. All she could see was a book, some kind of pamphlet and a piece of cloth. She took the book out first. It was called *For Whom the Bell Tolls* and was by Ernest Hemingway. Once she'd outgrown her Nancy Drew phase Jeanne hadn't really been much of a reader, but she knew enough to know that Hemingway was quite a big deal in the literary world. Next, she took out the pamphlet. The title on the front read: INSTRUCTIONS FOR AMERICAN SERVICEMEN IN BRITAIN 1942.

"I'm not sure why I kept that," Wendell said with a smile. "I guess I wanted a souvenir from my time there."

Jeanne opened the pamphlet to the introduction on the first page. *YOU are going to Britain as part of an allied offensive*, the first line read. *To meet Hitler and beat him on his own ground.*

"I think it's awesome that you fought in the war," she said softly.

"You do?" He looked at her hopefully.

"Yes, it must have taken a lot of courage."

He shook his head. "There were plenty of folks a whole lot braver than me."

Deciding not to press him further on this, she flicked through the aging pages, smiling at the numerous instructions for American servicemen on how to get on well with the British and not cause offense. "I never knew that bum meant backside in the UK."

Wendell chuckled. "Uh-huh. A lot of us made asses of ourselves with that one!"

" 'The British don't know how to make a good cup of

coffee,'" Jeanne read out loud. "'You don't know how to make a good cup of tea. It's an even swap.'"

"Ain't that the truth." Wendell grinned.

Jeanne smiled back at him. It was good to see him looking happier again. She put the pamphlet down and took the piece of cloth from the box. "What the heck is this?" She shook the fabric out. It was like a tiny pillowcase in faded stripes of pink, yellow, blue and green.

Wendell chuckled. "That, my dear, was one of your first dresses."

"What?" Jeanne studied the piece of cloth and, sure enough, there was a neck-sized hole at the top and arm-sized holes in each side, clearly handmade. "I take it you didn't buy it at Bloomingdale's."

His expression turned wistful. "It was what you were wearing the night I rescued you."

"From France?"

He nodded.

Jeanne traced her finger along the tiny stitching around the hem. Had her real mom made this for her? She shivered at the thought.

"By the time you were born, the Germans had been occupying France for three years," Wendell explained. "They plundered the country, leaving the French with barely a thing. I guess your mom had to make your clothes from whatever she could lay her hands on."

Jeanne nodded, too emotional to speak. It blew her mind to think that she had once worn this dress in a country occupied by the Nazis.

"There's something else in there." Wendell nodded at the box. "For you."

"OK." Jeanne put the tiny dress down and looked inside the box. At the bottom, there was an old yellowing document and a long iron key. "What is it?" She held the document up to the light, but the writing appeared to be in French. Her eyes were drawn to what seemed to be an address, set out separately in the center of the page:

LE DISPENSAIRE DE LIVRES
PLACE DE LA VILLE
VALLÉE DU CERF

"It's a deed," Wendell explained.

"To what?"

"Your mom's store."

"But how do you have it?"

He glanced around anxiously as if looking for the right reply. "It—uh—it was with you when I came to get you, tucked inside your blanket."

"But why? Why didn't Laurence keep it?"

He shrugged, but Jeanne's Spidey senses began to tingle. He knew more than he was letting on, she was sure of it.

"I had an idea, last night..." He grabbed hold of her hand. "What say you and I take a vacation together, to France, to try to find the store and...and to find out some more about your mom?"

"But it was so long ago, do you think we'd be able to find anything?" She felt a thrilling mixture of adrenaline and fear bubbling up inside her. It was a feeling she hadn't experienced since leaving work and it was like the return of an old friend.

"You're a detective, aren't you?"

"Not any more."

Wendell frowned. "Honey, just because those assholes forced you to quit, it doesn't change the fact that you're one of the best cops Chicago has ever seen."

"Huh, tell that to Captain Fitzpatrick."

"That chump can eat my shorts."

Jeanne couldn't help laughing. "Don't you think you're a bit too old for the Bart Simpson quotes?"

"That little yellow dude is my hero." Wendell grinned. "Look, I don't know what happened in that last case you worked on, and I know you don't want to talk about it, but one mistake does not cancel out thirty years of service, not to mention all the commendations you've received."

"Yeah well, depends what the mistake was," Jeanne muttered.

"Forget about it, honey." He looked at her, his eyes sparkling. "To my way of thinking, we're both in urgent need of a vacation, and I . . . well, I want to make it up to you for not telling you about your real mom sooner. And I'd love to find out more about her too," he added softly.

"Really?" She felt the adrenaline begin pulsing through her veins.

"Absolutely. I'm telling you, Jeanne, this could be the most important investigation of your life."

6

LAURENCE—MAY 1940

Dear Laurence,

Thank you so much for your latest update on the play rehearsals—you have no idea how much they help lift my spirits. In your letter you asked me how I am truly feeling. I know this isn't a very heroic thing to have to admit, but the truth is, I have this overwhelming sense of foreboding that something terrible is about to happen. I can't explain why, I just feel a dread deep in my bones.

I keep reciting your poetry prescription—I've read that Rilke poem so many times now, I know it by heart. I'm sure I'm not telling you anything you don't already know, but for someone who has never really understood poetry, I want you to know that I finally see what the big deal is. Poems are like the eau de parfum to the eau de cologne of a novel; you don't need nearly as many words to have such a powerful impact. Anyway, now I am fixated on the line where God urges the reader not to lose Him. I fear I am losing Him, Laurence. I fear that soon the

Germans will unleash their fury upon us and I do not understand how a loving God could allow this.

I'm sorry. I don't mean to infect you with my gloom; I probably won't even send this letter. I'll just use it as an opportunity to pretend that I am talking to you on one of our idyllic walks through the forest. Oh how I miss the forest! Oh how I miss you! Please forgive me. I know I have failed you. I know I'm not the romantic hero you dreamed of spending the rest of your life with, and now I feel that my cowardice has confirmed this. But is it so wrong to be afraid of dying? Is it so wrong to not want to fight?

Perhaps I should send this letter after all, to tell you that I release you, that you no longer have to think of me as your beau if you don't want to. I have always loved you, Laurence, and always will. But sometimes the most loving thing to do is to let someone be free and I want you to be free to be truly happy. So please do not feel guilty.

All my love,

Luc

I sit on the steps outside the post office, my eyes swimming with tears. *No!* I want to yell at the ink on the page, as if it will somehow magically transmit to Luc. *Don't give up!* It no longer matters to me that I was having doubts about our relationship. Faced with the specter of a real war, my romantic wishes seem silly and selfish. All that matters is that Luc is happy and comes home safe.

I wipe my eyes and look back at the page. It breaks my heart that, after all my years of nagging, he should finally come to appreciate the power of a poem in such terrible circumstances.

Ever since he left, his letters have been so cheery and positive. Even when the Germans recently bombed a garrison not far from his, he remained resolute and upbeat. Has his fear been there all along? Was he just trying to protect me from it?

I look at the newspaper stand outside the post office. The headlines all report the Luftwaffe's latest attacks on Belgium and France. My gaze drifts to the poster on the wall by the post office door. *THE VALLEY PLAYERS PRESENT: ROMEO AND JULIET*, it proclaims in bright red font.

Tonight is opening night. We are only doing a run of three nights—Friday, Saturday and Sunday—rather than the customary full week, due to the fact that half the town are now absent.

My thoughts return to Luc. I must write back immediately with a new prescription for him. But what should I choose?

Back in the store, I riffle through the shelves, but I'm all a-jitter with nervous energy, making it impossible to concentrate. *Please let Luc be wrong*, I say to myself over and over, *please let nothing terrible happen*.

In the end, there's only one thing for it—only one person who can possibly calm my ragged nerves. I turn the sign on the shop door to CLOSED and make my way over to the church. Inside, the air is blissfully cool and smells faintly of incense. Even on the hottest of summer days, the church remains as cool as a cellar, its thick stone walls soaking up the heat from the sun. I walk across the gray flagstones, worn smooth by the feet of so many worshippers over the years, and head to the confessional.

As a small child, I was obsessed with the confessional, and its intricately carved dark wood, the thick velvet curtain and the mystery of what happened inside, the faint murmur of voices. Once I was old enough to understand and take my first confession, I loved the drama of it all. I spent weeks mulling over which sin I ought to confess first to Père Rambert. Should it be the piece of cheese that I stole when Maman wasn't looking, or the night I stayed up reading by the light of my flashlight after I'd been told to go to sleep? They all seemed so boring. In the end, inspired by a swashbuckling story I'd been reading about the dread pirate Anne Bonny, I confessed to Père Rambert that I had stolen ten pieces of eight from a Spanish ship. There was a long silence and then the Père's deep voice came through the lattice partition. "You do know that it is also a sin to lie, Laurence." Shame coursed through me hot as lava. I had sinned during my very first confession! Surely there would be a very special place in hell for people like me. I began to weep. But thankfully Père Rambert assured me that if I said three Hail Marys each morning my sin would be absolved.

Now I see that the curtain is drawn on the Père's side of the confessional and I slip into the other side and kneel on the step.

"Bless me, Father, for I have sinned. My last confession was..." I frown. "Er, six months ago?"

"I think you might find that it's been a little longer than that," the Père replies.

Damn, caught lying again. "I'm sorry."

"You are forgiven."

I clear my throat. "I fear that I have hurt someone I love very much," I say quietly, and again my eyes fill with tears. "Someone kind and caring and who deserves so much better."

"I see," Père Rambert replies, and I can tell from his voice that he's moved closer to the lattice partition. "And tell me, did you intend to hurt them?"

"No! But..." I break off. Luc and I first started courting right after Maman died. Falling into his arms was such a comfort in my dark tunnel of grief. It was only as I slowly started to see the light at the end of the tunnel that I was also able to see that Luc was not the right one for me. I could have ended things then, at the first sign of my doubt, but I didn't. I was too scared to. "I fear that I've hurt them by trying not to hurt them, if that makes sense," I finally say.

"I think I understand," comes the Père's reply. "Tell me, has this person forgiven you?"

I think of the love flowing through the ink of Luc's letter.

"Yes."

"Then you must forgive yourself."

"But don't I need God's forgiveness too?"

"God knows your intentions were true. Grief is a powerful thing, Laurence. It can make us do and say things we can come to regret. The death of your mother was a huge loss; any decisions you made then weren't necessarily coming from the soundest place of judgment."

"Yes." I nod heartily, then stop. "Wait, how did you know?"

"Matters of the heart can be a very complicated thing," he replies, then chuckles. "They make me glad I've taken a vow of chastity."

I laugh and wipe away my tears. "I think I might follow Jeanne of Arc's example and remain a maid. Life was a lot simpler when I was married only to my books."

"We'll see," Père Rambert replies sagely. "Sometimes the most loving thing to do seems like the most painful thing, but it isn't. How can it be? In the end, love always heals any wound it creates."

I let his words sit with me for a moment, as if savoring the flavors of a good coffee. "Thank you, Père."

"God bless you, Laurence. And good luck tonight with the play."

"Oh, yes, thank you." I laugh. "I think I'll need it."

I walk back outside. It's only just gone nine o'clock, but already the heat is oppressive. I gaze around the square at the people having their breakfast outside the café, and queuing at Madame Bonheur's for her freshly baked croissants and baguettes. I see Leon the blacksmith smoking a cigarette on the town hall steps, his eyes closed and face tilted toward the sunshine. I see Monsieur Tissier inspecting the work of the boy cleaning the hotel windows. It seems so cruel that life should be continuing almost as normal here while Luc and the other men are enduring so much.

I go back into the bookstore and turn the sign to OPEN. Then I turn on the radio on my desk, in need of some music to lift my spirits. But instead of music the shop is filled with the clipped tones of a newsreader. "This morning at dawn the Germans began an assault on Belgium, Luxembourg, the Netherlands, and France," he announces gravely. "The phoney war is over!"

7

LAURENCE—JUNE 1940

"The government have left Paris!"

All eyes in the hotel bar turn to look at Violeta standing, breathless, in the doorway. All eyes apart from those belonging to Père Rambert, which remain fixed on his wine glass.

"They've left Paris for Tours," Violeta continues. "What do you think it means?"

"It means they're making way for the Germans," Gigi replies from her bar stool where she's nursing a Martini.

I get a sinking feeling. When Gigi returned home two months ago, I pooh-poohed her ominous predictions. But now I can't help feeling she was right, especially after this latest news.

"What should we do?" Violeta asks.

All eyes turn to Père Rambert. When he realizes that he has become the focal point of our attention, he takes a sip of his drink and clears his throat.

"I suggest that you hide your most treasured possessions."

I'd been expecting him to say "pray." While his telling us to hide our most treasured possessions might be a more practical measure, it's infinitely more terrifying because of the implication. We must hide our treasured possessions because the Germans might take them. The Germans are about to invade. I shudder as I think of what the Nazis might do to my beloved books. Didn't they demand the burning of books in their own country and Austria a few years ago? I cried the day I saw the photographs in the newspaper. The thought of all those ideas and imaginings going up in smoke practically cracked my heart in two.

"But I have so many valuable possessions!" Violeta exclaims, looking aghast.

"Who cares about things," Gigi snaps, before draining the rest of her drink. "What about the people of Paris? How must they be feeling, being deserted by their own government?"

I think of my friend Michel. What will become of his book-stall on the Seine if the Germans take over Paris?

Gigi slips from her stool and straightens her skirt before marching past Violeta and out of the bar.

"Well, really, there was no need for that," Violeta huffs.

I've been so desperate for any sign of my old friend Gene-vieve, I chase after her like a hound following a scent.

"Gigi, are you all right?" I call as I run down the hotel steps.

She stops and turns and I can see that beneath her makeup her face is ashen. "A lot of people I care about live in Paris," she says. And even though this is only to be expected, it takes me by surprise. She's said so little about her life in Paris since returning home, it led me to believe that she didn't really care about leaving it at all.

"I'm sorry. Is there anything I can do?"

I'm fully expecting her to say no, but to my surprise she looks thoughtful for a moment then nods. "Perhaps we could go for a walk—in the forest?"

Again, I'm surprised. Despite having spent so much time there as a child, Gigi hasn't mentioned the forest since her return. But then again, she hasn't really mentioned anything much, despite us spending weeks in rehearsal and three nights on stage together.

"Of course," I reply, hoping that a visit to our childhood haunt might rekindle our former closeness.

We walk through the square and down the hill, past the station, neither of us saying a word. I guess we're both too shocked at the news. Finally, the road narrows to the bumpy track leading into the forest.

As soon as we're beneath the canopy of branches, the air cools and I breathe in the Christmassy scent of pine. The forest still fills me with same sense of magic I got when I was a child. It still feels as if I've walked into an illustration from an old leather-bound collection of fairy tales and at any moment I could happen upon a house made from gingerbread, or catch a glimpse of a red-hooded cloak darting between the trees.

"Do you have any news about Luc?" Gigi asks, carefully picking her way over the uneven ground in her heels.

"Still no word," I reply, trying to quell the panic that has been building in me for the past month. "Although, according to the BBC, many French soldiers were evacuated from Dunkirk."

"Do you think he could be among them?" Gigi looks at me so hopefully I feel the sudden urge to hug her. I manage to fight it. I've learned that, unlike Genevieve, "Gigi" doesn't care for displays of affection—or at least not from me.

"I don't know." The truth is, it's highly unlikely Luc would have ended up in Dunkirk, given where he was stationed, but I can't bear to think of the other possibilities.

We walk on in silence until we reach the stream. The water shimmers with sunbeams dancing through the trees.

"Do you remember when we used to play here as kids? And we'd try to catch fish from pieces of cotton tied to sticks."

"You and Luc would," she mutters. "I would be in charge of

making our camp nice and cozy." There's a bitterness to her tone that makes me glance at her. Gigi always preferred to have a less rough-and-tumble role in our adventures—or at least I thought she did.

We carry on walking deeper into the forest and it becomes darker and cooler as the trees thicken. Even the sounds change, with the sweet song of the larks being replaced by the cawing of crows. Although we haven't said as much, we're instinctively following the trail to our childhood hideaway, a path so well-trodden we still remember it after all these years.

"Look, there's Monseigneur Oak!" I exclaim, pointing ahead of us to an ancient oak tree. I'm hoping that the sight of our beloved friend might prompt a smile from Gigi, but it's not to be. Her mouth is set firmly in a frown. "I wonder if our carving is still there."

I hurry on ahead and walk around the huge gnarled trunk until I find the place where the bark is missing. And there, sure enough, are the carved initials: LS and LH. Laurence Sidot and Luc Hamoncourt. But where is Gigi?

"Where are your initials?" I ask as Gigi joins me.

"I didn't do it." She shrugs. "Luc only gave his knife to you."

"Oh." I feel embarrassed that I don't remember this and concerned at the bitterness in Gigi's tone.

We walk on, down an even narrower path, so overgrown it wouldn't be visible to the untrained eye, and I travel back along the same path in my mind, some thirteen years, and I see Luc and I, our faces streaked with mud, Gigi following behind, dressed like a doll in her frilly dress, her long hair a sheet of gold upon her back. *"Wait for me,"* I hear her girlish voice calling, ghostly, through the trees. *"Wait for me."*

Finally, we reach the end of the trail, emerging into a wide clearing, surrounded by a wall of trees. This clearing with its sprinkling of daisies and toadstool rings was always the most enchanted part of the forest to me, especially if we were here at sunrise or sunset and the sky above became streaked with shades of violet, red and tangerine. In all of our years of playing in the forest, we never encountered another person in the clearing, so, of course, in my fertile imagination it became a portal into a mysterious realm.

"It's as if no time has passed," I murmur, slowly turning to take in the view. High above us, a solitary bird swoops and soars in the cloudless sky, and just for a moment, I completely forget about the war.

"Huh, for you maybe," Gigi mutters and something inside of me snaps. I'm so tired of her constant sniping.

"You're not the only one to have had a life, you know." My words come out harsher than I'd have liked but still . . .

She stares at me. "What do you mean?"

"For your information, things *have* changed for me. My mother died for one thing—not that you bothered reaching out to me. Was my losing a parent not exciting enough for you? Were you having too much fun in Paris to even take a moment to write to me?"

The silence in the clearing becomes so thick, it feels as if I could slice it with a knife. But I'm determined that this time I won't be the one to break it, however awkward it might be.

"I'm sorry I didn't write," Gigi says finally. "I was going through a difficult time myself."

"Really? Why?" I ask softly, relieved that she might finally be about to open up to me.

"If you must know, I'd just found out that my husband-to-be was betraying me."

"Your husband-to-be?"

"Yes."

"But I hadn't heard that you were getting married." If there'd been any mention of Gigi's engagement in the press, it would have been around town like wildfire.

"That's because he didn't want his family to find out." Gigi stares straight ahead.

"Why not?"

"Because he's Jewish."

"And?"

"And I'm not. And he's not supposed to marry out, apparently his family won't allow it. But now it's not a problem because, conveniently, the whore he cheated on me with is also Jewish."

She spits out the word "Jewish" like she's spitting out a worm and I think back to the time outside the café when Gigi spoke so bitterly. This must be the reason. Her personal hurt is making her blame an entire people.

"I'm sorry."

"Yes, well, now you know." She takes her cigarettes from her purse and lights one. "Can we go?"

"Of course." I'm about to turn to leave when I hear a gentle thud on the ground. "Wait," I whisper, placing my hand on her arm. "I think it's the deer." There's a rustle in the trees and then, at the far side of the clearing, a deer flits like a shadow through the trees. Followed by another, and another. It's a sight that still makes me shiver with excitement and I know that it will be having the same effect on Gigi; I remember how she'd gasp with awe any time we were lucky enough to see them. "Maybe it's a lucky omen," I whisper. "Maybe the French will still beat the Germans."

She gives a loud snort and the deer freeze, startled, before racing back into the cover of the forest.

I turn and stare at her, perplexed. "You scared them away."

"So what? They're only deer, they're not some magical beings." She shakes her head. "Honestly, Laurence, you've spent way too long with your nose stuck in books. Life isn't a fairy tale, you know. Of course we aren't going to beat the Germans—even our government are running away from them." And with that, she stalks back into the trees.

I follow behind her, trying—and failing—to stop the angry thoughts buzzing like hornets in my head. *How dare she speak to me like that?*

As we walk past Monseigneur Oak, I glance at the faded carving and feel a sense of loss so strong it almost takes my legs out from under me. I have no idea if Luc is alive or dead and Genevieve may as well be dead. It's as if all of the foundation stones in my life are crumbling to dust, even the French government, as the Germans begin infecting our country like a plague. I feel in my pocket for Maman's Nénette doll, but even she brings little comfort.

I become so mired in my thoughts of loss and despair, Gigi and I are back at the edge of the forest before I know it. We remain deadly silent as we march back along the road leading to the station. I focus on the cloud of steam billowing from the platform to try to distract myself. But as we draw closer, the sound of voices fills the air. Agitated voices, so *many* voices. I crane my neck and peer over the hedge to try to see what's going on. A train is standing at the platform from Paris, full to the brim with people.

"What the . . . ?" I quietly exclaim as I look at the faces pressed against the windows and hanging out of the doors. Then I see a sight so surreal I think I must be hallucinating. A row of women are crouching on the adjacent track, holding their skirts up. "What are they doing?" I mutter.

Gigi has stopped just ahead of me and she's peering over the hedge too. "Going to the toilet," she murmurs.

"But why?"

"Maybe because the train is so overcrowded with people fleeing from Paris," she replies snippily, as if this ought to be obvious.

I turn away, ashamed at intruding on such scenes of desperation, and for a moment I feel the burning urge to make amends with Gigi. In the face of such a shocking sight, our bickering seems so childish. But she is walking on again, faster now.

"Goodbye," she mutters over her shoulder as she takes the fork in the road leading to her parents' chateau. Something about the way she says it feels as final as a full stop.

8

LAURENCE—JUNE 1940

For the next few days, I have the radio on permanently in the shop. But instead of playing my usual music, I have the dial fixed to news broadcasts, either from France or from the British via the BBC. In light of what is happening, I'd been expecting few, if any, customers, but the opposite proves true, as The Book Dispensary becomes a hub for townsfolk seeking consolation. All day long, I'm issuing prescriptions of stirring poems to try to raise their spirits or epic adventures to give them a distraction.

On the morning of the fourteenth of June, I come downstairs to see that someone is in such urgent need of a book prescription they're actually queuing outside the door. Then I realize from the wiry hair that it's Père Rambert. My heart sinks. If even the town priest with his direct line to God is coming to me for consolation we're in trouble for sure.

"Good day, Père," I say as gaily as I can as I open the door.

"Laurence," he says, in the same grave tone he greeted me with the day my mother died. My stomach tightens.

"Is everything all right?" I stand back as he enters the shop. Something is definitely wrong; he's forgotten to put on his white collar.

"I'm afraid I have some very bad news."

"Not Luc?" My hands start to tremble.

He nods.

"No." I back away until I'm leaning against my desk, letting it support my quivering legs.

He looks down at the floor. "I've received news that his unit were bombed by the Luftwaffe several days ago."

"No. No. No. No." The only thing that has kept me hopeful these past few days since the German invasion is the thought that Luc might have been beating a retreat from the front and making his way back home. I'd imagined him, dirty and unkempt and possibly even wounded, walking into the store. I'd pictured myself throwing my arms around him and telling him that I loved him. I'd even bargained with God in my prayers— *If you just bring him back to me, I promise I'll love him fully.* And God answers my prayers with this? Anger burns through my shock. "But I prayed," I stammer. "I prayed that he would be saved."

"I'm sorry," Père Rambert replies and I see that the whites of his eyes are streaked pink, as if he has been crying. "If you like, we could pray for him now, together."

"What's the point?" I snap. "When God doesn't listen."

"God always listens," he replies gently.

"So God doesn't care then?" I feel like a belligerent child, but I can't stop. I have to do something with this rage before it consumes me. Luc was the most good and kind person I've ever known. How is it right that he should be killed in such a horrific way? What kind of God would allow this to happen?

"God loves us all very much."

His words fade and I stare blankly at the door, thinking of all the times I've seen Luc walk through it over the course of my lifetime. As a child, when he'd come calling for me to come out to play, and as an adult, when he'd call in with pastries on his lunch break, or pop by to see if I'd like to go for a walk. And then, in the past year, when he'd turn up in his overalls to help me refurbish the store. The notion that I'll never see him walk through that door again is so hard to comprehend it takes my breath away. And then I think of what happened the very last time he walked through that door and it's as if I can feel my heart splintering.

"The last time I saw him . . ." I break off, unable to speak for sorrow and shame, and I begin sobbing uncontrollably.

"There, there." Père Rambert comes closer and I catch a waft of his pipe smoke woven into his cassock, so comforting and familiar.

"How do you know?" I ask, desperately grasping at straws. "How do you know for sure?"

"I received word from his commanding officer early this morning. Several men from the town were killed in the bombing."

"Oh no!"

"It's a terrible business, but he died fighting for what is right."

"Really?" I frown at him through my tears. "Nothing feels right about it to me. Nothing feels right about any of this."

Père Rambert's expression is the gravest I've ever seen. "Evil has come to France, Laurence, and we must do everything we can to prevent it. Are you sure you don't want me to pray with you?"

I shake my head. I'm too numb to know what to do.

"All right, I must go and inform the other families."

I think of Luc's parents, who moved to Provence a couple of years ago. "What about Luc's mother and father?"

"A telegram has been sent to them."

"Oh." I have nothing left to say. There *is* nothing left to say.

"Please come and see me later, if you need to."

"I will. Thank you."

I watch him leave the store, then I finally regain the use of my legs and hurry over and lock the door. I cannot open today. I cannot imagine doing anything. I'm barely capable of thinking.

I sit behind my desk and turn on the radio. The news is terrible. German troops have now gathered outside of Paris, but I feel immune to it. As tears stream down my face, all I can think of is Luc.

A sharp rap on the door startles me to my senses. I look up to see Madame Bonheur standing there, her face pressed against the glass, peering inside.

"Laurence, my dear," her voice booms. "Open this door at once!"

It's as if I'm five years old again and she's hollering at me to stop dipping my fingers in the barrel of sugar at the back of her bakery. I numbly obey her command and unlock the door.

"Oh, my dear, my poor sweet girl." She steps inside and wraps her warm, doughy arms around me. "I just heard the news from Père Rambert. I'm so sorry."

At first, I fight her embrace, remaining stiff as a board, but her cinnamon smell is intoxicating, and I find myself melting into her, convulsing with sobs.

"I can't believe he is gone. I can't believe I'll never see him again."

"I know, my dear, it is a tragedy."

"He was too good to die—too kind. He was only just starting his life. He had so much left to do!"

"I know." She puts her hands on my shoulders and looks me in the eye. "He loved you so very much."

I know she's trying to console me, but the effect of her words is crushing.

Outside in the square, the town hall clock strikes nine and the presenter on the radio announces the main headline as if they're announcing the end of the world: "Paris has fallen!"

"My God!" Madame Bonheur exclaims, clutching her hands to her chest.

Before we can say another word, there's a commotion outside. Madame Bonheur spins round and looks outside.

"The Germans are coming!" I hear a child cry. "The Germans are coming!"

I look past Madame Bonheur and see one of the butcher's sons, Noa, pedaling furiously on his bike through the square.

"What do you mean?" Madame Bonheur calls back to him. "Where are the Germans?"

Noa stops his bike. More and more people come out onto the square.

"Have you seen them?" Monsieur Tissier calls from the top of the hotel steps.

"Yes," Noa replies. "I was fishing in the stream by Dove Meadow and I saw them coming down the road at the top of the hill."

Dove Meadow is one of my favorite places in La Vallée du Cerf, situated just a mile out of town. Bile burns at the back of my throat at the thought of the Nazis—the people who murdered Luc—so close to us, and getting closer by the minute.

"Thank you, my dear," Madame Bonheur says to Noa. "Now hurry home, you hear?"

Noa nods and starts pedaling back in the direction of the butcher's.

Monsieur Tissier starts slamming the shutters closed on the hotel windows and the handful of people eating breakfast outside the café scurry away. Abram collects their still full plates and hurries inside, slamming and locking the door behind him.

My heart pounds as the enormity of what is about to happen hits me. Madame Bonheur places her hands on my shoulders.

"You must close the shutters and lock the door, and hide anything valuable," she tells me.

I nod, dazed. All around the square, the rap rap rap of shutters being closed is the only sound to break the stunned silence. Even the birds seem to have stopped singing.

As Madame Bonheur leaves I close the shutters, go inside and pull the blind down over the door, plunging the store into darkness. I sit back down at my desk and focus on my breathing. So much has happened in such a short space of time, my brain feels like a gramophone whose handle is in urgent need of turning. Then I think of what Madame Bonheur said about hiding anything valuable. My beloved books are my most valued possession, but I have far too many to be able to hide them all, and I've never been one for jewelry. Then I remember the pendant Luc gave me the day he left. I'd been so ashamed of the way I reacted when I saw the jewelry box, I've not looked at it since. Now, I take the box from the top drawer of my desk and open it with trembling fingers. Looking at it no longer fills me with shame; it fills me with love as it's my final connection to Luc. As I take it from the velvet cushion, I feel that the back is rough, as if something has been etched into it. I turn on the desk lamp and hold it up to the light. Sure enough, there's a border of tiny writing all around the edge. *I am not afraid. I was born to do this.* My favorite quote from Jeanne of Arc.

"Oh, Luc," I whisper, holding the pendant to my lips.

And then I hear a rumble like thunder coming from outside. I turn off the lamp and radio and realize that it's the sound of engines, accompanied by a sharp, rhythmic clicking. I go over to the door and push the blind slightly to the side. The square is now completely deserted as the sound gets louder and louder. And then I see a line of motorcycles complete with sidecars sweeping into the square. But instead of a person sitting in the sidecars, there are mounted machine guns.

My stomach churns. It's the strangest feeling; after all of these months reading about the Nazis in the papers and hearing about them on the news, to see them arrive here, in my beloved home town, is like being unable to wake from the very worst of nightmares. Behind the motorcycles comes a fleet of gleaming black cars, with tiny flags bearing swastikas fluttering either side of the hoods. And then come columns of marching soldiers. I watch in horror as they begin filling the square, a tide of murky gray green. What should I do? What will *they* do? Are we all about to be killed? My body remains frozen while my mind races.

Outside in the square, there's the sound of a trumpet blast and a man begins speaking in French with a German accent through a megaphone. "Attention. This is the German army," he says. "We are now in charge here. You must all report to us tomorrow and hand in your rifles and your radios."

I look at the radio on my desk, my one connection to the outside world. There is no way I'm giving it to the Germans, but where should I hide it? Then I remember the loose floorboard at the back of the store. I take the radio over to the poetry nook, lift the rug and the loose floorboard and hide it beneath. Then I stand for a moment in the dark, thinking of what Père Rambert said about Luc dying fighting for what is right, fighting evil, and I hold the pendant tightly, as if trying to absorb Saint Jeanne's words of courage through my fingertips.

"I am not afraid. I was born to do this," I whisper into the darkness.

9

LAURENCE—JUNE 1940

After taking a moment to gather my courage, I go back over to the door and peer outside. Several of the townsfolk have come out into the square to listen to the German with the megaphone, who has stationed himself at the top of the town hall steps. I see Monsieur Tissier standing in the doorway of the hotel and Abram is holding the café door slightly ajar.

I take a deep breath and open the door a few inches. My breath catches in my throat as I glance around the square. It's now full of Germans, on foot, bikes and horses, and in cars, lorries and, right at the rear, a line of tanks.

"You will now be living on German time," the soldier with the megaphone announces, and as if by magic another soldier appears holding a ladder. He hurries over to the clock on the town hall wall, races up the ladder and moves the clock hands forward by an hour.

I hear a tut from along the street and see Madame Bonheur in the doorway of her boulangerie, shaking her head.

"You are also now being placed under a curfew and must remain at home between nine o'clock at night and five o'clock in the morning," the soldier continues.

I feel the urge to retch. The very people who killed Luc and Jacques and God knows how many other townsfolk will be living amongst us.

"Now go about your business," the soldier orders. "Heil Hitler."

I jump as the other soldiers yell, "Heil Hitler!" and raise their arms in that chilling salute.

I remain, watching in the doorway, as several soldiers hurry over to the hotel and start talking to Monsieur Tissier. Others peel away and start walking around the square, their jackboots clicking loudly on the cobbles. I see a couple heading toward Madame Bonheur and I step back out of sight, but still keeping the door ajar.

"Good day," I hear one of them say. "Are you the owner of this boulangerie?"

"I most certainly am," she replies curtly.

"Very good. We must inform you of the new rules."

Having no desire to listen to their new rules, I start pacing around the store. Should I open as usual, or wait and see if they visit me too? I'm still pacing a couple of minutes later when there's a rap on the door.

"Good day . . ." The door opens and a German pokes his head inside. Unlike the fair hair of so many of his fellow soldiers, his is as black as coal and his eyes are a piercing shade of blue. "Aha, a bookstore," he says in perfect French with a beaming smile upon his face. The notion that a book-burning Nazi should be happy to see my store completely throws me. "May we come in?" His politeness throws me too.

I nod and he and another soldier step inside. The other soldier rattles something off in German, then the dark-haired one begins to translate.

"Are you the proprietor of this store?"

"Yes." My voice comes out like a squeak.

"And do you live on these premises?"

"Yes. Upstairs."

"And how many bedrooms do you have here?"

"One," I reply, puzzled that this should be of any interest to them.

I wait as he translates my answer to the other soldier. He nods, turns on his heel and leaves.

"Thank you very much," the translator says with a smile. He clicks his heels together in a parting salute and turns to go.

"Excuse me." Again, my voice comes out pitifully weak. "Should I . . . am I allowed to open the store?"

"But of course." He turns and smiles back at me. "The world would be a much duller place without bookstores."

I am so speechless by this response, I stand gaping after him.

I'm still standing gaping when Madame Bonheur comes bustling in, a few moments later, her rosy cheeks even redder than usual.

"Are you all right?" she whispers, as if the Nazis might still be lurking behind one of the bookshelves.

"Yes. No. I don't know. It's all so much to take in."

She nods.

"What did they say to you?" I ask.

"They say I am to bake their bread, and that feeding them must be my priority." She clutches her hands together. "Oh, Laurence, how has it come to this?"

"I don't know."

"I feel terrible asking this when you are going through such a hard time but . . ." She glances around the store. "Do you have something for me? Something that will help save me from despair?"

"Of course." I go over to the poetry nook and take down a hardback collection of Emily Dickinson poems, frantically leafing through the pages until I find her poem "Hope." As my eyes scan the words, I realize that it will probably make the perfect prescription for most, if not all, of the townsfolk. I hurry

over to my desk, take a sheet of prescription paper from the
drawer and feed it into the typewriter. As I type out the poem, it's
as if the words take root inside of me and I can see a bird called
Hope perching in my soul. It's a bright yellow canary, singing oh
so sweetly, and never stopping, not even in the face of loss—or
the arrival of a deadly enemy. I only hope it has the same effect
on Madame Bonheur. Beneath the poem, I type: READ EVERY
MORNING WHEN YOU WAKE AND EVERY NIGHT BEFORE YOU
SLEEP, and hand it to her.

I watch as her eyes scan the words and slowly she nods before
hugging me.

"Thank you. Now I must go, but I'm just next door if you
need me."

"Thank you."

I follow her to the door and peer out into the square. The
armed motorcycles and black cars are still parked in front of the
town hall. The lorries and tanks are driving off, in the direction
of the hill overlooking the town—in the direction of Charlotte's
farm and Chateau Blanc. Gigi!

Even after everything that has happened since she returned,
my first instinct is to protect her. I put on my coat, lock up the
shop and hurry through the square. *Just be natural,* I tell myself,
do not panic. You are just going for a walk to visit a friend. Thankfully, the soldiers left in the square are now gravitating toward
the hotel and none seem to notice me. I turn down the road
toward the station and see a sight that turns my blood to ice: a
group of German soldiers on motorcycles have gathered at the
junction with the road leading up the hill. I'm about to turn and
try going the long way round instead when I realize that they've
noticed me.

"*Guten Tag!*" one of them calls to me, loosening the strap on
his motorcycle helmet.

These are the same people who killed Luc, is all I can think.

The soldier takes off his helmet and grins, as if they've just popped by for a friendly visit rather than occupied our country. He says something else to me in German that I don't understand. The other men chuckle. Then one of them shouts, *"Tres jolie!"* in a mock French accent.

I want to turn and run, but then I remember the pendant in my pocket and I think of Jeanne of Arc and how she fearlessly led the French army into battle against the English at just seventeen. *I am not afraid. I am not afraid,* I repeat to myself as I keep on walking. To my surprise and relief, they let me pass. I hurry up the hill, feeling sick from a mixture of fear and adrenaline. Even the beauty surrounding me when I reach the lane leading to the chateau seems to have lost its charm in the light of what's happened. The sunlight pouring through the trees is too bright. The air too humid. The smell of honeysuckle cloying. Finally, the snowy turrets of the chateau loom into view.

As I approach the house, I'm not sure what to expect. Will Gigi and her parents know about the Germans' arrival yet? And how will I break the news about Luc? I pull on the rope handle beside the door and the bell clangs, making me jump. Every sound feels magnified. I hear footsteps from inside the house and the door opens. The pale face of Maud, the Fontaines' lifelong housekeeper, peers out at me.

"Yes?" she says, her eyes nervously darting this way and that.

"Good day. Is Gigi here?"

"Who is it?" I hear Gigi call from somewhere upstairs.

"It is Laurence," Maud replies, stepping back and ushering me inside.

Maud has always been tall and thin, but where she once used to be as straight as an exclamation point, the top of her spine is now curved like a question mark, and her black hair is streaked with gray. Behind her, I see Gigi coming down the wide curved staircase, holding an ebony-framed hand mirror. She's clad in a scarlet satin robe, with a pink towel wrapped around her hair like a turban.

"Have you heard?" I say.

"Paris has fallen," she replies. "I know, I heard it on the radio."

"No, the Germans are here, in the valley."

Maud gasps and Gigi's icy façade cracks slightly and I see a look of fear flicker across her face. "What do you mean?"

"They're in town now, a couple of hundred of them at least, and it looks as if they'll be staying. You need to tell your parents."

Gigi gives a dry laugh. "My parents have left."

"What do you mean, they've left?"

"They've run away like the government, down south."

"Why didn't you tell me?" I look around the vast hallway with its polished checkered floor and huge chandelier. "Will you be all right here, on your own?"

"Of course! And anyway, I'm not alone, I have Maud."

Maud gives a terse nod.

"There's something else," I say, my mouth going dry. "Some other news."

"Yes?"

I would rather not tell her in front of Maud, but it appears I have no choice. "Luc—he . . . he's dead."

A terrible clatter breaks the silence as Gigi drops the mirror she's carrying and it shatters into tiny diamond-like pieces on the floor.

"Oh no!" Maud cries, throwing her hands up, and I'm not sure if it's the news about Luc or the mess on the floor causing her distress.

"Come," Gigi says, ushering me inside.

I follow her along the wood-paneled hallway to the living room at the back of the house, or the sunbeam room as I used to call it as a child, due to it being bathed in sunshine for most of the day. Little has changed about the room since we were children. The walls are still covered with paper decorated with pink roses and eggshell-blue hummingbirds. An old clock still ticks way too loudly for its size on the mantelpiece, and a fern-green chaise longue still sits facing the fire. The only real difference I can see is the record player perched on top of a side table by the back door and countless records spilling out all around it on the floor. Oh, and a half-drunk tumbler of what looks like whisky and an overflowing ashtray. These must be Gigi's touches as her austere parents had no time for such vices—or any other kind of fun, come to think of it.

"How . . . how did he die?" Gigi asks. Now that we're out of the darkness in the hall, I can see a deathly pallor on her normally rouged cheeks.

"His company—they—they were bombed by the Luftwaffe," I stammer, barely able to bring myself to utter the words.

She sits down on the chaise longue and lights a cigarette with a cube-shaped table lighter made from marble. "I'm sorry," she murmurs.

I perch on one of the ornate, stiff-backed chairs. "I can't believe he's gone. And that the Germans are here too . . . It's too much to comprehend."

"You've seen them?"

I nod. "They're in the square now. They've said that we all have to register at the town hall tomorrow, and hand in any rifles and our radios. Our radios! Can you believe it?"

I look to Gigi for a similar sense of indignation, but her face remains as inexpressive as a mask.

"Well, at least now it might mean an end to the fighting," she eventually says, picking up the tumbler of whisky and taking a swig.

I glance at the clock on the mantelpiece. It's still only ten in the morning—or eleven now, according to the Germans. Why would Gigi be drinking so early? Maybe it's a bohemian actor thing.

"Yes, but at what cost?" I reply. "Who knows what the Germans are planning on doing to us."

"I have a feeling that you and I will be just fine," she responds in her patronizing town mouse tone.

"Why?" I really don't want to get into yet another fractious conversation with her, especially today.

"Well, we're not . . ." She breaks off.

"What?"

"Jewish."

"Yes, but millions of our fellow countrymen and women are. Abram in the café is."

She shrugs and takes another drag on her cigarette. How can she be so indifferent?

"Look, I know your husband-to-be was Jewish, and I know he hurt you, but surely you can't want every Jewish person to be punished just because one man betrayed you."

"You have no idea what that man did to me! And that woman! She was supposed to be my friend." She takes another swig from her drink.

"No, I don't," I say, trying to remain patient, although I feel certain Gigi would try the patience of a saint. "But surely it would be better—your life would be easier—if you were able to forgive."

"Forgive!" she splutters. "You've been spending too much time with Père Rambert. There's no way I'm forgiving that ignorant pig."

The sun comes out from behind a cloud, causing a beam of light to fall on her face and even though she's undeniably beautiful, all I can see is bitterness oozing from every pore of her porcelain skin and I know there's no way I'm going to get through to her.

"I need to go," I say, standing.

"Very well," she replies coldly.

For a moment I think she's going to leave me to see myself out, but she reluctantly gets to her feet.

We walk silently into the hall, where Maud is still sweeping up the remains of the mirror.

"Are you going already?" she asks, looking up at me.

"Yes, I need to get back to the store."

"Well, thank you very much for calling by," Gigi says stiffly.

"You're most welcome," I mutter.

As she opens the door, I hear the sound of a car making its way up the drive, accompanied by the rattle of a motorcycle and my throat tightens.

"My God!" I hear Maud gasp from behind me as a convoy of two cars and a motorcycle displaying flags bearing swastikas comes into view. I glance at Gigi, who tightens her satin robe, but her face remains expressionless.

We stand like a trio of statues in the wide doorway as the vehicles park in front of us and the motorcyclist disembarks and takes off his helmet.

"Good day, proprietor of the house I speak with please?" he asks in broken French.

"That's me," Gigi replies, stepping forward.

He eyes her up and down and grins lasciviously. Then he marches over to one of the cars and says something in German. The rear door opens and we all watch as first one and then two shiny black boots swing into view. The soldier gets out and I can tell straight away from the adornments on his uniform that he's clearly high-ranking. He marches over to us and bows his head and clicks his heels in a salute. High above us, a crow scratches the air with its harsh caw.

The soldier says something in German. His voice is quiet, but eerily rather than comfortingly so. When he has finished speaking, the solider from the motorcycle translates.

"This is Kommandant Muller," he barks. "Staying here he will be."

Maud gasps.

"What do you mean, he'll be staying here?" Gigi asks crisply, appearing completely unfazed. But then she clasps her hands behind her back and I see that her fingers are trembling.

"We are requisitioning accommodation for to stay in our soldiers," he replies in broken French. "We are told that yours is one of the largest houses in the town, so the Kommandant and his men they must stay here."

"How many men?" Gigi asks.

"There will be seven in total. How many bedrooms you have?"

"Nine."

"Very good." He says something to the Kommandant in German.

"And what about me, and my housekeeper?" Gigi nods at Maud.

"You are welcome to stay here too, and she can be our housekeeper also." He smirks.

"Surely you can't stay here with them," I whisper to her. "Come and stay with me."

"And give up my home?" She looks at me as if I'm insane. "Not all of us French run away, you know." She turns on her heel and goes inside. "I'll get dressed, then I'll show you to your rooms," she calls over her shoulder as if welcoming relatives to stay rather than the enemy.

The motorcyclist looks me up and down. "And you are?"

"Just a friend," I reply, although as I trudge off down the driveway, nothing could feel further from the truth.

10

LAURENCE—JUNE 1940

For the next couple of days, I'm in a strange kind of trance. I think the whole town is, as we try to come to terms with our new world order and the sight of German soldiers everywhere. The truth is that they're far more courteous than I think any of us would have imagined. Nodding politely when they pass, chatting and laughing with the children, even giving them sweets and fruit, and according to Violeta, who has had several soldiers billeted to her large house, being immaculately behaved guests. Not that I would trust them for a second. These are still the vermin who have killed so many of our men. They have also taken over the town hall and the hotel, using the bar as a place to congregate for evening meals.

For the first couple of days after their arrival, I barely see a customer in the bookstore and on the morning of the eighteenth of June I'm contemplating closing up and going for a walk in the forest, but then Charlotte appears. She's holding a wicker basket and clad from head to toe in widow's black, including a floor-length mourning veil. She'd stopped dressing in mourning for Jacques about a month ago, so I'm assuming that this is her way of protesting against the Germans. If so, she has my full support.

"Oh Laurence," she says by way of greeting.

"Are you all right?"

She looks around furtively to check the store is empty. "No! I have three of those brutes staying at the farm. Can you imagine? Members of the same army who killed Jacques now living with me, living in his house! And I'm expected to attend to them. It's too much."

"I'm so sorry. It all feels like a terrible dream."

"I was so sad to hear about Luc. Are you all right?"

"Yes. No. I don't know. I think I'm still in shock. If I didn't have so many books to lose myself in I think I would have gone completely mad." I gesture around at the shelves.

"That's how I felt too when Jacques died." She pats my arm. "I brought you something." She places her basket on the desk in front of me and pulls back the cloth cover. All I can see is her purse and a folded newspaper. She reaches beneath the paper and pulls out a couple of eggs with straw still stuck to them and a pat of butter wrapped in brown paper. "It's not much, but I'd rather you have it than them."

"Oh Charlotte, thank you."

"Nonsense. After all you've done for me with your book prescriptions, it's the least I could do. Speaking of which . . ." She glances at the shelves. "I don't suppose there's anything you can prescribe for me now, to help me get through?"

"But of course." I reach into the desk drawer and pull out one of the copies of "Hope" by Emily Dickinson that I'd typed up for just such an occasion. I've typed about twenty copies now and not just for my fellow townsfolk. I need to keep writing those words to make the sentiment really sink in, and keep my bird of hope singing. I hand Charlotte the poem and watch as she reads.

"It's beautiful," she whispers.

"It helps if you try to picture an actual bird perching inside of you," I say. "Mine is a canary. I think of it every time I see one of them." I nod out of the window at four German soldiers patrolling the square.

"I think that my hope shall be a hummingbird," Charlotte says with a small smile.

"Excellent choice."

She slips the poem into her basket. "Thank you so much."

"You're welcome."

"I'd better get back. I'm worried about leaving Raul on his own. You know he is a communist?"

"I didn't, no."

"The Communist Party are supposed to be neutral about the Germans because of the pact they have with Russia, but he really detests the Nazis and he's finding it very hard to hide his feelings. You know how blunt he can be."

"I do." I see her to the door. "*Bon courage.*"

"Thank you, and you too."

Once she's gone, I put the food she brought in the pantry. The thought of Charlotte having to live with the people who took Jacques' life is atrocious. It makes me grateful that after Papa died, Maman had to sell our house and we moved into the room above the store. If I had a German soldier billeted with me, I don't know how I'd be able to control my temper.

I hear the bell over the door tinkle and hurry back into the store. The German translator with the black hair is standing by my desk, smiling warmly.

"Good day. I thought I might treat myself to a book," he says.

"Most of them are in French," I reply shortly, "and I have some in English, but none in German."

He doesn't seem to pick up on my hostility and continues smiling. "That is not a problem. I love French writers."

"Oh really? Such as?"

"Balzac is one of my favorites."

I frown. Balzac is one of France's most well-known writers. Is he just saying this to try to gain favor with me?

"Oh yes, and what have you read by him?"

His smile grows as if he's enjoying this literary challenge. "*Le Père Goriot.* Although I also like his *Louis Lambert.*" He gazes into the middle distance, as if retrieving a memory. " 'He devoured books of every kind ... even taking delight in reading the dictionary if no other books were available.' " He looks back at me. "I was like this also, as a child."

"Me too," I blurt out, remembering how I would read Maman's sewing patterns if there was nothing else to read. Then I remember who this man is and what he represents and shame pulses through me.

"Perhaps you could recommend something to me?" he asks.

"I'm sure someone as well read as you will be just fine," I reply curtly, sitting down behind my desk.

While he browses, I feel increasingly nauseous. How has the world come to this? How is a member of the same force that killed Luc and Jacques now walking around the store, walking in Luc's very footsteps? By the time he reappears at my desk, I can barely see straight from confusion and anger.

"I will take this, please," he says, placing a French translation of *Faust* by Goethe in front of me. "I have read it in German obviously, but it will help with my French to read this edition."

"Very well," I reply.

"I am Gerhard by the way." He looks at me expectantly.

"Laurence," I say crisply.

"Thank you, Laurence." He looks at the price written on the inside sleeve of the book and places the money on my desk. "What does this mean?" He points to the sign beside my typewriter.

"It is nothing, just a little service I offer my customers."

"I like the sound of a book prescription." He smiles.

"Very good," I mutter.

His smile fades. "Well, I suppose I must get back. I've been billeted to the chateau up on the hill."

"Chateau Blanc?" I can't help asking in spite of my desire to ignore him.

"Yes, you know it?"

"I know the family who own it."

"Gigi?"

"Yes." I feel a stab of concern as I think of Gigi and Maud on their own up on the hill with a group of German soldiers.

"I see. Well, thank you for your time and the book." He tucks it into his pocket.

"No need to thank me. You bought it."

"Yes, but still." He clicks his heels together and bows his head. "Until we meet again."

I watch as he leaves the store and listen to the sound of his boots on the cobbles fading into the distance. Hopefully he won't come back. Hopefully I made him realize that he isn't welcome here.

For a long time after the soldier has gone, I feel uneasy. When I can't bear it any longer, I close the store and head to the church, trying to ignore the soldiers goose-stepping in formation across the square.

Thankfully, the church with its beautiful stained-glass light and incense-infused air doesn't appear to have been contaminated by our occupiers, yet at least. I see Père Rambert by the altar tending to a vase of wild flowers.

"Oh Père," I sigh as I reach him. "I don't know how much more of this I can take."

He glances beyond me to the large oak doors, as if he's expecting someone to walk in on us.

"How are we supposed to live with the people who have killed so many of our own—the people who killed Luc and Jacques? Why is this happening?" I implore.

"There, there, my child," Père Rambert says in a hushed

tone, patting me on the shoulder. "There is no denying it is a very challenging time, but we have to remain steadfast."

"But how?"

"Do you remember what Jesus cried out when he was on the cross?"

I nod, although in truth I have forgotten.

"He asks God why he has forsaken him," Père Rambert says, as if he can read my blank mind.

"What, even Jesus thought God had forgotten him?"

"Yes, but of course He hadn't. God is like the sun."

"How?"

"On those days when it is cloudy has the sun ceased to exist?"

"No, but—"

"It is still there, waiting for the clouds to clear."

"But what if it feels as if they'll never clear?"

"Like last winter?"

"Yes."

"Did spring not come? And then summer? Is the sun not shining now?" He looks up at one of the stained-glass windows. Shafts of light are pouring through the blue cloak of the Virgin Mary.

The church door creaks open and Violeta comes in. She bobs down and crosses herself before kneeling in one of the pews.

"At least now we have an end to the fighting and killing," Père Rambert says in a loud voice. "At least now we can live in peace."

"But—"

His bushy eyebrows knot together in a frown and he places his hand on my arm. "The sun is still there," he says firmly.

I stare at him, bewildered. Has he not read the papers or listened to the news? Is he unaware of what the Nazis have done in their own country and Austria and Poland? Is he unaware of the millions of French soldiers they've killed or taken captive? He'll be telling me next that we ought to love our enemy. Disappointment seeps through me. "I need to get back to the store," I mutter and turn to leave.

Back in the store, I pace up and down, wishing Luc was there with a force that hurts. He was always so good at calming me. "What should I do?" I whisper into the empty shop. "How will I live like this?" But, of course, Luc doesn't reply because Luc is dead. He's dead. And those monsters killed him. I don't think I've ever felt so impotent. "I can't give up," I sob, slumping down at my desk. "I can't let them win."

Then don't . . . a voice seems to whisper back at me, or maybe it's coming from within me. It's impossible to tell. *Don't let them win. Don't give up.*

"But what am I to do," I whisper back, "when even our government have capitulated?" I close my eyes, and wait, and listen.

Keep saying no, the answer comes from some deeper, wiser place. *Keep saying no.*

That night I think of the only way of saying no that is left to me and I take the radio from its hiding place in the store and bring it upstairs to my bedroom. Feeling the slightly paranoid desire to keep my actions hidden, I drape the covers over the bedpost, creating a makeshift tent, just like I used to when I was a child reading by flashlight after bedtime. Oh how innocent that seems now! Oh to go back to those days and somehow stop this nightmare from happening.

I switch the radio on and turn the dial until I hear the clipped British tones of a BBC announcer. I instantly feel some relief. The British troops might have been driven from France, but they are still at war with the Germans. They could still *beat* the Germans, especially if they persuade the Americans to join with them.

I curl onto my side and fetch the Jeanne of Arc pendant from my pocket, clutching it to my chest. I'm about to turn the radio off and go to sleep when I hear a man speaking in French and it's like a bolt of lightning coursing right through me.

"It is quite true that we were, and still are, overwhelmed by enemy mechanized forces," the man is saying. "But has the last word been said? Must we abandon all hope? Is our defeat final and irremediable? To those questions, I answer—no!"

My skin erupts in goosebumps as I remember the words I heard inside my head earlier. *Keep saying no.*

"For remember this, France does not stand alone. She is not alone!" the man continues in an impassioned tone, but who is he? And why is he speaking on the BBC?

"I, General de Gaulle, now in London, call on all French officers and men who are at present on British soil, or may be in the future, with or without their arms; I call on all engineers and skilled workmen from the armaments factories who are at present on British soil, or may be in the future, to get in touch with me. Whatever happens, the flame of the French resistance must not, and shall not, die. Tomorrow I shall broadcast again from London."

As the broadcast ends, I lie back and frown. Who is this person calling himself General de Gaulle? It sounds like a made-up name to me, for wasn't Gaul the old name for France? Could there really be a person called the General of France? But does it matter who he is? Surely all that matters is what he said, and on the BBC no less. *The flame of the French resistance must not, and shall not, die.* I feel his words burning deep inside me.

. . .

I wake the next morning with the hazy feeling that something important has happened, but I can't quite remember what. Then I feel the sharp edge of the radio next to me in the bed and it all comes flooding back. The mysterious man on the BBC calling himself the General of Gaul, and more importantly, his rousing words of resistance. I wonder if anyone else in town heard the broadcast. I'm pretty sure I'm not the only one to have refused to hand my radio in to the Germans. Speaking of which, I need to hide it immediately. I would have done it last night, if I hadn't been so excited.

I get out of bed and make my way downstairs. Thankfully, the blackout blinds mean that no one is able to see me from the street. I hide the radio beneath the floorboard then I ponder venturing to the café for breakfast. I haven't been there since the Germans arrived, I'd been far too downhearted to want to see any of them up close, but last night's broadcast has got my canary of hope singing.

For the past few days, I've paid very little attention to what I've been wearing and I haven't gone near my cosmetics, but this morning, as I apply a coat of dark pink lipstick, it feels like an act of defiance. The French resistance must not be extinguished and I am determined not to let those Nazis see how they have rattled me. I kiss my Jeanne of Arc pendant and slip it into my pocket next to the Nénette doll.

Outside, the sun is already warm but made bearable by a gentle breeze. My heart sinks as I see that every table outside the café is occupied by German soldiers dressed in their dreary gray green, but I will not be thwarted. I lock the shop door and stride across the square. All heads outside the café turn toward me as I draw close.

"*Guten Tag,*" one of the soldiers says in a slightly suggestive way and a couple of them snigger.

I force myself to smile—a feat so hard it feels as if my face might actually creak from the effort. "*Bonjour,*" I reply. *You hideous toad*, I continue in my mind.

"Day lovely, *ja?*" he says in broken French.

"Yes," I reply. *And it would be even lovelier if you would all drop dead.* I give an inner smirk, enjoying this new game.

Inside the café, I find Abram standing behind the counter, drying a plate with such force it's a wonder he hasn't rubbed the paint off. Thankfully, there are no Germans inside; they're all too busy stealing our sunshine.

"Good day, Abram, how are you?"

He looks at me and I see fear in his eyes.

"Are you all right?" I ask quietly as I reach the counter.

"Yes," he mutters. "What can I get you?"

"Do you really need to ask?" I joke, but he doesn't smile. "Did you hear the broadcast last night, on the BBC?" I whisper.

"I no longer have a radio. We were supposed to hand them in," he whispers back, clearly unnerved.

"I will be handing mine in today," I lie, realizing that it's probably not best to broadcast the fact that I have disobeyed the German toads. "But I listened last night and a French general was giving a speech—on the BBC—to France! He said that the French resistance shall not die!"

The door opens and a pasty-faced soldier comes in.

"Take a seat. I will bring your breakfast over," Abram tells me before turning to the soldier. "Yes, sir?"

I sit down, feeling slightly sick. How must it feel to be Abram, or anyone Jewish in France for that matter, having to serve the monsters who are intent on persecuting your people?

"Coffee and croissant," the soldier barks, no please or thank you. He slings some money on the counter, then marches back outside.

I try to catch Abram's gaze to give him a sympathetic smile, but he's already turned away to make the coffee, his shoulders slumped.

After breakfast, I call into the church to see if Père Rambert has heard anything of last night's broadcast. I find him kneeling in the front pew praying, so I take a seat and look up at the statue of Jesus nailed to his cross above the altar. I used to wish that the church chose more joyful versions of Jesus for their statues, like him turning water into wine, but now his suffering feels strangely comforting. Finally, the Père finishes praying and stands.

"Laurence," he says upon seeing me.

"Good day, Père." I glance over my shoulder to make sure there's no one else in the church. "Did you hear the broadcast last night on the BBC?"

"What are you doing, listening to the radio?" the Père hisses, also glancing around the church. "We are supposed to have handed them in."

"I'm not giving those poisoned toads my radio," I reply defiantly.

"Oh Laurence, you must be careful. You don't know what they are capable of."

"Yes, yes I do." To my annoyance, tears fill my eyes. I blink them away. "They murdered Luc, didn't they?"

"Of course, I'm sorry."

"I thought you said we should do everything we could to prevent their evil," I hiss. "But ever since they got here, you've been acting like a coward." I see hurt in his eyes and feel a stab of guilt. Calling a priest a coward, and in his church, is surely an unforgiveable sin.

"Come," he says, nodding to the confessional.

Is he serious? I stare at him as he strides over to the ornately carved booth, the bottom of his cassock swishing on the stone floor.

I trudge after him like a sulky child and kneel in my side of the box. "Forgive me, Father, for I have sinned. It has been..." I quickly try to work it out. "...quite some time since my last confession. I'm sorry I called you a coward," I whisper through the latticed partition. "I was just so excited last night to hear a French general tell us that all is not lost, that France has not lost. I wanted to share it with you."

I close my eyes and wait for him to dole out my punishment. I hear a creak from the other side of the box and then his whispered voice right by the lattice partition.

"What you have to realize, Laurence, is that it is now very dangerous to share such things."

My eyes spring open in surprise.

"I heard the speech," he continues. "But we have a very long and treacherous road ahead of us. And we no longer know who we can trust."

We, he's saying *we*. My skin prickles with excitement. Does this mean . . .

"Is your radio well hidden?" he asks.

"Yes," I whisper back.

"Good. Keep it that way. And for now we must wait, and watch and listen."

"What for?"

"For further instruction."

"All right," I say obediently.

"And you must trust no one, do you understand? So no more talk about what you heard on your radio."

"I understand." I pause. "Do you think he was right, the French general?"

"About what?"

"About the flame of French resistance not dying, about us not losing the war."

There's a moment's silence and the Père clears his throat. "Yes. God willing."

11

JEANNE—1993

As the cab chugged its way up the cobblestoned hill, Jeanne drank in the pretty white cottages either side, their walls draped with amethyst bursts of wisteria and thin wisps of smoke coiling from their chimneys.

"This place is beautiful," she murmured to Wendell, beside her on the back seat.

He nodded, gazing silently out of the window. It was the quietest he'd been all journey. On the plane, he'd been so taken with the in-flight food and entertainment and Jeanne had been so caught up in her own feelings of apprehension, she'd forgotten that this trip was bound to be nerve-wracking for him too. She still hadn't got him to tell her what had happened to Laurence. All she'd been able to deduce was that she, Jeanne, had had to leave France in a hell of a hurry as a baby and then Wendell had been posted back to an airbase in the US so that her gram and gramps could take care of her until the war ended. And when the war ended, Wendell married Lorilee and the rest, as they say, was history. Whenever Jeanne tried quizzing Wendell about what had happened to Laurence, he closed up like a clam, pleading ignorance and telling her to wait until they got to France. Her skin tingled. What if her birth mom was still alive? What if they were able to find her?

The cab driver, a heavy-set man with dark gelled hair, muttered something in French as they reached the top of the hill and emerged onto a large square lined with ornate buildings all made from the same creamy stone. He drove around the square and parked outside a building with rows of shuttered windows, bearing the sign "Hotel Belle Vue."

"Looks like we're here," Jeanne said, but Wendell was still staring blankly at the square.

Jeanne got out of the cab and said, "*Merci,*" to the driver, hoping she'd pronounced it correctly.

He nodded and went to get their cases from the trunk and Jeanne hurried round to help Wendell out.

"Well, I'll be damned," he muttered as he gazed around.

"You OK?" Jeanne asked, concerned.

He nodded. "It just feels so strange—being back here—and seeing it in the daylight."

"Oh." Jeanne made a mental note to ask what he meant as she fumbled in her purse for some of the French francs she'd gotten at the airport's money exchange.

The driver said something unintelligible and she held the money out helplessly, all of her hard-earned Chicago street smarts instantly worthless as he took a bunch of the notes from her. And then he was driving off and Jeanne, Wendell and their suitcases were left standing there, in a square, in the middle of France.

Jeanne glanced around. Next to the hotel, there was a café with a row of small round tables lined up outside, the seats all facing outward. An old man sat on the floor beside the café playing the accordion, his eyes closed and his head swaying in time with the melody. On the other side of the hotel, a majestic building towered over the square, French flags fluttering on poles either side of the sweeping steps leading to the entrance.

Nestled slightly behind the building, there was a beautiful old church, its spire reaching like a pointed finger into the clear blue sky. She turned to the opposite side of the square, where there was a row of tiny stores. People were gathered in clusters outside them, looking in the windows and laughing and chatting.

"So Laurence's store would have been somewhere on this square," Jeanne said, her stomach churning. What if the store was still there? What if her mom still owned it? What if she'd just sent the deeds with Jeanne for safekeeping?

"Yes. Although I'm not exactly sure where it was," Wendell replied, leaning on his cane. He looked exhausted.

The clock on the wall of the building with the flags said that it was coming up to one o'clock in the afternoon. Jeanne checked her watch. It was approaching six in the morning Chicago time; they'd been traveling for over twelve hours.

"What say we check in, then maybe we could go get a coffee in the café next door?" she suggested.

"Sounds like a plan."

The hotel lobby was dark and cool and smelled of furniture polish, which figured, as everything in the place, from the reception desk to the coffee table and the grandfather clock in the corner, gleamed in the soft lamplight. The reception desk was opposite the entrance, and to the left there was an archway leading to a bar, and to the right, another archway opening onto a restaurant. The soft murmur of chatter and clinking of cutlery filled the air.

A woman with hair as shiny and brown as the furniture stood behind the desk and she greeted them with a warm smile. Her understated makeup was immaculately applied and her peach satin blouse and black pencil skirt fitted her hourglass figure perfectly. Jeanne guessed this was what was meant by the term "French chic" and she instantly felt underdressed in her faded Levi's and Bob Seger tee.

"Hey, I don't suppose you speak English?" she asked hopefully as she approached the desk.

To her relief, the woman nodded. "Yes, of course."

"Awesome. We have a reservation for two rooms in the name of Jensen."

"Ah, yes." The woman looked down at a register on the desk. "Welcome to the Hotel Belle Vue."

"Thank you."

"Howdy," Wendell said to the woman with a twinkly-eyed grin, tipping his baseball cap in greeting.

The woman beamed back at him and took two keys from a rack on the wall. "You are on the third floor, so you will have some excellent views."

"I hope you guys have an elevator," Wendell quipped, waving his cane.

"We do indeed." The woman pointed to a small elevator door in the corner of the lobby and handed Jeanne the keys. "Are you here on vacation?"

"Kind of," Jeanne replied.

The woman looked at her quizzically.

"We're here on a bit of a fact-finding mission too," Jeanne explained. Someone my daddy—uh—used to know lived here during the Second World War. We're trying to find out more about her."

The woman's smile faded. "That was a very dark time here."

There was something about the way she said it that made Jeanne shiver.

"Anyway, I hope you find what you've come for," she said, her smile returning.

"Thank you."

Jeanne and Wendell crammed inside the tiny elevator with their suitcases.

"Breathe in," Wendell joked as the door slid shut. Jeanne smiled. Her whole life she'd seen her mild-mannered dad as the supporting actor in the Lorilee show, always floating around in the background, never taking center stage. But since his revelation about Laurence, she was getting to see a whole other side to him. They might have come to France to find out more about her real mom, but hopefully this vacation would give her a chance to get to know her real dad better too.

The elevator pinged and the door slid open onto a narrow corridor with oak-paneled walls and a plush burgundy carpet. They reached the first of their rooms and Jeanne unlocked the door. The furniture inside was old-fashioned but full of character and the window looked out onto the back of the square, revealing a panorama of green.

"Wow, look at all those trees," Jeanne said, pointing to the dense forest blanketing the hills.

Wendell muttered something and sat on the end of the bed. "This room will do me fine, honey. Do you mind if I don't join you for a coffee? Pesky jet lag's got me beat."

"Of course. You take a nap, Pops, and I'll see you later."

Jeanne's room was at the other end of the corridor. Ordinarily, she would have found the pale pink wallpaper and matching floral bedspread and curtains a little too girly for her taste, but here in this beautiful town, it only seemed to add to the magic.

She put her case down and went over to the window. The room overlooked the square and the lilting strains from the accordion player drifted up on the warm breeze to greet her. She gazed down at the statue of a soldier leaning on his rifle in the center of the square. She wondered if it was connected to the Second World War. Then she looked beyond the statue to the row of shops. They were all so tiny compared to American stores, but that just added to the charm of the place. Could one of them have been Laurence's bookstore? Could it *still be* her bookstore?

She watched as a man came out of one of the stores holding a stick-shaped loaf of bread and her stomach rumbled. Unlike

Wendell, she didn't take any delight in airline food and had barely touched her alleged "chicken" in its plastic tray. But now she was in France, a country renowned for its cuisine. Her stomach rumbled again and she picked up her purse and headed for the door.

Once outside, Jeanne made a beeline across the square to the "boulangerie," according to the sign above the door. As soon as she was within a couple of meters, she caught the waft of the most delicious smell and her hunger grew. The curved bay window was full of tiny round cookies in every color of the rainbow. Behind them was an arrangement of wicker baskets crammed full of pastries and sticks of bread. They looked almost too good to eat. Almost, but not quite.

She was about to step inside when she noticed the building next door. It was completely boarded up and someone had painted the word LIBERTÉ in red on the central board. She spotted a jar of wilting red roses on the ground by the door and felt a strange tingling in the pit of her stomach. She stepped back to get a better look at the building. There were two small dark windows on the first floor and what must have been the store's sign running across the building beneath them. It had clearly been battered by the elements over the years and what was left of the paintwork was chipped and peeling, but she could just make out the word *Livres*. She felt a jolt of recognition. Wasn't that in the name of Laurence's store on the deeds Wendell had shown her?

She took her English–French pocket dictionary from her purse and turned to the words beginning with L. *Livres* meant books. Her heart began to pound. Had this relic of a building been her real mom's bookstore? But why was it boarded up, and why had someone painted LIBERTÉ on the front? And why were there flowers outside of it, like it was some kind of shrine? A feeling of alarm surged through her. What had happened there?

12

LAURENCE—AUGUST 1940

For the next couple of months, all thoughts of resistance feel slightly anticlimactic as I heed the Père's advice and watch and wait and listen. To my disappointment, all I seem to hear from many of my fellow townsfolk is the refrain, "At least there is no more fighting," as they sink into a weird kind of apathy. It's impossible to know what people are really thinking and it's the strangest thing, living in a town you've spent your entire life in, with people you've known forever, but now, suddenly, there's a silent question hanging in the air between us: *Whose side are you on?* As it's too dangerous to ask the question directly, you're left to guess at the answer. This is easier with some people than with others. Sadly, it seems that Gigi has taken the side of our occupiers. According to Violeta, she's now a regular guest at the Kommandant's table in the hotel bar. Apparently, the soldiers love basking in the glow of a star of the Paris stage. The only way I'm able to reconcile this revelation with my memories of my childhood friend Genevieve is to pretend that she died along with Luc and this Gigi character is an interloper, just like the Germans.

On the first Monday in August, I open the store with a

heavy heart. Every night I listen to the broadcasts from the BBC, but I want to do more than listen, I want to take action, but what can I do? I decide to rearrange the window display to try to lift my spirits. I'm midway through arranging an assortment of Dickens' novels around the mannequin when I hear the sound of boots on the cobbles and two soldiers appear. I'm just placing an open copy of *Oliver Twist* in the mannequin's hand when one of the soldiers bangs on the window, causing me to practically jump out of my skin, and the book goes flying to the floor. The soldier barges through the door and barks something at me in German, then points to the copy of *Oliver Twist* on the floor. In the midst of his barrage of German, I recognize the words "Charles Dickens" and then he says, "*Jude*" three times. I know enough German by now to know that *Jude* means Jew.

"But Dickens wasn't a Jew," I say.

He reaches past me and grabs the book. "*Jude,*" he says again, and he begins tearing the pages out and throwing them onto the floor.

I'm about to leap at him when I see the gun holstered to his belt, and the other solider, now standing sentry-like at the door. Once all of the pages are on the floor, he flings the empty cover back at me. It ricochets off my hip and lands at my feet. The soldiers march off. As I pick up the hollow husk of the novel, it triggers a bottomless sense of loss inside of me and I'm unable to stop myself from crying. I cry for the book, I cry for our town, I cry for our country and, finally, I cry for the loss of Luc. Ever since I received word of his death I've been trying to press down my grief but now it all comes spilling over and out of me, searing and raw.

I know I need to get out of the window. I don't want those monsters to see what they've done to me, but it's as if I've become paralyzed by sorrow. Through the haze of my tears, I see a figure walk past, then stop and come back. I wipe my eyes and, to my horror, I see Gerhard staring in at me. Since arriving in the Valley he's become a regular customer in the store but I've studiously avoided being drawn into his attempts at conversation and he's the last person I want to see now.

"Laurence!" he mouths through the glass, clearly shocked.

I stumble to my feet, knocking the mannequin sideways, and make my way out of the window.

"What is wrong?" Gerhard asks as he comes through the door. He looks at the crumpled pages on the floor. "What has happened?"

You Nazis, that's what's happened, I want to scream at him, but all of the fight has gone out of me.

He crouches down and picks up a couple of the torn pages. "Oh, *Oliver Twist*," he says knowingly. "Who did this?"

"One of your fellow soldiers," I mutter.

"I see." He picks up all of the pages and places them on my desk. "This book, it is banned in Germany."

"Why?"

"It features Jewish characters."

"Jewish . . . what, you mean, Fagin?" I stare at him in disbelief. Fagin is hardly the most sympathetic portrayal of a Jew; if anything, I would have expected the psychopath Hitler to have enjoyed it.

Gerhard nods. "He shouldn't have destroyed your book. He should have simply asked you to remove it. I'm sorry."

His apology means nothing; if anything, coming from one of *them* it only makes things worse. "So what am I supposed to do?" I gesture around the store. "Get rid of everything and only stock *Mein Kampf*?"

He looks shocked and shakes his head. "No!" There's something about the vehemence of his response that takes me by surprise. Why would he not want me to sell Hitler's book? "Wasn't *Mein Kampf* banned here?" he asks.

"Yes." I cast my mind back a few years to when a publisher named Fernand Sorlot brought out a French edition of the book. Bizarrely, Hitler had taken him to court to have the edition banned.

"You don't need to stock *Mein Kampf*," Gerhard says firmly. "And if any other soldier bothers you about your books—or anything else for that matter—you must tell me, do you understand?"

I nod, but I'm not really focusing on what he's saying. Why had Hitler banned Sorlot, who was rumored to be anti-Semitic, from publishing his book? Why did Gerhard react so vehemently to my sarcastic suggestion? Maybe it's because I'm seeking a distraction from my grief, but after he leaves, my mind is like a dog with a bone, gnawing away on this question. What if there was something in the Sorlot edition that Hitler didn't want us to see? That the Germans still don't want us to see. If only I could get my hands on a copy. If there is something sinister hidden in those pages, I could let people know and maybe shake them from their apathy. And surely this would be an act of resistance, the kind General de Gaulle speaks about in his radio addresses. I consider seeking Père Rambert's advice but decide against it, for fear that he might talk me out of doing something. I've waited, I've watched and I've listened—now is the time for action. But where would I find a copy of Sorlot's book?

The answer comes to me instantly—the place I always go when I'm searching for book treasure, my friend Michel, the Paris *bouquiniste*. But how would I get to Paris now that the Germans have restricted travel? I could say that I need to buy new stock for the store. Surely self-proclaimed book lover Gerhard would be sympathetic. He clearly felt bad about one of his fellow soldiers destroying *Oliver Twist*. Hopefully, he would be grateful for a chance to make amends. And maybe I could sweeten the deal by asking him if there are any books he would like me to find for him. Now that I have the seed of a plan, I'm way too excited to sit in the store, so I lock up and set off around the square to see if I can find him.

As luck would have it, I find Gerhard almost immediately, having breakfast at a table outside the hotel.

"Hello again," I say gaily as I approach Gerhard's table. It's amazing how much easier I find it to be friendly now that I have a cunning plan to help fan the flames of resistance.

"Laurence!" he greets me with a warm smile. "Would you care to join me for some coffee?"

"No!" I reply a little too harshly, but there's no way I want people thinking that I fraternize with the enemy. "I have a lot of work to do, I'm sorry," I add quickly. "Actually, that's why I was looking for you."

"You were looking for me?" He seems too pleased by this for my liking, but I try to ignore it.

"Yes. I need to go to Paris to get some new stock for the shop and I was wondering if there was anything in particular you'd like me to get for you. You have become one of my best customers after all." My God, who knew I was this good at acting?

His smile grows. "That is so thoughtful of you. Perhaps you could keep a lookout for anything by Balzac?"

"But of course." And now for the crucial part of my plan. "Can you tell me, do I need any kind of paperwork to take the train to Paris for business?"

He shakes his head. "Don't worry about that. I will see to it that you get the necessary document. I'll bring it to the store later."

"Thank you."

"Oh, good day." Gigi appears on the hotel terrace, radiant in a cornflower-blue dress and pearls. She looks shocked to see Gerhard and me together.

"We were just discussing bookstore matters," I tell her.

Gigi sits down at Gerhard's table without being invited.

"Are you sure you don't want to join us for a coffee?" he asks me.

"No, I need to get back to the store. Thank you for your help."

He stands as I prepare to leave. "No, Laurence, thank you."

I hurry off, internally groaning. I really hope I haven't made him think that we're going to be book-loving bosom buddies.

As I cross the square, I see Madame Bonheur and a couple of other women standing in front of The Book Dispensary laughing heartily. Such unabashed merriment is a rare sight these days so, I'm instantly intrigued.

"Good day, ladies," I call as I approach them. "Please tell me the joke? I'm in urgent need of something funny."

Madame Bonheur points a chubby finger at the shop window. The mannequin is sprawled across the chair where I knocked her, her dress up around her waist, revealing a pair of lacy bloomers. "These ladies told me what you have done with your display and I had to come and see for myself," Madame Bonheur says. "Really, it is too funny."

"It is like she is drunk," one of the other women says.

I'm about to tell them that it was actually an accident, but why ruin their fun? And I'd far rather them think it was intentional than caused by a fascist Nazi toad. "She *is* drunk," I tell them. "Drunk on books!"

"Oh Laurence!" Madame Bonheur grabs me and plants a kiss on my cheek. "You are all the entertainment we need. Now I must get back to my customers."

As she hurries off next door to the boulangerie, I unlock the store door and, to my joy, the other women follow me inside.

"In all of this business, I'd forgotten how much joy a book can bring," I hear one say.

"Me too," says the other, as they start browsing around.

I hurry over to help them, and for the sweetest moment, I

am like Alice falling down her rabbit-hole, thinking of nothing but my wonderland of books.

Gerhard is good to his word and provides me with a travel pass, so the very next day I find myself on a train to Paris. It's been months since I was last in the city and I'm very apprehensive about what I might find. Just the thought of seeing swastikas draped all over our beloved capital buildings makes me feel sick to my stomach. But at least now I'm doing something to try to resist, I remind myself as I stare out of the window at the countryside rolling by. Gazing at the hills and fields bleached pale gold by the summer sun is strangely therapeutic. For a while, I'm able to imagine that the Germans aren't here, that the nightmare isn't real. But then I see a field in the distance dotted with their planes, like sinister mechanical birds grazing for worms, and I realize that nowhere is safe from them.

As soon as I arrive in Paris, the German occupation is all too apparent in the form of an armed checkpoint at the ticket barrier. I take my papers from my bag, my heart pounding. *I am in Paris on business, I have done nothing wrong*—I remind myself. *Yet, at least*. But if I do manage to find a copy of Sorlot's *Mein Kampf*, how will I manage to get it through any checkpoints on the way back? Have I been foolish and naïve coming up with such a scheme? Has my desperation to do something, *anything*, clouded my judgment?

As I wait while the queue of passengers inches closer to the checkpoint, I try to reassure myself. As long as I'm able to find Michel, all will be well. He'll be able to advise me.

Finally, it is my turn to have my papers checked. Of course, I have the more sour-faced of the four soldiers on duty, but after what feels like an age, he shoves the papers back in my hands and waves me through. The relief I feel is like the fizz from champagne. But it is short-lived. As I emerge from the station, the Paris I see before me reminds me of the destroyed copy of *Oliver Twist*. With its normally bustling streets practically empty of cars and people, it is like a hollowed-out husk of a city—all of the walking, talking, living stories stripped from it.

I make my way toward the Seine, past shuttered-up shops and open but almost empty cafés. What if I've made a terrible mistake coming here? What if the Nazis have driven the *bouquinistes* from their stalls on the banks of the river? Just the thought makes me despair. There have been people selling books on the banks of the Seine since the sixteenth century. People joke that it is the only river in the world to run between two bookshelves.

By the time I'm a block away, it takes everything I've got not to break into a run, but I mustn't draw attention to myself from the German cars and bikes and foot soldiers patrolling the streets. Finally, I see the glimmer of water and . . . I crane my neck. The green booths are still there! There are less of them, I notice, spaced out rather than all together. *Please, please, let Michel's still be there.* I hurry along the pavement, glancing into the green booths. It is such a relief to see the magazines suspended on pegs from the slanted roofs and the lines of books displayed on the tables. But where is Michel?

I smell him before I see him, the sweet aroma of his pipe smoke causing my canary of hope to trill. I follow my nose to his box and find him perched on his stool behind the table. As always, he is wearing a brightly colored bow-tie—scarlet today— teamed with a pink shirt, brown corduroy jacket and dark green trousers. It has only been around four months since I last saw him, but he looks thinner and his auburn hair is grayer at the temples.

"Michel!" I exclaim.

When he sees me, he flings the magazine he's been reading into the air. "Laurence! My dear! You are still alive!"

I'm so happy to see that the Germans haven't suppressed his theatrical tendencies, I grin from ear to ear.

"I've been so worried about you," he continues as he hurries out of his booth to greet me.

"And I you!"

He hugs me to him. "How did you get here?"

"Train. I got a travel permit to come and buy some stock for the shop."

"That is wonderful. I have a treat for you." He goes back behind his stall and pulls a book from under the table. "*The Hunchback of Notre Dame*, first edition."

"Ooh la la!" I exclaim, turning the book over in my hands. I open the front cover and see that someone has inscribed it: *To my darling Michelle, with all my love, Walter, Christmas 1831.* I feel a wistful pang as I think of this Michelle and Walter and how they must now be deceased, although, given what has happened to the world, maybe they are in a better place. "I will buy it for sure," I say, fumbling in my bag for my purse.

"No, no." He shakes his head. "It is a gift."

"Michel, you have to earn a living, especially in these times."

"I know. But hopefully you will buy something else from me, no?"

"Of course."

"Would you care for a coffee?" He fetches a flask and two tin beakers from beneath the table.

"Yes please. Actually . . ." I glance either side to check for Nazis. "I have a rather unusual request."

"Yes?" Michel pours the coffee and hands one of the beakers to me.

I lean across the table and lower my voice to a whisper. "I am looking for a copy of *Mein Kampf*."

Michel splutters his mouthful of coffee back into his cup. "What? Why?"

"Not for me," I say quickly. "I mean, not for my reading pleasure, obviously. I am just—I am curious about something."

"About Hitler?" He looks at me as if I'm a stranger to him. I know what he must be thinking and I need to set him straight instantly, before he pushes me into the river. Michel is a communist and even though Russia have their pact with the Germans, I know that he abhors Hitler.

"Yes. Why did he get Sorlot's original French edition of the book banned? Do you remember the court case?"

Michel nods. "I do. But why are you curious about this?"

"Because it doesn't make sense to me. Sorlot is known to be right-wing and anti-Semitic. Surely theirs would have been a publishing match made in heaven."

"Yes, but Hitler needed a publisher he could manipulate," Michel replies bitterly.

"What do you mean?"

"In 1938, Hitler allowed Fayard to publish a French edition of his literary monstrosity. It is just 347 pages. Sorlot's translation was completely unabridged, and it was 687 pages."

"But that's almost twice the size," I exclaim.

"Exactly."

"So what did Hitler ask Fayard to edit out?"

Michel leans so close I can smell the coffee on his breath. "All of the sections talking about Hitler's desire to destroy France," he whispers.

"So Hitler took Sorlot to court because he didn't want the French to know of his plan?" A shiver runs up my spine.

"Exactly. And now, here we are, six years later, and his plan is almost complete."

"But if the French knew that he wants our destruction, maybe they wouldn't be so quick to collaborate with the Germans."

"Maybe."

"Would it still be possible to find a copy of Sorlot's book?"

"Oh yes, he continued to sell it covertly after the ban. I've seen copies of it for sale along here, but that was before the Germans arrived of course. Now we have to be so careful about what we sell, or they will take our permits away."

"Yes, I have experienced similar."

"In your store?"

I nod. "We have a German company billeted to our town. Yesterday they told me that I can no longer sell *Oliver Twist* because it features a Jewish character."

"My God!" He shakes his head. "What is the world coming to?"

"Is there anywhere I could go to try to find a copy of the book?"

He looks thoughtful for a moment, as if he's trying to decide whether to let me in on a secret. "You could try the café."

"De Flore?"

"Yes."

"It is still open?" I feel a burst of joy. Café de Flore is one of my favorite spots in all of Paris. As the preferred haunt of some of my most beloved writers and artists, why would I not love it? Michel and I had lunch there several times before the war, which was an exercise in self-restraint, I confess, especially the day I realized that the one and only Pablo Picasso was sitting sipping absinthe at the table right behind me!

"Of course it is." Michel grins. "Even the Nazis cannot break the Flore spirit. Now, when you go there, you must ask at the bar for Pierre Duras, and you must tell him that I sent you."

"OK."

"If anyone can get that book for you, it will be Pierre. But what do you plan to do with it?"

"I will show my sleepy townsfolk what the Germans really think of them and want for our country. Maybe then they will wake up and start to resist."

Michel smiles. "You have been listening to the broadcasts from London too?"

"Yes." I hear the clip of boots on the pavement behind me and quickly start browsing the books on display. "Tell me, do you have anything by Balzac?" I say loudly.

"It just so happens that I do." Michel takes a copy of *La Duchesse de Langeais* from a pile of books behind him.

"Wonderful, thank you." I glance sideways and see a group of four of soldiers walking past.

"Tell me, how is your friend Luc?" Michel whispers as soon as they have gone. "I hear they have taken many of our men prisoner."

"Luc . . . he was killed." Saying those dreadful words out loud brings a lump to my throat.

"Oh no, I am so sorry."

"Yes, well, it is providing me with much motivation to resist."

"I can imagine." He places his hand on my arm. "You take care, you hear? These are very dangerous people."

"I know." I pay for the Balzac novel and hastily buy some other books to confirm my cover story of buying stock for my store. "Pierre Duras," I say, checking I've remembered the name correctly.

"Yes. And remember to say that I sent you."

"Of course."

We hug goodbye and I feel a sharp tug of sorrow. Under the shadow of the swastika, simple farewells are now laden with a haunting subtext: *What if we are saying goodbye forever?*

13

LAURENCE—AUGUST 1940

I hurry along the tree-lined Boulevard Saint-Germain, trying not to notice how much it has changed. Unfortunately, I fail—it's impossible not to notice. The normally bustling sidewalks are almost empty and the apartments above the stores all have their shutters firmly closed.

Finally the cream-colored awning of Café de Flore comes into view. Situated on the junction with Rue Saint-Benoît, the café is one of those interesting corner buildings that widens like a triangle from its entrance, and the perfect place for sitting at one of the little round tables outside and watching the world go by. But I have no desire to sit and watch this new world go by, so I hurry inside.

To my surprise and relief, the air is filled with chatter, and a thin film of cigarette smoke rises from the long tables. The large stove in the middle of the room, apparently there to encourage writers to make themselves at home, is not lit, but, of course, there's no need for it in the August heat. I make my way over to the bar, trying not to feel self-conscious. On the few occasions I've been here before, I've been with Michel, who seems to be a part of the furniture. It's strange being here on my own, like I've entered a club I'm not a member of. I smile nervously at a woman behind the bar.

"Would it be possible to see Pierre Duras?" I ask in what I hope is the sophisticated yet nonchalant tone of a woman about town. "Michel Allard sent me."

She looks me up and down, then nods to a nearby table. "Take a seat."

Almost as soon as I've sat down, a waiter is at my side, placing a little paper mat embossed with the green Café de Flore font upon the table. "Can I get you a drink?"

"Yes, *petit noir*, please."

The waiter hurries off and I glance around the place, again trying to appear calm and worldly. Unlike the rest of Paris, it is exactly as I remember it before the Germans came, and just as busy. Groups of people are clustered around the bench tables, talking quietly but animatedly. Most of the men wear turtlenecks and corduroy jackets, their long hair reaching their shirt collars, and the women, ooh la la! It is as if they have never read a women's magazine, and the countless silly articles telling us how we need to wear lipstick to raise morale, or if they have read them, they are willfully choosing to ignore them. Most of them are completely free of cosmetics, displaying a wilder, more natural beauty instead, one that comes from within. I watch as a woman with flame-red hair wearing a men's trouser suit holds court amongst a group. Her spirit is infectious even from two tables away.

I take a napkin from the table and discreetly wipe off my lipstick. I want to be like this woman. I *was* going to be like this woman, I remind myself, before the war and Luc's death knocked me sideways. I sit back in my chair and close my eyes and inhale the chatter and smoke and the energy. Whilst I love the peace and space of the valley, coming to Paris is like filling the tank of my imagination with gasoline. And never have I needed it more than I do today.

The sound of someone clearing their throat breaks me from my reverie and I open my eyes to see a thin young man with a wispy brown beard standing in front of me.

"I understand that you want to see me," he says, looking at my dreary dress and hat. Why, oh why, did I not wear something with a little more flair, something a little more bohemian?

I nod. "Yes, Michel Allard said you might be able to help me."

My connection to Michel clearly makes me appear slightly less dull and provincial. He nods and sits in the chair opposite me. "How do you know Michel?"

"He has always been my favorite *bouquiniste* in Paris. I have my own bookstore in La Vallée du Cerf and he helps me find the more limited or out-of-print editions. When I saw him today, he told me that you might be able to help me find a book."

"Oh yes?" He looks at me wryly. "And what book might that be?"

I lean forward and lower my voice. "I'm trying to find a copy of Sorlot's edition of *Mein Kampf.*"

Unlike Michel, Pierre remains completely expressionless at my request. "And why is that?" he asks.

"I want to know why Hitler was so scared of the French seeing it," I whisper.

His face is poker-straight. "And why do you want to know that?"

"Because I want other people to know." I lean even closer. "I want them to see that despite what their posters might say, the Germans have not come to rescue an abandoned population, they have come to destroy us."

Finally, there's the faintest flicker of a reaction and the smallest of smiles plays upon his lips. "So, you are some kind of book detective?"

I laugh. "I guess you could say that."

"Very good." He nods.

The waiter arrives at the table with my coffee.

"Drink that and I will meet you on Rue Saint-Benoît in two minutes," Pierre instructs, getting to his feet.

"OK."

I drink the coffee so fast I burn my tongue. But I don't care. Finally I am doing something. Finally I have some kind of purpose after two months of dazed inaction. It's only when I get outside that I realize he didn't tell me *where* to meet him on Rue Saint-Benoît.

I start walking slowly down the road. There's no sign of Pierre and for a horrible moment I wonder if I've been the victim of a prank and he's back in the café laughing with his friends about the stupid country mouse who asked him for Hitler's book. I'm about to give up when I hear someone whisper, "Psst." I turn and see Pierre lurking in a doorway. He beckons at me to follow him inside.

Like so many doorways in Paris, it leads to a hidden courtyard with apartments in a square all around it. Pierre starts going up a set of stone steps to the right, his long thin legs taking them two at a time. I follow him up three flights and along a narrow passageway until we reach a door at the end. He unlocks it and we go inside.

"Whoa!" I exclaim the second I cross the threshold. The hallway, which was already narrow, is made even thinner by teetering walls of books either side. The musty smell of old paper is instantly intoxicating to me. I close my eyes and inhale deeply.

Pierre looks back at me. "Are you all right?"

"Yes, oh yes!" I gaze in awe at the walls of books, catching glimpses of old friends on the spines: *Madame Bovary*, and *Thérèse Raquin*, and what looks like an original edition of *Down and Out in Paris and London*.

"Come," he says, beckoning me into a room at the end of the hallway. Two threadbare armchairs sit either side of a small fireplace—the mantelpiece has been turned into an impromptu bookshelf, as has the table by the blacked-out window and both alcoves either side of the hearth.

"This is the apartment of my dreams!" I blurt out. "The apartment of a true bibliomane!"

"Hmm," Pierre replies. "I hope not like Flaubert's bibliomane!"

"I hope not too." I chuckle, as I think of Flaubert's story of the book obsessive who becomes a crazed serial killer. "'He had but one idea,'" I quote from memory, "'one love, one passion . . .'"

"'Books,'" Pierre continues the quote with a grin. "'He sleeps among them, gazes at them . . .'"

"'Savors their dust and smell,'" we say in unison.

"How can I deny it?" Pierre laughs and looks around the room. "The evidence is everywhere."

"Even in the coal bucket." I laugh, looking at the battered copy of *Das Kapital* by Karl Marx poking over the top of the pail.

"I am guilty. I confess!" He shrugs his thin shoulders and gestures at one of the seats. "Please, sit."

I sit back in the chair, feeling way more relaxed now that we've bonded over being fellow bibliomaniacs.

"Although I have to confess that I do not love all books," Pierre says, pulling some books from one of the shelves in the alcove, revealing another layer behind them. He takes one of the hidden books out and shows it to me. The black gothic font on the orange cover sends a chill down my spine: *MEIN KAMPF.* And beneath it, in plain font: *MON COMBAT.* My struggle. The thought of Hitler talking about his struggle when he has caused so much pain to the world makes me want to retch. "All right, book detective, here is the evidence you are looking for." Pierre crouches beside me, leafing through the book until he points to a page. "Here Hitler calls France 'the mortal enemy of our nation.' And here he calls for the destruction of France.

And here he calls us 'the most terrible enemy.'" He hands the book to me. I feel simultaneously sick and vindicated.

"This is excellent evidence," I reply. "May I purchase it from you?"

"Are you sure?" He looks at me, concerned. "If you get caught with it, you could get into a lot of trouble."

"I am already in a lot of trouble—we all are."

He has no answer to that and looks at my case. "Do you have somewhere you can hide it?"

I open the case and show him a hole in the fabric lining at the bottom. "I could put it under here. How much do you want for it?"

He shakes his head. "Nothing. If you are taking it to help educate people about our oppressors, then I will gladly give it to you for free. May I make a suggestion though?"

"Of course."

"Rather than showing the book to people, why don't you make a leaflet containing the quotes?"

"A leaflet?"

"Yes. You could deliver them to people's houses at night, anonymously. That way, you have less chance of being caught and you get to show it to more people."

Something tells me he is speaking from experience, and again my bird of hope begins to sing. Could it be that he and other people like him are beginning to embark upon similar acts of resistance? I know better than to ask him outright, but I hope with all my heart that it is so.

"Thank you very much for your help," I say, as I tuck the dreaded book inside the lining of my case.

"It is nothing," he replies with a shrug.

If only he knew the truth. If only he knew that today he has given me so much more than a book.

. . .

Thankfully, the journey home passes without incident and I return to La Vallée du Cerf feeling like a changed woman. Or rather, feeling more like the woman I used to be. Not even the sight of the German soldiers practicing their maneuvers in the fields by the station can dampen my spirit. I have finally heeded General de Gaulle's call and have begun my own personal contribution to fanning the flames of resistance.

I get back to the store to find a note pinned to the door. I can tell that it is from Madame Bonheur before I even open it, due to the flour and greasy fingerprints. *You need to water your plants*, her curly writing says cryptically. The only plants I possess are in pots out the back. I go through the kitchen into the small yard I share with the boulangerie and I spy a brown baguette-shaped paper bag tucked inside the pot of rosemary. Madame Bonheur has written, *Thank you for making me laugh* on it.

A warm glow of gratitude fills me. I've been feeling so lonely recently, but the truth is, I still have good friends who really care for me. The smell of the baguette instantly makes me ravenous. I tear a bite off and go back inside. It's time to write my leaflet.

I check the blackout blinds are firmly shut before lighting the lamp on my desk. At first, I think of writing the leaflets on my book prescription paper but soon realize the stupidity of this idea. Half of the town have received at least one of my prescriptions by now—using the thick creamy paper would be like placing an arrow on my head for the Germans to find me. Then I remember the sketch pad I bought a couple of years ago after seeing Picasso in Café de Flore and fancying that I might one day follow in his footsteps. Sad to say, my attempts at cubism left a lot to be desired, but I'm certain I wouldn't have thrown the pad out. Sure enough, I find it lurking beneath the ledgers in the bottom drawer of my desk. Using my metal rule, I tear the large pages into quarters, the perfect size for a leaflet.

I set the copy of *Mein Kampf* in front of me and start copying out the offensive statements. Thankfully, Pierre has dog-eared the relevant pages for me so I don't have to read any more than is absolutely necessary. Then I start mulling over what I ought to write on the leaflet. I need something as powerful as the posters and leaflets the Germans have bombarded us with, pretending to be our friends.

In the end, I choose *ATTENTION POPULATION* as the heading, in a deliberate play on their use of POPULATION ABANDONED.

THIS IS WHAT HITLER WROTE IN HIS MEIN KAMPF, I type. THIS IS WHAT OUR OCCUPIERS REALLY THINK OF US. Then I type out the quotes about the French. AND THIS IS WHAT THEY WOULD LIKE TO DO TO US . . . and I add in the quote from Hitler calling for the destruction of France. The irony isn't lost on me as I type his words of hate at the very same desk I use to write my book prescriptions filled with love and hope. But if it only per-suades a handful of townsfolk to resist, it will have been worth it, I reassure myself. I complete the leaflet with a line from General de Gaulle. THE FIRE OF THE FRENCH RESISTANCE MUST NOT AND SHALL NOT DIE!

I sit back and re-read the text. Is it powerful enough? Will it cause my fellow townsfolk to sit up and take notice? I don't know. All I know is that at least I have done something. I pick up the copy of *Mein Kampf* and take it over to the fireplace. The only book I will have no problem destroying, I think to myself as I light a fire and throw it onto the flames.

I spend the rest of the evening typing up leaflets. There are ten pages remaining in the sketch pad, so I'm able to make forty. Obviously this will only cover a tiny portion of the town's popula-tion, but it's a start. And if I deliberately target the people I know love to gossip, they will help spread the word for me.

It's almost two in the morning when I'm done. I check the fire and see that thankfully *Mein Kampf* has been reduced to a pile of ashes. I stand for a while, staring at the glowing embers, pondering when I ought to deliver the leaflets. Part of me wants to put it off, but I have the horrible feeling that if I don't strike while the iron is hot—or the print is fresh—I'll lose the momentum I gained today, along with my courage. But if I get caught wandering around town after the curfew, I could get stopped and searched. I decide that the safest time would prob-ably be between four and five in the morning, just before the curfew ends, as then I can feign ignorance and say that I'm out that early because . . . I gaze around the store for inspiration. I could say that I'm delivering a book for a customer, and I have to do it early before the store opens. But why would I be deliv-ering a book to someone? I think of Esme Chapelle, an elderly customer who lives at the bottom of the valley. She was complaining recently that her legs aren't what they used to be and she's been struggling walking up the hill. If I get stopped by the Germans, I could say that I'm bringing her the latest novel by her favorite romance writer, and I'm doing it so early because I have a lot of work to do in the store later. It's not exactly a cast-iron cover story, but it's the best I can come up with.

I lie in my bed completely unable to sleep until I hear the cockerel's crow echo down the valley. I spring out of bed and, inspired by the women I saw in Café de Flore, I put on a pair of trousers and a plain blouse and black beret. Then I hurry down-stairs and put the book for Esme in my basket, with the leaflets hidden in between the pages. Outside, the approaching sunrise is turning the sky above the forest a deep shade of indigo. I feel for the tiny Nénette doll and the Jeanne of Arc pendant in my pocket. "I am not afraid. I was born to do this," I whisper to myself.

Thankfully, the square is deserted and there's no sign of any Germans. Hopefully they're all fast asleep after their maneu-vers last night. I head down the hill to the rows of tiny cottages belonging to the farmhands and the poorer townsfolk. As far as I know, no Germans have been billeted here, so it should be relatively safe. I don't think I've ever felt fear like it as I post the first leaflet. As I make my way up the path to the cottage, every sound seems magnified in the stillness of the early morning. My feet sound like a marauding elephant and even my breath seems to roar. My hands are trembling so much I almost drop the leaflet. *I am not afraid, I am not afraid,* I say over and over inside my head, as I crouch down and tuck it beneath the door.

Slowly but surely, I make my way along the narrow, twisting streets delivering my leaflets. As much as I would love to post one to the town's chief gossip, Violeta, it's way too dangerous as she has several soldiers staying with her, so, just as the sun is starting to rise, I do the next best thing and deliver one to her charlady, Ines, as her tongue is almost as loose as her boss's.

I'm just slipping the leaflet through her letterbox when I hear the distant putt-putt of a motorcycle. My entire body becomes rigid with fear. The sound grows louder and mercifully I regain the ability to move and crouch behind Ines' coal bunker. Peering through a slit in the wood, I see the motorcycle make its way up the street. One soldier is on the bike and another is in the sidecar, holding a rifle across his lap, as if poised and ready to shoot. I take a deep breath to try to calm myself and feel the tickle of dust at the back of my throat. *Damn it! I mustn't choke.* But the sensation is too overwhelming and I can't help spluttering. I close my eyes and begin praying with all my might. *Please, please, don't let the soldiers have heard me.*

14

LAURENCE—AUGUST 1940

As the tickle in my throat grows, my eyes start streaming and my heart pounds. *Please, please, please don't let me be caught!*

Is it my imagination or is the motorcycle slowing down? I can't bring myself to look. I need to focus all of my attention on not choking. After what seems like hours but must only be seconds, the putt-putt sound begins to fade. I collapse against the wall of the bunker and give a small cough. But the relief I feel is short-lived as I hear a noise from inside the house. I picture Ines finding my leaflet in her letterbox and discovering me hunched over spluttering in her coal bunker. I don't think even my vivid imagination would be capable of explaining that away.

I peer around the bunker to make sure the soldiers are out of sight, then race back down the street in the other direction, coughing and spluttering as I go.

Thankfully, I make it home safely, although my nerves are in shreds. All morning, I sit behind my desk, watching the square and waiting for something to happen. I'm not exactly sure what I'm expecting, I mean it's not as if my leaflets are going to spark some kind of instant insurrection, but I'm crackling with nervous energy. Then, at just before midday, a convoy of black cars sweeps into the square, parking outside the town hall. I go over to the door and look out. Gerhard is standing at the top of the town hall steps, holding a megaphone.

"Attention," he calls.

My heart plummets. Do the Germans know about my leaflet already? Is he going to say something about it? And will he remember me mentioning *Mein Kampf*? Will he realize that it is more than just a coincidence? My face flushes as I realize how stupid I have been. I was so desperate to do something, I forgot to think it through with a calm head.

"We are introducing a new form of rationing," Gerhard continues.

I gasp with relief.

"You will all need to come to the town hall to be issued with your tickets."

Then I realize what he is saying and my relief fades. If they are bringing in new rationing, then surely this will mean even less food—for the French at least. The injustice of us French having to be grateful for the crumbs the Nazis throw us, while they feast like kings in our hotels, restaurants and cafés fills me with outrage. I'm glad I made my leaflet. There's no way Gerhard could prove that I produced it, and anyway, surely the Germans wouldn't think a mere woman capable of such things. Now, hopefully, the combination of less food and discovering what Hitler really thinks of us will be enough to wake my sleeping fellow townsfolk from their apathy.

Gerhard finishes his announcement and the soldiers swarm inside the town hall. I pop my head outside the door and see Madame Bonheur standing in the doorway of the boulangerie holding a rolling pin.

"Swines!" she mutters.

I nod.

"Do you know what they call us French?" she whispers.

I shake my head.

"The most terrible enemy."

"Really?" My spirits soar. I hadn't delivered a leaflet to Madame Bonheur as I was worried she might work out that it was from me, but somehow she has heard about it already.

"Yes. Hitler says so in his book."

"How do you know?" I ask, my heart pounding.

"Violeta told me, when she came to buy bread for those Nazi pigs she has staying with her this morning. She said I should put poison in the dough. I'm sorely tempted!" She turns on her heel and goes back into her store.

I return to my desk. Ines and her loose tongue have exceeded my wildest expectations. Violeta knows about the leaflet already—and now so does Madame Bonheur. This is as good as putting up a poster in the town square. And, even better, Violeta, the walking town gossip column, appears to be on the side of the Resistance. My leaflet seems to have lit a spark.

The best way I can describe the next month is like a vise slowly tightening. The Germans keep up their façade of friendliness, but the smiles seem more forced—on both sides. The new rationing scheme is brutal, especially to a nation of food lovers, and I find myself remembering Maman's declaration that *"We need stories more than we need food"* on a regular basis to try to console myself. Every time my belly rumbles, I look around the store and seek sustenance from the shelves. Today for lunch I am dining on an appetizer of *Little Women* before a hearty feast of Flaubert. Ever since my meeting with Pierre in Paris, I have been re-reading Flaubert's novels and I am currently engrossed in the adventures of Emma in *Madame Bovary*. Every so often, I stop and gasp, intoxicated by the poetry of his prose. I'm just scribbling down a quote about how humans long to make music capable of melting stars—melting stars!—when the door bursts open and two German soldiers march in. Although it's been a month since I distributed my leaflet and the Germans don't seem to have discovered it, it's the first thing I think of. They've come to question me or, even worse, accuse me of treason. I snap my book shut and force a smile upon my face.

"Good day, gentlemen, how may I help you?" I hope they can't detect the tremor in my voice.

One of them marches over to my desk and I see that it's the same soldier who destroyed my copy of *Oliver Twist*. This does not bode well. I place my ledger over the copy of *Madame Bovary*, as if shielding a child from a bully. He pulls a document from his pocket and slams it down on my desk.

"*Liste Otto*," he barks, pointing at the document.

I breathe a sigh of relief. This would appear to have nothing to do with my leaflet.

"*Liste Otto*," he barks again, so forcefully I can smell the stale onions on his breath. He points at the document, then gestures around the store at the books.

I look down at the document. Beneath the title: LISTE OTTO, it reads, *works withdrawn from sale by publishers*. My stomach churns as I realize that this must be a list of books banned by the Germans.

The soldier says something else and I catch the name Otto Abetz—the German ambassador to France. So this must be his doing. The soldier prods the document, points to me, and then to the books.

I nod to show that I've understood and try my hardest to hide my fury. "Thank you," I squeeze out through gritted teeth.

He gives me the most token of salutes and they leave.

I open the document with trembling fingers, dreading the prospect of seeing some of my most beloved books contained within. The list is divided according to publisher. I quickly scan the pages. Some of the names I see bring little surprise.

Communists Karl Marx and Rosa Luxemburg are present, as is the former French Prime Minister Léon Blum, who has committed the crime of being both a socialist *and* a Jew.

The bell above the door rings and Charlotte hurries in.

"Laurence, are you OK?"

"Yes, thank you."

"I was queuing outside the boulangerie and I saw the soldiers come in here. What did they want?"

"They came to deliver me this." I show her the list.

"Works withdrawn from sale . . ." she reads.

"Yes."

"*All Quiet on the Western Front* is on this." She frowns at me. "But isn't that about a German soldier? Why would they want to withdraw it?"

I shrug. "I guess because it is too realistic."

"What do you mean?"

"It shows how awful war can be. It shows a German soldier destroyed by the fighting."

"It sounds good to me."

"I know." I go over to the shelves and take down the three copies of the novel I have in stock.

"Why should they dictate what we can and cannot read?" Charlotte asks. "Isn't it bad enough that they control our movements and what we eat?"

I nod, then I look down at the books in my hands. "Maybe we don't have to obey their every command."

"What do you mean?" She looks at me curiously.

"What if we read this book as . . ." I break off, remembering Père Rambert's warning. As much as I'm certain Charlotte isn't a fan of the Nazis, I probably shouldn't utter the word "resistance" until I'm completely certain.

"As an act of resistance?" she whispers.

"Yes!"

She clutches my arms, her eyes sparking with excitement. "Have you been listening to the broadcasts too?"

I nod, relief surging through me at the discovery that I've had an ally right under my nose all along.

"I've been feeling so helpless, not knowing what to do," she says.

"Me too."

"But this..." She looks at the books. "This could be something."

"We could resist through reading." My canary of hope trills so loudly at this prospect, I'm surprised Charlotte isn't able to hear it singing. Judging by her beaming grin, her hummingbird is hovering happily about the place too. "Here." I hand her one of the books. "I'll re-read it too."

"And what about the other copy?"

"I'll ask Madame Bonheur if she'd like to join us. She can definitely be trusted."

"Perhaps after we've read it, we can meet to discuss," she suggests hesitantly.

"Yes!" I reply eagerly. "And we can revel in the words the Germans have tried to ban."

Charlotte tucks the book into the bottom of her basket. "Oh Laurence, thank you! You have no idea how happy you've made me." For the first time since Jacques' death I see the faintest sparkle in her eyes.

I look at her and smile. "I think I do."

And so, a couple of weeks later, Charlotte, Madame Bonheur and I meet for a walk in the forest early on a Sunday evening. At first, we chit-chat about trivial things, just in case anyone is listening. But once we reach the part of the forest where the trees become thicker and the light fades, we lower our voices.

"What a book!" Charlotte whispers. "I felt as if I was there in the trenches."

"Me too." Madame Bonheur shudders. "That part with the huge rat, when it was swinging on his bread. Ooh la la!" She throws her hands up in horror.

"The bit that really moved me was when he was guarding the Russian prisoners of war," I say. "And he realizes that an order has turned these men into his enemies, but another order could just as easily turn them into his friends again."

"And isn't that exactly what happened?" Charlotte says. "With the Russians making their pact with the Germans." She sighs. "Reading it made me so sad about Jacques all over again. It all seems like such a waste."

"It made me feel the same about Luc." I nod in agreement. "When Paul realized that the other soldier is just the same as him, with exactly the same fears, it broke my heart. It makes their deaths seem so futile."

"It is all so futile." Madame Bonheur wipes a tear from her eye.

"Are you OK?" I place my hand on her arm.

She nods. "I lost someone I loved very much on the Western Front."

"Really?" I look at her curiously. Madame Bonheur has never married. At one time, there was a rumor, started by Violeta no doubt, that she preferred the company of women, but I've never seen any evidence to prove this. Could it be that she lost a sweetheart in the Great War?

"No wonder the Germans want to ban this book," Madame Bonheur says.

"I feel like they want to stop their own soldiers from reading it rather than the French," I reply.

"Yes, indeed," Madame Bonheur agrees.

I'm about to ask the others what they thought of the book's ending when I hear a woman's giggle coming from the footpath up ahead of us. We all stand dead still as we hear a man's voice. He's speaking in French but with a German accent. My heart races as I think of the copy of *All Quiet on the Western Front* tucked inside my bag. I'd brought it along in case anyone wanted to share a favorite quote from the book. What if I'm searched? How will I explain why I've brought it on a supposedly innocent stroll?

"Quick!" Charlotte whispers, tugging on my sleeve, and the three of us scramble behind a cluster of bushes. I bite my lip to stop myself from gasping in pain as a bramble tears into my leg.

As we crouch there in silence, the voices grow louder.

"You're so talented," the woman says and the hairs on the back of my neck stand on end as I recognize Gigi's voice.

The man coughs. "Not really," he replies and I realize that it's Gerhard.

"Oh, but you are, speaking so many different languages."

To my horror, they come to a standstill just as they draw level with us. I daren't look at the others. I hardly dare breathe.

"Would it be awfully impudent of me to . . ." Gigi breaks off.

"What?" Gerhard asks.

Through the leaves, I see her feet position themselves facing his and the pointed heels of her shoes lift off the ground as she stands on tiptoes. "Kiss you," she replies breathlessly.

I hear Madame Bonheur tut under her breath and I glare at her. Gigi fraternizing with the enemy might be horrifying but not enough to risk getting us arrested by the Nazis. Again I think of the book in my bag and my skin erupts in a cold sweat.

"That was nice," Gigi says.

"Yes, yes it was," Gerhard replies slightly stiltedly. "Shall we go back now, get something to eat?"

Yes! I silently implore. *Go back immediately!*

"If you insist," Gigi replies coquettishly.

Please, insist!

I'm practically delirious with relief as I watch their feet disappear off along the footpath.

"Phew! That was close," Charlotte whispers.

"That slut!" Madame Bonheur hisses.

But as we clamber back out of the bushes, I'm less concerned about Gigi and more troubled by the fact that being in possession of a book had me fearing for my life. How on earth has it come to this? Then I have the awful thought that the others won't want to meet up again at such a risk, and our fledgling book club will be over before it even began.

"Maybe this was a stupid idea," I say reluctantly. "Maybe it is too dangerous."

"Nonsense!" Madame Bonheur snorts. "Now more than ever we need to fight for our liberty."

"Really?" I grin with relief, then turn to Charlotte.

"I agree," she replies, her voice wobbling slightly.

I take hold of both their hands. "To reading for liberty!" I whisper.

"Reading for liberty!" they whisper back, and high above us a bird starts to sing.

15

JEANNE—1993

Jeanne hurried inside the bakery. A young man was standing behind the counter looking at his pager.

"Hey, what's the deal with the building next door?" she asked, so eager for information she momentarily forgot that she was in a foreign country.

The young guy stared at her blankly.

"I'm sorry, do you speak English?"

He shrugged and shook his head.

Jeanne was about to give up when a woman of about her age came bustling out from the back. She was wearing an apron over a rose-printed dress and her black hair was held up in a bun with a pencil.

"*Bonjour!*" she greeted Jeanne with a warm smile.

"*Bonjour,*" Jeanne replied. "I don't suppose you speak English?"

"*Oui,* a little." The woman nodded.

"Great. I was just wondering what was going on with the building next door."

Instantly, the woman's smile faded. "What do you mean?"

"Why is it boarded up? And what's with the flowers outside?"

"I'm not sure. I only bought this place a couple of months ago. Perhaps people leave them there, in—how do you say—memorial?"

"In memory of someone?"

"*Oui*. Why do you ask?"

"Oh, no reason, I was just curious." Jeanne decided not to reveal too much until she had a better lay of the land. "Could I get a couple of those cookies in the window please?"

"The macaroons?"

"Yes." As Jeanne put some French money on the counter, her mind raced. Why would people be putting flowers outside Laurence's store? If it was Laurence's store of course, she still didn't know for sure. And why would they have painted the word LIBERTÉ on the board?

Back outside, she examined the boarding over the door and saw that it was locked shut with a padlock. Wondering if there was a back entrance, she started walking nonchalantly along the parade of stores as if she was just out for a casual stroll. She passed a gift shop with a window full of trinkets and a shoe shop that smelled of warm leather and a florist's with buckets of vibrant flowers on display before reaching a narrow alleyway. Checking no one was looking, she slipped down the passage to the back of the buildings. Following the smell of fresh bread, she made her way back to the derelict store.

She stood on tiptoes and peered over the gray stone wall into a small backyard. Unlike the front of the building, the back door hadn't been boarded up. She thought of the long iron key that had been in the box Wendell gave her. He'd told her it had come with the deed to the store, also tucked inside the blanket Jeanne had been wrapped in when she was rescued. Could it be for the back door? She'd brought the key to France with her. Perhaps she could try it later.

． ． ．

"So, I think I might have found Laurence's store," Jeanne announced to Wendell across the table.

It was five p.m. French time and they'd come down to the hotel restaurant for dinner. Wendell was looking sprightly after his nap, his silver hair still damp from the shower. Jeanne, on the other hand, was now feeling wired from adrenaline and a lack of sleep.

"Really?" He put down his knife and fork, his expression deadly serious. "How . . . how does it look?"

"Kind of like a derelict shrine."

"What do you mean?" Was it her imagination or was there a tremor in his voice?

"Well, it's all boarded up, but someone's left a jar of flowers outside of it."

"Oh."

She studied his face for any clues as to what he was thinking or how he was feeling. Shaken up would probably be the best way to describe it. She took a sip of her wine. "I was thinking I might try that key you gave me tonight, see if it unlocks the door."

"I thought it was boarded up."

"The back door isn't. Don't worry, Pops, I already cased the joint."

He smiled weakly. "You can take the girl out of the police force . . . I'm not sure it's such a good idea to go sneaking in there at night, though. What if you get arrested?"

"Show a little faith, Pops. I learned how to break into a building from some of the best in the business."

He sighed. "I don't doubt it. But wouldn't it be easier to go to the local authorities in the morning and show them the deed and see what they have to say?"

Jeanne frowned. Was he really worried about her getting

into trouble or was he afraid of what they might discover? "But what if they say no—or *non*, or whatever—what if there's a load of red tape? What if they need more proof that I'm Laurence's daughter?"

"Hmm."

"Come on, Pops, I thought we came here to find out more, get some answers. We'll be in and out of there in no time, I promise."

His eyes widened. "You want me to come too?"

"Of course!"

"Holy cow, when I suggested a vacation, going on a crime spree wasn't exactly what I had in mind!" But, to Jeanne's relief, he began to grin.

"It's hardly a crime spree. Just think of it as the perfect daddy-daughter bonding experience." She raised her glass of wine and clinked it against his.

They set off as soon as darkness fell.

"Just going out for an evening stroll," Wendell called loudly to the hotel receptionist as they made their way through the lobby. "Don't want to arouse suspicion," he muttered to Jeanne.

"Hmm, I was kind of hoping we could have slipped out unseen," Jeanne replied as all eyes in the lobby watched them go. She linked her arm through his and they made their way down the steps. "OK, so I'm pretty sure the store used to be in that boarded-up building over there," she said, leading him past the statue in the middle of the square. "It has the word *livre* in the sign. And look, there are the flowers someone left." She pointed to the jar of roses.

"Well, I'll be damned." Wendell stopped walking and stared at the store. "*Liberté*," he whispered.

"I'm not sure why someone painted that on there. Graffiti, I guess?"

He shook his head. "No. I think it might be something to do with Laurence."

"Really?" A shiver ran up Jeanne's spine as she looked at the building and tried to imagine it without the boards and with the sign freshly painted. "What do you think *Le Dispensaire de Livres* means?" she asked.

"It means The Book Dispensary." Wendell gave a sad smile. "She thought of books as being like medicine. She'd type her customers prescriptions for their reading, just like a pharmacist."

Jeanne laughed. "I guess I didn't inherit her reading gene then."

"I don't know, when you were a kid, you always had your nose in a book."

"True. I did love a good Nancy Drew or Hardy Boys mystery."

"You're so like her. It . . ." He broke off as an elderly couple walked past.

"*Bonsoir*," the old man said, lifting his hat slightly.

"*Bonsoir*," Wendell replied, raising his cane in greeting.

"It what?" Jeanne asked. Hearing him say she was like Laurence brought up mixed feelings for her. On the one hand, it felt great to be compared to a woman who was some kind of war hero, but on the other, there was still the mystery over why Laurence had sent her away. Had she done it to protect Jeanne or because she was the kind of kick-ass freedom fighter who didn't want to be tied down with a baby? Jeanne felt an awkward twinge as she thought of her own decision to never have children because of her career. Was this something she'd inherited from her birth mom too?

"Doesn't matter. So, are we going to commit a felony on our first night in France or what?"

"Stop saying that, Pops." Jeanne chuckled.

She led him round to the back of the buildings. With no delicious aroma of baking to guide her this time, Jeanne counted the backyards they walked past—the florist's, the shoe shop, the gift shop—she stopped and peered over the wall. The yard was steeped in darkness.

"This is it," she whispered.

"I remember," he whispered back.

"You do?"

"Not sure I'm going to be able to leap over the wall this time round though."

"What do you mean this time round? You've leapt over it before?"

"This is where your mom hid me, after my plane came down. We snuck in the back way. Ah, the bravery of youth. Not to mention the stupidity." He shook his head. "The place was crawling with Germans."

Jeanne shuddered. It was impossible to believe that somewhere so picturesque and tranquil could have once been home to the Nazis.

A noise from the end of the alleyway caused them both to jump. Jeanne turned and saw a fox scurrying away. "Come on, we've got to get over there before we get busted." She crouched down and linked her fingers, forming a stirrup with her hands. "Step into this and I'll give you a lift."

Wendell leaned his cane against the wall and placed one of his feet into her hands.

"Ready?"

"As I'll ever be!"

Slowly and carefully, she lifted Wendell up. He put his hands on top of the wall and somehow managed to hoist his other leg over, sitting astride the wall. Jeanne passed him his cane and hoisted herself up. She quickly jumped down on the other side and looked around the yard.

"Hey, don't leave me up here like John Wayne. Help me down," Wendell hissed.

"Easy, cowboy, hold your horses," Jeanne quipped, finding

an empty crate and placing it beneath him. "Here, step onto this."

"Step onto this, she says, as if I'm some lithe-limbed kid," Wendell muttered to himself, but he managed to swing his other leg over and slid down onto the crate. "Geez!" He wiped his hands on his jeans and looked around.

"You OK?"

He nodded.

"Right, now for the moment of truth." She took the old key from her pocket and placed it in the lock. "Well, it went in."

"As the actress said to the bishop."

"Pops!"

"Sorry. It was something the guys in the RAF used to say. Being here is bringing back a bunch of memories."

Jeanne tried to turn the key. At first it wouldn't budge, but when she applied more force, it suddenly turned, the click echoing in the silence. "It worked." Jeanne's pulse quickened.

"Oh lordy!" Wendell exclaimed.

The door opened with a loud creak, made even louder by Jeanne's nerves.

Get a grip, she told herself sternly. *It's just an empty building. You've been in way scarier situations than this.*

The first thing she noticed as she stepped inside was the musty smell. She wondered how long it had been left locked and boarded up. She shivered. It felt a little like walking inside a tomb. As her eyes adjusted to the pitch dark, she was able to see the outline of a sink.

"I remember this," Wendell whispered, coming in behind her. "This was the kitchen."

It was barely bigger than a closet.

Jeanne crept through the doorway. There was a flight of steep narrow steps to her right and straight ahead was a larger space.

"That was her store," Wendell said, pointing ahead. "Look, the shelves are still there on the walls."

Jeanne put her hand out and felt a thick wooden shelf running along the wall beside her. It was so dark due to the boards on the window she could barely make out a thing. If only she had a flashlight. Then she remembered her cigarette lighter and took it from her pocket and flicked it on.

"Whoa!" she gasped as she slowly moved the lighter in an arc. Dark wooden beams ran across the low ceiling and every inch of wall space was covered with empty shelves, apart from the wall to her left, which housed a fireplace. Two old armchairs sat either side of it, adding to the spooky feel. Jeanne imagined Laurence sitting there in front of a roaring fire, the shelves full of books, and she felt a wave of sorrow.

She turned to her right and saw a wooden desk housing an old-fashioned typewriter, the kind folks had before electric word processors had been invented. But as she got closer, she saw that it had been trashed. All of the keys were springing out at different angles as if someone had taken a sledgehammer to it. Another shiver ran up her spine. What happened here? What happened to Laurence?

She turned and shone her lighter to the back of the store, where Wendell was scratching his head and gazing at the floor.

"You OK?"

"Uh-huh. I just remembered something. She had a hiding place. I'm sure it was here, under one of the floorboards."

Jeanne hurried over, her skin prickling with excitement.

"I think it was under this rug," he said, poking at the edge of a frayed old rug with his cane.

Jeanne knelt down and lifted the rug, trying to ignore the moldy smell rushing up to fill her nostrils. She relit her lighter and shone the flame over the boards. They all looked pretty tightly nailed down. Then she noticed that one of them had no nails. She gripped the edge of the board with the tips of her fingers, but she couldn't get enough leverage on it. "I need something flat, like a ruler."

"How about this?" Wendell took a steel comb from the back pocket of his jeans and passed it to her.

"Thanks." She eased the comb into the gap between the floorboards and slowly she managed to raise the board. Once again, she had the feeling of being in a mausoleum. Hadn't the guys who'd raided Tutankhamun's tomb all gotten cursed? She tried not to think about it as she reached down into the pitch dark.

At first, she felt nothing, but then her fingertips brushed against something solid.

"I got something," she cried, leaning forward and trying to find something to grab a hold of. Feeling some type of handle, she lifted the object up and out. "What is this?" she asked, flicking her lighter on.

"It's her radio," Wendell replied softly.

"Her radio? Why would she hide it?"

"The Germans banned radios as soon as they occupied France. Folks got killed for having them."

Jeanne stared at him, horrified. "But why?"

"The BBC used to broadcast coded messages to the Resistance, giving them information about weapons drops and suchlike."

"Weapons drops?" It sounded like a line from a spy movie.

"Uh-huh. And explosives. We'd drop them in the forest. Sometimes we dropped people too."

Jeanne stared at him in disbelief. "Who?"

"Special undercover operatives. A lot of them were women as they aroused less suspicion." He sighed. "I've never seen bravery like it."

"Geez." Jeanne put the radio down and reached beneath the

floorboard. This time she found something softer. "I think I've found a book."

"Yeah, there might be a few down there."

"Why would she have hidden books?"

"The Germans banned some of them too."

Jeanne pulled out several books and shone her lighter on them. They all had French titles. She recognized the names of the author on one of them, though: Ernest Hemingway. She showed it to Wendell.

"There was a Hemingway book in that box you gave me too." She'd brought the book with her to read on the plane but had never gotten round to it.

Wendell grasped the book as if he'd been handed a priceless jewel. "Yeah. I bought my own copy of it when I got back to the States. Something to—uh—remember her by." He cleared his throat and looked away.

Jeanne made a mental note to read his copy of the book as soon as possible. Clearly it meant a lot to both her parents; perhaps it would contain some clues about their relationship.

She reached back into the hole and found something small and cold and metal. She took it out and saw that it was a silver pendant with a soldier on it. There was some tiny writing in French around the edge.

"Recognize this?" she asked, showing it to Wendell.

He shook his head.

Jeanne tucked the pendant in her pocket then put the floorboard back in place and covered it with the rug. When she stood up, she saw that Wendell was slowly making his way up the narrow stairs. Then she heard him gasp.

"What is it?" she asked, hurrying up behind him. She flicked on her lighter and found him in what had obviously once been a bedroom. A brass bedstead stood in the middle of the room, stripped of its bedding.

"This was . . . this was where . . ." Wendell whispered, leaning on the bedpost for support.

"Where what?"

"Where everything happened," he replied, and as she shone the lighter upon him, she saw tears rolling down his face.

16

LAURENCE—OCTOBER 1940

"How much longer must we queue for?" Violeta cries, surely voicing the plaintive thoughts of every woman standing in the line outside the town hall. Along with hunger, dread and fear, queuing has become a new French pastime, and one that, I have to say, I'm not very good at.

Damn those toads and their rationing system, I think bitterly as I watch a tank trundle past in the drizzling rain. For every hour I spend queuing for meat or milk or fruit or bread, I could be serving customers in the store and earning money. Not that business has been great, for all of my customers are in the same situation. The Germans are now beginning to show their true colors, turning as cold and unforgiving as the weather.

The queue moves forward slightly and I reach the shelter of the town hall doorway. A red-framed sign saying *RAUCHEN VERBOTEN!* meaning SMOKING FORBIDDEN! has been stuck to the wall. It makes me want to start smoking, just to disobey them. *Verboten* seems to be the favorite word of the Germans, especially when it comes to anything fun.

I stare at the letters, trying to find other words hidden inside them to relieve the boredom. The first word I find is *verte*. I used to love the color green because it reminded me of Mother Nature, but now it's yet another thing the toads have ruined, with their murky green uniforms. I study the word *RAUCHEN* and find the word race in English.

Ha! I chuckle to myself. The green race, that is what the Germans really are, in spite of what Hitler might claim about the so-called superior Aryans. Knowing that there is a joke on them hidden within their stupid sign makes me feel slightly better.

Finally I reach the hall where the ration tickets are being issued and I see Gigi standing at the front of the line. It's the first time I've seen her queuing for anything since rationing was introduced in August; I assume she normally gets Maud to do it.

A door at the far end of the hall opens and the Kommandant comes marching out, accompanied by Gerhard. As they walk past Gigi, both nod in greeting, and I hear her gaily calling, "Good day!" Clearly she is still getting along swimmingly with her house guests, and way too well with one of them. And to think that I'd been worried about her.

As the soldiers draw close, Gerhard smiles at me. I look away, but it's too late.

"Good day, Laurence," he says warmly. "I must come to your store soon. I have run out of reading material."

I squirm as I picture the women in the queue next to me and what they must be thinking.

"Very well," I mutter, still looking at the floor.

Someone barks something in German, causing an immediate silence to fall. I look up and see the Kommandant staring at me, his pale face flushed with anger. He repeats what he said and I realize that he was yelling at me. I have no idea what he's saying, though. I look to Gerhard, who is shifting awkwardly. The Kommandant snaps something at him.

"He—uh—says that you are to look at a German officer when he addresses you," Gerhard mutters in French.

"I didn't know he was about to address me," I reply.

"He meant me." Gerhard at least has the good grace to look embarrassed.

"Oh, I see. I am most humbly sorry," I reply loudly, staring right into Gerhard's bright blue eyes, hoping that sarcasm is apparent in any language.

"Apology accepted," he says.

At exactly that moment, Gigi approaches. Clad in a figure-hugging lavender dress and a glossy fur jacket, she looks more like she's off for a night at the opera rather than queueing for ration tickets. She frowns at me.

Gerhard says something to the Kommandant and he nods curtly and strides off.

"Good day, Gerhard," Gigi says, gazing at him through lowered eyelids. "I hope you enjoyed your breakfast."

He glances at me before moving on. "Yes, I did thank you."

"That's wonderful," she gushes.

As they leave the hall, my heart rate returns to normal.

"Well done," the woman behind me whispers.

But my bravado soon fades as I think of what Père Rambert would say. I was wrong to be sarcastic. I mustn't do anything to arouse suspicion. Will I ever learn to keep a lid on my temper?

Once I've got my tickets, I come back outside to see yet another queue snaking around the square from Madame Bonheur's boulangerie. At least this is one queue I do not have to join. Madame Bonheur has been leaving me a baguette every day in our shared backyard.

I walk through my store and into the yard and, sure enough, I find a baguette hidden behind my pot of mint. I go into the kitchen and make a cup of the insipid coffee substitute we're now expected to drink. Rumor has it that it's made from acorns. I carefully tear off one third of the bread for my breakfast.

I can tell from the crisp golden crust and fluffy interior that it's freshly baked that morning and I feel awash with gratitude. Only the Germans are meant to get freshly baked bread now. We French are meant to make do with their stale leftovers. This is more than an act of kindness on Madame Bonheur's part, it's an act of bravery, for the Germans have been making it very clear that they will show little mercy if we break any of their stupid *verboten* rules.

I savor every morsel of the bread before going through and turning the sign on the store door to OPEN. I'm barely back at my desk when the bell jangles. I look up, hoping for a customer, but instead I see Gigi.

"Good day," I mutter, sitting down at my desk.

"Good day." She glances over her shoulder before coming over. Judging by the over-powering waft of Chanel accompanying her, she clearly has no concerns about her perfume running out.

"Can I help you?"

She shakes her head. "I'm not here to buy anything, I'm here to warn you."

"Warn me? About what?"

"About the way you acted today, in the town hall, in front of Gerhard and Franz."

"Franz?"

"The Kommandant."

"Very friendly," I can't help sniping.

She looks at me crossly. "They are living at the chateau—of course I have got to know them."

"Of course."

"Look, do you want my help or not?" She taps her immaculately manicured nails on my desk.

Not really, I think, but I force myself to nod.

"We have to be courteous to them."

Again, I have to fight the urge to say, *But why?*

"They are our occupiers," she continues.

This time I'm unable to hold my tongue. "They are trespassers," I hiss.

"Laurence!"

"What?" She hasn't made the effort to talk to me in months so why does she think I'll listen to her now?

"Do you want to get into trouble?" she hisses. "If you're polite to them, they are no problem at all. In fact, some of them are very nice."

"Very nice?" Her words are a red rag to my bull-like rage. "Are you saying that the same people who murdered Luc are very nice?"

"But they aren't the same people. He was killed by the Luftwaffe."

"My God!"

She shakes her head and sighs. "Well, don't say that I didn't warn you. I was just trying to be a friend."

"A friend?" The red mist in front of my eyes thickens as I think of her cooing all over Gerhard in the forest. "You're no friend."

She frowns. "What do you mean?"

"Ever since *they* arrived, I've barely seen you. Rumor has it you spend most of your spare time entertaining your new friends the Nazis."

"But—I . . ." Gigi stammers, but before she can say any more, the door opens. The cheery tinkle of the bell has never felt more inappropriate and I want to groan out loud when I see Gerhard coming in.

"Good day, Laurence. Oh, hello, Gigi." Is it my imagination or does he look slightly less enthused to see her?

"Gerhard!" she exclaims as if he's her lifelong friend, not I. "What a coincidence to see you here. Are you a book lover too?"

The bread in my stomach starts threatening to make a reappearance as I squirm at her gushing display.

"I am indeed," he replies, "As Laurence will vouch, I'm sure."

As he smiles at me, she gives me the fierce type of glare that ought to come accompanied by a crack of thunder.

"Why don't you two have a browse," I say. "I have some paperwork to attend to." I take the sales ledger out of the desk drawer and flick absently through the pages. Stupidly, I had forgotten that Luc used to do my accounts and the sight of rows of his neat little numbers forms knots in my stomach. Out of the corner of my eye, I see Gigi following Gerhard to the poetry section.

"Ah, Rilke," Gerhard exclaims and rage courses through me. Rilke might have written in German, but his words of love and wisdom couldn't be further removed from the cruelty of the Nazis, just like Erich Remarque and his poignant *All Quiet on the Western Front.* I think of my resistance book club and my anger fades slightly. This month, we are reading *Souvenirs sur l'affaire* by our former Prime Minister Léon Blum. It's not the kind of book I'd normally read if I'm honest, but just knowing that the Nazis want to ban it enhances the flavor of the words, like garlic in a stew.

I hear Gigi giggle and it sets my teeth on edge. When the Germans first arrived, it had been impossible for me to imagine how any French citizen's life could be happy under their occupation, but now I realize that Gigi can be happy anywhere, as long as she is able to trade on her beauty.

Once more I'm cast back to my childhood, to when I was about twelve years old and fighting tears as Maman tried to detangle my matted hair. "Why can't I have hair like Genevieve," I sobbed. "Why does it always end up looking like a bird's nest? Why can't I look perfect too?"

"Who wants to look perfect?" Maman replied with a snort. "Imperfect is so much more interesting. Look . . ." She took two books down from my overcrowded shelves—a brand new copy of *Little Women* in paperback and an old leather-bound English edition of *Great Expectations* we'd found in a market. "Which of these books looks the most appealing to you?"

"The Dickens one of course."

"Why of course?"

I turned the book over in my hands. "Because it is so old and the pages are so soft from years of turning and they smell like . . . like stories. And it is so interesting to think of all the people who must have read this book over the years, to wonder what they thought of the story and why they turned down the corners of certain pages. It's full of mystery."

"Exactly!" Maman smiled at me triumphantly.

I stared at my reflection in the mirror. "So are you saying I'm more mysterious because my hair looks like a bird's nest?"

"Of course! Who wouldn't be intrigued by a girl with birds nesting in her hair?"

Now, the memory of us both laughing makes me smile.

"What are you thinking?"

Gerhard's voice brings me back to the present with a jolt. He's standing right in front of me at my desk.

"What am I thinking?" I echo, confused.

"Yes, to make you smile so."

Gigi appears at his side, scowling.

"I was just remembering something."

"Well, it must have been a very happy memory." Gerhard puts a copy of *The Book of Hours* by Rilke on the desk in front of me, along with some money.

"It was," I reply defiantly. Then I remember that I'm supposed to be keeping my disdain for the Germans under wraps. "Thank you," I say politely, picking up the money.

"You are welcome."

"Are you going back to the chateau?" Gigi asks Gerhard.

"No, I have to get back to work," he replies. "We have some busy days ahead. Goodbye, Laurence, and thank you again."

I watch as Gigi follows him out of the store like an adoring puppy dog, without as much as a backward glance.

The following morning I'm woken by a commotion coming from the square. I stumble, bleary-eyed, to the window and pull back the blackout blind. It's still dark, but thankfully the silvery light from an almost full moon makes it possible to read the time on the town hall clock. It's just coming up to six—or five in real time, I remind myself. Regularly reminding myself of the real, *French* time is another act of resistance I've adopted, if only in my head. The noise is coming from the other side of the square—the café to be precise. About ten German soldiers have gathered outside and some are hammering on the door. Nazi pigs, I think to myself, so greedy they cannot wait for their breakfast while the rest of us are forced to go hungry. I hear someone shouting in German and then another man's voice, speaking in French. I open the window a crack.

"You need to come out," the German speaking in French calls. It sounds like Gerhard.

I squint through the darkness and see a figure I assume must be Abram, standing in the doorway of the café, silhouetted against the light inside.

In the middle of the commotion, I hear the words "Polish" and "Jew."

"But why?" I hear Abram cry. "What about my café?"

"It is no longer your café," the soldier replies in French and now I'm certain that it's Gerhard.

I crouch by the window, barely able to breathe. What are they doing? Why is it no longer Abram's café? Surely the Germans aren't starting to requisition our businesses in the same way they've taken our food.

The voices quieten and I'm no longer able to hear what they're saying. Then suddenly a scuffle breaks out. I open the window wider and see the soldiers hammering on the café door again. Abram must have gone back inside and locked them out. *"Bon courage!"* I whisper, trying to send a comradely gift of strength across the square to him. The sound of the Germans battering on his door grows louder. It must have woken everyone. I picture my neighbors peering through their blinds like me and then I see a flash of light from inside the café as the soldiers break down the door. A shot rings out and I feel sick to my stomach. Surely they haven't killed Abram? Some of the soldiers pour into the café, shouting in German, while others carry what looks like a body into the square.

"Oh no, oh Abram," I gasp. But then I see the other soldiers coming out of the café, dragging someone with them. The soldiers carrying the body come closer, to a car parked near my store. I move back slightly and see from the uniform that they're carrying one of their own. Was he accidentally shot in the melee, or did Abram shoot him? Did Abram shoot a German? I clamp my hand to my mouth in horror. What will they do to him if this is the case?

As the soldiers reach the car, I hear someone moan in pain and see that the person they are carrying is alive and clutching his leg. I breathe a sigh of relief for Abram as I watch them put the injured soldier into the back of the car and speed off. Then I look back at the café and see the other soldiers dragging someone toward the war memorial in the center of the square. As they get closer, I see that it is Abram. The soldiers force him to stand by the stone steps of the plinth, then they form a line in front of him. My throat tightens as they draw their guns. Oh no! No! No! A volley of shots tears through the silence, causing my ears to ring. Abram's body judders and jerks in a terrible dance before falling in a heap on the floor.

As the ringing in my ears fades, one of the soldiers walks over to Abram's crumpled body and prods it with the toe of his boot as if kicking a piece of rubbish. And in that moment, I feel something inside of me close, like a set of shutters coming down tight around my heart. One of the soldiers puts his gun back in its holster, turns away and as the silvery moonlight catches his face, I see that it is Gerhard. Gerhard is one of Abram's killers.

He glances up and our eyes meet. My anger hardens and I don't look away. I want him to know that I have witnessed his crime. *You are just the same as all the rest*, I spit at him in my mind. *Murderer!*

Gerhard wipes his face with the back of his hand and turns back. Another of the soldiers climbs the steps of the memorial and looks around the square.

"This is what happens to traitors who disobey," he shouts in French. "Let this be a warning to you."

I stay at the window, not caring if they see me. A figure hurries across the square from the direction of the church. It's Père Rambert and he's clutching what looks like his Bible to his chest. My hands clench into tight fists. What if they shoot him too? Ignoring the soldiers, the Père kneels by Abram's lifeless body and begins to pray. Mercifully, the soldiers slink off into the shadows.

As I listen to the soft lilt of the Père praying, something within me feels forever changed. Finally, I understand how Saint Jeanne found her bravery. I know now that I will do anything to rid France of this evil. I know now that I am willing to die to save my beloved country.

17

JEANNE—1993

The next morning, Jeanne woke with a jolt, momentarily disorientated by the abundance of pink flowers swimming before her eyes on the quilt. As the events from the night before began filtering back into her mind, she rolled onto her side and looked at the pile of "evidence" she'd gathered on top of the dresser. It was impossible not to see the things she'd discovered last night as evidence. Going into the store with Wendell had been as heart-stopping and adrenaline-fueled as any crime-scene investigation, and the items she'd found hidden beneath the floorboards were bound to contain clues, not only to Laurence's life but also, possibly, to her death. Jeanne was starting to believe that Wendell really didn't know what had happened to Laurence, and he'd been so shaken up at seeing the bedroom above the store, there was no way she could have questioned him more. But it was looking increasingly likely that something bad had happened. Why else would Laurence have left those things in her hiding place? Why else would the store have been abandoned all these years? And why else would people be leaving flowers outside of it? Jeanne's skin erupted in goosebumps. What if the store really was a crime scene? What if it was where her mother had been killed by the Nazis? The smashed-up typewriter would certainly indicate that some kind of violent act had occurred there.

She went over to the window and opened the curtains. The rising sun was casting the cobblestones and buildings in a buttery gold glow. As she looked around the square, she tried to imagine it full of German soldiers. Her gaze fell upon the boarded-up store and she pictured her dad hiding there with Laurence right under the nose of the enemy. What would they have done to him if they'd found him? She dreaded to think.

She heard the sound of metal scraping on the ground below and looked down to see a tall slim man with wavy brown hair placing chairs and tables outside the café next door. The thought of a coffee in the early-morning sunshine was very appealing. Jeanne quickly got dressed, scribbled a note to Wendell telling him where she was in case he woke, pushed the note under his door and made her way downstairs.

As Jeanne emerged from the hotel, the clock on the wall of the building with the flags struck six. She hoped the café was open this early. The door was open so that was promising. She took her little French phrase book from her purse and looked up coffee.

"*Bonjour!*" The man behind the counter greeted her with a cheery grin.

"*Bonjour! Café?*" she asked, leafing through the pages of the book. "Uh—*si . . . vu . . . plait.*"

"*Oui.*" He then rattled something off in French so fast she had no hope of being able to translate it.

"I'm sorry," she said, shrugging helplessly. "I don't understand."

"Would you like cream and sugar?" he replied in perfect English.

"You speak English!"

"Yes, but it was so much fun to see you trying to speak French with your book." He chuckled.

"Oh man!" She grinned back at him. After the heaviness of last night, it felt good to kid around, even if it was at her expense. "No thank you, just black."

"Ah, so you are a true coffee lover."

"Absolutely."

"Please take a seat and I will bring it to you."

"*Merci!*" Jeanne replied in a deliberately strong French accent.

He laughed. "Very good."

She went outside and sat at one of the tables. How long had it been since she'd laughed like that with a guy? She honestly couldn't remember. Her career had always been her first love. When her first couple of serious relationships didn't work out, mainly due to the all-consuming nature of her profession, she'd convinced herself she couldn't have both and had spent most of her forties enjoying the occasional hook-up with a guy called Chad in Forensics. Chad had commitment issues, so it seemed like the perfect arrangement for both of them. But now her career had hung her out to dry, had it really been worth the sacrifice?

She thought of her brother Danny and his wife and kids. She used to tell herself she'd die of boredom if she had to squeeze herself into a life like theirs, but she was starting to feel like someone who'd just discovered that she'd been the punchline to her own joke.

She sighed and felt inside her purse for her cigarettes. Her fingers brushed against something metallic and she pulled out the pendant. She'd forgotten to put it on the dresser with the rest of last night's haul. She held it up to the sunlight and noticed some tiny writing in French around the border. She wondered who the solider was and why Laurence would have had the pendant, why she would have hidden it.

Just then, the café owner came out holding a small carafe of water and a glass, which he placed on the table in front of her along with a paper napkin.

"*Merci*. Hey, I don't suppose you could tell me what it says on here?" she asked, showing him the pendant.

"Aha, Saint Jeanne," he said knowingly.

Jeanne started at the sound of her name.

"Or, as you guys would call her, Joan of Arc."

"It's a woman?" Jeanne looked back at the figure.

"Yes, and one of the bravest women France has ever seen." He took the pendant and studied the tiny writing. "It says: 'I am not afraid. I was born to do this.' It is a famous quote of hers."

"I see." As he handed the pendant back to Jeanne, she felt a shiver of excitement. Had Joan of Arc been a hero of her mother's? Is that how she'd ended up with her name? As the man went back inside, Jeanne held the pendant tightly. Ever since she'd found out the truth about her real mom, it all felt like some kind of weird dream, but now, for the first time, she felt a proper sense of connection with her.

She carefully tucked the pendant inside the zip-up pocket in her purse and took out her cigarettes and her dad's copy of *For Whom the Bell Tolls*. Perhaps it would provide her with some more answers. But just as she was about to start reading, she saw a movement in the corner of the square. An old lady was slowly making her way along the parade of stores opposite. With her long baggy clothes and lank greasy hair, she looked like one of the vagrants who inhabited the arches beneath the railway bridges back home. Judging by her fuller figure, this woman wasn't going hungry though. Jeanne watched as she made her way past the florist, the shoe shop and the gift shop.

"Your coffee," the café owner announced, reappearing holding a white cup.

"*Merci*," Jeanne murmured, keeping her gaze fixed on the old woman.

"Have a nice day," the man said in a mock American accent.

"Ha, very good. You too," she replied with a grin.

When she looked back across the square, she saw that the old woman had stopped by Laurence's store. Jeanne watched as she started rooting around in her bag—and took out a bunch of fresh flowers and a bottle of water. The woman knelt down, took the old flowers from the jar, tipped out the stale water and refilled it from the bottle. Then she put the fresh flowers into the jar and knelt in front of them, crossing herself, as if she were in church. What the hell?

Jeanne stood up, her heart pounding. Had this woman known her real mom? She hurried across the square. As she got closer, she could hear the woman muttering something over and over in French like some kind of mantra. Jeanne cleared her throat and the woman practically jumped out of her skin. She stumbled to her feet, saying something in French, spitting out the words as if she was cursing. Up this close, Jeanne could see that her face was caked with makeup and her lipstick had obviously been applied with a shaky hand, making her mouth look more like that of a clown's. She could also smell the woman's cloying floral perfume mixed with the sour scent of stale liquor.

"*Bonjour*," Jeanne said softly. "Do you speak English?"

The woman began backing away, still muttering at her in French.

"Please don't go," Jeanne pleaded. "I want to talk to you."

But it was no good, the woman was hurrying off the way she'd come like a startled rabbit.

Jeanne looked down at the jar of fresh flowers and sighed. Just when she thought she was learning more about Laurence, the mystery grew deeper.

18

LAURENCE—MAY 1941

I place my pendant on my dressing table next to the cup-sized vanilla cake Madame Bonheur has baked for me and close my eyes. The sweet sound of birdsong drifts through my bedroom window on the warm breeze and for a moment I relax. Then I hear the rumble of a truck and the sound of marching boots and my body tenses. It's the thirtieth of May—the Feast Day of Jeanne of Arc—which has, of course, been declared *verboten* by the Germans.

I bring my hands together in prayer as an act of defiance. "Saint Jeanne of Arc, patron of France, my patron saint," I whisper, "I ask you now to fight this battle with me by prayer, just as you led your troops to victory in battle. Grant me the courage and strength I need to endure this constant fight. Oh Jeanne, help me to be victorious."

I sit for a moment, contemplating Jeanne and her bravery, but the silence is rudely interrupted by my stomach growling in hunger. I open my eyes and look at the cake. It's supposed to be an offering to Saint Jeanne, but the sweet smell of vanilla is making me drool. Surely she would understand if I took a nibble. Surely she would want me to be fortified in my battle. I take the cake from my makeshift altar and bite into the soft sponge. It is so long since I have had cake, I feel instantly drunk on the sugar.

"Oh Jeanne, please forgive me," I gasp, before taking another bite, and another. In seconds, the cake is gone. "I'm sorry," I whisper to the etching on my pendant, before putting her back in my pocket. "But now I've had the sustenance I need, I shall resume my battle for liberty with renewed vigor!"

I get dressed into a short-sleeved blouse and trousers, fastening the belt to its tightest notch. All of us are getting thinner; even Madame Bonheur's skin is slacker, falling in empty pouches from her neck and arms.

Downstairs in the store, I take a black crayon from my desk drawer and wrap it inside one of Maman's old handkerchiefs with a daisy embroidered in the corner. As I tuck it into my pocket, I wonder what she would have thought of how I'd end up using it. I hope she would have approved, although I'm pretty certain she would have urged me not to do anything so dangerous.

I unlock the door and step outside. The brightness of the early-morning sun is promising a hot day ahead. It's the perfect day for a walk in the forest, but I can't think of such things. I have urgent business to attend to. I glance around the square and see that it's completely deserted. There's not even a sign of any patrolling soldiers. I hurry down the hill toward the post office. There, on the wall, are the latest posters from the Germans, this time featuring a hideous caricature of a Jew. I shiver as I think of what happened to Abram. It turned out that the soldiers had gone to his café that terrible morning to requisition it following a new statute banning Jews from certain professions. Abram had shot one of the soldiers in the leg, trying to defend his property, and that is why they set upon him like a pack of wild dogs.

I look both ways to make sure no one's about, then hurry

over to the posters. I take the crayon from my pocket and write a huge letter V in one of the blank spaces. I check again that no one is coming, then start filling the letter out, making it bigger and bolder.

In a broadcast from London in March, Winston Churchill instructed the French to start writing V for victory signs anywhere we could as an act of resistance. To my delight, I've not been the only person in the valley to do so. V's have been appearing in chalk and even paint on the pavements and walls all around town. They've even been carved into the trunks of some of the trees. Of course, as fast as we put them up, the Germans take them down, but still. It warms my heart to think that there are other people in town just like me, tiny sparks of resistance that hopefully one day will join together to form an indestructible flame. I keep filling my mind with thoughts like these as I write a V sign on the other poster. It helps to keep my fear at bay as the Germans have now declared that defacing their posters is punishable by death.

I slip the crayon back into the handkerchief in my pocket and make my way back up to the square. I see one of their SMOKING FORBIDDEN posters on the wall of the corset shop and I cannot resist. Checking once again that no one is coming, I quickly make thick black lines through certain letters until *RAUCHEN VERBOTEN* has been transformed into *RACE VERTE*. The green race. Ha! I chuckle to myself. I hope my fellow townsfolk enjoy the joke.

As I return to the square, I hear the sound of shutters being opened and see Gigi standing in front of the café—Abram's café. After they murdered him, the Germans offered Gigi the job of managing the café, an offer she seemingly had no trouble accepting. Obviously I haven't eaten there since. I wait by the corner until she goes back inside. The last thing I need is for her to see me out and about so early, no doubt she would run straight back to Gerhard or the Kommandant, telling tales.

The thought of Gerhard makes my skin clammy from a mixture of hatred and dread. Ever since that terrible day, it's as if we've been engaged in an awkward dance. He's been polite yet distant, almost as if he is ashamed, although obviously I know that the Nazis feel no shame when it comes to murdering Jews. Didn't they arrest thousands of foreign-born Jews just a couple of weeks ago and send them off to God knows where? It's as if they see them as being lower than vermin. Well, I know who the real rats are here.

Gigi goes back into the café and I hurry across the square to my store.

Later that evening, I prepare for the monthly meeting of our resistance book club. This month, in honor of Jeanne of Arc's Feast Day, we have been reading the play *Sainte Jeanne* by the Irish writer George Bernard Shaw. I was only able to acquire two copies of the play on my last trip to Paris, one from Michel and one from Pierre, so we had to rotate the copies amongst the group, which has now grown to four members; we have now been joined by Charlotte's cousin, Odette, a milliner with a great gift for both hat-making and sarcasm. This evening, we are meeting in the store, in the brief window of opportunity after it has shut but before curfew, and should we be rudely interrupted by any Germans, our cover story is that the other women are helping me conduct a stock check.

I make sure the blackout blinds are firmly in place and light a couple of candles on the mantelpiece, as it's far too warm for a fire. So as not to arouse suspicion, all of the book club members have been allocated different times to arrive. I wait perched on the edge of one of the armchairs until I hear the coded knock on the door. We're using the same code the BBC use at the start of their broadcasts to Europe, mimicking the first four notes of

Beethoven's Fifth Symphony, which is also the dot-dot-dot-dash Morse code for V—for victory.

I hurry over and peer through a crack in the blind to see Charlotte standing there nervously. I quickly let her in and lock the door behind her.

"Oh, Laurence, what a day it has been!" she exclaims, quickly embracing me before slumping down in one of the armchairs. "I don't know how much longer I'm going to be able to control Raul. He's chomping at the bit, wanting to take revenge on the Nazis."

"What have they done now?"

"They have taken his favorite horse."

"Not Rosa?"

"Yes. It's as if they want to make him crack so that they can do to him what they did to Abram."

"You have to tell him to stay patient. The Resistance is growing; my friend in Paris told me that the British are getting ready to send people and weapons to help us. He'll be no good to France if he loses his temper and gets himself killed."

"I know." Charlotte wrings her hands. "I don't know what I'd do if I didn't have him at the farm. Now Jacques is gone, he's become such a comfort and a help to me."

A sharp dot-dot-dot-dash at the door causes us both to jump and then laugh.

"I am so jittery these days," Charlotte sighs.

"Me too."

I hurry over to the door and let Odette in. She and Charlotte embrace, then she turns to me.

"Oh Laurence, thank you!" As she takes off her pink cloche hat, I see that her face is full of gratitude.

"What for?"

"This month's book. It was like a rallying call to my spirit."

"Mine too," Charlotte agrees and my heart swells. "If only I could get some of Saint Jeanne's courage," Charlotte sighs. "If only I could hear God telling me what to do."

"Hmm, if you start hearing voices, I fear it might be time for you to see the doctor," Odette quips.

"Very funny." Charlotte removes the cloth cover from her basket. "Well, I might not be as brave as Jeanne, but I do have a talent for sneaking food out from under the Germans' noses."

As if on cue, my stomach rumbles, causing the other two to giggle.

"I feel as if French stomachs must now be noisier than our voices," I say, my eyes on stalks as Charlotte produces two apples and a chunk of cheese. I go and fetch some plates and a knife from the kitchen.

As Charlotte starts slicing the apples, there's another knock at the door, but instead of the Beethoven code, it's just two sharp raps. We all freeze, staring at each other in fright. Charlotte shoves the food back into her basket.

"Quick," I say, "go to the shelves, make it look as if you're checking the stock."

They do as instructed and I head for the door, my heart thudding. I peer through the crack and see Madame Bonheur standing there.

"It's all right," I whisper to the others before opening the door. "Why didn't you come the back way? Why didn't you use the code?" I hiss as I pull her into the shop.

"Oh, I forgot! Why do I need a secret code anyway? I am not a spy." She comes bustling into the shop holding a bag. I can see some bread sticking out of the top and the sight makes me both salivate and fume.

"What if the Germans saw you bringing this?" I say.

"Well, if you don't want it—"

"Of course we want it," I interrupt.

"We want it!" Charlotte and Odette cry in unison.

"Very well then." Madame Bonheur tuts. "Stop being so fussy."

Does she think I enjoy being so uptight? I hate it. I hate how the Germans are changing me from a free spirit into this person made of "but"s and "what if"s. "I just don't want you to get killed," I mutter.

She puts her arm round me and pulls me close. "Those pigs will not kill me. Who else would make them such delicious bread?"

"Good point." I chuckle, and it feels so good to laugh and relieve the tension.

Charlotte retrieves the apples and cheese from her basket and Madame Bonheur places not one but two baguettes on the plate beside them.

"It truly is a feast!" I exclaim. "Saint Jeanne would be proud."

Odette and Madame Bonheur sit in the armchairs and Charlotte and I sit cross-legged on the floor before them, forming a circle of sorts. I place my copy of *Sainte Jeanne* in the center.

"So, what did everyone think?" I ask.

"I wasn't sure about the end." Madame Bonheur sniffs. "When she says that she never wanted to be a saint."

"That was one of my favorite bits," I cry. "To me, it showed the hypocrisy of the leaders, allowing her to burn at the stake but then canonizing her. And don't you think it is the perfect metaphor for what's happening today, with Pétain allowing France to burn?"

Odette nods. "Yes, if only we could have leaders like Jeanne, who put their country first, and above any personal gain."

"My favorite part was where she said she cannot be frightened by being told she is alone because everyone, even God, is alone," I say, helping myself to a slice of apple. "It helped me to see my own solitude as a form of strength."

"You are not alone, Laurence," Charlotte says, looking at me with such love in her eyes it warms me to the core.

"No, you are most definitely not," Madame Bonheur agrees.

"Thank you," I reply. But, in truth, and in spite of their friendship, I've never felt more alone than I have this past year without Luc by my side.

"I loved the part where Jeanne talks about nothing being crueler than people doing nothing in the face of heresy," Odette says. "There are a few people in this town I'd like to read that line to!"

"Yes, and make them keep reading it until they realize the error of their ways," I agree, thinking of Gigi.

I take one of the cubes of cheese and allow it to melt on my tongue. The contrast between the sharp taste and the creamy texture is divine.

We all sit in silence for a moment, savoring the food.

"Isn't it wonderful," I say eventually.

"What?" Charlotte asks.

"This." I gesture at our group. "That, in spite of everything, we have still found a way to find joy." The others nod and I continue, on a roll. "Who would have thought that simply reading a book would become such an act of resistance!"

Madame Bonheur chuckles. "And to think that I was always such a reluctant reader. Hitler and his cronies have done more for my literacy than any teacher ever did!"

We all laugh.

"I have to say that's the strangest reason for becoming a book lover, but it's wonderful too." I grin.

"Do you want to see something even more wonderful?" She smiles back at me.

"Of course!"

We all watch as she reaches into her bag and produces a bottle of wine.

"Ooh la la!" Odette cries.

I fetch some glasses and Madame Bonheur pours us all a drink.

"To Saint Jeanne," I say, raising my glass.

"To Saint Jeanne," the others echo. But just as we're clinking glasses, there's a loud knock on the door.

"Shit!" Odette exclaims and we all look at each other in shock.

"Are you expecting anyone else?" Madame Bonheur whispers.

"No!"

She springs to her feet and beckons to the others. "Come with me, out the back. We can go into the boulangerie."

The others tiptoe through the kitchen and into the yard.

There's another knock on the door, louder this time. I quickly scoop up the plates and glasses and sling them into the kitchen sink, praying whoever it is won't come out here. Then I smooth down my hair and hurry to the door. I peer through the blind and see Gerhard standing there. Thankfully he's alone. I unlock the door and open it slightly.

"Good evening," he says. "Please, may I come in for a moment?"

"The store is shut."

"I know, but I need to talk to you about something."

I glance beyond him into the square. The last thing I need is anyone seeing a German solider paying me a private visit. Thankfully, even though there's still about half an hour until curfew, there's no one about. I open the door wider.

"Thank you," he says, walking past me into the shop.

"How may I help you?" I say in the stiff, cordial voice I've used ever since I saw him take part in Abram's murder.

He glances at the candles flickering on the mantelpiece and, to my horror, I notice that Madame Bonheur has left her copy of *Sainte Jeanne* on the armchair. I watch as his gaze falls upon it.

"George Bernard Shaw," he mutters. I hold my breath,

waiting for him to make the connection between the subject matter of the play and the fact that it is Saint Jeanne's forbidden Feast Day. But instead he smiles. "I am a fan of his *Pygmalion*. The German director Erich Engel made a very good adaptation."

"Great," I say politely, my jaw clenched. I think I would have preferred him reprimanding me for celebrating Saint Jeanne's Feast Day than trying to be my friend. "So, how may I help you?"

"I am looking for something to read. Something uplifting."

Why, to help you overcome your guilt at being a murderer? I want to snap at him. The prospect of helping a Nazi feel "uplifted" is appalling. "Why don't you take a look then," I manage to mutter instead.

"Is there anything you might recommend?" He smiles at me hopefully.

Keep calm, I tell myself. I'm already treading on thin ice with a book celebrating Jeanne of Arc on display. "Perhaps a romance," I say sarcastically, thinking of his evening stroll with Gigi in the forest.

His smile fades, but I don't care. I can't bring myself to be friendly with him after what I saw him do. Perhaps he thinks that by leaving it this long, I will have forgotten, but, if anything, the time has made me even more bitter.

As he heads to the poetry section at the back of the store, a terrible thought occurs to me. What if he sees the glasses in the kitchen sink?

"Apparently the latest novel by Paul Morand is very entertaining," I call after him. "I have a copy of it here."

To my relief, he comes back over. "Thank you." He smiles gratefully as I hand him the book.

He puts the money on the desk and as I go to take it, he places his hand on top of mine. It takes everything I've got not to openly flinch.

"I didn't do it, you know," he whispers.

"Do what?" I reply, praying he'll remove his hand before I'm forced to shove him away.

"Shoot him. I intentionally missed." He tucks the book inside his coat pocket. "Goodnight, Laurence."

I watch, speechless, as he leaves.

19

JEANNE—1993

Wendell arrived at Jeanne's room at just before nine, looking a whole lot better than when they'd parted the night before. Over a breakfast of delicious, warm, buttery croissants and rich coffee in the hotel restaurant, Jeanne told him about the strange woman she'd seen leaving the flowers outside the store.

"I can't figure out why she got so upset," she said, spreading some apricot preserve on her pastry.

"Maybe she was a close friend of your mom's," Wendell suggested. "Maybe she wanted to be left alone to remember her."

"Do you think Laurence is dead then?" Jeanne asked quickly, studying his face for any tell-tale change in expression.

"I . . ." He looked down at the table, his face etched with sorrow—or was it guilt?

"Yes?" she asked softly.

"I guess I'd always hoped . . ." Again he broke off.

"Hoped what?"

"For a miracle." He gave a sad smile.

Deciding not to press him further, Jeanne took the pendant from purse. "I did find out more about this, though." She placed it on the table. "The engraving is of Joan of Arc. Or

Jeanne d'Arc as they say here." She looked at Wendell hopefully. "Do you think Laurence named me after her?"

Wendell nodded. "I reckon so, it would definitely make sense that she was your mom's hero, she was an awesome warrior. She led the French army to victory against the English when she was just a teenager."

Jeanne looked down at the pendant. "I found out what the writing means too."

"Geez, all this before I got up?" Wendell raised his eyebrows.

"Yeah well, you snooze you lose." She showed him the pendant. "It says, 'I am not afraid. I was born to do this.'" As Jeanne said the words out loud, she felt strangely emboldened.

Wendell nodded. "That's exactly the kind of thing I can imagine Laurence saying too."

As Jeanne watched him go misty-eyed, she experienced a strange twinge of envy. The more she discovered about Laurence, the more she wished she could have known her. At least Wendell had his memories of their time together. She had nothing, other than a random assortment of objects to scour for clues. And whatever had happened to Laurence, it didn't look great for Jeanne. Either her real mom was dead or she'd deliberately abandoned her.

"What say we take the deeds to the store to the town hall this morning, see if they can help us any?" Wendell suggested. "Veronique told me it's the building with the flags."

"Veronique?" Now it was Jeanne's turn to raise her eyebrows.

Wendell's cheeks reddened. "The gal on reception. I got chatting to her while I was waiting on you to come back from the café."

Jeanne laughed. "Good work, Pops. I say that's a great idea."

. . .

Trying to get help at the town hall was easier said than done as it turned out no one at the reception desk could speak English, or at least not fluently enough to understand what they were trying to say.

"We need an interpreter," Wendell muttered.

"Wait here," Jeanne replied. "I have an idea."

She ran across the square to the café. Now it was mid-morning, the tables on the terrace were filled with people eating and drinking in the sun. She went inside to find the man from earlier standing behind the counter. A couple of young women were working beside him, one drying glasses and the other serving a customer.

"Hello again," he said with a grin when he saw Jeanne. "In need of more coffee already?"

"I'm always in need of more coffee," Jeanne replied, "but I was actually wondering if I could ask you a favor? My dad and I are trying to get some help over at the town hall, but no one can understand us."

He shook his head in mock outrage. "Oh the horror—imagine people not being able to speak English—in France."

"Please, it's really important."

Thankfully, he seemed to sense the urgency of her plea and said something in French to one of the other staff before turning back to Jeanne. "OK, lead the way."

Back in the town hall, Jeanne found Wendell performing his disappearing dime trick to a young woman behind the reception desk. She giggled coquettishly as he produced the dime from behind his ear. Clearly Wendell's charm with the ladies transcended all language barriers.

"Hey, Pops, this is . . ." She turned to the man from the café. "I'm sorry, what's your name?"

"Yitzhak."

"Yitzhak?" Jeanne echoed. She was no expert, but it didn't sound very French.

"Yes, it's Polish. I'm Polish, originally." Yitzhak turned to Wendell and shook his hand. "So, you are a magician?"

Wendell laughed. "Only in my spare time."

Yitzhak turned back to Jeanne. "So, what is it that you'd like me to tell them?"

"My birth mother used to live in this square. She owned a bookstore, opposite the café—the building that's all boarded up."

Yitzhak's smile faded. "Your mother owned that store?"

"Yes. She left it to me when she died, but for, uh, various reasons, I haven't been able to come and claim it until now. We have the deed to the property right here." She took the aging document from her purse. "We just want to check with someone official that everything's in order before we enter the building."

Yitzhak whistled through his teeth, then shook Wendell's hand again. "Your wife, she was a very special woman."

Jeanne watched him intently. What did he mean, she was a very special woman? And how did he know? He didn't appear to be any older than Jeanne. He couldn't have known her mother personally.

"She wasn't...We never married," Wendell stammered. "We met during the war."

Yitzhak nodded. "And you are from America?"

"Yes. I was in the air force during the war, stationed in Britain."

"Wow." Yitzhak looked back at Jeanne. "You're alive," he whispered, as if she was some kind of miracle.

"Er, yes, obviously," she joked, but her head was filling with even more questions. Before she could say anything, the woman behind the desk asked Yitzhak something in French.

"We have our passports, if that would help," Wendell said, taking his passport from his pocket and placing it on the desk. Jeanne added hers to it, along with the deed to the store.

As Yitzhak spoke to the woman, Jeanne noticed a similar

look of shock and awe pass across her face. Then she took the documents and disappeared into an office behind the reception desk.

"She's just going to get someone to come and see you," Yitzhak explained.

A couple of minutes passed and then a barrel-shaped man wearing a tight-fitting suit appeared, looking highly excited. He said something to Yitzhak, then shook Jeanne and Wendell's hands vigorously.

"He is welcoming you to the Valley," Yitzhak explained. "He is very pleased to see you. Very pleased indeed."

The man took them through to a plush office and invited them to sit down. Jeanne had been preparing herself for a fight, or some kind of interrogation at least, but this guy was treating them like royalty. He went to a cabinet and pulled out a file, then said something to Yitzhak in French.

"These are the details of the person who has been taking care of the property in your absence," Yitzhak explained. He looked at Wendell. "There is also a document naming you as the father of Laurence's daughter, Jeanne, so it all checks out with your passports. The woman who has been taking care of the property has the keys, so she will be able to grant you access."

Jeanne exchanged a shifty glance with Wendell. Now would probably not be the best time to tell them they'd already gained access to the store.

"That would be awesome. I cannot wait to see it!" Wendell said, with way too much feigned enthusiasm. Jeanne sighed. He'd make a terrible undercover cop.

As they emerged back into the sunshine, the square was now bustling with people and a busker was tuning up his guitar on the steps by the statue of the soldier.

"It's hard to imagine the things that went on here during the war," Yitzhak said, gazing gravely at the busker.

Jeanne nodded, although she still didn't know exactly what

had happened to her mother. Perhaps the person who'd been taking care of the store could help solve the mystery. She looked down at the name on the piece of paper: Charlotte Martel.

"If you like, I can drive you to the farm where she lives," Yitzhak offered. "It is quite a walk from here." He looked at Wendell's cane.

"That would be great, thank you," Wendell replied.

"Are you sure?" Jeanne asked. "You've already done so much for us. I don't want to keep you from your work."

"It would be an honor," Yitzhak replied dramatically.

Jeanne frowned. Why was he treating them with such reverence? And what had he meant when he'd exclaimed, "You're alive!"? But before she could ask, he was hurrying away down a side street.

"Wait here," he called over his shoulder. "I'll just get my car."

Jeanne looked at Wendell. "Is it my imagination or are folks acting a little weird now they know who we are?"

Wendell shrugged. "Maybe it's just the French way of being hospitable."

But Jeanne remained unconvinced. People were definitely acting strange around them. Before she could ponder any more, a battered blue car shaped like a bug came chugging up the street. The front bumper appeared to be hanging from a thread. Jeanne fought the instinctive urge to book the driver immediately.

"Holy cow, take a look at that jalopy!" Wendell exclaimed.

The jalopy came juddering to a halt up beside them and Yitzhak leaned out of the window. "Jump in!"

"I doubt that thing would survive if we did any jumping in it," Wendell muttered.

"Shhh, Pops," Jeanne hissed, fighting the urge to laugh.

There were no doors in the rear of the car, so she opened the front passenger door and looked for some kind of lever to pull the seat forward.

"Stand back!" Yitzhak commanded, before whacking the back of the seat, sending it flying forward.

"Well, I guess that's one way to do it," Jeanne muttered as she climbed into the back.

Yitzhak jerked the passenger seat back and Wendell got in and tapped the floor with his cane. "Just checking it isn't a foot-mobile like in *The Flintstones*."

"Pops!" Jeanne exclaimed.

Thankfully, Yitzhak laughed loudly. "This car has got me all the way to Poland and back many times." He thrust the gearstick into first and they juddered off along the cobbled street.

As they drove down the hill, Wendell and Yitzhak fell into a conversation about cars and Jeanne gazed out of the grimy window. The valley was pretty as a painting, with its winding streets lined with old stone buildings, all framed by the rolling green wall of the forest in the distance. She tried to picture her real mom walking these same streets. It must have been a great place to grow up—until the war happened at least. Yitzhak drove past a small railroad station and onto a narrow country lane. The trees either side had grown over the road, forming a tunnel, and the sunlight was filtering through, casting lace-like patterns on the ground. After a couple of miles, they reached a junction and he turned onto a dirt track, the seemingly suspension-less car feeling every bump.

"I'm sorry," Yitzhak said to Wendell as he gripped onto the dashboard.

"No problem," Wendell replied. "This feels just like landing a Lysander during the war."

"You flew a Lysander?"

"Yes siree Bob."

"But weren't those the planes that were used for secret missions?"

Wendell nodded.

Jeanne couldn't help smiling at how impressed Yitzhak

seemed by this. She was impressed too. She was seeing a whole other side to her Pops on this trip.

Finally, the dirt track opened out into a yard and they came to a halt in front of an old, gray stone house. A black and white collie dog that had been sleeping in a patch of sunlight by the door sprang to its feet and let out a yelp, but it was more in welcome than warning.

Yitzhak hurried round to help Wendell out, then he gave the passenger seat a whack. Just as Jeanne was clambering out, the door of the house opened and a petite woman with white hair in a long braid came out. She was wearing a green dress, white apron and slippers.

Yitzhak said *"Bonjour"* to the woman, then turned back to Jeanne. "Do you have the paperwork, the deed to the store?"

"Sure." Jeanne handed him the document along with her passport. The woman was staring at her intently.

Yitzhak went over and started talking rapidly in French. As he showed her the paperwork, she took a step back, gasping and clasping her hands to her chest. Then she pointed at Jeanne.

"Jeanne? Jeanne?"

Yitzhak nodded. "This is Charlotte," he said to Jeanne. "She was a very close friend of your mother's."

Before Jeanne could respond, Charlotte was running toward her, arms outstretched. "Jeanne! Jeanne!" she cried over and over before clutching hold of her, her eyes full of tears.

20

LAURENCE—JULY 1941

"I didn't realize you smoked," Michel says, as I take a tin of tobacco and a pack of cigarette papers from my purse.

"I didn't—until the Germans and their puppet government in Vichy made it *verboten*," I reply, sprinkling some tobacco upon one of the tissue-thin papers. "To be honest with you, I enjoy the act of making the cigarette far more than smoking it—I find it strangely liberating."

Michel laughs and takes a sip of his coffee. It's the end of a hot summer's day and we've come to Café de Flore for something to eat. My official story is that I'm in Paris to buy stock for the shop; the real story is that I'm here to get copies of the latest title for my book club. This month, the Germans banned all books by British and American authors, so we will be reading *For Whom the Bell Tolls* by Ernest Hemingway. Michel has already sold me two copies; now we're waiting to meet with Pierre, who shall hopefully have acquired two more.

"I have to do something," I continue before lighting the cigarette. "Who are they to say that women can no longer have tobacco rations for *moral* reasons? Where is their morality when they round up the Jews like cattle and execute people in the street?"

"They have no morality," Michel replies gravely.

I inhale a lungful of smoke and splutter over the table.

Michel chuckles. "Perhaps you could find a way to resist that is less bad for your health?"

I shake my head. "Never! I shall learn to enjoy smoking if it kills me! It's bad enough that they've forbidden women to wear trousers. If Pétain had his way, he'd have us all chained up in the kitchen, chanting *'travail, famille, patrie'* endlessly."

"There will only be one true motto for France," Michel says.

"Indeed. Liberty, equality, fraternity," I reply.

"Ah, that is like music to my ears!" Pierre cries, as he arrives at our table and sits down beside me.

I take another puff on my cigarette and again end up choking.

"Laurence is now smoking as a form of resistance." Michel grins.

"Good for you," Pierre replies.

"Thank you." I place the cigarette in the ashtray, hoping it will burn away on its own without me having to inhale any more of the foul smoke. "So, do you have the books?"

"I do indeed." He gives a dry laugh. "Who would have thought it would come to this in France—the home of liberty. Who would have thought that reading Hemingway or Faulkner should become a crime?"

"It is ridiculous," I reply with a sigh. "I only wish there was some other way I could fight back. I mean, what will my little book club achieve against the Germans? What difference will it really make?"

"It's making an important difference," Pierre replies gravely. "Because you are not letting them win in here." He taps his head. "Or here." He taps his heart. "And you are helping others to do the same."

"I know, but still . . ."

I see Pierre and Michel exchange a glance across the table, and Michel nods. It's almost imperceptible, but it feels as if they've just exchanged a silent message. I take another puff on my cigarette to try to make out that I didn't notice, and this time I don't even try to inhale, storing the smoke in my mouth for a moment instead.

"Please remind me, where is it that you live?" Pierre asks.

"La Vallée du Cerf," I reply.

"I see." Again, he and Michel exchange a pointed glance. "And that's by La Forêt de Soleil, no?"

"Yes." I smile at the mere mention of the forest. "My favorite place in the whole world. Apart from your stall, obviously," I quickly add with a smile to Michel.

"Obviously." He chuckles.

"So, you know the forest well?" Pierre continues.

"As well as I know my own hand," I reply. "I practically lived there as a child."

"And you have a small group of people in your book club—people you know you can trust."

"Yes. I can trust them absolutely."

"Very good."

Again the men exchange a look.

"Do you think that these people would be prepared to help with the Resistance?"

"Of course. Why do you ask?" Excitement bubbles up inside of me.

Pierre glances over his shoulder, then leans closer. "The British government have started sending help."

"What kind of help?"

"Undercover operatives, and weapons and ammunition."

"We need volunteers to help get these people and goods to the right places."

"We?" I look at them both questioningly.

"Now that the Non-aggression Pact between Germany and the Soviet Union is over, the communist groups here in France have been able to join the Resistance," Michel explains.

"And we have all come together to form one group," Pierre adds.

"So you two are helping the British?" I whisper.

They both nod.

"This is excellent news!"

"So, what do you say?" Pierre asks. "Would you be able to recruit people in your town to help us too?"

"Of course." My body courses with adrenaline. Finally, after months of resisting through reading books and defacing posters, I might have something more impactful to do. "I can ask the others when I give out the books for our next book club meeting."

"Excellent," Pierre replies. "And when will you be able to come back to Paris?"

"Next week?" I suggest.

"Good. Then we can let the British know."

I take a celebratory puff on my cigarette and cough so hard I almost retch.

"And perhaps once you are helping us you won't feel the need to choke yourself to death," Michel says wryly.

For the rest of the day I am so high on excitement, I no longer feel the weakness from hunger I've become so accustomed to. As soon as it's light the next morning, I spring out of bed and fill the lining of my basket with the four copies of the Hemingway novel. After a quick and tasteless breakfast of stale baguette, I set off. Charlotte and I have arranged to meet at her henhouse on the farm as it's out of sight of the main house and any of her German guests. This will also enable her to smuggle the book inside the house beneath the eggs. As I walk up the track to the henhouse, I see her hovering outside. As soon as she sees me, she comes running over.

"Oh Laurence, you made it back safely!" she exclaims. "I always get so worried now when you go to Paris."

Seeing the genuine concern on her face warms my heart. The one silver lining of this past year has been my deepening friendship with Charlotte.

"There's no need to worry," I tell her as we embrace. Then I lower my voice. "The one advantage to the Germans and the Vichy government thinking that us women are good for nothing other than being mothers and homemakers is that they would never suspect I am up to anything *verboten*."

She nods. "Did you get the books?"

"I did."

We make our way over to the henhouse and go inside. I try my hardest not to breathe in the smell of stale straw and excrement. The chickens are all roosting together on a raised wooden platform. Charlotte goes over to two large wooden boxes filled with straw and starts pulling out eggs, placing them carefully on the floor beside her. "They've stopped laying as much as I'm finding it hard to get feed," she says with a sigh.

"I know the feeling." I laugh. "It has been about three months since my last period."

"Mine have stopped too," Charlotte cries.

"Well, at least we don't have to bother with sanitary napkins."

She pulls a face. "Yes, that is definitely a good thing." She has another rummage in the straw but finds nothing. She sighs. "I was hoping there would be more so that I could give you some, but I only have enough for the soldiers' breakfast."

"It's OK." I take a copy of *For Whom the Bell Tolls* from its hiding place in my basket. "Who needs food when you have great stories?"

Charlotte smiles. "Indeed."

"I have some other news too, but you mustn't breathe a word of it to anyone."

"Of course." Charlotte puts the Hemingway novel under a cloth in her basket and starts placing the eggs on top of it.

I lower my voice to a whisper. "Yesterday, when I was in Paris, the friends I get the books from told me that they are helping the British."

"What?" Charlotte stares at me in shock. "How?"

"The British have started sending people and supplies into France, to help the Resistance."

"Oh, that is wonderful news."

"I know. They asked me if I would help too—and enlist the help of other people here in the Valley." I look at her questioningly.

"Doing what?"

"I'm not exactly sure. I think they're trying to establish some kind of network."

Charlotte's eyes become glassy with tears. "Finally!"

"I know. So, would you be prepared to help if you were needed to?"

"Of course. And I know for a fact that Raul would. Only last night he was talking about how badly he needed to do something."

"That's fantastic. I'm going back to Paris next week, so I'll let them know and then hopefully we can get something started."

Charlotte clasps my hands in hers. "Oh Laurence. Do you think it is possible? Do you think we will beat the Germans?"

"Yes," I reply firmly. "Yes, now, I really do."

But our excitement is rudely interrupted by the sound of a man clearing his throat outside. Charlotte's grip on my hands tightens and I can feel her nails digging into my palms.

"Is it Raul?" I hiss.

"I don't know," she whispers.

I think of the Hemingway books in our baskets and my heart pounds.

"Excuse me," a man calls in French but with a German accent.

Oh no! It feels as if my stomach has dropped right out of me down onto the floor. How long has he been out there? Did he hear what we were saying? I replay our conversation in my mind, my skin growing clammier with every fateful word. *Helping the British . . . establishing a network . . . Resistance . . . beat the Germans.* Clearly Charlotte is having exactly the same thoughts as her face drains of all color.

"Y-yes?" she stammers, and we cling to each other as we await his response.

21

LAURENCE—AUGUST 1941

It turned out that the man was one of Charlotte's "guests," impatient to know where his breakfast was. But the whole experience was a stark reminder of what we are risking and so we hold the next meeting of the book club deep in the forest, away from the prying eyes of any Germans. In preparation, I gave each of the members a hand-drawn map with slightly different routes to Monseigneur Oak. I get there first and straight away I trace my fingers over Luc's initials in the gnarled trunk of the ancient tree.

"We are finally doing something, Luc," I whisper into the warm summer air. "You won't have died in vain."

A breeze rustles through the leaves and for a moment it feels as if Luc is whispering back to me. Then I hear footsteps approaching and quickly hide behind some bushes. Peering through the leaves, I see Odette walking along the footpath.

"Psst!" I whisper and she hurries over to join me.

"I just saw Brigitte Bernard in the meadow with a German," she whispers. "She is as bad as that whore, Gigi."

My heart sinks a little as I remember that for every member of the Resistance, there appears to be someone equally eager to collaborate, including one of my former best friends. "At least you and I will be on the right side of history," I whisper. "In years to come when they write about this, we will be the ones people admire, not them. Not the cowards." I hope against hope that I am right.

Odette nods. We hear more footsteps and Madame Bonheur appears, cursing under her breath as her faded daisy-print dress gets caught on some brambles.

"Over here," I whisper from behind the bush.

She curses again as she fights her way through the undergrowth to join us. But before she's able to complain any further, I hear more footsteps, but this time it sounds like more than one person and I hear someone cough—I hear a *man* cough. The three of us stand frozen to the spot behind the bushes. All I can think is, what if it is Brigitte and her German, and the horrible irony that we would be the criminals rather than her, fraternizing with the enemy. As I peer through the leaves, I see Charlotte and Raul and I instantly relax. Odette and Madame Bonheur look at me questioningly.

"It is all right," I whisper. "Charlotte told me that he wants to help too."

I step out from behind the bush.

"Good evening, Laurence," Charlotte greets me. "I hope you don't mind, but Raul saw my copy of *For Whom the Bell Tolls* and asked me how I got it, so I told him about our club, and he . . . he would like to join, if that's OK?" She looks at me hopefully.

"It is an excellent book," Raul says gruffly.

"You read it?" I'm unable to hide my surprise, remembering what Violeta once said about him being illiterate.

"Yes, I am a great fan of Hemingway."

"That is excellent." I curse myself for having believed that tittle-tattler Violeta. "Come . . ." I beckon at them to follow me into the small clearing behind the bushes.

Madame Bonheur, who has known Raul since he was a child, greets him warmly. Odette looks a little more suspicious.

"It's all right," I tell her. "He's one of us."

"I brought a gift," he says, reaching one of his shovel-sized hands inside his baggy jacket and producing a bottle of wine.

"Ooh la la!" Madame Bonheur exclaims and Odette's icy expression thaws slightly.

"And on a Sunday too." I laugh. "What better way to resist." Back in June, the Germans banned drinking wine in France on a Sunday. I don't think it's any coincidence that support for them and Pétain seems to have definitely been on the wane ever since.

"We didn't bring any glasses, just in case we were stopped," Charlotte says.

"That's all right. It feels fitting to all drink from the same bottle," I say. "It's like we are all members of a secret society. Blood brothers and sisters . . ." I taper off, feeling embarrassed at my overexuberance.

We sit in a circle on the dusty ground and Raul uncorks the bottle. I catch a waft of the wine—a delicious mixture of autumn berries and woodsmoke—and feel intoxicated from the smell alone.

"This was all I was able to bring," Madame Bonheur says, producing one baguette from her bag. "Those pigs have eaten everything."

"That's all right, we have bread and wine—enough for communion," Raul jokes, although I'm pretty certain I've never seen him set foot in the church.

"Indeed," I reply. "So, what did everyone think of the book?"

"I found it dull," Madame Bonheur mutters. "So much talk of weapons and bull-fighting and blowing up bridges."

"They were the best bits!" Raul exclaims.

"Yes, well, you would feel that way, wouldn't you?" Madame

Bonheur replies sniffily. "You're an 'obscenity unprintable' man."

We all burst out laughing.

"Why did Hemingway write 'obscenity' or 'unprintable' instead of the actual curse word?" Odette asks. "I found it really off-putting."

"I found it funny," I say. "I suppose it was his way of getting around the censors."

"Hmm, he shouldn't have bothered," Madame Bonheur mutters.

"I really liked the descriptions of Robert Jordan and Maria's love affair," Charlotte says, her face flushing slightly. "Especially the part where he talks about how he no longer cares if he lives for seventy years or seventy hours now he's experienced their love. And the bit about the earth moving out from under them . . ." She blushes even redder. "It made me think of Jacques." She looks at me, her eyes shiny with tears. "Did it make you think of Luc?"

I nod, although, in truth, the love I felt for Luc was nothing like the love Hemingway's Robert Jordan describes, so full of fire and passion. My love for Luc was, and is, less of an earth-moving thing, more sturdy and steady. Just like Monseigneur Oak, I think, gazing up into the wide canopy of his branches. "I really liked the descriptions of the pine forest," I say. "It made me think of this place."

The others nod in agreement.

"I loved the fact that they were fighting against fascism, even if it was in Spain," Odette says. "Oh, to be able to fight the fascists here. To be able to blow up a train or a bridge."

Raul nods enthusiastically. "Perhaps one day soon we will."

"Yes, and on that note, I have some good news for you," I say, lowering my voice.

"You do?" Charlotte looks at me expectantly.

"Yes. I had confirmation last week from my friends in Paris

that they would like our assistance in helping the British with their operations here in France."

"Are you serious?" Odette looks delighted. Raul is beaming too.

"I'm so happy we can finally do something," Charlotte says, smiling at Raul.

"Me too," he mutters. "I know other people who would like to help also."

We all look at Madame Bonheur. "I'm not sure," she says, looking troubled. "It sounds very dangerous."

"Life is already very dangerous," Raul replies bluntly.

"I know. I just . . . I don't want to lose any of you."

I take hold of her hand, trying to ignore how much bonier it now feels. "But surely we have to do something."

She nods. "But I'm not as young as I used to be. I don't know if I'd be capable of blowing up trains and bridges."

"That's all right." I smile at her. "You can make sure we don't starve instead. It will require a lot of energy to fight the fascist Germans."

At this, she smiles warmly. "Yes, I will do anything I can to help you fight those obscenity unprintables."

The next week, I return to Paris first thing on Thursday morning, officially to browse Michel's stall for books, unofficially to receive my first instruction as part of the network. As I come out of the station, I have to refrain from swinging my empty case from side to side, such is my enthusiasm. Any signs of high spirits would stick out like a sore thumb in this new, occupied Paris, where people hurry by, shoulders stooped and faces drawn. The roads are emptier than ever now that gasoline is so hard to come by, so when I do hear the roar of an engine my skin erupts into goosebumps as there's every chance it will belong to the Germans. I try to avert my gaze and stare straight ahead as truck after truck loaded with soldiers races by. *Has something happened? Is something happening?*

It must be some kind of routine maneuvers, I try to reassure myself, quickening my pace.

When I reach the Left Bank of the river, I see Michel standing in front of his stall rearranging the books and chatting to a customer. As I draw closer, I hear him wishing the man, *"Bon courage,"* and they embrace as if they might never see each other again. I hang back until the man has gone before approaching the stall.

"Good day," I call cheerily for the benefit of any collaborator who might be eavesdropping. "What literary treats do you have for me this week?"

"Laurence, you made it!" He sighs with relief.

"Of course. Why shouldn't I?" I think about the trucks of soldiers I just saw and I move closer. "Has something happened?"

He nods before going back inside his booth. "Apparently a German soldier was shot at Barbès–Rochechouart Metro station this morning. I thought you might have a problem getting into Paris."

"Shot? By who?"

"A member of the Young Communists." He shakes his head. "They are fools. I said to Pierre this will only make things worse for us. The Germans have already executed three Parisians in reprisal. We will never beat them if we start killing them now. We need to play the longer game."

I take a moment to digest what he just said, my initial joy at this victory for the Resistance quickly turning to dismay.

"Are you sure you want to do this?" Michel asks. "Things are going to get a lot worse before they get better."

"I'm sure," I say, thinking of Maria in *For Whom the Bell Tolls* and how much I related to her need for revenge against the fascists in her country.

"Good." Michel reaches beneath his table and pulls out a large leather-bound atlas. "Is this what you are looking for, mademoiselle?" he asks loudly, as a couple of men walk by. They're wearing ordinary suits, but these days you can't be too careful.

"Oh yes, that looks perfect," I reply loudly.

He opens the book and I see a piece of paper tucked inside the pages containing a hand-drawn map.

"This is a map of the forest by your town," he whispers. "Pierre has been in touch with another contact of his there, who tells us that this clearing should be just large enough for a plane to land and take off." He turns the map so it's facing me and points to a clearing. It takes me a moment to get my bearings.

"I know that clearing," I whisper excitedly. "I'm not sure if it's big enough to land a plane in, though."

"Apparently they only need about three hundred and twenty meters."

"That should work then, just about."

Michel snaps the atlas shut and fetches an old copy of *The Merchant of Venice* from under the table. "Take this book with you."

"But it's by an English writer, what if I get stopped and searched?"

"Shakespeare is the one enemy dramatist Hitler hasn't banned. And he is a great fan of this particular play."

"But why?"

"Shylock. He sees him as being the perfect anti-Jewish propaganda."

I feel sick as I wonder what William Shakespeare would have made of his work being used by an evil dictator to justify his crimes.

"If you get stopped and searched on your way home, I'm sure this will win you favor with the Nazis," Michel says with a grim smile.

"OK." My skin prickles with an icy sweat at the thought of being stopped and searched by the Nazis, especially as they will be seeking revenge for the shooting of one of their own.

"You will find two words underlined in pencil inside," Michel continues. "One of the words represents your location and the other means that the drop will be happening that night. When you hear a personal message containing both words during the Radio Londres broadcast, it means you must go to the clearing that night. It should be happening around the time of the next full moon—the RAF pilots need the moon to be able to see where they're going. You are to go to the clearing at midnight and take a flashlight."

"A flashlight?"

"Yes. Pierre's contact will explain more when you get there."

"Right." My mind starts racing. For so long I have yearned to be able to do something, but now that time has arrived, I feel sick with nerves.

"Are you sure you still want to do it?" Michel asks as if sensing my fear.

"Yes, absolutely," I reply determinedly, trying to channel my hero Jeanne of Arc.

"Right. Let me give you some more books and an invoice for your cover story."

"Thank you."

Once we've packed my case with books, he comes out from behind the stall and embraces me. *"Bon courage,"* he whispers and I think of the man I saw him saying the exact same words to earlier. Could he have been another member of the Resistance?

"And you too," I reply, hugging him tightly.

All the way back to the station, my fear grows. So far I've been lucky on my trips to Paris. Could today be when my luck ends? No, I tell myself, there's no way I'm being thwarted by the Germans before I've even properly begun my mission.

As I take a shortcut down a side street, I see a poster on the wall that has been defaced. Pétain's new motto for France: *TRAVAIL FAMILLE PATRIE* has been crossed out and underneath someone has written: *TRAHISON FAMINE PRISON* in bold red. BETRAYAL FAMINE PRISON. Yes, that just about sums up the new France. I think of the person who defaced the poster, just as I have defaced the posters in the Valley, and I feel part of an invisible network. This thought emboldens me and I march on to the station.

My courage soon disappears, however, as I find the forecourt swarming with soldiers. I instinctively feel in my pocket for my pendant. *I am not afraid, I was born to do this. I am not afraid . . .* I chant in my mind as I force myself to keep on walking. As soon as I get close to the soldiers, one of them yells at me to halt. *I am not afraid. I am not afraid. I am not afraid.*

"Good day," I say cheerily.

He returns my smile with a scowl. "Where are you going?" he asks, looking at my case.

"Back home, to La Vallée du Cerf," I reply.

"And what were you doing in Paris?"

"Getting new stock for my bookstore." My heart pounds.

"Books," he says with a sneer.

"Yes."

"Open your case."

I put the case on the table in front of him and click the clasps open with trembling hands. What if I had a forbidden book hidden in the case? But I don't, I remind myself. Thankfully, for once, none of the books in my possession are on Otto's List. The soldier rifles through them, and when he picks up the copy of *The Merchant of Venice*, my heart almost stops. What if Michel was wrong? What if, because it is by an Englishman, the soldier will think it is banned?

"Papers!" he barks, a tiny piece of his spit landing on my dress.

"What? Oh . . . oh . . . yes, of course." I hurriedly produce my papers from my purse.

He looks at them, looks at me, then shoves them back in my hand. "Go!"

I don't need to be told twice. I shut the case, only locking one of the clasps in my haste, and hurry on through.

Thankfully, my train is waiting on the platform. I get on and find an empty compartment, then I take *The Merchant of Venice* from my case and start flicking through the pages, searching for the underlined words. I need to find them as soon as possible just in case I'm searched again and someone takes the book. In my haste, I don't find anything at first and start to panic. What if there's been some terrible mistake and I miss the message on the radio?

I take a long deep breath and start going through the pages again, slower this time. As the train judders and squeals out of the station, I spot the faintest of penciled lines beneath the word "wrinkles" and I breathe a sigh of relief. The train picks up speed and starts chugging out of Paris, the buildings soon melting into fields. I spot another faint line beneath the word "gilded." Gilded and wrinkles. I have my secret code!

I sit back in my seat and repeat the words in time with the rhythm of the train on the tracks to really let them sink in. *Gilded and wrinkles. Wrinkles and gilded.* As I do so, I realize the bittersweet irony. Shakespeare's wonderful words might have been twisted to fit Hitler's hate, but now they are being used to help France resist. In spite of my tension, I can't help smiling, as yet again I am reminded of the magical power of books.

22

LAURENCE—SEPTEMBER 1941

For the next few days, I pay special attention to the moon, watching as it grows fatter and rounder. Every night, I take my radio from its hiding place and listen to the broadcasts from London and the bizarre coded messages, listening out for the two key words, "wrinkles" and "gilded." Even though the personal messages make no sense, things like: "John is bringing whisky" and "Yvette likes big carrots," they make my skin tingle with excitement at the thought of what they represent. They also make me laugh, thinking of the Germans trying in vain to decipher them.

On the night of the full moon, the sky is clear and filled with stars, the silvery light making the perfect conditions for flying. I turn on my radio and listen to the first four notes of Beethoven's Fifth Symphony, followed by the opening announcement: "This is London! The French speaking to the French. Before we begin, please listen to some personal messages..."

I sit upright on the end of my bed, listening intently for my words.

"Jean has a long mustache," the announcer declares, causing me to giggle, mainly from nerves. "There is a fire at the station." As I'm pondering what that could mean, I hear the words that get my nerve endings tingling. "Caroline has gilded wrinkles."

Gilded wrinkles! Gilded wrinkles! I leap to my feet, my heart racing. "Calm yourself," I tell myself sternly, recalling the next part of my instructions from Michel.

I set off for the clearing at just past eleven, with my flashlight in one coat pocket and the Jeanne of Arc pendant and Nénette doll in the other. Across the square, I can hear the laughing and cheering of German soldiers in the hotel bar. *Our* hotel bar, I think to myself as I skulk along in the shadows. Thankfully, I'm able to use the darkness of the blackout to my advantage. I've dressed in a sweater and trousers for practical reasons, reasoning that if I get caught out after curfew I'll already be in trouble so it'll make little difference that I'm not wearing a dress.

Once I get out of town, my breathing steadies, and by the time I reach the forest I'm almost giddy with relief. Stage one of my mission is complete. Although who knows what stage two will bring. I wonder who will be there in the clearing—which of my fellow townsfolk is a contact of Pierre's. My money is on it being Raul. I only hope it isn't Leon the blacksmith. I'm not sure I could be alone in the forest after dark with that letch, even for the good of France.

As I make my way to the clearing, the path seems littered with twigs cracking underfoot at an extraordinary level of decibels. *I am not afraid. I was born to do this*, I whisper in my head, trying to drown out the sounds. Somewhere close by, an owl hoots, causing me to jump. "I am not afraid, damn it!" I whisper. As I pass Monseigneur Oak, I stop to run my fingers over the carving of Luc's initials for good luck, and instantly I feel calmer, as if the essence of Luc is somehow etched into the sturdy trunk. I picture him walking beside me, as he has done so many times before, his warm hand steady on the small of my back, gently pressing me forward.

Finally I reach the clearing. Now what? I think to myself, scanning the open space. There's no sign of anyone. What if Pierre's contact doesn't arrive? What if I'm here alone, with no clue what to do? I hear the rustle of something moving on the other side of the clearing and I flatten myself against the trunk of a tree. After a couple of seconds, I pluck up the courage to peer out and I see a figure flit between the trees across the clearing from me. A tall, broad figure I'd recognize anywhere.

"Hello?" I call softly.

"Laurence?" he calls back, clearly surprised, and I hear him making his way around to me. When he reaches me, we both stand staring at each other in shock.

"Good evening, Père," I say, finally breaking the silence. My mind races, trying to work out why on earth he is here. Perhaps he is out for a late-night stroll. Perhaps it is just coincidence. "What . . . what are you doing here?"

"I was about to ask you the very same thing." He's wearing trousers and a shirt and sweater, with no sign of his cassock or even his collar.

I desperately try to think of what to say. I know that the Père is against the Germans, but surely he cannot be a member of the Resistance.

Clearly he is having a similar thought process as a look of realization dawns upon his face. "Have you been sent here?" he whispers.

"Yes. And you?"

He nods. "Oh Laurence. Do you know how dangerous this is?"

"Yes. Do you?" I'm unable to disguise my indignation.

"Please don't tell me you've been listening to Pétain's nonsense. Just because I'm a woman it doesn't mean I'm incapable of doing dangerous things."

"I know. I know." He smiles. "You certainly are as stubborn as your mother."

I laugh. "Well then, you will know that it is pointless trying to argue with me."

We both start at the sound of footsteps. I turn and see Raul lumbering into the clearing, holding a handful of long sticks.

"It's OK," the Père says, placing a hand on my arm to reassure me. "He is with us."

"You know Raul? You and he are part of the Resistance?"

"Yes," the Père replies. "Do you have your flashlight?"

"I do."

He takes my arm. "Come."

We go over to Raul. He nods to us, showing no surprise at all, which makes me think that he must have known I was coming, so he must be Pierre's other contact in the valley, and that dark horse Père must be Raul's contact.

"We need to get ready," Raul says, looking at his watch. He hands the Père and I a stick each. "Fix your light to the top like this," he instructs, showing us his own flashlight already bound with string to the top of a stick. He hands me a piece of twine. It takes a couple of attempts to tie it due to my fingers quivering. "From now on, we must use our code names with anyone we might meet," Raul says looking at me. "The Père is Julien and I am Fabien, and you—"

"Can I be Jeanne?" I interrupt, hoping that if I am named after my heroine I'll be able to inherit some of her bravery.

"I don't see why not," Raul replies. "Père, you stay here and, Laurence, you come with me." He leads me to the opposite end of the clearing. "Stand here," he tells me. "When the plane flies over, the pilot will flash a letter in Morse code. I will then use my light to flash the code back. Only when you see me do this should you turn on your own light and hold it up, like so." He holds his stick aloft. "This way we create a flare path to help the pilot land."

"I see." My pulse quickens at the thought of a pilot trying to land in such a confined space, and with such a makeshift landing strip.

Raul hurries off and takes his position at the other side of the clearing, the three of us now forming an L shape. I hear the distant hum of an engine and my stomach churns as I think of the Germans in the Valley. What if one of them is in the forest and they hear the plane? What if they see it landing? Don't be stupid, I tell myself. Why would any Germans be all the way out here? They're far too busy gorging on our wine and food.

The hum grows louder and suddenly a plane appears like a giant moth above the trees. A light from the plane blinks three times in quick succession. I watch as Raul flashes his light in exactly the same sequence. I quickly turn on my flashlight and at the other end of the clearing Père Rambert does the same. Holding the stick aloft, I whisper a furtive prayer. "Please let him land safely—and preferably not on top of me!"

The plane circles the clearing, then approaches on a sharp descent, the sound of the engine getting louder and louder, and the trees start swaying in the breeze, as if doing some crazed welcome dance.

"Please don't let him land on me!" I whisper, barely able to watch.

There's a clanging noise and a couple of bumps and suddenly a tiny plane is sitting right in front of me. It's somehow managed to come to a standstill almost instantly and I watch, stunned, as the propeller on the front slows to a halt. I see the reassuring circular symbol of the British Royal Air Force on the side, along with the letter J. Two machine guns have been mounted on the wheel arches.

Raul and Père Rambert turn off their flashlights so I quickly do the same. There's a creaking sound as the cockpit hatch at the rear of the plane opens and a figure appears holding a suitcase. The person drops the case to the ground with a thud, then climbs down a ladder attached to the side of the plane. I hear a British man's voice calling, "Good luck, old girl," from the cockpit.

"Thanks, Bunny," a woman replies in English.

I can't help gasping. The person who has been dropped from the plane is a woman!

The engine rattles back into life and I see the Père and Raul turn their flashlights back on, so I do the same. The plane taxis around, then bumps its way back across the clearing and up, up, up . . . But will it get high enough in time to clear the trees? I hold my breath, willing the little plane to gain enough height and speed. Thankfully, the pilot manages it, but only just.

As the plane disappears off into the night sky, I shine my light on the woman in front of me. She's young, about my age, and smartly dressed in a skirt, blouse and jacket. She looks as if she's ready for a day's work in an office rather than being dropped by plane in the dead of night in the middle of a French forest. I hurry over to greet her.

"Hello," I whisper. "Welcome to France."

"Thank you. I am Juliette," the woman replies in perfect French.

"Welcome," Raul says as he and the Père reach us. "I am Fabien and this is Julien"—he nods at Père Rambert—"and this is Jeanne." I'm struck by the strangest sense of déjà vu as I think back to all the times I was called Jeanne as a child in this very same forest. Perhaps all of those pretend battles were a dress rehearsal for this. "Jeanne, you are to take Juliette to your store," Raul continues. "She will stay there tonight and tomorrow some-one will come to fetch her."

"OK."

"You will know it is them because they will ask you for a copy of *Cyrano de Bergerac*. You are to tell them that you don't think you have any in stock but you will check upstairs. When the coast is clear, you must bring Juliette downstairs and they will leave the store together."

"*Cyrano de Bergerac* . . . check upstairs," I echo, trying to make sure I retain my instructions.

"Now we must split up," Raul continues. "Ladies, you go first. The Père and I will take the longer way round. If you are stopped by any soldiers, Juliette is your cousin who has come to visit."

"All right." My throat tightens at the thought of being apprehended so late after curfew with my mysterious cousin. Judging by her somber expression, Juliette is feeling equally apprehensive. "Here, let me take this," I say, picking up the suitcase. "Goodness, what do you have in here?" I say without thinking, flinching at the weight.

"I can carry it if you like," she offers.

"No, no, it is fine. I'm your host after all." I start leading her along the trail, cursing myself for asking about the contents of the case and hoping she doesn't think me stupid. I decide to try to make conversation to help break the ice. "Is this your first time in France?" I whisper.

"No," she whispers back. "I've spent many summers in Provence. My mother is French but my father is English."

"I see." I feel a wave of relief. Hopefully she will be able to do a convincing impression of a French woman. "How was your flight?"

"Terrifying," she replies. "We got shot at just as we made it across the Channel."

I say a silent prayer that the pilot and his plane will make it back in one piece.

"If we get stopped and questioned, I will say that you are my cousin on our mother's side of the family," I tell her. "And obviously don't call me Jeanne in front of anyone here as that is not my real name."

"Of course."

Once we reach the town, we skulk along the darkest edges of the streets and when we get to the square, I gesture at Juliette to wait in the doorway of Odette's hat shop while I check to see if the coast is clear. I break out in a cold sweat as I see a couple of soldiers patrolling the other side of the square. Thankfully, they're walking in the opposite direction. I wait until they disappear down a side street before gesturing at Juliette to follow me. As I let her into the store, I don't think I've ever felt so relieved to be back home.

"You live in a bookstore!" she gasps, eyes wide, as I lock the door behind us.

"I do indeed." I check the blackout blinds are shut tight, then light the lamp on my desk and turn to look at her. She has a nice, open face, the kind that indicates a warm and honest heart.

"How wonderful," she whispers as she gazes around at the books.

I smile at her. "You are a fan of books?"

"Oh yes. I love them." She goes over to the nearest shelf and runs her fingers along the spines; this, along with sniffing the pages, is the sign of a true bibliomane indeed and I feel an instant connection to her.

I think of why she is here and the bravery it must have taken. I wish I could ask her what she'll be doing in France, but I know that for the sake of both our safety I can't.

"What is this about?" she asks, pointing to the sign for book prescriptions on my desk.

"It is something I do for my customers. They tell me their needs or ailments and I prescribe them a book or a poem."

"What a lovely idea." She looks at me with real urgency in her eyes. "Would you prescribe something for me?"

"Of course. What is it that you need?"

"Fortification," she replies, her voice trembling slightly.

"I would be honored. Come . . ." I take her by the arm and guide her upstairs to the bedroom, where I light the candle on the nightstand. "I'm afraid I only have one room—and one bed. But you are welcome to it. I can sleep on the floor."

"No, no." She shakes her head. "I'm happy to share if you are."

"As long as you don't snore," I joke, trying to relieve the inevitable awkwardness caused by the prospect of spending the night with a total stranger. "Make yourself comfortable and I'll go and get your prescription."

I go back downstairs and put some paper in the typewriter. Outside, I hear the sharp clip of soldiers' boots marching closer. *They're just on their evening patrol,* I try to reassure myself as my pulse quickens. *They don't know I have some kind of undercover agent hiding upstairs in my bedroom. I have an undercover agent hiding in my bedroom!* As the enormity of that fact hits me, the sound of the soldiers' feet reaches the store—and stops. My heart practically stops too as I wait and listen. *She is my cousin on my mother's side,* I start mentally rehearsing. *She's just here visiting.*

I hear the sound of a match being struck and then the boots move off again. They must have been stopping to light a cigarette. I'm so shaken up by now it's hard to feel any relief. Juliette and I still have to make it through the night. She still has to leave without being apprehended in the morning.

I focus my attention back on the typewriter and begin typing "Invictus" by the English poet William Ernest Henley. It's a poem I recently prescribed to Charlotte after one of the Germans staying with her helped himself to a pocket watch that had belonged to Jacques. As I type the poem's message of being the master of one's fate and the captain of one's soul, I feel the empowering sentiment burning away my READ THIS WHENEVER

YOU'RE IN NEED OF FORTIFICATION, ESPECIALLY THE FINAL STANZA, I type beneath the poem.

Once I've finished, I turn out the lamp and make my way back upstairs, where I find Juliette sitting up in bed, her hands clasped tightly in her lap.

"*Voilà!*" I announce gaily to try to disguise my fear, and I hand her the prescription.

"Thank you." She takes the poem from me and begins to read.

For modesty's sake, I go next door to the bathroom to change into my nightdress. Just as I'm finishing, I hear a loud sniff. I hurry back into the bedroom to find Juliette wiping tears from her eyes.

"It's beautiful," she whispers. "I only hope that my soul is unconquerable."

"Me too," I whisper, getting into the other side of the bed. Suddenly our situation doesn't feel quite as strange as I feel the common bond between us grow. "Thank you."

"What for?" she asks.

"For helping us. For helping France. I will never forget it. And I will never forget you." I lean over and blow out the candle.

We lie in silence for a few minutes, then she starts tossing and turning beside me, clearly as anxious as me. I think of what Maman used to do whenever I was too nervous or fearful to sleep and I shift up onto my elbow.

"If you like, I could tell you a story? To help you get to sleep." As soon as I say it, I feel embarrassed. This situation is already odd enough without me offering a grown woman a bedtime story.

"Yes please," she replies enthusiastically, causing me to grin with relief.

"Very well." I prop myself up against my pillow and clear my throat. Of course, there's only one story befitting a woman in need of fortification—or rather *two* women in need of fortification.

"Once upon a time, there was a French peasant girl named Jeanne..." I begin.

23

JEANNE—1993

After their slightly awkward embrace—for Jeanne at least—Charlotte invited them into the house and led them through to a beautiful, country-style kitchen, complete with stone floor, a large open fireplace and a pine dresser lined with plates, cups and bowls in bold shades of yellow, blue and green.

"Please," Charlotte said, gesturing at them to take a seat at a round pine table. As soon as Jeanne sat down, Charlotte shook her head and said something to Yitzhak in French.

"She says that you look so much like your mother," he explained.

"Tell me about it," Wendell muttered.

Charlotte continued talking.

"She and your mother were the best of friends," Yitzhak translated. "They became close during the war." He listened for a moment and smiled. "Apparently, they were in a book club together. They read books that had been banned by the Germans, so they had to do it secretly. It was their act of resistance."

Jeanne turned to Wendell. "Pops, do you think the books we found under the floorboards were the books they read?"

He nodded. "Makes sense."

"Can you ask her if one of the books was by Hemingway?" Jeanne said to Yitzhak. *"For Whom the Bell Tolls."*

As he translated, Charlotte's face lit up and she nodded. Then she said something else.

"Oh wow," Yitzhak exclaimed.

"What?"

"Apparently she was supposed to have been your god-mother."

"For real?"

Charlotte nodded, her eyes gleaming with tears.

The notion that this woman should have known Jeanne as a baby filled her with a new sense of urgency. *Tell me everything,* she wanted to cry. *Help me fill all the blank spaces.*

"You were a very joyful baby—an angel," Yitzhak said with a grin. "You gave them so much hope at a time when they desperately needed it."

If I was such a joyful baby, such an angel, then surely Laurence wouldn't have willingly abandoned me. The urgency that had been building in Jeanne reached boiling point and she suddenly and completely inappropriately started to cry.

"Honey, what's wrong?" Wendell asked, concerned.

"I'm sorry," Jeanne gasped.

Charlotte came hurrying over and held her tightly, but rather than feeling comforted, Jeanne felt as if she was coming undone. In all of her years pretending to be her mother, Lorilee had never, ever held her this tenderly. It was all too sad, too much. Charlotte said something softly in French as she stroked Jeanne's hair.

"There's something she wants to give you, something that belonged to your mother," Yitzhak explained.

Jeanne nodded and wiped away her tears. He'd said "belonged" to your mother, past tense. So Laurence *was* dead. She glanced across the table at Wendell. He looked ashen-faced, clearly having come to the same conclusion.

Charlotte left the room, returning a couple of minutes later with what appeared to be a tiny bundle of yarn.

Charlotte began speaking animatedly as she handed it to Jeanne.

"It's a Nénette doll," Yitzhak translated. "They were very popular in France during the First World War. People saw them as lucky charms. This one belonged to your mother's mother."

"Well, I'll be darned," Wendell softly exclaimed.

"What is it, Pops?" Jeanne asked.

"I never thought I'd see her again."

Jeanne looked down at the woolen bundle in her hand. Now she knew that it was a doll, she could make out its red arms and the blue stitches of its eyes. The white of the body had yellowed with age, and there was what looked worryingly like a bloodstain on the doll's face. She shivered.

"She's a lucky charm all right," Wendell murmured.

But Jeanne wasn't able to see beyond the stain. Was it her mother's blood? And if so, how had it gotten there?

Charlotte placed her hand on her shoulder and said something.

"She wants to know if there's anything she can do to help you? Anything you'd like to know?" Yitzhak explained.

Jeanne nodded. "I want to know what happened to my mom. Why did she send me away to the UK? Why did she send the deeds to her store with me? Is she dead? And if so, how did she die?" In spite of her tears, she noticed a look of concern on Yitzhak's face before he translated.

Charlotte paused before speaking.

"She says there is someone you need to see," Yitzhak told Jeanne. "Someone who knew your mother better than anyone. Someone who can answer your questions."

A shiver ran up Jeanne's spine. Finally it seemed that the mystery surrounding Laurence was about to be solved, but was she ready to hear the answers?

24

LAURENCE—MARCH 1942

The winter of 1941–42 is harsh and unforgiving. Every day a fierce wind tears through the valley, stripping everything back to the bone. Food, fuel and even automobiles are all taken away from us. The last of the phoney good cheer from the Germans has faded too. After the shooting of their naval cadet at Barbès Metro station and the assassination of the Feldkommandant of Nantes by the French Resistance in October, Hitler ordered the immediate execution of fifty French hostages. Fifty more were subsequently killed. So when I return to Paris in March of 1942 for the first time that year, it is with a greater sense of apprehension than ever before.

I find Michel hunched in his booth, clad in a greatcoat and fur hat, with an old woolen blanket tucked around his knees. His face is pale and his cheeks hollow, but I'm relieved to catch a glimpse of a jaunty yellow polka-dot bow tie poking over his collar. I've come to see Michel's bow ties as a symbol of his spirit. The day he stops wearing them is the day I really start to worry.

"Laurence!" His face lights up as I reach the stall. "It is so good to see you." He reaches his mittened hands across the table and grasps mine in greeting.

"And you too." I take a piece of cheese wrapped in brown paper from my coat pocket. "I brought you this. I'm sorry it isn't much, but food is becoming so scarce, even in the country. I had crow soup for the first time last week." I mimic being sick.

He throws his hands up in horror. "It is too much! My land-lady has started breeding guinea pigs."

"To eat?" I ask, horrified.

He nods before taking a bite of the cheese. "Ooh la la!" He rolls his eyes as if in ecstasy. "But enough about food. I have the perfect literary feast for your book club."

"You do?" This is excellent news. All the way to Paris, I'd been worried that he might not have been able to get any new stock.

"Yes." He leans forward to check no one's coming, then produces a book from beneath the table. It is a thin volume with a plain, cream cover and the title printed in bold in the middle. *LE SILENCE* in black and *DE LA MER* in blue beneath it.

"*The Silence of the Sea,*" I read the title out loud before looking at the top of the cover for the author's name. "Who is Vercors?"

"It is the author, or rather it is their *nom de Resistance,*" Michel replies, giving the words "*nom de Resistance*" extra the-atrical emphasis.

"*Nom de Resistance?* You mean . . ." I lean forward and lower my voice. "This book is written by someone in the Resistance?"

"Yes, and it is published by a Resistance publisher too."

I look at the bottom of the cover, where the name of the pub-lishing house is printed beneath a small star. *Les Éditions de Minuit.* "The Midnight Editions," I whisper and it sends a shiver down my spine.

"I can only give you one copy, as they have only printed

three hundred and fifty so far. But you are one of the very first people to see it, as they haven't distributed them yet."

"That's fine. We can share it around the group." I hold the book to my heart. "This really is the greatest gift."

"I know." Michel nods enthusiastically. "Finally the writers of the Left Bank are getting organized. Otto Abetz can go to hell with his lists."

"Is it a novel?" I ask, hurriedly hiding the book in the lining of my case.

"Yes. It tells the story of an old French man and his niece, who have a German officer sent to stay with them."

"Ha! Some of my group will certainly relate to this."

"I thought so." He smiles. "The officer is perfectly polite and a great fan of France, but the man and his niece refuse to speak to him. It is their way of resisting, see? By greeting him with a sea of silence."

"This is exactly what my group need. Some of them are becoming quite dispirited. The cold and lack of food aren't helping. It's making everyone so weary."

Michel gives a sympathetic nod. "It's been such a harsh winter. But this book should be just the sustenance they need."

"Thank you!"

"And I have a message from Pierre for you."

Instantly, my pulse quickens. I haven't had to do anything for the Resistance since hosting Juliette and making sure she got collected safely. "Oh yes?"

Michel takes a copy of *In Search of Lost Time* by Marcel Proust from a pile of books behind him. "One of our couriers will be passing through your town on Friday and he will have something for you. He will be posing as a customer and he will ask for this first volume of Proust's book. He will tell you it is for his aunt's birthday. Only if he mentions his aunt and asks for the first volume are you to give it to him."

"Understood." After a lull in activity, it feels great to have a job to do. And one that sounds relatively easy too. I put the book in my case. "Thank you."

I return to the Valley feeling newly inspired and I can't wait to share the new book with our group so that they can feel reinvigorated too. Just as I reach the square, I hear a roar from the sky and look up to see two planes flying over. But they aren't German, they're British. As I look at the round RAF symbols, my new-found optimism grows. "Good luck," I whisper as they fly past.

When I reach my store, I glance across the square to the café, where a couple of German soldiers are sitting huddled in their long coats at a table outside. Gigi comes out and they say something to her. I'm too far away to hear what they say, but her giggle peals out as loud as the church bell. Gigi is the only woman in the Valley not to have lost her curves this winter. She has officially become a BOF—short for *Beurre Oeufs Fromages,* the nickname given to the wealthy who can still afford to eat on the black market, or in Gigi's case, due to her sucking up to the Nazis, a sight guaranteed to make me lose my appetite.

I go into my store and lock the door behind me, keeping the blackout blinds firmly closed. I put the copy of *In Search of Lost Time* into my desk drawer, then settle into one of the armchairs in front of the unlit fire, with my papa's old coat draped over my legs like a blanket. Fuel is so scarce now, I've taken to only lighting a fire on the very coldest of days. The constant hunger doesn't help much either, with barely anything in our stomachs to warm ourselves from the inside. I push the gnawing thoughts of food from my mind and open my copy of *The Silence of the Sea*, the very first book to have been written for the Resistance. It gives me such a thrill to think of the mystery author "Vercors" sitting at his or her desk typing away. I wonder if it is a well-known author. Perhaps I'll be able to identify them from their prose. I begin reading eagerly—the book detective in me, as Pierre would call it, delighted to have another case to try to solve.

The story is a wonderful read, and in many ways the complete opposite of the books our group has read recently, with their focus on the more violent side of war. Although the story is about resisting passively through silence, it's no less powerful for it. It's so short I read it within an hour or two, but that's no bad thing as it means we'll be able to pass our one copy around the group quickly. I'm unable to detect who has actually written it, but I don't mind at all as it was such a thought-provoking read. At first, reading about a German officer who is so well mannered and such an avid fan of France made me want to vomit. *Why are you making a Nazi so sympathetic?* I kept yelling at the author inside my head. But by the end of the novel, I was able to see why they chose to do this and how it made the story all the more powerful. The French man and his niece were still able to resist through their silence *in spite* of him being so friendly, which was surely a much harder task than ignoring an openly hostile Nazi. Even when it becomes clear that the German and the niece have fallen for each other, she doesn't give in to her feelings and maintains her silence, only uttering the word "*adieu*" to him when he is about to leave.

As I put the book in my hiding place in the poetry section, I wonder if any kind German soldiers really do exist. Certainly the soldier in *All Quiet on the Western Front* was very sympathetic and it isn't that long since the Great War when it was set. But these are just fictional characters, I remind myself as I go upstairs. I've yet to see any evidence of caring hearts beating away beneath the murky green uniforms of the soldiers stationed here in the Valley.

· · ·

On Friday I wake at the crack of dawn, too excited to sleep. Even though I haven't touched it since I got back from Paris, I check the desk drawer to make sure that the Proust novel is still there before opening the store. *Volume One, aunt's birthday,* I repeat the coded message in my head.

In desperate need of something to calm my nerves, I decide to rearrange the window display. The poor mannequin has been neglected all winter, as my hunger and exhaustion led to chronic lethargy. But now I'm feeling tentative sparks of hope again, I change the mannequin into another old dress of Maman's—one of her favorites, in sky blue cotton. I sit her upright in the armchair and put a copy of the children's book *The Wind in the Willows* in her hands, making sure that the cover, featuring a group of animals including a toad, is on prominent display. I'm hoping that Madame Bonheur will get the joke at least, as she knows that "toad" is one of my favorite nicknames for the Nazis.

While I'm in the window, I look out into the square. It's one of those cusp-of-spring days, and the pale blue sky is streaked with wisps of cloud. Some soldiers are sitting outside the café eating their breakfast, Gigi is hovering around them like a hummingbird waiting to take their orders. No, she isn't a hummingbird, I correct myself, she's a cuckoo. Aren't they the parasites who lay their eggs in another bird's nest? An image of Abram's body twisting and jerking as he's shot comes into my mind and I force myself to focus back on my window display.

After I've rearranged the window, I go back into the store and sit at my desk. Then I get up and tidy some of the books in the history section, then I even dust the legs of my chair. Anything to keep myself busy. I'm just checking that the poetry section is in strict alphabetical order when the bell above the door jangles. I hurry out, my heart thumping, to find Gerhard standing by my desk.

"Oh," I say, unable to keep the disappointment from my

voice. Since his confession that he deliberately avoided shooting Abram, he has steered clear of me and the store. I'd put this down to him being fearful about confessing such a thing. Not that he has any reason to be afraid. Even if I did tell his superiors, they're hardly likely to believe me.

"Good day," he says. It's the first time I've seen him up close in a long time and I notice that he's paler than usual and there are lead-gray shadows beneath his eyes.

"Good day."

"I was wondering if you had anything new in stock? Maybe from one of your trips to Paris?"

My throat tightens. What does he mean by this? Is he on to me? I think of the copy of *The Silence of the Sea* under the floorboard in the poetry nook. What if he looks under the rug and finds my hiding place?

"I'm in desperate need of some literary inspiration," he continues and I relax a little. "It has been a very long winter."

The thought of him, a Nazi, stealing our food and fuel all winter, and then complaining, while we French were shivering and starving, well... The blood in my veins bubbles like lava. *Stay calm, Laurence,* I imagine Père Rambert saying. *Think of the bigger picture,* I imagine Michel saying. *Don't let him get to you,* I imagine Luc saying. I am hugely grateful to know such calming influences!

I take a breath and compose myself. "Perhaps some poetry would soothe your soul?" I say, not caring if he can detect my sarcasm.

"Good idea!" As he walks past me, I'm sure I can smell stale liquor on his breath. Ah, what a long and arduous winter it must have been, partying in the hotel bar night after night.

I stomp back over to my desk. It's only as I sit down that I remember the special customer who is meant to be calling today. What if he arrives while Gerhard is here?

The bell above the door jangles and Gigi comes in.

Normally this sight would fill me with dread, but in the context of the bigger picture, it fills me with relief.

"Good day," she says curtly. "Is Gerhard here? I thought I saw him come in." She looks flustered, and her normally immaculate eye makeup is slightly smudged.

"He's in the poetry section." I gesture to the back of the store.

She marches through and I hear her mutter something. She's speaking too quietly to make out what she's saying, but from her tone, she doesn't sound happy. Could it be that they are having a lovers' tiff? Violeta's housekeeper, Ines, was overheard in the queue outside the butcher's saying that she had it on good authority that they were now sleeping in the same bed.

"Why are you always here then?" I hear her snap at him.

His reply is too faint to decipher. Why does Gigi have such a bee in her bonnet about Gerhard coming here? But before I can ponder this question, the door opens and a man walks in. A man I've never seen before. My mouth goes dry. If this is the man from the Resistance, it couldn't be worse timing. Gerhard probably wouldn't realize that he's a stranger in town, but Gigi definitely will.

"Good day," the man says, looking around. He's wearing a slightly baggy suit. Slightly baggy clothes are now de rigueur due to our starvation diet, so at least he blends in in that regard.

Gigi and Gerhard have fallen silent, but because they're out of sight in the poetry nook, the store must look completely empty to the man. I stand as motionless as the mannequin in the window, unsure what to do. The man could be a perfectly innocent customer—if I start pulling faces and pointing in alarm at the poetry section, I will look like a crazy person. But if he is from the Resistance, how can I warn him?

"I was wondering if you had a copy of *In Search of Lost Time* in stock?" he asks. "The first volume."

As I stare at him my mouth becomes even drier, until I'm barely able to swallow.

"I would like to buy a copy for my aunt," he continues. "For her birthday."

Say something, you dummy! a voice yells inside my head. *Warn him!*

"What a lovely gift," I reply, willing Gigi and Gerhard to start arguing again so the man realizes they are in the store. "I happen to have a copy right here," I continue, taking the book from my desk drawer. As long as he doesn't say anything else, all should be OK.

"Thank you, Jeanne," he replies with a knowing smile.

At exactly that moment, Gigi appears.

"Jeanne?" she asks, raising her eyebrows.

My face flushes in a distinctly indiscreet way.

"Yes, why did you call me Jeanne?" I say to the man with a frown.

Thankfully, he's clearly a lot harder to ruffle than me. "I'm so sorry. When I asked someone just now for directions to the bookstore, I'm sure they told me that the proprietor was named Jeanne."

"Huh, must have been one of our childhood friends," Gigi says sniffily. "Laurence was always playing at being her hero Jeanne of Arc back then."

I want to hug her for unwittingly providing the man with the perfect excuse. But my relief is short-lived as Gerhard emerges from the poetry nook.

"Are you new in town?" he asks in French but with his strong German accent.

This time I see a flicker of fear on the man's face before he quickly composes himself and greets Gerhard with a warm smile. "Yes, I'm here to visit my aunt for her birthday." He says it with such conviction I almost forget that he's lying.

"Very nice." Gerhard nods. "And Proust makes the perfect gift." He nods to the book on my desk.

There's a moment's silence, which seems to stretch for an eternity.

"I must get back," Gerhard says, heading for the door.

"You didn't find anything?" I ask casually, trying to mask my relief.

"No. I was distracted." He looks pointedly and, it has to be said, quite frostily, at Gigi. Then he nods to the man and me. "Goodbye."

We all watch as he leaves. Gigi heads after him, then stops at the door. "So, who is your aunt?" she asks, looking the man up and down.

Once again, I'm gripped by fear.

"Jacqueline," he replies without missing a beat. It's a good choice to be fair, what with Jacqueline being one of the most popular female names in France. There are at least two Jacquelines that I know of in town. Neither of them would be old enough to be this man's aunt though.

"Oh yes, which one?" Gigi asks.

God damn it! "Enough!" I say, pretend jokingly. "If you keep interrogating my customers like this, I'll have none left."

She shrugs her shoulders and finally, *thankfully,* she leaves.

I breathe a huge sigh of relief and look at the man, hoping to exchange comradely grins about what a close shave that was, but his face remains blank.

"Payment for the book," he says, pushing a ten-franc note across the desk to me.

"Oh but . . ." I'm about to say, *Surely you don't have to pay?* when I realize that he must be giving me the note for a reason. "Thank you."

"I'm sure you will find it helpful," he says cryptically.

"Yes," I reply confidently, although I'm not entirely sure what he's getting at.

"Especially tonight. Listen for the messages," he whispers before turning on his heel and heading out the door.

. . .

That night, I sit perched on my bed with the radio and ten-franc note in front of me. While I wait for the Radio Londres broadcast to begin, I study the note. On one side, there's a picture of a miner in a helmet with a pick slung over his shoulder. On the other is a picture of a peasant woman in a white headscarf, holding a baby to her chest. It's the perfect depiction of Pétain's France, where men are men and women are only good for becoming mothers. I hold the note up to the lamplight and the watermark appears—Jeanne of Arc in her helmet ready for battle. The one woman in France who's apparently still allowed to live life on her terms—before she was burned alive, of course.

I hear the by now all too familiar notes from Beethoven and a shiver runs up my spine. "This is London!" the voice crackles over the airwaves. "The French speaking to the French. Before we begin, please listen to some personal messages . . ."

I hold the note tightly and wait.

"Caroline's ten-franc note has wrinkles," the announcer reads. *Wrinkles*—the code word for the clearing. This must be my message. I'm to go to the forest tonight.

When I get to the clearing, I keep my eyes open and ears peeled for any sign of the others, but no one shows up. I stand pressed against a tree, trying to stay calm, but the forest which has brought me so much comfort and joy previously now seems intent on terrifying me. Every sudden rustle in the undergrowth and flutter of wings in the trees causes me to jump out of my skin. And even worse are the unanswered questions flapping like bats in my head. *Why has no one else come? Have they been caught? Could this be a trap?*

I feel in my pocket for Maman's doll and my Jeanne of Arc pendant. *I am not afraid. I was born to do this,* I silently chant to try to drown out my fears.

Finally, I hear the hum of a plane and step into the clearing with my flashlight at the ready. *But how will the pilot be able to land with only me here to guide him?*

I remember what Raul told me about the Morse code signal and keep my eyes fixed on the sky. The plane comes into view and a light flashes three times. I flash the same signal back before holding my stick aloft. I wonder if the fact that there's only one light will cause the pilot to abandon the mission and turn and go back.

The plane circles the clearing and I see something that causes me to break out in a cold sweat. There's a bright orange light coming from the rear. The type of orange light that looks just like a flame! I clap my hand to my mouth, hardly daring to breathe. Is the plane on fire? It begins making its descent. *Please, please, please don't explode,* I silently beg, holding my stick aloft and forcing myself to keep my eyes open rather than squeeze them tightly shut in dread.

The plane touches down in the center of the clearing. I turn my flashlight off and watch by the light of the moon as the cockpit hatch opens and a man springs out with the stealth and agility of a cat. He's wearing an air force uniform, complete with leather helmet and ear flaps. A scarf is wrapped around his neck and a pair of huge goggles are perched on top of his head. He runs round to the rear of the plane and I hear him cursing under his breath.

"Is everything all right?" I ask in English as I step from the shadows.

"The darn exhaust's on fire!" he replies in a soft American drawl. "I don't suppose you have any water, do you?"

I shake my head.

"And there isn't a river or lake or something nearby?"

"No, sorry."

"Shoot!"

We both stand motionless for a second staring at the plane.

All I can think is that at any moment it could explode, sending flames shooting into the sky, like a beacon telling the Germans where to find us. Then a vague memory comes back to me, of Luc and me making a campfire as kids, and him telling me that one of the best ways to put out a fire is to starve it of air.

"Could we smother it somehow?" I ask.

He looks thoughtful for a second, then his face lights up and he slaps me on the back. "You're a genius!"

"I am?"

"Yes. I need to go get my Mae West." He races back up the ladder into the plane.

"You need to get Mae West?" I echo, completely bewildered. Why on earth would he want the famous actress to put out a fire? Surely she isn't on board the plane? I stare up into the darkened cockpit.

"Yes, to stick inside the pipe," he calls down.

This only heightens my confusion.

Please hurry, I silently implore as I watch the flame flicking from the pipe like a serpent's tongue. If it explodes now, the pilot will stand no chance of survival.

He pops back out of the cockpit and throws something down to me. It's a bright yellow vest made of a rubbery material with various canvas straps hanging from it. The pilot jumps down and I hand it back to him. He hurries round to the pipe and stuffs the vest inside.

"I don't know if you're the praying type, but right about now would be a good time to start," he says.

I hold my breath and silently pray, *Please, please, let it work!*

The night air is filled with the acrid aroma of smoldering rubber, but thankfully the flame seems to have been extinguished.

"Holy cow!" the pilot exclaims. "That was a close shave."

"I know! I thought the whole thing was about to go up in flames."

"But you didn't run away," he says.

"No." We look at each other and I note that he has a really friendly, boyish face, with the kind of dimples either side of his mouth that hint at a wicked sense of humor.

Now that I'm no longer fearing death—imminently at least—I take a better look at the plane. It's painted matte black, with the RAF symbol on the side and the letter B. As with the other plane, there are machine guns attached to the wheel covers.

"I'm still not sure what Mae West has to do with anything," I say, trying to break the awkward silence.

"It's what we call our life preservers."

"But why?"

"Let's just say that when we put them on, they make us look very well-endowed in the chest department." He chuckles.

"Ah, I see." I can't help grinning at the image.

"Anyway, it's very nice to meet you." He extends his gloved hand.

"You too," I reply, shaking it. My hand looks tiny in his.

"What happened? I was told there would be three lights to land by."

"There were supposed to be, but the others didn't turn up. I'm sorry."

"Hey, no need to apologize. I'm just glad I made it down in one piece." He climbs back into the plane and re-emerges holding a case. "This is for you. Are you sure you'll be OK carrying it on your own?"

"Of course," I reply indignantly. Then I pick the case up and I can't help wincing at the weight.

"I'd offer to carry it for you, but I'm not sure I'd be all that welcome in these parts."

"No, that is certain."

He goes back round to the rear of the plane and gingerly fishes the remains of his vest from the exhaust pipe. "Rest in peace, Mae West," he says with a mournful grin as he holds the smoldering fabric at arm's length. "Here's hoping I don't come down in the Channel—that's if I can get the old bird back in the sky." His smile fades as he looks at the plane.

"Do you think it will work?" My mind starts racing as I wonder what on earth I will do if the plane is grounded. How will I hide a pilot *and* a plane?

"I sure hope so."

Without even thinking, I take Maman's doll from my pocket and hold it out to him. "Here."

"What's this?"

"It's a Nénette doll. My father gave it to my mother during the First World War. They're meant to bring good luck."

"But don't you want to keep it?"

I think of him trying to fly a broken plane over the Channel back to Britain, and without a life preserver, and I shake my head. "I think you need it more."

He steps close to me and takes hold of my hand. His expression now deadly serious. "Thank you."

"You're welcome." I feel a strange sensation pass through me, then he lets go of my hand and it's gone.

He tucks the doll into his pocket and I watch as he climbs back into the cockpit. "I will return it to you, I promise," he calls down to me softly.

"You'd better," I say, trying to keep the wobble from my voice. "*Bon courage.*"

"*Merci.*" His smile fades and for a moment we maintain eye contact before he pulls the door of the cockpit shut.

The plane's engine stammers into life, then almost immediately cuts out. Dread builds inside me and in the ensuing silence my heart thuds like a drum. Again and again the pilot tries bringing the engine back to life, and again and again it splutters and dies. My pulse is throbbing so frantically I feel as if my every vein might be about to burst. Then, just when I'm about to abandon all hope, the engine coughs into life again and this time it holds.

Adrenaline courses through my body as the little plane bumps its way away from me and suddenly takes off. The luck of the Nénette doll worked! I watch as the plane disappears over the trees and into the night. I only hope that Nénette will continue to work her magic and carry him safely all the way home.

The long walk back to town is made even slower by the weight of the case, but I'm strangely buoyed up by my encounter with the pilot. To distract myself from my fears of getting caught, I think of him instead. I've never met an American before and after reading so many American novels and watching so many of their movies, I have to admit that I'm more than a little thrilled. I wonder which part of America he's from. His accent didn't seem as sharp and nasal as a New Yorker's; it was more soft and languorous.

As my arms begin to ache, I distract myself from the pain by inventing an entire backstory for the pilot. He probably has an American name, like Joe or Walter or Eugene, and judging from his ability to land a plane in the most difficult of conditions, not to mention putting out an on-board fire, I'd guess that he joined the air force as soon as he left school—and of course he would have been one of the most popular boys in his American high school. I picture him eating burgers and drinking milkshakes in a diner with his "folks," as he would no doubt call them. Once I've created an entire family for Joe / Walter / Eugene, I move on to the story of how he came to be flying to France. He's obviously one of the many American airmen who've been sent to Britain since the US entered the war at the end of last year. I picture him arriving in a quaint English village, saying things like "gee whiz" at how different it all is. Then I remember how I felt when he held my hand and I get that same fluttering feeling in the pit of my stomach. The thought of Maman's Nénette protecting him as he makes the perilous journey back to Britain brings me a strange kind of comfort.

I'm just reaching the edge of the forest when I hear voices. *German* voices. I hide behind a tree, pressing myself into the trunk and cursing my bad luck. Perhaps it was for the best that no one else showed up tonight. If I'm about to be caught, at least Raul and the Père will be safe. But it's only small consolation. I've heard rumors of how the Germans like to torture members of the Resistance—before they execute them. My empty stomach churns and bile burns at the back of my throat. I hear the strike of a match. Great. Why of all places did they decide to come here for a smoke? Thankfully, the voices don't come any closer. From what I can make out, there are two men, both speaking quietly. I can't understand what they're saying, so I try to decipher the tone of their conversation instead. Whatever they're talking about, it sounds intense.

"*Nein, nein, nein,*" one of them says loudly. Wait, is it Gerhard? I'm so used to hearing him speak in French, I can't be certain.

The other man says something and, in contrast, his tone is gentle, reassuring. Then I hear the first man laugh softly and now I'm certain it's Gerhard. But what is he doing here?

I focus on staying as still as possible, as quiet as possible. High above me in the trees comes the sudden beating of wings and somehow I manage to refrain from crying out in shock. The men fall silent. Have they gone? I didn't hear any footsteps. Very slowly and very carefully, I lean to one side and peer around the tree. At the opposite end of the small clearing, I see the men silhouetted in between the trees. They're hugging. I'm so startled to see two Nazis in such an affectionate pose I'm unable to move.

Gerhard says something to the other and suddenly they're

kissing. *They're kissing.* And it's not the kind of kiss you would give to a comrade or even a family member. It's the type of passionate kiss I used to dream of Luc and I sharing, instead of the slightly awkward shuffle our mouths would engage in. But if they're kissing in this way, they must be . . . My stunned brain tries to process this development.

After the Night of the Long Knives in 1934, Hitler made any sexual acts between men a criminal act. Apparently thousands of gay men have been imprisoned in Germany since then. So what on earth are Gerhard and this other man doing? What are they risking by doing this? And why is Gerhard being seen around town with Gigi as if they are an item? Could it be that she is some kind of unknowing cover story for him?

I press myself into the tree, hoping this will be enough to make me invisible in the darkness, and suddenly a line from *All Quiet on the Western Front* comes back to me. It's when the main character looks at the body of the man he has just killed and realizes for the first time that he is a human and not just an abstract idea. I think of Gerhard deliberately avoiding shooting Abram. I think of him tenderly embracing the other soldier. I think of him also harboring a secret life that could possibly get him killed. And for the first time since he's arrived in the Valley, I don't see him as my enemy.

But he *is* your enemy, I remind myself. If he found you hiding here with a case full of God knows what, there's no way he'd let you go. Just as I'm contemplating this, there's a sudden burst of sound as a bird starts beating its wings in the tree directly above me. Everything in me freezes as the two soldiers stop embracing and Gerhard stares through the darkness directly at me. Can he see me? I fight the instinct to move, knowing that if I do so, I'll be seen for sure.

The other soldier says something and Gerhard replies, then takes him by the arm and they start walking away. Their voices grow quieter and quieter until the only thing I can hear is the whisper of the wind between the leaves, accompanied by my sigh of relief.

As soon as I get back to the store, I lug the case up the stairs into my bedroom and place it on my bed. I undo the catches and peer inside. What I see makes me step back in shock. The case is packed full of what at first glance appear to be huge pale brown cigars. But these are no cigars. Each one is stamped with the word DYNAMITE.

25

LAURENCE—MARCH 1942

It's safe to say that I don't get a wink of sleep for the rest of the night as my mind hums with questions. Why did the American pilot deliver a case full of explosives? Did he know what he was bringing? What are the British and Americans expecting us to do with them? And what will happen to me if I'm caught with a case full of dynamite in my possession? How can I get it out of my possession? And why didn't any of the others turn up for the drop? What has happened to Raul and the Père?

I hear the cockerels in the valley begin to crow. After examining the contents of the case last night, I shoved it under my bed. Now, as I get up and put Papa's coat on over my nightdress, it feels as if I have a live bomb ticking away in the room. I go downstairs and into the kitchen. What I really need now is one of Abram's delicious coffees. That would jolt some sense into me. But instead I have to make do with the insipid acorn substitute. Much as I love oak trees, their fruit makes a pathetic cup of coffee.

I'm standing by the stove waiting for the kettle to boil when there's a sharp rap on the back door. I pull Papa's coat tighter round me, my heart pounding, my head filling with fear. The

Germans know about the explosives—perhaps Gerhard did see me in the forest—and they've come to arrest me.

There's another knock on the door and then I hear Raul's gruff voice calling my name.

I practically fold in on myself with relief. I open the door a crack and peer out. Raul is standing in the backyard with the wheelbarrow he uses to deliver eggs and milk to the boulangerie. "Did you go last night?" he whispers.

"Yes," I whisper back. "But I was the only one. What happened?"

"I'm so sorry I couldn't make it. One of the German swine staying at the farm saw me leaving to go to the forest."

"No!"

"It's all right. I told him I was going to check on the sheep as it's lambing season."

"Did he believe you?"

"Not at first, so I made him come to the barn with me." He grins. "Luckily, one of them had just started giving birth. The lamb was in the wrong position and had got stuck." He chuckles. "That Nazi pig regretted doubting me once he'd seen me with my hands inside a ewe!"

"I can imagine!" I grimace.

"Did the plane manage to land? Did you get the drop-off?" he whispers.

"Yes."

The kettle comes whistling to the boil and I go back inside and take it from the stove.

Raul follows me into the kitchen. "Where is it?" He looks at me hopefully.

"Upstairs in my bedroom."

"You didn't look inside, did you?"

I turn to fetch the pretend coffee from the cupboard so he won't see me frowning. Why does he not want me knowing what's inside the case? Does he think that I can't be trusted?

Does he think that, as a woman, I shouldn't know about things like explosives? "No, I did not," I reply coolly.

"Very good. Can I go and get it?"

"Sure. It's under my bed."

While Raul clomps up the stairs to my bedroom, I stir my frustrations into the coffee. On the one hand, I am angry that he thinks I can't be trusted, especially as I am the only one who ended up risking my life to collect the stupid explosives last night. But on the other hand, I will be very relieved to see the back of them.

Raul returns, carrying the pack as effortlessly as if it contained nothing but air.

"You did very well, carrying this on your own for so far," he says.

"Yes, we women are not quite as weak as you men seem to think."

"I don't think you're weak, Laurence," he answers gravely. "Not at all. I just want to keep you safe." In spite of his hulking size and brute strength, I see softness and warmth in his gaze and I instantly regret being so short with him.

"Thank you," I murmur.

Raul takes the pack into the yard, puts it in his wheelbarrow and covers it with old potato sacks. I think of him having to wheel it back through town in broad daylight, past countless German soldiers, and I feel a stab of concern.

"Good luck," I whisper.

He nods and pulls his cap down tightly. "Thank you."

I remain distracted for the rest of the morning, wondering if Raul has made it back to safety and what he will do with the case once he does. It doesn't help that a hazy rain has begun to fall, so I have no customers or even passers-by to watch. When I can't bear my own anxious thoughts any longer, I close the store and hurry across the square. It's the kind of rain that seems to fall horizontally, driving into my mouth and eyes and settling in a film on my skin.

As always, reaching the church brings an instant, welcome relief. I look around for any sign of the Père and hear the low murmur of voices coming from the confessional. Not wanting to intrude, I sit on a pew at the back of the church and wait. Finally there's a sign of movement from the ornate box and, to my surprise, Gigi appears. I bow my head as if in prayer as the sharp click of her heels echoes on the stone floor.

"Laurence," she says curtly as she draws level with me.

"Oh hello," I say, pretending I hadn't seen her.

She carries on marching past, leaving only a vapor trail of her perfume. I'm so shocked to see her in church—and in the confessional too—I forget my own reason for being there and stay seated on the pew.

"Good day, Laurence."

The sound of the Père's voice breaks me from my thoughts and I scramble to my feet. "Good day, Père." I hurry down the aisle toward him, relieved to see that all appears to be well. "Can we?" I nod to the confessional.

"Of course."

I hurry inside and kneel before the lattice partition. I want to pour my heart out to him the way I used to, but just as I'm about to speak, I realize that if I tell him about the explosives, I could be putting his life in danger too. I don't even dare ask why he didn't show last night. Seeing Gigi here has unnerved me. What if she has come back into the church and is listening?

"Is everything all right?" he whispers through the partition.

"Yes. No. I don't know."

"Ah, one of *those* days!" The sound of his soft chuckle makes me want to weep. This new life under German occupation is so relentlessly terrifying, I'm not sure how much more I can take. I miss Maman and Luc with an ache that reaches bone-deep.

"Can I ask you a question?" I whisper.

"Yes, of course."

"Is it ever right to take another person's life?"

I hear a soft exhale from the other side of the booth. "Can I ask you why you are asking this?"

I lean closer to the partition and lower my voice further still. "What if we are called to kill in the name of the Resistance?" I think of the German soldiers in *All Quiet on the Western Front* and *The Silence of the Sea,* and how perfectly normal and decent they seem. I think of Gerhard, unable to shoot Abram and kissing the other man so tenderly. Just like Paul in *All Quiet on the Western Front,* I no longer see the Germans as an abstract idea—a heartless, soulless enemy—or at least, not all of them. What if, in a few years' time, our countries are officially friends again? How would I feel if I'd used a stick of dynamite to kill one or some of them? "I'm not sure I'd be able to do it," I whisper. "I'm not sure I'd be able to take another life."

"Oh Laurence. Hopefully it would never come to that."

"But what if it does? What if the Resistance ask me to?"

"There are many different ways to fight."

I think of the man and his niece in *The Silence of the Sea,* and how they never give in to their desire to fraternize with the enemy.

"Perhaps in this situation, choosing not to take a life is the strongest thing," the Père continues. "I am just so sorry that you are having to think of such things. And at such a young age. Can I recommend you do something?"

"Of course." I prepare myself for the usual prescription of prayer.

"Keep defeating them in your mind. Keep choosing to love."

"Love the Germans?" I ask incredulously.

He laughs. "Maybe that is a step too far. But keep choosing to love books, to love nature, to love your friends. Don't let them defeat you in your mind. That is the one place they can never get without your permission, do you understand?"

"Yes," I whisper, close to tears.

"My greatest prayer for you is that you keep that spirit of yours free."

I'm so moved by his words, I'm barely able to speak. "Thank you!" I whisper, tears streaming down my cheeks.

I stumble out of the church to discover that the sky has brightened and the rain has cleared. I look across the square to The Book Dispensary. Somehow, in spite of two years of German occupation, my store is still open and the prescriptions I'm issuing are more important than ever. I see Charlotte coming out of the boulangerie and I hurry over to her.

"Ah, Laurence," she cries, before lowering her voice. "I was just coming to find you. Do you have our new book?"

"I do indeed, and I think you will love it."

I unlock the store door and we step inside. "Tell me, have you seen Raul this morning, after he made the delivery to the boulangerie?" I ask casually.

"Oh yes, he got back a long time ago. I left him busy tending to the new lambs."

I breathe a sigh of relief. Raul is OK and hopefully the contents of the air drop are well hidden. Now I must push them from my thoughts too, and get on with doing what I'm supposed to be doing. I go over to my hiding place in the poetry nook and take out the copy of *The Silence of the Sea*.

Next month, when I go to Paris and walk along the Left Bank of the Seine, I cast my mind back to the first time I met Michel. It was my sixteenth birthday and Maman had brought me to the big city as a birthday gift. When I discovered the *bouquinistes* selling their wares alongside the river, I truly thought that I'd died and gone to heaven. Michel had been the first *bouquiniste* I spoke to and I was instantly drawn to his vivid auburn hair, jaunty bow tie and welcoming smile.

Picturing the Michel of ten years ago as I arrive at his stall now is a bit like the advertisement for Maybelline lipstick featuring two pictures of the same woman, one drab and dreary, the other a riot of color, accompanied by the tagline: *See what a difference Maybelline makes!* Only in this case, the tagline would be: *See what a difference the German occupation makes!* with the present-day Michel a pale ghost in comparison to his former self.

Don't let them win, I urge myself, remembering the Père's advice, and trying to ignore the bags beneath Michel's eyes and his sunken cheeks. Thankfully, as soon as he sees me and breaks into a smile, the tension in his face seems to fade.

"Laurence!" he cries. "I have the greatest gift for you!" His smile vanishes at the sound of boots clicking on the pavement.

I pick up a random book and pretend to be engrossed. The clicking grows louder, and slows for a moment. As I'm facing the stall, I'm not able to see the soldiers, but I imagine them staring at us and my face flushes. *Keep calm, Laurence, keep calm.* I glance up at Michel and I see him nod in greeting to the soldiers. Thankfully, after what feels like an eternity but was probably no more than a couple of moments, they move on. I glance after them and see that it wasn't soldiers after all but French police. They stop at the next stall and ask to see the *bouquiniste*'s papers.

"They are becoming as bad as the Nazis," Michel whispers. "Ever since the British bombed the Renault plant last month, they have been rounding up more Jews. I heard they've been sending them to an internment camp in Drancy."

I shudder as I think of a suburb of Paris being used for such a terrible purpose. "You need to be careful," I whisper back.

"Perhaps you shouldn't bring me books any more. It's too dangerous."

"No way!" he exclaims before leaning forward to check that the police have gone. "Wait until you see what I've got for you this time."

I have to admit that his excitement is infectious and my desire to see this new mysterious book soon outweighs my fear.

"I'm sure it can't be better than last month's choice," I reply.

"Did you like it?" He looks at me hopefully.

"I loved it. And so did the rest of the group. Those of them who have Germans staying with them found it very therapeutic." Well, Charlotte did at least. Raul was less impressed by the idea of using silence as a weapon, saying he would much prefer to use his fists. "So, put me out of my misery, what do you have for us this time?"

"*Poetry and Truth*," he reveals, in a dramatic whisper.

"*Poetry and Truth*"? I echo, very much liking the sound of this.

"Yes, come close." We lean together across the table.

"Paul Éluard has published a clandestine collection of poems," Michel whispers.

At the mere mention of a clandestine collection of poems, my skin tingles. Has there ever been a more intriguing combination of words?

"For the Resistance?" I whisper.

Michel nods before looking either way to check that the coast is clear. I open my case, ready, and he takes a book from his inside coat pocket. It has a plain cream cover with *POETRY AND TRUTH 1942* emblazoned in red upon the front. "Before you hide it, take a look at the first poem," Michel urges.

I quickly open the book and see a poem titled "Liberté." It's a fairly lengthy poem, comprised of four-line stanzas, all listing the different places Éluard has written a certain person's name. On a notebook, on a desk, in the desert, on snow, on fields, on a lake of moonlight and even birds' wings; the list is magical and all-encompassing. Then finally, on the very last line, Éluard reveals the mystery name—a name he claims he was born to write: "Liberté." I stand speechless for a moment and let the power of the poem sink into my being.

"Isn't it wonderful?" Michel exclaims.

"Yes, yes!" My eyes swim with tears.

"Éluard initially wrote it for the love of his life," Michel explains. "But then he realized that since the German occupation, the only word on his mind was Liberty, so he made that the subject of his love, the subject of the poem."

"I'm so glad he did." I wipe my eyes and stuff the book into the hiding place in the lining of the case. "I'm going to read it and read it until I know it by heart," I declare.

Michel nods in approval. "That's exactly what I did—and I believe that was his intention. That way, we will be able to share it with others without even having to risk printing it."

I think back to what Père Rambert said about the most important form of resistance being in the mind and I imagine my beloved France full of people silently chanting Éluard's call to freedom in the face of the German oppression without them ever knowing. It's a thought that fills me with joy and I'm even more delighted that I will be able to do my bit, spreading the word "liberty" throughout the Valley.

26

JEANNE—1993

If riding in Yitzhak's car had been a hairy experience with three of them on board, with four it was even more nerve-wracking as it chugged and bounced along the dirt track. Jeanne glanced at Charlotte on the back seat beside her. The old woman was still staring at her intently, her eyes as dark and alert as a bird's. Somehow, the little car made it up the steep hill and onto a road running parallel with the forest.

"It sure is weird to see that place again," Wendell murmured.

"Is that where you crash-landed your plane?" Jeanne asked.

"Uh-huh. And I did a couple of drop-offs there before that. The first time I landed in that forest, my exhaust pipe caught fire!"

Jeanne stared at him, shocked. "How did you put it out?"

He shifted in his seat to look at her. "I stuffed my Mae West in the pipe."

"Mae West?"

He laughed. "That was exactly your mom's response. She was there when it happened; it was the first time we met. Mae West was the nickname us air force boys had for our life preservers."

"But how did you manage to fly out after the fire? Wasn't the plane damaged?"

"No, it worked just fine—eventually. Your mom gave me that yarn doll to take for the journey. Yup, she was a lucky charm all right." He gazed back out of the windshield at the trees. "That forest was the last place I ever saw her. I just wish . . ." He broke off and took a handkerchief from his jacket pocket.

"What, Pops?" Jeanne asked gently.

"I wish I hadn't left her behind." His voice broke. "Things could have been so different."

Jeanne leaned forward and placed her hand on his shoulder. He put his hand on top of hers and gave it a squeeze.

Charlotte said something in French and Yitzhak glanced at Wendell. "She says that Laurence loved you very much."

Rather than console Wendell, this only made him more upset. "I'm so sorry," he gasped over and over, wiping his eyes, but Jeanne wasn't sure if he was talking to them or Laurence.

As soon as he fell silent, Charlotte spoke some more.

"Laurence told her that the father of her baby was someone she knew from Paris," Yitzhak explained. "She only found out the truth after the war—from the person we are going to visit now."

"Why would she have said he was from Paris?" Jeanne asked.

This time Yitzhak didn't need to ask Charlotte and responded immediately. "Members of the Resistance had to keep everything like that secret. If your mother had told her the truth, it could have put her life in danger too."

Jeanne leaned back in her seat. She couldn't begin to comprehend how terrifying it must have been living under German rule. And even for those lucky enough to escape, like her father, the emotional scars clearly ran deep. She wondered what he meant by wishing he hadn't left Laurence behind. Had he had the opportunity to rescue her too? Clearly whatever happened had left him with a huge burden of regret and guilt.

As they carried on driving past the forest, she gazed out at the panorama of green and thought back to how depressed she'd been over her enforced early retirement. She'd made a sloppy mistake at a crime scene, contaminating a crucial piece of physical evidence. At the time it had felt like the end of the world, or her world at least, but compared to what Laurence and Charlotte and her dad had been through, it was nothing. The perpetrator had still been found guilty in spite of her mistake. She'd had a successful thirty-year career; she'd gotten a generous retirement package. Her ego had been bruised, that was all. She felt ashamed for feeling so mistreated.

After a while, they arrived in a small village. Yitzhak consulted his map, then drove through some ornate iron gates onto a long gravel driveway. At the end of the driveway stood a huge old house made from sand-colored stone. Perfectly manicured hedges ran around the front of the building and two round turrets stood sentry-like either side. An official-looking sign by the door indicated that the house was some kind of institution rather than a family home.

As Yitzhak parked up, Charlotte began to speak.

"The person we are here to see is very old," Yitzhak translated. "So they might be asleep."

They'd better not be, Jeanne thought.

As she clambered out of the back of the car, she glanced at Wendell. He looked so pale and anxious. She went over and linked arms with him. "It'll be OK, Pops," she whispered. "At least this way we'll get some closure, right?"

He nodded but he didn't look convinced.

They trooped into the entrance hall and over to a desk, where an officious-looking woman sat sorting through some computer disks. Charlotte said something to her in French and pointed at Jeanne.

The woman looked at Jeanne curiously, then came out from behind her desk and led them along a hallway and into a large sunny room at the back of the building. The room was dotted with armchairs and looked out onto a terrace, and beyond that a beautifully landscaped garden. The woman went over to a high-backed chair facing the garden and spoke softly to the occupant, then she looked back at the others.

"He had to have a minor surgery yesterday, so he is still very drowsy," she said in perfect English. "Come, come." She beckoned to them.

Jeanne stepped forward to see a frail old man with white wiry hair sitting in the chair. His clothes hung loosely from his thin frame as if from a hanger. Charlotte said something to him in French and he looked up at Jeanne and clasped his hands together.

"Jeanne?" he asked, his voice cracking.

Jeanne nodded and his pale blue eyes filled with tears.

Charlotte started speaking to Yitzhak.

"This is Père Rambert," he explained. "He was the town priest during the war. He knew your mother her whole life. He was like a father to her."

The priest slowly raised a gnarled hand and beckoned at Jeanne to come closer. She crouched down on the floor in front of him and he started saying the same sentence over and over again, his voice cracking.

"He says you are a miracle," Yitzhak translated.

Then Charlotte spoke, placing a hand on the Père's shoulder.

"He is the one who saved you from the Nazis, who got you to the forest so you could be rescued," Yitzhak explained.

"Holy cow," Wendell whispered, looking at Jeanne. "He must be the guy who handed you to me."

Jeanne looked from Wendell to the priest and back again,

her body tingling at the thought of the three of them having met before in such a fateful way.

Yitzhak said something in French to the Père before turning to Wendell. "I told him that you are Jeanne's father."

"*Pilote?*" the Père said, looking up at him.

"Yes, *oui*," Wendell replied.

"Laurence—she loved you," the priest said in faltering English. He looked from Wendell to Jeanne. "Loved you both, very, very much."

"So she's definitely dead then." The words burst from Jeanne's mouth. She hardly dared move as Yitzhak asked the question in French.

"*Oui*," the priest said softly, and Jeanne didn't need Yitzhak to translate to know that all hope of ever meeting her birth mom had been terminated by that one tiny word. She felt a bone-deep mixture of disappointment and loss.

"I'm sorry," Yitzhak whispered.

Wendell choked back a sob.

"It's OK, Pops." Jeanne stood up and gripped his arm, swallowing down her own tears. She needed to be strong for him.

"I'd been hoping . . ." Wendell gasped.

The priest leaned forward and said something, pausing every now and then to catch his breath.

"He says that the war was a terrible time," Yitzhak explained. "There was so much cruelty. But you . . ." He nodded to Jeanne. "You were love."

The old man leaned back in his chair looking suddenly exhausted. "*Amour*," he whispered again.

"Could you ask him how my mother died?" Jeanne said to Yitzhak.

As Yitzhak translated, the priest visibly recoiled. For a moment, Jeanne thought he wasn't going to reply. Finally he said a few words.

"He says she died a hero."

And with that, the old man closed his eyes and his breathing slackened.

"What I don't understand is why I needed rescuing from the Nazis," Jeanne said, trying to make sense of everything she'd just learned. "I was just a baby."

Yitzhak asked the question in French, but the Père appeared to have fallen asleep. Charlotte said something, though, her expression deadly serious.

Yitzhak cleared his throat. "Because . . . because they wanted to kill you."

At the start of summer, I come up with the idea of running a story time for kids in the store. Seeing the town's children become so thin and raggedy makes me compelled to do something to lift their spirits. I fetch my old dolls and stuffed toys from the storeroom upstairs and give them a wash, then I place them in a circle around the mannequin, who is sitting in the armchair holding an open, leather-bound edition of *Grimms' Fairy Tales*. Then I stick a poster in the window advertising my idea:

Story Time Thursday 4 P.M.
Only Those Age 10 And Under Allowed To Attend!

A few minutes before my event is due to start, I arrange some cushions on the floor by the hearth in front of one of the armchairs. I only hope that the seats will be filled and I won't be reading fairy tales to myself!

Thankfully, at just before four, the bell above the door jangles and Violeta's niece, Claudette, and the hairdresser's daughter, Beatrice, come marching in.

"We're here for story time. We're both under ten. I am nine and three quarters and Beatrice is eight," Claudette announces, looking around the place as if she's about to give it a thorough inspection. Clearly the apple hasn't fallen far from Violeta's tree with this one.

"Very good," I reply and point to the cushions. "Please, take a seat."

Claudette races over to the armchair, and sits on it like a queen on her throne, her short, thin legs swinging off the end.

"Actually, that's where I'm going to be sitting," I tell her gently. "How about you join Beatrice on the cushions?"

Claudette gives a dramatic sigh and plonks herself down beside Beatrice, who is sitting smiling up at me shyly, twisting a long strand of her fair hair around her finger.

For the next few minutes, the bell rings constantly as more and more children are deposited by their weary and grateful mothers. When at last my audience is settled, I pick up the copy of *Grimms' Fairy Tales* and sit down in the chair.

"Today I am going to tell you the exciting, the spine-tingling, the riveting tale of Little Red Riding Hood," I say in the kind of theatrical delivery Michel would be proud of.

"I already know that story," Claudette sighs like a world-weary woman of ninety rather than a girl of nine and three quarters.

"So do I," says a little boy named Tomas, whose mother is one of my best customers and a huge fan of romantic fiction.

"Ah, but do you know the *real* story?" I say, determined not to be thwarted.

"A little girl wearing a red hood gets tricked by a wolf and he eats her and her grandma and a woodcutter comes to save them, the end," Claudette rattles off in a bored tone.

"Yeah, he chops the wolf's belly open!" Tomas says, a little too bloodthirstily, I note.

"Ah, but that is not the real story," I reply enigmatically.

The children all sit upright, now fully attentive. Even Claudette stops sighing and yawning. But before I can say any more, there's a knock at the door and I see a local seamstress named Hanna and her son Mordecai. As I go over to let them in, I notice something that makes me sick to my stomach. Both of them have yellow stars with the word *JUIF* printed in black pinned to their clothes.

I look up from the star on Hanna's thin cotton jacket and meet her gaze. "I'm so sorry," I whisper.

"Why are you sorry?" Mordecai asks. "Why is she sorry, Maman?"

"She's sorry that we are late," Hanna replies firmly, giving me a knowing look.

"Yes," I say quickly. "But don't worry, I haven't started the story yet, so you haven't missed anything."

"Phew!" Mordecai rushes over to the other children and sits on the floor.

"Thank you," Hanna whispers.

I clasp hold of her hands and squeeze, trying to convey so much without words. She blinks and looks away.

Once Hanna has gone, I lock the door and turn to see Mordecai and Tomas about to come to blows.

"Boys, what's going on?" I exclaim, hurrying over.

"Tomas was making fun of Mordecai's star," Claudette informs me.

"Tomas, why would you make fun of a star?" I ask, pretending to be shocked. "A star is one of the most amazing things in the entire universe."

"It is?" Mordecai asks with a sniff.

"Yes!" I quickly wrack my brains for everything I know about astronomy. "Stars are like compasses—and they tell stories."

"No they do not!" Tomas replies grumpily.

"Of course they do." I hurry over to the non-fiction section and take an encyclopedia from the shelf, turning to the page about the constellations. "Look at this," I say, showing some of the illustrations to the children. "These stars are the famous flying horse, Pegasus. And here is Orion, named after the Greek hunter." Thankfully, Tomas starts looking vaguely impressed. "And this is the North Star, Polaris. It's my favorite star of all because people use it to find their way to places, just like a compass."

"Really?" Mordecai wipes his eyes.

"Yes." I place my hand upon the cursed star on his chest and force myself to smile. "So now you have your very own star, you should never get lost."

"I wish I had a star," Claudette says sulkily.

"I think it's time we got on with our story," I say quickly.

Mordecai sits upright and puffs up his chest.

Of course, I hadn't planned on having to rewrite the tale of Little Red Riding Hood for my unforgiving audience, so I have to think frantically as I read. When I get to the part where the wolf pretends to be the grandma, a little girl called Maria puts up her hand.

"Yes, Maria?"

"I think the Germans are just like the wolf," she says.

"Shh!" Claudette hisses. "You mustn't say things like that."

"But they are," Maria persists. "They pretend to be nice, but really they just want to gobble up our food."

There are murmurs of agreement among the group and I don't know whether to laugh or cry. Have I somehow inadvertently started a junior branch of my resistance book club? But then I think of how Hitler used the young people in Germany to spy on their own families and my desire to laugh fades.

"Back to the story," I say loudly, "and the very exciting, *real* ending!"

Thankfully, they all fall silent and gaze up at me. But what should the real ending be? If some of them think that the wolf is like the Germans, what message could I secretly convey?

" 'What big eyes you have,' Little Red Riding Hood said to the wolf." I clear my throat and deepen my voice. " 'All the better for seeing you with,' " I growl.

" 'And what big hands you have,' Little Red Riding Hood continued. 'All the better for hugging you with,' the wolf replied. Little Red Riding Hood frowned. These hands looked more like paws and there was no way her grandma had gigantic claws!"

Some of the children giggle; the rest look gripped.

"Little Red Riding Hood sat very still," I continue. "There was only one place she'd seen those paws with claws and it wasn't on her grandma—it was on the big bad wolf! Little Red Riding Hood thought for a moment. 'Don't you want to tell me what a big mouth I have?' the wolf asked impatiently. 'Not yet,' Little Red Riding Hood replied, for she realized that if she mentioned his mouth, the wolf would use it as an excuse to eat her and there was no way she wanted to be eaten. But one thing that Little Red Riding Hood had that the wolf didn't was her brain." I look up from the book and smile at the children. "Did you know that children have much cleverer brains than grownups?"

They all shake their heads and Claudette frowns.

"But aren't children's brains smaller?" she asks.

"Yes, but they aren't so full of nonsense," I reply. "And that means that children are able to think of much more interesting and exciting ideas than grown-ups."

"Hmm." Claudette frowns.

"When was the last time you played a really exciting game with a grown-up?" I ask.

Some of the children shrug.

"Have you ever seen a grown-up pretend that a tree is a tower or a cave is a castle, or a cow is a mooing monster who likes to squirt milk at its enemies?"

The children start to giggle and shake their heads.

"Their brains are too full of dull old nonsense, like what time children should go to bed, and how much everything costs, to think of such enjoyable things," I continue. "But because Little Red Riding Hood was a child and had a much more fun and imaginative brain she was able to come up with an excellent idea to help her escape from the wolf. Can anyone guess what it was?" I ask, trying to buy myself some more time.

"Did she bake him in a pie?" a girl called Rose asks.

"No, but only because she knew the wolf had eaten her grandma and she didn't want to bake her too."

"Did she say, 'What a big bottom you have?'" Mordecai asks. "And while the wolf turned to look at his bottom, she ran away."

The children start really laughing now.

"What a big bottom you have!" Tomas yells.

Mordecai looks at his backside and growls, "No I haven't!"

"Yes! Yes, that's it! Well done, Mordecai!" I exclaim. "And while the wolf is busy looking at his backside, Little Red Riding Hood runs out to the woodcutter and grabs his ax and comes back and chops the wolf open. And the wolf doesn't see her coming because he's too busy moaning that his bottom isn't big!"

Now the children are rolling on the floor in hysterics and it's such a tonic. I wish I could bottle their laughter to listen to whenever I need reminding that it's still possible to create moments when hunger and Nazis and their cursed stars don't matter, thanks to the magical power of stories.

After the children have been collected by their parents, who all seem equally shocked and grateful for their offspring's revived spirits, I decide to close the store early and go for a celebratory walk. But just as I'm locking the store door, I hear the hum of a plane approaching. I shelter my eyes with my hand and look into the sky. When I see the round Royal Air

Force symbol, the joy inside me grows. I picture the American pilot sitting in the cockpit, with Maman's Nénette tucked inside his pocket. It isn't the first time I've thought of him since our meeting. The truth is, I think of him most days. My mind has been so desperate for a distraction from the relentless doom and gloom, I've gotten into the habit of creating little stories about us in my head, partly inspired by Robert Jordan and Maria in *For Whom the Bell Tolls,* it has to be said. But unlike Hemingway's Maria, I don't stay in a cave, preparing food and washing socks. In my stories, I'm no "little rabbit," I'm fighting fearlessly alongside the pilot, often in my very own plane. Perhaps it is crazy to dream about a virtual stranger like this, but there was something about the dramatic way in which we met that makes me feel connected to him. And the fact that he is now in possession of Maman's doll only deepens that connection.

"Good luck," I whisper up at the plane and I notice a flock of birds swirling in the sky beneath it. I blink hard to check that I'm not seeing things. The flock appears to be growing. But how? Then I realize that they aren't birds at all, they're pieces of paper! Hundreds and hundreds of pieces of paper, tumbling and twirling down through the air. I stand, gaping in amazement as they start landing all over the square. What are they?

One lands right by my feet and I pick it up and gasp in shock. It's a poem—and one that I know by heart. But why on earth are the air force dropping it here? I blink hard and look back at the paper. No, I'm not hallucinating. Éluard's love poem to liberty has been dropped from the heavens, like the most perfect of gifts. As I scan the stanzas, my bird of hope sings along. Once again all of the power and the passion of Éluard's words flow from the page and into me. *Liberty. Liberty. Liberty.* And now, all around the square, people are scrambling like ants picking up the pieces of paper. I watch, reveling in their expressions of surprise and then, as they read the poem, beaming smiles. Outside the hotel, a soldier who'd been dining in the sunshine suddenly jumps to his feet.

"Halt!" he yells. "Do not touch them!"

But, to my delight, most people ignore him, stuffing the poem into their pockets and hurrying on their way. I can barely contain my glee. Thanks to this mystery plane and its magical cargo, most of the town will now be sharing this month's resistance book club read.

About an hour or so later, I'm about to tidy away the cushions from story time when I hear a commotion out in the square. I look out and see Madame Bonheur standing at the door of her boulangerie, her face flushed from the heat.

"What's happening?" I ask quietly as I watch a crowd of soldiers swarm up the steps of the town hall. Just at that moment, Violeta appears, hurrying across the square right into the melee. I watch with my heart in my mouth. Much as Violeta and her forked tongue can annoy me, there's no way I want her getting into trouble with the Nazis, and judging by their angry shouts, they're not in the best of moods. Thankfully, she makes it over to our side of the square, shaking her head and sighing.

"What is it?" I ask. "What's happening?"

"Apparently one of their cars has been stolen," Violeta replies, fanning herself with her identity papers. "So they've taken someone hostage in retaliation."

"Oh no." I think back to the hostages that were taken by the Germans last year in Paris, in retaliation for the shooting of one of their soldiers. Over one hundred hostages were killed. But surely they wouldn't kill one of our townsfolk over a stolen car.

"Who is the hostage?" Madame Bonheur asks.

"Charlotte's farmhand," Violeta replies briskly.

"Not . . . not Raul?" I gasp.

She nods.

More people have come out onto the square now to see what's going on. The melee outside the town hall calms down and one of the soldiers steps forward holding a megaphone. It's Gerhard.

"Attention!" he calls and an ominous silence falls. "Last night a car was stolen from our company. We have now taken a hostage in retaliation for this theft, and unless the car is returned and the real culprit comes forward, the hostage . . ." He clears his throat. ". . . the hostage will be killed first thing tomorrow morning." He steps back and joins the crowd of soldiers going into the town hall.

I look around the square. Like me, everyone seems to have been stunned motionless, then they hurry back inside, like mice scuttling from the light.

"I don't know how Charlotte's going to cope, managing that farm on her own," Violeta says with a sigh before bustling off, no doubt eager to spread this bombshell piece of news.

I turn to Madame Bonheur, panic-stricken. "Do you think the person who stole the car will come forward? They have to come forward. They can't let Raul be killed for something he didn't do. And what about Charlotte? Do you think she knows?"

Madame Bonheur shakes her head. "They only just took him, from here in the square. I saw them apprehend him outside the café."

"Right. I need to go to her at once." *Before Violeta gets to her,* I think.

She nods. "I will go and see Père Rambert. See if he can talk some sense into the Germans."

"That's a great idea, thank you." I feel the faintest glimmer of hope. If anyone can talk some sense into the Germans it will be the Père.

. . .

All the way to the farm, I feel a growing despair. There's no way the real culprit will come forward now that they know certain death is waiting for them. But how would they be able to live with themselves with Raul's death on their conscience? Of all the Nazis' evil schemes, this killing of hostages is one of the cruelest, and the injustice is breathtaking.

Thankfully, when I reach the farm, there's no sign of Charlotte's German "guests." I suppose they must all be too busy tormenting their innocent prisoner. I find Charlotte tending to the vegetable plot beside the farmhouse. She looks so content in her own little world watering the tomato plants, I want to turn and run away. But of course I can't.

"Laurence!" she calls happily when she sees me, putting down her watering can and heading over.

"I'm afraid I have bad news," I say, and instantly she stiffens. "It's Raul."

"Oh no!" She claps her hand to her mouth. "Please tell me he isn't dead."

"No, but . . ."

"But?"

"The Germans have taken him hostage." As I explain what has happened, it's as if all of the color is sucked from Charlotte, all of the life too.

"They can't kill him," she keeps saying over and over. "They can't."

I want to tell her that they won't, reassure her that there must be some way out, but the Germans have been here too long now; we know what they're capable of all too well.

"What if they shoot him like they shot Abram?" she says, echoing my own worst fear. "In front of everyone in the square."

My stomach lurches. This is exactly what they would do. They would want to make an example of him, and terrorize us all further.

"Madame Bonheur has gone to see Père Rambert, to ask him

to try to talk some sense into the Germans," I say, trying to calm her.

Charlotte laughs scornfully. "As if they will listen to someone like him, someone kind and decent."

It's horrible seeing her so disillusioned. "I just don't know what else we can do."

"There has to be something. I can't lose him as well as Jacques. I can't . . ."

I grab hold of her arms. "I'll think of something, I promise. But in the meantime, you have to stay calm, especially when your bastard guests come back here this evening."

"Don't you mean your 'obscenity unprintable' guests?" She smiles weakly.

"Yes, of course—sorry, Hemingway." But the joke falls flat. I hug her goodbye and head back for town, feeling more hopeless than ever.

28

LAURENCE—JUNE 1942

When I get back to the store, the sight of the cushions on the floor practically cracks my heart in two. How can it be that just a few hours ago the store was filled with the sweet sound of children's laughter, but now all I feel is the specter of death hanging over us? This plunging from joy straight into despair is too much to bear. Raul can't die. He mustn't die. But yet again, faced with the cruelty of the Germans, I feel completely impotent.

I pick up the copy of *Grimms' Fairy Tales* and shove it in the desk drawer. Who was I trying to kid, imagining I could help the children through a simple story, when kids like Mordecai are being made to wear stars like a curse, when they may end up witnessing whatever barbarous act the Nazis have planned for Raul? What is the point to any of this? I look around the store in despair.

But stories always win. A wiser voice speaks from somewhere deep inside of me. *Why else would the Germans want to ban books? Why are they so scared of them? Stories live on far longer than any humans.*

I slump down at my desk and take a breath. I can't lose my faith in the written word. If I do that, I have nothing.

I barely sleep a wink all night and at the first sound of a cockerel I sit up with a start, feeling tired to my bones. If only I could rescue Raul. But how? My mind slips into one of its daydreams about the American pilot. He and I are in a plane flying high above the square and we let down a rope to try to hoist Raul to safety. I sigh. It's a ridiculous fantasy. Our only hope is Père Rambert. Perhaps he was able to work a miracle and get the Germans to show some compassion. But before I'm able to gain any kind of comfort from this prospect, I hear the sound of hammering out in the square.

I go over to the window and peer through the blackout blind. In the center of the square, next to the memorial to the Great War, some German soldiers are hammering what look like two beams of wood together. As they slowly raise the structure, bile burns in my throat. They are making a gallows! No! No! No! The thought of them shooting Raul in front of us was bad enough but to hang him . . .

I run downstairs and into the yard and knock on the back door of the boulangerie. Madame Bonheur opens it, looking as white as flour.

"Have you seen what they're doing?" I gasp.

"Yes." She pulls me inside and hugs me, rocking back and forth. "Oh Laurence. What is happening to this world?"

"We have to stop them," I mumble into her chest, but I know my words are futile.

Madame Bonheur makes me a sweet tea, then I go back home so she can get on with her baking. I picture them feasting on our freshly baked bread whilst they execute one of our own and I feel sick to my stomach.

I cannot be here for this, I think to myself as I pace up and down inside the store. *I cannot witness Raul's suffering.* But I can't run away from it like a coward, either. Raul is a member of my book club, a key member of the Resistance here in the Valley. I have to be there for him, to show my solidarity. I'm wrenched from my tortured thoughts by a sharp knock on the door. I open it to find Charlotte standing there, trembling.

"They . . . they're going to hang him," she sobs.

I pull her into the store and into my arms. "I'm so sorry."

"What should we do?" she wails.

"We need to be strong," I say, with a determination that catches me by surprise.

"But how?"

I think for a moment, and then the answer comes to me. I fish the poem from my pocket. In all of the drama, I'd completely forgotten about the plane flying over yesterday. "The British Air Force dropped copies of this from a plane yesterday. It's 'Liberté' from our *Poetry and Truth* book. We need to read it again."

"OK." Charlotte sniffs.

"Hopefully it will give us strength," I say, holding the poem in front of us. "Because we need to be strong for him. We need to be there for him, if . . ." I can't bring myself to say the words, but Charlotte nods. "Come, let us read it together, out loud."

We look down at the poem and start reciting Éluard's words. Our voices quiver at first, but as the poem builds, they grow stronger and by the time we reach the final line, we practically shout the word "liberty."

I put the poem back in my pocket and look Charlotte in the eye. "Ready?"

She nods and we head to the door.

The gallows is now complete and one of the soldiers is placing a small stool beneath it. Another soldier is holding a coil of rope with a slip knot tied in one end.

"Oh no," Charlotte murmurs.

"Stay strong," I whisper, linking arms with her and pulling her to me.

As we walk over to the memorial, soldiers start going around the square hammering on doors, yelling at people to come out. *Liberty, liberty, liberty,* I repeat in my head and I imagine myself becoming the Éluard poem, painting that precious word all over the square. On the hotel awnings, on the Nazi posters, on the war memorial, on the gallows. *Liberty, liberty,* everywhere.

As Charlotte and I stand in front of the gallows, Père Rambert comes hurrying over, holding his Bible.

"Did you talk to the Germans?" I whisper.

He nods. "It was no good," he whispers and a cold sweat erupts on my skin. My bird of hope plummets silently to the floor of my soul.

Gradually, the square fills with people looking dazed and confused. Finally, the Kommandant marches over to the gallows, accompanied by an ashen-faced Gerhard. He shouts something in German.

"This is the last chance for the thief of the car to step forward," Gerhard translates.

Nobody moves.

The Kommandant mutters something to the group of soldiers beside him and they start marching toward the town hall.

I feel so sick I'm barely able to swallow and I can feel Charlotte quivering next to me. *I am not afraid. I am not afraid.* I clutch the pendant in my pocket. But I *am* afraid. I'm terrified of what the Germans are about to do.

I look around the square and see Gigi standing in the doorway of the café. *Abram's* café. My stomach drops as I think of what the Germans did to him on this very spot.

Watching him get shot was horrific enough, but watching Raul get hung... *How do you like your new friends now?* I want to yell at her.

Charlotte lets out a soft groan.

"On the marches of death I write your name," I whisper, quoting from the Éluard poem. "I was born to know you, to name you..."

"Liberty," Charlotte whispers.

I feel someone bustling through the crowd behind me and turn to see Madame Bonheur. She might be thinner, but she's still a solid presence, and with her beside me and Père Rambert beside Charlotte, it feels as if we are being supported by a pair of cast-iron bookends.

Please, please, please, I silently pray. *Please let there be a miracle. Let the real thief come forward.*

But no one moves and no one says a word. Apart from the German soldiers congregated around the Kommandant, chatting away as if nothing is happening. And then finally there's the sound of boots coming down the town hall steps and making their way across the square. I catch a glimpse of Raul's dark mop of hair as they frogmarch him through the crowd. And then he's being bundled up the steps of the memorial to the makeshift gallows, his hands tied behind him. For a moment, I think my legs might give way, but then I notice how Raul is standing, so bold and upright, as he stares straight ahead. There's something so powerful about his courage that I feel it seeping into me.

"We must be as strong as he is," I whisper into Charlotte's ear, tightening my grip on her arm.

She nods and wipes her eyes.

The Kommandant starts barking something in German and Gerhard steps forward to translate.

"Now you will see what happens if you disobey us," Gerhard begins.

As the Kommandant says something else, Raul looks down at Charlotte and me. He gives us the smallest of smiles, then looks away, staring intently across the square.

"Every time someone commits a crime against us, you will be made to pay," Gerhard continues.

I keep my gaze fixed on Raul and I hear Père Rambert murmuring the Lord's Prayer under his breath.

The Kommandant yells something and one of the soldiers pushes at Raul to get up onto the stool. The silence in the square thickens. The compulsion to cry out builds inside of me, but I clench my jaw tightly. *Liberty, liberty, liberty,* I silently chant, hoping that Raul is somehow able to hear.

The soldier puts the noose around his neck, but Raul stands even taller, his chest expanded. "Victory to France!" he yells, piercing the silence. The soldier pulls on the rope while another kicks the stool away.

Charlotte lets out a whimper.

Père Rambert's praying grows louder and Madame Bonheur joins in. "Thy will be done, thy kingdom come . . ."

I clench my fists and keep my gaze fixed on Raul. "Liberty, liberty, liberty," I whisper under my breath.

Raul kicks and writhes and wriggles, and for a moment I think that he might actually be strong enough to defy the Germans and their noose. But then he makes a terrible choking sound and I see a wet patch darkening in the crotch of his trousers, spreading and spreading, just like that dark stain of blood on the floor when they shot Abram. Raul's eyes close and his body falls limp. I retch and turn away.

The Kommandant says something and he and the other soldiers march over to the town hall. Only Gerhard remains. He shifts awkwardly from one foot to the other and clears his throat.

"His body is to be left here until we remove it," he says,

looking down at the floor. "To remind you of what happens to traitors."

"He wasn't a traitor," I can't help crying. "He was an innocent hostage."

"Shh," Madame Bonheur and Père Rambert say in unison.

As I blink away my tears, I think of what I saw Gerhard doing in the forest with that other man. How can he of all people be a puppet for such barbarity? He quickly slips down from the memorial and hurries over to the town hall.

I look at Raul's once strong body hanging limp as a rag and now I understand how Robert Jordan in *For Whom the Bell Tolls* could dedicate his life to blowing up bridges, fighting the fascists in Spain. Against these monsters, violence is the only way to win.

29

JEANNE—1993

By the time Yitzhak brought Jeanne and Wendell back to the square, the sun was starting to set, casting the cobblestones in an amber sheen and the cool air smelled sweetly of woodsmoke.

"Thank you so much for all you've done for us," Jeanne said as she clambered out of the back of the car.

Wendell nodded in agreement. "Yes, I really appreciate it."

"It was an honor," Yitzhak replied. He shook Wendell's hand, then turned to Jeanne. "Do let me know if there's anything else I can do."

"I will."

As Yitzhak went into the café, Jeanne and Wendell continued on to the hotel next door.

"What a day!" Jeanne exclaimed as they entered the lobby.

"Uh-huh." Wendell yawned.

"You OK?" Jeanne asked, concerned at how pale he looked.

He nodded. "It's just stirred up a lot of memories and . . . and a part of me had always hoped there'd been some kind of miracle and she'd survived. It was such a crazy time, so much chaos, so many people sent to the camps. I'd hoped that maybe the message from the network had been a mistake."

"What message?" Jeanne hardly dared breathe, praying he wouldn't clam up again.

"The one saying she'd been killed," he muttered, looking down at his feet.

"So you did know what had happened to her!" Jeanne stared at him in disbelief.

"Yes, but I never found out any of the details, so I'd always entertained this fantasy that maybe she'd escaped. I was clutching at straws, I guess." He looked at her anxiously. "I'm sorry, honey. I didn't want to dash your hopes until we found out for absolute certain."

Jeanne nodded. "It's OK, I get it." And she did. Hadn't she also hoped against hope that Laurence might still be alive, even though it defied all logic? Wendell had clearly loved her so much. Telling himself that she might have survived had been a way of protecting himself from the full enormity of the loss.

"I think I might go take a nap. I'm beat."

"Of course." She went over to the elevator with him and pressed the call button. "I'm too wired to sleep. I think I'll go to the bar, have a drink."

"Sure, honey." He looked so dejected it broke her heart. The thought of him clinging to that hope, however tenuous, for fifty years was too sad to fully comprehend.

After seeing Wendell into the elevator, Jeanne went through to the hotel bar and ordered a large glass of red wine. She took it out onto the terrace and looked across the square. Slowly but surely, the mystery surrounding her real mom was being solved. Like Wendell, she'd been hoping for some kind of miracle and the discovery that Laurence had somehow survived the war. The confirmation that she'd died was achingly sad, but at least she now knew for sure that her real mom hadn't abandoned her. That was some small consolation.

She took a sip of her wine and closed her eyes, enjoying the feeling of warmth as it trailed down her throat. Not all of today's

discoveries had been negative. She'd instantly warmed to Charlotte and she loved the idea of Laurence running a book club for
the Resistance and fighting fascism through books. But there
were still crucial pieces of the jigsaw missing. How did Laurence
die? And why had the Nazis wanted to kill Jeanne when she was
just a baby? This last revelation had left her feeling sick to her
stomach.

She sat down at one of the tables, deciding that it might be
more effective and less stressful to approach these unanswered
questions with the detachment of a cop working on a case. She
began mentally sifting through the evidence, as if writing notes on
the whiteboard in an incident room. There was the smashed-up
typewriter and the bloodstain on the doll and the strange old lady
who left the flowers outside the store. There was the way the guy
in the town hall had fawned all over them as if they were royalty,
as if her mother had been someone important. The one person
who might have been able to tell her more about Laurence and
her death, the priest, had conveniently fallen asleep rather than
answer her question.

To try to stop her mind from going round in endless circles,
she took Wendell's American edition of *For Whom the Bell Tolls*
from her purse. It would be good to read something she knew
her mom had read, another tenuous link to her, just like the pendant. As she turned to the first page, she thought of Laurence and
Charlotte and whoever else was in their secret book club, risking
their lives to read these exact same words.

Jeanne soon became so immersed in the world of the
Hemingway novel she didn't notice dusk falling or the waiter
coming to light the candle in the top of the empty wine bottle on her table. She murmured her agreement at his offers of
another drink and occasionally stopped to light a cigarette, but
otherwise she was transported to Spain and the world of Robert
Jordan and his fellow freedom fighters. With each new chapter,
she tried to imagine what Laurence would have made of it. Had

it inspired her in her own fight against fascism? Would she have related to the Jordan character? Would she have been moved by the plight of Maria? Would she have laughed, bemused, as Jeanne had, by the use of words like "obscenity" or "unprintable" instead of actual cussing?

It was only when the town hall clock struck eight that she put the book down and looked out across the square. The statue of the soldier was now silhouetted against the soft glow of the old-fashioned street lamps. Jeanne wondered again if it had been put there as some kind of memorial to the Second World War. Then it occurred to her that it might contain some kind of clue about her mother.

She finished her drink, put her book back in her purse and hurried over to the statue. As she walked up the stone steps, she saw some names carved into the plinth beneath the soldier. The dates beside the names all seemed to be from between 1914 and 1918, so it had to be a memorial to the First World War. As she studied the names, she saw a sight that instantly triggered her detective instincts. There was a pockmark in the stone that looked as if it might have been caused by a bullet. She crouched down and ran her fingers over the hole. Had there been some kind of gunfight here in the square during the war? She made a mental note to ask Yitzhak in the morning. Shivering, she hurried back to the warmth of the hotel.

30

LAURENCE—SEPTEMBER 1942

As I enter the confessional, I don't even bother with the "Bless me, Father, for I have sinned" rigmarole. In the three months since Raul was killed, I have less and less time for such pointless things. The church, which used to be such a sanctuary for me, now feels like just another building, as my faith in God has been tested to the limit, pulled as taut and thin as a drum skin.

"Any news?" I whisper through the lattice partition.

"Hello, Laurence," Père Rambert replies before lowering his voice to a whisper. "Yes, there is meant to be a drop tonight. They said it would only require one person to collect."

"OK, I'll do it."

"Are you sure?"

"Yes. I want to. I need to—for Raul . . ."

"I understand." I hear him shift closer to the partition. "You are to take it to your store and it will be collected in the next day or so. The code for tonight is 'Jean Claude had sausages for breakfast.'"

"Right." I no longer laugh at the bizarre messages either. I can't remember the last time I found anything funny.

"Shall we pray?" the Père asks.

"All right," I reply flatly and close my eyes.

"Dear Father, please watch over Laurence tonight," the Père whispers, "and keep her safe from harm. And please protect all of France from this evil within. Help us to overcome it, Father, bless us with your love, mercy and strength. Amen."

"Amen," I mutter, before stepping out of the box and hurrying from the church.

As soon as I sneak out of the back door of the bookstore later that night, I notice the moon. It's impossible not to, it's hanging so low and full, but it's the fact that it's glowing as orange as a flame that makes me catch my breath. What's the point of admiring its beauty? I think bitterly. The Nazis will surely think of some way to ruin the moon, just as they've ruined the earth. I've come out the back way in order to avoid being spotted by any soldiers patrolling the square, which means I have to climb over the wall. As I hoist myself up, I notice how weak my arms have become due to lack of food. But what I might lack in physical prowess, I more than make up for in mental fortitude, I remind myself. Ever since Raul was murdered there's been a hardness growing inside of me, like the stone in a peach. I jump down into the narrow alleyway that runs behind the shops and wipe my hands on my trousers.

"Please, Saint Jeanne, send me some of your courage," I whisper, clutching my pendant in my pocket for good luck, before setting off.

All is quiet in town, so I make it to the forest without incident. As I creep through the trees, I keep looking up for glimpses of the fiery moon, to reassure and guide me. Finally I reach the clearing and fetch my flashlight from my pocket and wait. And wait. At least an hour passes and my legs start to ache. I sit down in between the roots of a tree and try to think of something to pass the time, but my mind remains a blank slate. It's been this way for weeks now; it's as if my imagination has gone on strike, unwilling to dream again until the world regains its sanity.

When my backside becomes numb from too much sitting on the hard ground, I stand up and stretch my legs. Surely the plane should be here by now. Perhaps it hasn't been that long, I try to reassure myself. It's only because I'm on my own and I've become such dull company that it feels like it's been forever. Somewhere in the distance, an owl hoots. Oh, to be an innocent woodland creature, I think wistfully, with nothing more to worry about than where you're going to nest or find food.

More time passes and the moon journeys right over the clearing. The plane should definitely have been here by now. Did I get something wrong? Did I mishear the message? The announcer on Radio Londres definitely said that Jean Claude had sausages for breakfast. But was it sausages that Père Rambert told me, or was it croissants or bacon or . . . ? At the thought of such a menu, my mouth starts to drool and my empty stomach lets out a loud rumble of hunger.

I hear the crack of a twig from somewhere behind me and instinctively I hide behind the nearest tree. It's probably a rabbit or a fox, I tell myself. Don't panic. But then there's another sound and as much as I want to deny it, it most definitely sounds like a footstep. A *human* footstep.

I remain frozen to the spot. I can't look around the tree for fear of being seen, but whoever it is is so close now they will be upon me in seconds. I'm pressed so tightly to the tree, I can feel every gnarly nobble digging into me. The footsteps get closer and closer, then stop. I glance to my right and bite my lip to stop myself from crying out in fright. A man is standing about two yards from me, staring straight ahead. My first thought is one of relief; he's in ordinary clothes, not a uniform. But he could still be a German: an off-duty soldier, or even worse, one of their dreaded secret police. Perhaps he won't see me, I think, trying desperately to stay positive. If he just keeps looking and walking straight ahead, he might go right by me.

I close my eyes and focus everything I've got on not moving or even breathing. But then, of course, my treacherous stomach betrays me, letting out the kind of high-pitched gurgle that would be comical in any other circumstance but could now prove deadly. I keep my eyes shut, praying for a miracle. Perhaps the man is hard of hearing. Perhaps he thought it was his own stomach growling.

"Well, hello again . . ." a voice says softly. A strangely familiar voice with an American accent.

What? My eyes spring open and I have to blink twice to make sure I'm not hallucinating from fear, or hunger, or both. There, standing right in front of me, is the American pilot, the subject of so many of my escapist fantasies these past few months since we first met. But what the hell is he doing strolling around the forest in the middle of the night, in ordinary clothes, with no sign of his plane? I notice that he's holding a suitcase, as if he's just arrived on vacation.

"H-hello," I stammer.

"It sure was good of you to send me a guiding signal from your stomach." His grin grows.

"It wasn't intentional!" I exclaim. "I thought it was about to get me killed."

"Well, the night's still young," he quips.

I unpeel myself from the tree, rubbing my back where it aches. "What are you doing here?"

"Charming." He laughs.

"I'm sorry, I don't mean to be rude, it's just . . . you are not what I was expecting."

"Tell me about it! This isn't exactly what I was expecting either." He takes off his flat cap and runs his hand through his hair. In my daydreams of him, he always had dark hair, but in reality it's fair and curly where it's longer on top. "The engine in my plane failed. I ended up crash-landing in some trees about five miles north of here."

"My God!" I gasp. "Are you injured?"

He shakes his head. "No, just a few bumps and scrapes. I'm more worried about the plane."

"Do you think anyone saw it come down?"

He shrugs. "I hope not. It was in the middle of nowhere, in the heart of the forest."

"How did you find your way here, to the clearing?"

"I used the stars."

"Really?" His answer makes me think of Mordecai, and the star the Germans made him pin to his jacket.

"Yeah. Just like Captain Bligh after the mutiny on the *Bounty*."

"Who?"

He frowns. "You haven't seen the movie with Clark Gable and Charles Laughton?"

I shake my head.

"Wow. I thought you French were supposed to be cultured." He grins.

"We are—that's why we don't need your Hollywood movies," I quip back. "So who was he?"

"One of the most daring men ever to have sailed the seven seas. Anyways, I had to get back here to give you this." He takes Maman's Nénette from his pocket and I let out a gasp of joy and relief.

"I didn't think I'd ever see it again," I say, taking the tiny doll and clasping it to my chest.

"Are you kidding? I always keep my word—although this isn't quite how I imagined returning it to you."

We smile at each other and I feel that spark passing between us again. But before I'm able to reply, there's a sound behind me in the trees. I see my own horror mirrored in the pilot's eyes and fearful thoughts swarm into my head. *The*

Germans saw the plane come down. They've tracked him through the forest. They've heard us talking, heard his accent. There's no way on earth I'll be able to come up with a plausible cover story. The hairs on my skin stand on end as I hear the rustle of leaves and the soft thud of footsteps. The pilot glances over my shoulder in the direction of the sound and his mouth falls open in shock. I remain motionless, waiting for the click of a rifle or the bark of a soldier. But instead I hear a soft grunting, like that of an animal. I turn and blink hard, but no, I'm not seeing things. A deer with the largest, most ornate antlers I've ever seen is gazing at us through the trees. And the tableau is made even more mystical by the fact that its fur is as white as snow, like some kind of ghostly apparition.

"It's white!" I gasp. As a child, I'd grown up hearing the legend that a white deer lived in the forest, but try as I might, I'd never seen it. Until now.

"It's a lucky omen," the pilot whispers. "A white deer is meant to symbolize great change."

"Victory over the Germans maybe?" I whisper back.

"Maybe."

The deer looks at us a moment longer, then dissolves into the trees like an evaporating mist.

The pilot and I look at each other and maybe it's the fact that we just shared such a magical moment, but I feel that invisible current passing between us once more. Then the moment passes and I'm reminded of the harsh reality of our situation. I look him up and down, wondering what on earth I'm going to do with him. "Where is your uniform?"

"Back in the plane. We always wear civvies, as the Brits call them, under our flight suits just in case anything like this happens, so we can blend in."

"Hmm, I'm not sure how well you'll blend in with that accent."

"Yeah, sorry about that." He grins sheepishly. "I don't

suppose there's any chance you can help me out? Find me somewhere to hide until I can get word to Blighty that I need rescuing."

"Of course." I quickly wrack my brains for somewhere he could stay. Père Rambert's house is probably the best option as it's hidden away behind the church. But then if the Père got caught with an American pilot in his house it would mean certain death for both of them. I can't put the Père at that kind of risk, at least not without asking him first. "We can go back to my place tonight, then tomorrow I'll find somewhere else, somewhere safer, and try to get word to our network."

"Thanks," he says, his voice full of gratitude. "I feel as if I'm living in a *Boys' Own Adventure*."

"What's that?"

"It's an American magazine full of adventure stories for boys," he explains. "I loved it when I was a kid. Still love it as an adult too, if I'm honest."

I want to smile at the thought of him still reading his adventure comic, but I can't afford to smile right now. "I see," I say briskly instead. "Come..." I start leading him along the track, trying desperately to think of a cover story in case we're apprehended. "Do you speak any French at all?"

"*Non*," he replies. "That's about the extent of it, I'm afraid. Oh, and *merci beau cul*."

"Pardon?" I stop and stare at him.

"*Merci beau cul*," he says again. "It means thank you very much—doesn't it?"

"No, no, it does not."

"What does it mean then?"

"Thank you, beautiful ass."

"What?" He looks stunned for a moment, then bursts out laughing.

"Shhh!" I hiss. "Thank you very much is *merci beau*coup. Please, if we are stopped by any German soldiers when we get into town, let me do the talking. In fact, if we meet anyone at all, let me do the talking!"

"For sure." He gives me a sheepish grin and we carry on walking. "So, how many Germans have you got in your town then?" he asks casually, but I can detect a slight tension to his usual jaunty tone.

"We have an entire company billeted there, so a couple of hundred."

"Jeepers!"

"Indeed." I'm tempted to ask him where the word "jeepers" came from, but this is definitely not the time for idle chit-chat about vocabulary. I need to come up with a convincing cover story and quickly. I could say he is a cousin, or should I say he's a friend? A friend from Paris perhaps. But why on earth would we be out walking so long after curfew, and why would he be carrying a suitcase?

"What's in the case?" I whisper.

"It's what I was supposed to drop from the plane."

"Oh." I think of what was in the last case he brought me and this makes things a thousand times worse. If we get stopped by the Germans, we are dead for sure. To make matters worse, I can hear the first tentative chirps of the dawn chorus and the sky in the east is fading from black to deep blue. "We must hurry."

"Sure thing."

We make the rest of the journey through the forest in silence. I wonder if the pilot's having the same fearful thoughts as me, or if he's still seeing this all as some "boys' adventure." Oh, to be that fearless and light-hearted again, rather than hollowed out by hunger and death. I'm extremely grateful to have been reunited with Maman's Nénette, though, and I clutch her tightly for courage.

When we reach the edge of the forest, I come to a halt. Finally, I have thought of a cover story. "If we get stopped by any

Germans—or anyone at all—I'm going to say that you're my cousin, Vincent, visiting from Paris," I whisper.

"OK."

"You mustn't say a word though. I'm going to tell them that you're a simpleton."

He raises his eyebrows. "Gee thanks!"

"I'm sure you'll have no trouble playing the part," I can't help quipping. "I'll say that you didn't understand the concept of the curfew and I woke to find you missing, so I went out to look for you and found you wandering about aimlessly."

"All righty then." He gives me a nervous grin.

"OK, let's go," I say with far more authority than I feel. "And remember to stick to the darkest parts of the streets."

I take him the longer route home, avoiding the main street. Just as we start going up the hill toward the square, the town hall clock strikes five. Curfew is over. This is good news if we get caught by the Germans, as I can pretend that we've only just come out, but it's bad news too, as it means that the likelihood of us running into other people has now increased.

Sure enough, just as we're reaching the brow of the hill, I hear the sound of footsteps approaching from the other side. And not just any footsteps, but the sharp click of a soldier's jackboots.

"Quick," I hiss, pulling the pilot toward the wooden gate leading to Leon the blacksmith's yard. Thankfully, the gate isn't locked and we manage to cower behind it just in time. The footsteps get louder, but instead of the usual steady rhythm of marching, there's an unevenness to the sound, giving the impression that the owner of the boots might be staggering. To my horror, the feet come to halt right on the other side of the gate. I don't dare look at the pilot. I hardly dare breathe.

From the other side of the gate comes the sound of someone muttering in German. I feel the pilot link his little finger with mine. It's such a tiny gesture, but just to feel that connection fills me with much-needed strength. There's the sound of fumbling and the soldier starts humming one of the marching songs they're so fond of singing as they parade around town. I hear the sound of liquid trickling and then gushing. My heart sinks as I realize what must be happening. I look to the ground and see a dark puddle spreading beneath the gate toward our feet. We have no choice but to remain still. I feel the pilot squeeze my finger tighter and I return the gesture. It seems insane, but even in this moment, with a Nazi merrily urinating on our feet, I feel the same sense of intimacy we shared in the forest with the deer. This time, however, it isn't magic that bonds us together but horror. After what feels like forever the urinating stops, there's the fumbling sound of a fly being buttoned and the footsteps stumble and fade away.

"Holy cow!" the pilot exclaims under his breath. "I thought we were done for."

"Me too."

Our hands fall apart and I'm flooded with fear. How am I going to get him to the store without being caught? How am I going to hide him and then help him escape? It all feels too enormous to comprehend.

"You OK?" he whispers.

I nod and force myself to smile. He needs me to be strong. France needs me to be strong. *I am not afraid.*

I open the gate and peer out. Once I'm certain the coast is clear, we carry on up the hill and along the alleyway behind the square. Just as we draw level with the backyard of my store, I hear the back door of the boulangerie opening. Damn, Madame Bonheur is there already. I put my finger to my lips to signal to the pilot to be extra quiet and wait until I hear her go back inside. "Now," I whisper, and I hoist myself up and over the wall. He passes the case over to me and I almost buckle from the weight. I try not to think of what might be inside. Then he springs over with the ease of an athlete. I hear Madame

Bonheur humming to herself inside the boulangerie and realize that the door is still ajar. I hurriedly unlock the back door of the store and we both stumble inside. My heart pounds as I close and lock the door behind us.

"Phew!" the pilot exclaims, then he takes off his boots. "I guess I ought to wash these."

"Good point," I whisper back, kicking off my shoes. But before I'm able to catch my breath, there's a sharp rap on the door and I have to bite on my lip to stop myself from yelping in fright.

"Go up," I whisper to the pilot, pointing to the stairs. "Take the case and hide it under the bed."

As soon as he's gone, I open the door. Madame Bonheur is standing there in her apron, holding a stick of bread. She looks me up and down, in my forbidden trousers, sweater and beret. It must be abundantly obvious that I've been up to no good. I glance down and notice the pilot's boots on the floor beside me. I pull the door tighter to me and try to nudge them out of sight with the back of my foot.

"I thought I heard you," she says. "Is everything all right?" She stares at me. I know she's been worried about me since Raul was killed and I guess that my slightly wild appearance must only be adding to her concern.

"Yes, yes, I was just about to go for an early-morning walk, but then I remembered that we're no longer allowed to wear trousers, so I came back inside to change." I wonder if my excuse sounds as lame to her as it does to me. There's a moment's silence, which seems to stretch forever as she continues to inspect me.

"Are you sure you're OK?" she asks finally. "You know you can talk to me, if you need to?"

"Yes, of course. Thank you."

She waits for a moment, then hands me the bread.

"Thank you so much," I say again.

"Oh Laurence, I only wish there was more I could do." She kisses me on the cheek. "Remember, if you need anyone to talk to . . ."

"I know. Thank you."

As soon as she turns to go I shut and lock the door and stand there for a moment, feeling a sudden wave of exhaustion from the adrenaline and fear. But unlike my other missions to the forest, the danger isn't over by any means. If anything, it's even greater now that I have the American pilot upstairs in my bedroom. I put the bread in the pantry and head upstairs.

I find the pilot sitting on the very end of the bed in the dark. I light the candle on my nightstand and stand there awkwardly, unsure what to say or do.

"I see you only have one room," he says, taking off his cap and placing it in his lap. His boyish grin has gone. Clearly the enormity of the situation has hit him too.

"Now who's the one being rude," I joke to try to alleviate some of the tension.

"Oh no, I didn't mean to be ungrateful, I just meant, for sleeping." His face flushes, which instantly makes me warm to him.

"It's all right. I can sleep downstairs, in the store."

"You have a store?"

I nod.

"What kind?"

"Books." I watch his face to see his reaction. To my delight, his smile returns. "Do you like to read books?" I ask. "Or are you just a fan of boys' comics?" I don't know if it's nerves, but for some reason I feel the instinct to tease him. Thankfully, he takes it in good grace and chuckles.

"For your information, I used to love a good book. Before the war, that is. Can't seem to concentrate on anything much these days." He stands up and looks around the room. With him in it, the walls seem to shrink inwards, making the space smaller and smaller and us closer and closer. "I can't take your bed. I'll sleep downstairs."

"No, it's too dangerous! You have to stay up here, out of sight. I doubt I'll be able to sleep now anyway. And I'll need to go and see my contact in a couple of hours before opening the store, to see if I can find you somewhere safer to stay and get word to the network about what's happened."

"OK, thank you. Well, I might have a rest on the floor then, if that's all right?"

"Of course." I hurriedly scoop a pile of my discarded clothes from the floor. "Sorry for the mess, but I wasn't expecting to be bringing a visitor home with me, least of all to my bedroom." Now it's my turn to blush.

"No, I don't expect you were." He smiles shyly. "And please, you don't need to apologize for anything. I really appreciate what you're doing for me."

As if on cue, there's the sound of soldiers marching by outside.

"Germans?" he whispers, eyes wide.

"Yes."

"Whoa!"

"Don't worry, you should be all right up here. Sometimes the best hiding place is in plain sight," I say, trying to reassure myself as much as him.

"Yeah, I guess so." He doesn't sound entirely convinced.

I hand him a pillow and a couple of blankets and he creates a makeshift bed on the floor. I take off my shoes and get into bed fully clothed, sitting up against my pillow, pretending not to watch as he takes off his jacket and places his cap on my dressing table.

"You got one!" he exclaims.

"What?"

He takes my crumpled copy of "Liberté" from the dresser.

"Yes, a load of them were dropped from a plane one day in the summer."

"I know. One of my buddies was flying that plane. I was the one who dropped them."

"Really?" For the first time in what feels like forever, and certainly since Raul's death, I feel a spark of something very close to delight. "I'd wondered if it was you."

"You did?" He looks at me curiously and my face flushes again. I can't let him know that making up stories about him had become my way of coping.

"Yes. Well, only because you're the only pilot I've ever met," I bluster.

"Ah, I see," he replies with a twinkle in his eye which makes me suspect he's seen right through me.

"You have no idea how much that poem helped me," I say, quickly trying to shift the focus. "And many others too."

His face lights up. "That's awesome. Some of the guys at the base thought it was a dumb idea. They couldn't see how dropping a poem would help; they just want to drop bombs on the Germans."

"Trust me, sometimes a poem is more effective than the biggest of bombs."

He smiles and nods. "Maybe you'll tell me how it helped you later, after you've had some rest." He lies down on the floor and pulls the blanket over him.

"Of course."

I blow out the candle and lie still, listening to the slow steady rhythm of his breathing. Then I think of him up in his plane, sending poems fluttering to the ground like answered prayers, and how it brought Charlotte and me such strength in our darkest moment. Now that it's woven into the horrific story of what happened to Raul, this magical moment of serendipity shines like a thread of gold.

31

LAURENCE—SEPTEMBER 1942

Of course, the presence of the American pilot on my bedroom floor—the whisper of his breath, the soft sigh of the blanket as he moves—means that it's completely impossible for me to get a wink of sleep. As soon as I hear the sound of the soldiers arriving for breakfast at the café, I tiptoe over to my wardrobe and take out a change of clothes, before slipping through to the bathroom to have a quick wash. When I return to the bedroom, I find the pilot still lying on the floor, awake and staring at the ceiling.

"Good morning," he says, scrambling to sit upright as soon as he sees me.

"Good morning. Would you like some breakfast? I don't have very much, I'm afraid, but there is bread and acorn coffee."

"Say what?" He grimaces.

"It's best not to ask."

"That would be great, but please, don't give me much. I don't want you going hungry. Or *hungrier*. By the sound of your stomach last night, you need all the food you can get!"

"I was hoping you'd forgotten!" I exclaim.

"It was pretty funny."

"Not as funny as you thanking me for my beautiful ass." Again I'm taken aback by my impulse to tease him, but again he takes it in good grace, grinning sheepishly.

"Never let it be said that I don't know how to charm a lady."

After a hasty breakfast, during which the pilot is polite enough to pretend to like the coffee, I set off to see Père Rambert. It's a beautiful sunny September day, with the kind of vivid blues, golds and greens that make the world look like an oil painting. But, of course, it's impossible to relax enough to enjoy it. As soon as I see some German soldiers sitting outside the café, my stomach clenches. It's almost beyond comprehension that there's an American pilot hiding so close to them—and that I'm the one hiding him.

As I walk past the memorial statue, an image of Raul's lifeless body hanging from the gallows comes back to haunt me. What if someone finds the plane crashed in the forest? What if the Germans do a house-to-house search for the missing pilot? What if he's the next to be hung in the square—along with me? How can I ask Père Rambert to take the risk of hiding him? If he was caught and murdered by the Germans, I'd never forgive myself. As I hurry behind the church to the Père's house, I decide to only ask him to let the network know what's happened and I'll take care of the rest. Checking over my shoulder to make sure no one's looking, I knock on the door.

"Laurence," the Père says in surprise as he greets me. "Is everything all right?"

"I have the prayer book you were asking for," I say, for the benefit of anyone who might be hiding in a bush and listening, such is the state of paranoia I now live in.

"Oh, very good. Why don't you come in for a moment?"

He opens the door wider and I step inside.

"What happened?" he whispers as soon as he's shut the door behind me.

"I have an American pilot hiding upstairs in the store!" I exclaim, unable to keep my secret to myself a second longer.

"What?" He looks at me, horrified.

"His plane crashed last night, in the forest a few miles north of here. He managed to make his way to the clearing on foot, with the package he was supposed to drop."

"Oh my!" The Père scratches his head.

"We need to get word to the network, so that someone can come and rescue him."

"Yes, yes, of course. I'll see to it, don't worry." He frowns. "Is it wise to have brought him back to your place? Wouldn't it have been better to leave him hiding in the forest?"

"But that would have meant the risk of rousing more suspicion as we would have had to keep going there to check on him and bring him food. At least this way we can keep him safe without anyone noticing."

The Père still looks unconvinced. "Maybe he should come here."

"No. I'm not risking it. I'm not risking *you*. Let's keep him in one place until we've arranged his rescue."

He sighs. "All right, but if you need my help, you must come at once, do you understand?"

"Of course."

He takes hold of my arm and grips it tightly. "May God be with you."

I return to the store to find the pilot sitting on the edge of my bed. His shirtsleeves are rolled up and he's examining his hands, which, now the daylight is creeping in beneath the blinds, I can see are bruised and scraped.

"Are you all right?" I ask.

"Yup, I somehow managed to survive that coffee," he jokes.

"No, I mean your hands."

He nods. "I cut them climbing down from the trees, they just sting a bit."

"I'll get some iodine."

I go through to the bathroom and fetch a bottle of iodine and a piece of cloth.

"I'm sure I'll survive," he jokes when I return.

"Not if any of those scratches gets infected." I sit down beside him and open the bottle. "And a dead American pilot will be a lot harder to sneak past the Germans." As soon as I make the joke, I regret it for being so insensitive. "I'm sorry. I don't mean to be rude. I'm just . . . I'm a little nervous." I put some iodine on the cloth and dab at the cuts on his hand. His fingers are long and strong and for the briefest of moments I imagine them holding me. It's not an unpleasant image, but what the hell am I doing thinking it at a time like this? Clearly my anxiety is overwhelming me.

"I'll try not to take it personal."

We catch each other's gaze for a second and again the room seems to shrink.

"Right, I'd better go downstairs and get ready for work," I say, springing to my feet.

"How did it go with your contact?" He looks at me anxiously.

"He's going to get word to the network today."

"That's great. Am I going to be moved someplace else?"

"No, I'm afraid you're going to be staying here—for today at least." I'm worried he'll be disappointed at this, but to my relief he smiles and nods.

"Good."

"Good?" I echo.

"I like it here—with you."

Once again, I'm tempted to make a quip, but somehow I manage to bite my lip. "Excellent," I say quickly. "Now I must get to work."

All the way downstairs, my words echo in my head, taunting me. *Now I must get to work?* What on earth has happened to my conversational skills? I don't think I've ever felt as tongue-tied as I do with the pilot. But this is a very bizarre and tense situation, I remind myself.

I sit behind my desk and immediately hear the tread of his feet on the floorboards above. This is not good at all. I hurry back upstairs.

"Sorry to bother you," I say, as if I've only just encountered him here in my bedroom. "But please can you try not to move? I can hear the creaking floorboards down in the store and I don't want my customers getting suspicious."

"Of course—but what if I need to go to the bathroom?" His impish grin returns.

I think for a moment, then go over to the cupboard in the corner and pull out Maman's old chamber pot. For some bizarre reason, I was unable to part with it after she died. It's a very feminine and floral affair, covered in yellow roses. "Hopefully this will suffice?"

"Ah, my favorite flowers." He takes the pot from me and holds it to his chest as if cradling a baby. *"Merci beaucoup,"* he says, with extra emphasis on *"coup."*

We both laugh, and with my tension momentarily relieved, I try to make a more graceful departure this time.

"The store will be open from now until lunchtime, when I will close for an hour. Would you like a book in the meantime, to relieve the boredom?"

I'm impressed to see his face light up at the prospect.

"Yes please."

I reach under my mattress for my copy of *All Quiet on the Western Front*.

The pilot looks at me, bemused. "Why had you hidden it?"

"The Germans have banned it."

"They've banned books here?" The fact that he looks so horrified makes me like him even more.

"Yes. But I've made it my life's ambition to read everything on their banned list."

He laughs. "Attagirl!" Then he makes himself comfortable on the bed, with the book on his lap and the pot beside him. "I'm gonna enjoy reading this all the more knowing that I'm getting one over on Hitler."

"That's exactly how I feel when I read them." I grin, before heading back downstairs.

The morning passes relatively smoothly, although every time a soldier marches past the store my blood freezes. I place Maman's doll on top of my typewriter for courage and I try to process everything that has happened in the last few hours. Even though I'm now in an incredibly precarious position, the thick fog of despair I'd been feeling in the weeks since Raul was killed has finally lifted.

Just before midday, Charlotte appears. Silhouetted against the sunshine in the doorway, she looks thinner than ever. Raul's death has hit her even harder than it's hit me. She hasn't just lost a fellow member of the Resistance; she's lost her loyal companion at the farm.

"Good day, Laurence," she says bleakly, placing her basket down on my desk. "Ah, you have a Nénette." She points to the doll on the typewriter.

"Yes, it belonged to my mother. I'm hoping it will bring me luck." I long to tell her what has happened and how my Nénette has been to Britain and back, but that would mean putting her at risk too. "How is everything at the farm?"

"I'm so tired. Tomas has been a great help, but he's so much older and not nearly as strong as Raul." She sighs. "Oh, Laurence, I don't know what to do. I've all but given up hope."

"Don't say that!" I say, jumping to my feet. I'm about to try to hug some hope back into her when there's a loud crash from upstairs.

"What was that?" Charlotte looks up at the ceiling in fright.

"What?" I say, trying desperately to buy enough time to come up with an excuse.

"That crash upstairs. Don't tell me you didn't hear it."

"It . . . it must have been something blowing over."

"Blowing over?" She frowns.

"Yes, I think I left my bedroom window open. Let me just go and check . . ."

I race upstairs and find the pilot sitting on the bed looking shamefaced, the chamber pot upside down on the floor beside him.

"Sorry," he mouths as I glare at him.

"It's all right," I call loudly to Charlotte. "My vase had blown off the windowsill."

"I thought you had someone up there for a minute," Charlotte calls back with a laugh.

I grimace at the pilot before returning downstairs.

"Let me give you a prescription to help you feel hopeful again," I say, desperate to change the subject.

Like everything else, paper has now become an endangered resource. I put one of my last precious sheets into the typewriter and begin to type from memory.

"What is it?" Charlotte asks and I'm relieved to see the faintest glimmer of interest in her eyes.

"It's a poem called 'Dreams' by an American poet named Langston Hughes," I reply. "And reading it is a double act of resistance because he isn't just American, he's black too!"

To my delight, Charlotte grins. "Hitler would be livid."

"Indeed."

Once I've finished, I unwind the paper from the typewriter and hand it to her. As she reads, her eyes fill with tears. "This is exactly how my life has felt since Raul died—like a broken-winged bird."

"And that's why you need to hold fast to your dreams of liberty," I reply.

"Thank you, Laurence." She hugs me tight. "I love you."

"I love you too." As I kiss her on the cheek, I feel a sharp burst of joy at the fact that somehow, in spite of the darkness enveloping our country, Charlotte and I have managed to cultivate such a bright beacon of hope in the form of our friendship.

Charlotte takes two apples, four strawberries and a thin chunk of cheese from her basket and places them on the desk.

"Thank you!" I gasp, thinking of the two mouths I now have to feed.

"It really is the least I can do after all you have done for me. I'd better go and join the queue for bread before it's all gone. To liberty," she whispers before heading for the door.

"Liberty," I reply.

After what feels like the longest day in my entire existence, it's finally time to close the store. I pull the blackout blinds shut and breathe a sigh of relief. Then I put the apples, strawberries and cheese on a tray, along with a jug of water, two glasses and what's left of this morning's bread. When I get upstairs, I'm half expecting to find the pilot fast asleep as he's been so quiet all afternoon, but, to my surprise, I find him hunched over *All Quiet on the Western Front,* reading avidly.

"This is the best thing I've read in ages," he whispers as I come into the room. "And that's the best thing I've seen in ages," he adds, nodding at the plate of food.

I place it in the middle of the bed, and take a seat opposite him.

"So, we made it through the day," he says.

"Yes, thankfully there were no Germans in the shop when you dropped the pot!"

"You have Germans coming to your store?" He looks shocked.

"Well, there's only one who comes to buy books, but that's bad enough."

He nods gravely. "I can't imagine what it must be like to have to live with them. We keep hearing rumors that they're about to invade Britain. Their bombing's been bad enough, though."

"I can imagine." I pick up an apple and gesture at the plate. "Please, help yourself."

"Thank you." He tears off a chunk of bread.

I lean back against the bedstead and take a bite of my apple. The tart juice on my tongue instantly energizes me.

"There's so much I want to ask you, but I know I'm not supposed to," the pilot says.

"Me too. Perhaps if we avoid topics linked to the war . . ."

He nods before taking a piece of cheese. "Oh, this is delicious," he murmurs.

"It's freshly made, on my friend's farm."

"I'd like to be a farmer," he says with a smile.

"Really?"

"Yes, I love being outside, surrounded by space and plants and wildlife. Maybe I'll buy myself a farm once this is all over. If this is ever over . . ." He sighs and takes another bite of cheese.

"How long have you been a pilot?" I ask.

"Since leaving school. I wanted to be just like Charlie Lindbergh." He sighs. "Well, I got to fly to France. Shame about the circumstances."

I nod.

"So how about you?" he asks. "How long have you had the bookstore?"

"The store's been in my family my whole life. It belonged to my mother before, but she used it for her dressmaking. After she died, I decided to start selling books. I opened it three years ago, at the start of the war."

"Aw shucks, bad timing."

"Yes, that's what I thought at first, but actually it's been such a help." I long to tell him about my book club but know that I shouldn't.

"How?" The fact that he looks so genuinely interested makes it even harder not to tell him the truth.

"Well, it's kept me from being lonely for a start," I joke, "what with all of my book friends downstairs to keep me company."

But instead of laughing he looks concerned. "Do you not have any folks here?"

I shake my head. "I'm an only child and both my parents are dead. And my . . . my friend Luc was killed in the Battle of France."

"I'm sorry."

We sit in silence for a moment and I wonder what Luc would have made of me hiding a pilot in my bedroom.

"When you say friend . . ." the pilot continues, "was he . . . was it . . . romantic?"

"No . . ." I instantly feel a wave of guilt. "Well, it was and it wasn't." I try to disguise my awkwardness by taking another bite of apple.

"How so?" he asks softly. "Tell me to mind my own business if you don't want to say."

"No, it's fine. He and I were childhood friends and then after my mother died, we became closer, but . . . but I think that was a mistake."

He stops eating and stares at me intently. "Why?"

"I don't think we were meant to be together romantically. I think we were far better as friends—and I think he knew that too, deep down."

The pilot nods avidly, as if he really understands.

"How about you?" I ask. "Are you . . . do you . . . have anyone special in your life?"

He shakes his head and I feel strangely elated. "I have a friend, like yours, I guess. We've known each other since we were both knee-high to a grasshopper. I think everyone back home expects us to get married but . . ."

"But?" I hold my breath, aware that we're now engaged in a delicate verbal dance, and any misstep could send our growing closeness teetering off course.

"But she doesn't make me feel like . . . like flying a plane."

"What do you mean?"

Now it's his turn to look embarrassed. "Nothing makes me feel more alive than when I'm flying. The nerves, the adrenaline, the excitement. I don't know, maybe that's not how a relationship is supposed to feel, but I sure wish it was."

"I do too." I internally sigh. Oh to feel that way. "Although I've never actually been in a plane."

He looks at me. "Hopefully you will someday."

"I hope so too."

"Anyway, enough of this schmaltzy talk." He grins. "Didn't you say you wanted to know more about the incredible adventures of Captain Bligh?"

"I did." I take another bite of apple.

The pilot sits upright and clears his throat as if he's about to make an important announcement. "William Bligh was captain of a ship named the HMS *Bounty*," he begins and instantly my body relaxes. It's as if I'm a child again and Maman is telling me a bedtime story.

I lean back and close my eyes.

"Hey, don't fall asleep already!"

"I'm not. I like to close my eyes when I hear a story as it helps me to picture the characters and setting."

"All righty then. But if I hear you snoring, I'll be helping myself to your cheese." He chuckles. "Our story begins back in

1789. The *Bounty* had just left Tahiti in the South Pacific Ocean after picking up a consignment of breadfruit when some of the crew on board mutinied against their captain, led by a man named Fletcher Christian. The strangest thing about the mutiny was that Bligh and Christian had been good friends for many years."

"Why would he turn on his friend?" I ask, instantly thinking of Gigi.

"No one knows for sure. In the movie, they make out that Bligh was a bit of a tyrant, but all of the records show that he was actually a very fair captain. I think Christian was changed after they spent five months in Tahiti. They had so much freedom there I think he couldn't face going back to the harshness of life on board ship. He wanted to continue a life of wine, women and song. So he and his fellow mutineers put Bligh and the eighteen crew members still loyal to him into a small boat, with no charts and only enough food and water for a week."

I open my eyes, alarmed. "How did they survive?"

"They lived on half a pound of bread a day and rainwater."

"Sounds like France under the Germans," I mutter before closing my eyes again. "Carry on . . ."

"Yes, Your Majesty. Well, at first they set sail for an island named Tofua, where they sadly came to grief with some of the natives . . ."

He tells the story so vividly I can practically hear the sounds of the men fighting and the roar of the sea. Whether he knows it or not, the pilot is a born storyteller. By the time he reaches the end of the tale, with Bligh and his crew finally making it to safety using the stars to chart their course, all of the tension has left my body.

"That was wonderful!" I sigh.

He looks at me strangely. "For real?"

"Yes! Don't you just love the way stories give us the ability to travel anywhere in the world, at any time in history?"

"I guess I've never really thought of it like that."

I pop a piece of cheese in my mouth. "You should, it really helps, especially when times are tough."

"Go on then," he says, settling back against his pillow. "Why don't you take me somewhere with a story."

"With pleasure." I reach under the mattress for my copy of *The Silence of the Sea*.

"Do you have a whole library under there?" he jokes. "Is this another of the books banned by Hitler?"

"Yes, and even better, it was written and published in secret by the French Resistance."

The pilot whistles under his breath and it makes me feel proud to see him so impressed. I want him to know that not all French people have given in to the Germans like our so-called government in Vichy. I want him to know that many of us are doing everything we can to fight for our liberty.

"OK, but first you must close your eyes," I say. "I promise you it will make all the difference."

"All righty then." He folds his hands on his lap and closes his eyes and for a moment I'm able to see beneath the stubble on his jaw to the young boy he must have been, all curly blonde hair and dimply grin.

I read him an abridged version of the book, selecting the most powerful parts and summarizing the rest. When I reach the end, he's so still I think he might have fallen asleep, but, to my relief, he opens his eyes.

"So, when the niece finally speaks to the German, and tells him '*adieu*'..."

"She's letting him know that she has feelings for him too."

"And that's why the German smiles, even though he's going off to fight and probably be killed?"

"Yes, because he finally knows that, in spite of her silence, his love for her is reciprocated."

"Whoa." The pilot looks thoughtful for a moment. "I never realized so much could be said with just one word."

"Yes!" I exclaim. "And isn't that the sign of the most accomplished writer, that they can say in one word what would take us mere mortals pages and pages? One of my favorite authors, Flaubert, made it his life's work to find '*le mot juste.*'"

The pilot looks at me questioningly.

"It means 'the right word.' Sometimes he would spend weeks on just one page, trying to find the perfect words. It really paid off, though. His prose is like poetry!"

He stares at me and for a horrible moment I think he might start laughing. *Not everyone is as crazy about books as you are, Laurence,* I silently scold myself.

"I've never met anyone like you before," the pilot says quietly.

"Oh dear." I laugh nervously.

"No." He gazes at me intently. "That's not a bad thing. It's a very good thing, or leastways it would be . . ."

"It would be?"

He sighs. "If it weren't for this dumb war."

I see sadness in his eyes and I think of how utterly shattered I've felt ever since Raul's death. This past day with the pilot has made me feel alive again and I don't want to lose that feeling—not yet. "Then let's not be trapped here," I say softly. "Let's escape through stories."

"What do you mean?"

"Let's keep telling each other stories until we fall asleep."

To my relief, he nods enthusiastically. "OK then." He glances around the room. "Should I go down on the floor?"

"No. Not yet." I get under the blanket at my end of the bed and he does the same at his end. "It's your turn," I say, getting comfortable. "Tell me a story about your childhood . . ."

And so we spend our second night together, the pilot and I,

weaving a canopy of stories all around us. I learn of his imaginary childhood friends, a pair of elves named Spick and Span, who lived in the vegetable patch at the bottom of his parents' yard. I tell him of my own childhood games, pretending to be Jeanne of Arc fighting in the forest. He tells me the story of the first time he flew a plane and how exhilarating it had been to finally know what it felt like to be a bird. I share with him the moment I first saw the *bouquinistes* touting their wares on the banks of the Seine and how it sparked a desire in me to one day be a dispenser of books. We share stories of our dreams, hopes and fears and by the time we fall silent and his breathing slackens, I know one thing for sure. Just like Robert Jordan in *For Whom the Bell Tolls*, I realize that all the life I have is right here, right now, in this precious moment.

32

LAURENCE—SEPTEMBER 1942

I wake in the early hours of the morning to find the pilot's feet gently nestled against the small of my back. I know I should feel apprehensive about the fact that there's a strange man at the other end of my bed, but firstly, the pilot no longer feels like a stranger to me, and secondly, it is so reassuring to feel another human being's physical presence. Again, I am reminded of Hemingway's novel, but this time the certain knowledge that our time together is limited fills me with sorrow and I can't help letting out a sigh.

"Are you awake?" the pilot whispers.

"Yes," I whisper back, my sorrow growing. Now we're awake I suppose it will become awkward for both of us to be lying here together. Sure enough, he moves his feet away and instantly my back chills.

"I dreamed about you," he whispers and I see his silhouette shift in the darkness as he moves into a seated position.

I am hit by a wave of despair so great I'm unable to stop my eyes from filling with tears. It's been so nice to have his company, but it's made me realize how utterly alone I've become, and how lonely I will feel once he's gone. "What was the dream?" I ask listlessly as hot tears spill onto my cheeks.

"You were in my plane and I was flying you to safety in England."

This thought is so bittersweet I can't help letting out a sob. I cough quickly to try to disguise it.

"Hey, are you OK?"

"Yes," I squeak.

"Are you sure?"

"No," I cry.

I feel him lean toward me. "What is it?" His hand finds mine in the darkness and he squeezes it gently. "Have I done something to upset you? I'm sorry I fell asleep in your bed. You should have woken me and told me to move to the floor."

"No, it's not that. I'm glad you slept here. I loved feeling your feet on my back." *Why did you say that?* I internally groan.

"You did?"

"Yes. It felt so nice to have someone—to have *you*—so close to me." It's as if the cork on all of the grief, pain and fear I've been bottling up these past years has finally popped free and I dissolve into floods of tears.

"It felt real nice being so close to you too," he says softly. "But why are you crying?"

"I don't want it to end," I sob. "I don't want you to leave."

He moves even closer and suddenly he's lying beside me, his face so close to mine I can feel his breath on my cheek. "Can I hold you?" he whispers.

"Yes please," I whimper.

He stretches his arm across the pillow above my head and I nestle into the crook of his shoulder. He wraps his other arm around me and holds me tight.

"I'm sorry," I whisper again.

"Don't be . . ." He pauses. "I feel the same."

"You do?"

"Yes. Ever since the first night we met I . . . I've been thinking of you."

"Really?" I wipe my eyes.

"Uh-huh. Every time I looked at that doll, I thought of you and wondered how you were doing. And I looked at her *a whole lot*." He smiles.

"I've been thinking about you a lot too."

"Really?" he asks hopefully.

I nod. "Yes! When we met again in the forest, I had to pinch myself to make sure I wasn't having another of my daydreams about you."

He laughs. "I was the same. All the way to the clearing, I was praying you'd have been sent for the pickup. Although I have to admit, when I heard your stomach growling, I thought a bear had been sent." I laugh and he holds me closer. "You know what I said last night, about wanting to feel like I was flying a plane?"

"Yes."

"That's how you made me feel the first night I met you. It's how you *make* me feel."

And now I start crying again, but this time they're happy tears.

"Oh hell," he says.

"No, it's not oh hell, it's good, it's really good. I'm really happy," I wail.

"Hmm, you sure about that?"

"Yes," I sob.

"OK," he says slowly, clearly confused.

"I just don't want this to end. I've waited so long to meet someone who makes me feel like I'm flying a plane, or at least how I imagine flying a plane to be. I don't want us to have to say *adieu* like the German and the niece in *The Silence of the Sea*."

"We're not like the German and the niece at all."

I look at him hopefully. "Why?"

"Well, for a start, you've already said way more than one word to me. I reckon that the current tally must stand at least at a couple hundred thousand."

I laugh. "This is true."

"And was the German ever able to do this to the niece?" He plants a gentle kiss on top of my head.

"No," I practically moan as I'm taken over by a longing so strong I can barely breathe.

"Or this?" He kisses my cheek.

"No," I gasp.

"And how about this?" His lips touch mine and I feel a fluttering inside my chest, as if my bird of hope has hopped off its perch and is flying free inside of me.

I'm not sure how long we spend lying there in the dark kissing. All I do know is that with every kiss, I feel as if the pilot is breathing new life back into me. Finally, when I hear the rattle of shutters being opened around the square, I manage to tear myself from his arms.

"I must go and see my contact, see if there's word from the network."

The pilot groans and grabs hold of my hand.

"Don't worry, I'll be back soon. I'll try to get us some breakfast too."

"OK." He kisses my hand before letting it go.

As soon as I get out of bed, it feels as if a spell has been broken and the reality of our situation comes flooding back. I try my best to push it away. Hopefully Père Rambert won't have received word yet about the pilot's rescue. Hopefully we'll have another day together at least.

I'm just coming out of the store and locking the door behind me when I hear someone approaching.

"Good day, Laurence," I hear Gerhard say. Just the sound of his German accent sends fear coursing through me.

"Good day," I reply, turning and forcing myself to smile.

"I was wondering if I could . . . er . . . order a book."

I see Gigi come out of the café across the square. As soon as she notices us, she stands still and stares at us, hands on hips.

"What book would you like?" I ask.

"*The Notebooks of Malte Laurids Brigge* by Rilke. If it's not too much trouble. I understand it is inspired by his time in Paris."

"Yes, it is," I reply curtly. Then I remember that today of all days I must be polite to him. "I'll see what I can do." I force myself to smile and start walking across the square.

"Thank you." To my annoyance, he starts walking with me. "Are you going to the café? Can I buy you a coffee?"

Just as he says this, Violeta bustles by, holding her basket. She purses her lips and frowns at me.

"I'm afraid I can't this morning. I have rather a lot to do."

His face falls. "OK."

As we reach the church, I come to a standstill. Gigi is still watching us, whilst pretending to wipe one of the tables. "Hopefully I'll be able to get your book on my next visit to Paris. I'll let you know as soon as I do."

"Thank you. I really appreciate it." Gerhard heads off toward the café and I go into the church.

Père Rambert is standing by the altar looking up the aisle toward the door as if he's been waiting for me. He nods to the confessional before heading inside. I hurry over to join him and kneel down.

"Any news?" I ask, and I can't help adding a silent prayer that the pilot and I might have one more night together, however dangerous and selfish that might be.

"Yes. All being well, you are to take him to the forest tonight, to the normal place. I have the coded message for you. If you hear it on tonight's broadcast, it means the rescue is going ahead."

"All right, thank you." Even though I know this is the right thing, the safest thing, I can't help feeling a crushing disappointment.

The Père passes a tiny folded slip of paper through the lattice. I open it and read: *Margaret will be celebrating her birthday tonight.* Once I'm certain I've memorized it, I put the paper in my mouth and swallow it.

"Do you need anything in the meantime?" the Père whispers.

"No, it's OK."

"Very good. They also wanted to know if you received the package that was meant to have been dropped."

"Yes, I have it."

"Excellent. Someone will be coming to get it from the store in the next few days. I'll let you know more as soon as I'm able."

"Thank you," I reply flatly.

When I get back to the store, I keep the blackout blinds down and the closed sign on the door. I go through to the backyard and thankfully I find not one but two sticks of bread behind my pot of rosemary. I take the bread inside, place one of the baguettes on a plate along with a sliced apple, and put the kettle on. As I'm taking the food upstairs, I hear running water coming from the bathroom and then the pilot appears on the tiny landing, wearing nothing but a towel. His face instantly flushes.

"Oh hell, I'm sorry, I thought I'd have a quick wash while you were out."

"It's OK. It . . . it is nice that you are clean," I stammer.

"Yeah, I guess it is." He chuckles.

It is nice that you are clean! My cheeks start to burn at the stupidity of my words. I hurry into the bedroom and put the tray on the bed.

The pilot follows me into the room and grabs his shirt from the chair by my dresser. "Did you see your contact?" he asks, hastily getting dressed. As he buttons up his shirt, I can't help glancing at the sprinkling of golden hair on his chest.

"Yes. I'm to take you back to the forest tonight."

It could be wishful thinking, but I'm sure I can see my disappointment reflected in his gaze.

"I'll go and make us some coffee," I say, not wanting to get upset in front of him again.

"That would be great," he replies.

Down in the kitchen, I think once more of Hemingway's *For Whom the Bell Tolls*. I need to be like Robert Jordan and focus on the time the pilot and I do have together, instead of what will happen beyond tonight. But it's so hard. I need to reread those passages to make the sentiment sink in. I'm just going through to the store when I see the pilot in his shirt and trousers and bare feet at the top of the stairs.

"Do you need any help?" he whispers down to me.

"I was just going to get a book," I whisper back. "Perhaps you could keep an eye on the kettle for me."

"Sure thing." He creeps downstairs and into the kitchen while I go through to the poetry nook at the back of the store. I lift the rug, tug the floorboard up and reach into the darkness beneath. I don't need to see the book to find it; I know its shape and size by heart.

"More hidden treasure?" the pilot says and I turn and see him standing in the doorway.

"Yes." I put the floorboard back in place and pull the rug over it.

He shakes his head. "You shouldn't have to live like this."

"Hopefully I won't have to for much longer."

"Well, I'm sure as hell gonna do everything I can to try to make that happen."

If you make it out of here alive, I can't help thinking. But I mustn't think such things. "Come, let's have some breakfast and I'll tell you another story."

Of course, I'm far too embarrassed to read any of the romantic scenes in *For Whom the Bell Tolls,* but I do read the part where Robert Jordan realizes that he's willing to trade seventy years of his life for seventy hours with Maria and how lucky he feels for having those hours. I'm hoping that the pilot will recognize the subtext: that this is exactly how I feel about being with him too. But when I look up from reading, I notice that he's frowning.

"What's wrong?" I ask.

"I don't want just seventy hours with you."

"But this is the reality of our situation—the reality of war."

"I know but . . ." He takes the book from me and places it on the bed, then takes hold of my hands. "I want seventy years with you." This time, when he kisses me, it is with a new hunger. And this time when he caresses me, his hands move down from my face, exploring the rest of my body. As our clothes are discarded and our skin touches, I've never felt more alive, more desired, more grateful, more loved. And I finally understand what Hemingway meant, as the bed, the room, the very earth itself, moves out from under us.

After, as I lie in the pilot's arms, I try to make the moment last, but it's as if every second is a bead on a string slipping through my fingers and soon—soon there will be no more moments together left. Outside, I hear the world continuing as normal—the clip of soldiers' boots, the chatter drifting up from the queue outside the boulangerie, the birds singing, the sharp German dialect, so discordant against the lilting voices of the French.

"It didn't hurt, did it?" the pilot whispers in my ear.

"No, not at all."

At least now you have experienced the intensity of true love, I try to reassure myself. But this is a scant reward. The pain I'm going to feel when I have to say goodbye to him will be just as intense, if not more so.

"Please, don't be sad," he says, as if reading my mind.

"I just wish we had more time."

"We will."

"How can you be so sure?"

He shifts up onto his elbow and strokes my hair. "Because I think we were meant to meet."

"What do you mean?"

"Well, don't you think it's strange, the way our paths have kept crossing? That first night in the forest, then when I dropped the poems, and . . ." He breaks off, looking embarrassed.

"And?"

"Seeing the white deer. Maybe this is the great change it symbolized. You and I, being together."

"You think that our meeting was some kind of destiny?"

He gives a bashful laugh and looks away. "Why not?"

"I like that idea." The truth is, I love it.

"Good, then you'll realize that we're bound to meet again."

"Yes, I suppose so." My spirits lift a little.

"So, how about giving me another kiss—for destiny's sake." He grins.

"Ha! That's a good one." I move closer and kiss him with a passion I didn't know but had always secretly hoped I possessed.

That night at just before eight, I take the radio from its hiding place beneath the floorboard and place it on the bed.

"Radios are now forbidden in France too," I explain.

"What would they do if they found you with it?" the pilot asks.

"Kill me, probably."

"No way!"

"I've known people who've been killed for less." An image of Raul hanging from the makeshift gallows comes into my head and I shiver.

The pilot puts his arm around me and pulls me close. "I don't want to leave you here."

"We have no choice."

I switch the radio on and turn the dial to the BBC. This time when the notes of Beethoven's symphony ring out, all I feel is dread. Perhaps the message won't be broadcast, perhaps we'll have more time together, I silently hope. But more time together means more chance of capture—and death. We sit in silence as the messages play, and then finally, I hear the words that send adrenaline and dread coursing through my veins: "Margaret will be celebrating her birthday tonight."

"That's it," I say, turning off the radio, my heart heavy as stone. "It's happening tonight."

Returning to the forest with the pilot that night feels very strange. We've only been together for two days, but, due to the intensity of our time together, it feels like a lifetime. Both of us must be feeling the same sense of despondency, as we continue to walk in silence even after we've reached the safety of the trees. His fingers find mine though, and he grips my hand tightly. Finally, we reach the clearing. A slightly waning moon is shining brightly over the trees, silver this time.

"Who do you reckon is coming for me?" the pilot whispers, and I can tell that he's nervous.

"I'm not sure. Maybe someone from our network has arranged for you to go to another safe house."

He nods and pulls me to him. "I will come back to find you, I promise."

"If I don't find you first," I joke, and again sorrow floors me. I reach inside my pocket and pull out the poetry prescription I typed for him as soon as I heard the message on the radio, the poem "Farewell" by Anne Brontë. "This is for you. Read it when you're alone. It sums up how I feel about . . . about you."

"Thank you." He tucks the poem into his pocket.

"And here . . ." I hold out Maman's Nénette doll. "I want you to take her again—for good luck."

He shakes his head. "No, you need her more than I do." He clasps his hands around mine and the doll. "Whenever you look at her, you can think of me."

I lean into him and try to savor the remains of our precious time together. I can see why Hemingway kept writing the word "now" over and over during Robert Jordan's last night with Maria. Never have I been so acutely aware of the present moment. And then, in the distance, I hear a hum.

"Is that . . . ?" I fall silent as the hum grows louder.

"A plane," he finishes.

I take out my flashlight. "We have to stay hidden, in case it's the Germans."

The plane appears at the edge of the clearing and I see a light blink three times in quick succession. I flash the signal back. The plane circles the clearing and I hold my lit stick aloft.

"Will he be able to land with only one light?" I ask.

"Hopefully. The moon's pretty bright. Wait here." He takes the flashlight and steps forward, holding it over his head.

I watch as the plane circles once more, then begins descending rapidly.

"Dang, I think he might have overshot it," the pilot mutters before grabbing me and pulling me into the trees.

The tiny plane bumps down in the center of the clearing and comes juddering to a halt just a few feet in front of us.

"Holy cow, that was close!" The pilot steps out from the trees and I watch as the cockpit slowly opens and a man pops his head out.

"Bunny!" the pilot calls softly. "Boy, am I glad to see you. Although I thought you were about to mow me down there for a second."

"What do you expect when a fellow only has one landing light to go by?" the other pilot calls back in a strong British accent. "Anyway, you clumsy bugger, you should be thanking me for saving your skin. Get up here now before we have the Jerries swarming all over us."

"Hold on a second." The pilot turns back to me.

"Whatever you do, don't say *adieu*," I joke, trying desperately not to cry.

"No way." He hugs me tight and lifts me off my feet. "I'm coming back for you, do you hear? As soon as I can."

"I hope so."

"Of course I will." He cups my face in his hands and stares me straight in the eyes. "I love you."

"You do?" Joy cuts through my sorrow like a shaft of spring sunlight.

"Yes."

"I love you too!" I whisper, and then I laugh. "I don't even know your name."

"It's Wendell." He grins. "And who the hell are you?"

We both laugh, and he plants a kiss on my lips.

"I'm Laurence."

"Laurence." He nods as if he greatly approves. "Now I'll know what to call you in my daydreams." He kisses me again. "See you soon, Laurence."

"See you soon, Wendell." I utter the sentence with total conviction, as if by doing so it will have no choice but to come true.

As the pilot—Wendell—runs over to the plane, I can hardly

bear to watch, but I make myself as every second is still a second in his presence. He climbs up the ladder into the rear cockpit and the plane turns and begins bouncing its way back across the clearing. As I stand and watch it lift into the sky, I clutch Maman's doll and whisper his name again and again. "Wendell . . . Wendell . . . Wendell."

33

JEANNE—1993

Jeanne woke with a start, her skin clammy. She'd been dreaming that she'd been sent to save her mother, who was being held prisoner by the fascists in the Spanish mountains. In the dream, she could hear her real mom calling her name, "Jeanne . . . Jeanne . . ." over and over. She sat upright and looked around the hotel room to try to ground herself. The voice had been so loud, so clear, it took a moment to fully register that Laurence wasn't actually there with her. She took the little yarn doll from the nightstand and held it tightly. Her mouth was dry and her head was aching. She shouldn't have drunk so much wine last night.

She went over to the window and looked out. The clock on the town hall wall told her that it was almost seven, although it appeared much darker due to the banks of dark gray cloud hanging heavy in the sky. As her gaze drifted across the square, she looked at the memorial statue and remembered the hole she'd found in the stone. Could it have been from a bullet or had the wine and the Hemingway novel made her imagination run away with itself? Then she remembered her plan to ask Yitzhak if he knew anything about it.

After a quick shower, Jeanne made her way to the café next door, where she found Yitzhak drying some cups.

"Hey, could I get one of your awesome coffees?" she said, sitting on one of the stools at the counter.

"Good morning." He smiled warmly. "Of course."

As he filled a metal scoop with coffee grounds, Jeanne noticed a framed black and white photo of a man on the wall behind the counter. She wondered if it was Yitzhak's father. There was no doubting the resemblance in the large dark eyes and warm smile.

"Last night I had a look at that memorial statue in the middle of the square."

"Oh yes?" he replied, putting the coffee into the machine.

"Yes, and I noticed something strange."

"What?"

"It looked as if there was a bullet hole in the stone."

"A bullet hole?" He froze, still with his back to her.

"Yes. I'm a cop—or at least I was a cop until very recently. It's an occupational hazard, I guess, I tend to notice these things." She laughed to try to lighten the mood. But when Yitzhak turned round, he wasn't smiling. "Did something happen there, during the war?" she asked. "Was there some kind of fight?"

He shook his head. "Not that I know of. It was probably from . . . from one of the executions."

"What executions?" Her throat tightened.

"The executions carried out by the Nazis." She noticed him clenching and unclenching his fingers, clearly troubled about something.

"My Uncle Abram . . ." Yitzhak glanced at the photo on the wall. "He was shot there, by some German soldiers."

"Oh no. I'm so sorry."

"I didn't realize there was a bullet mark there. Maybe one of the cowards who shot him missed."

"I'm really sorry, I shouldn't have said anything, I didn't realize."

"It's fine. Working here, in his café, I'm always reminded of what happened to him. But I want to be reminded. I don't ever want to forget what can happen when people turn a blind eye to hatred and prejudice."

Jeanne nodded. "So this was his café?"

Yitzhak nodded and carried on making the coffee. "Yes. During the war, the French government brought in a statute forbidding Jews from owning businesses or working in certain professions. He was killed for fighting back when the Nazis tried to take the café from him."

"Geez." Jeanne looked back at the photo on the wall. When she'd studied the Second World War in her history class, she'd learned about the millions of Jews who'd been murdered and persecuted, but it hadn't felt real somehow. It had been too huge to comprehend. But thinking of this one man being forced from his business and then being executed in a public square in front of his friends and neighbors really brought the reality home. "So I guess your uncle would have known my mom."

He nodded. "He must have done."

Still looking at the photo, Jeanne imagined Laurence ordering a coffee from Yitzhak's uncle, perhaps even sitting in this very same spot, and she shivered.

"I have a feeling they would have been friends," she said quietly.

Yitzhak turned and gave her a sad smile. "I feel that way too."

Jeanne returned to the hotel to find Wendell in the restaurant regaling the waitress with tales from his air force days.

"I don't know, Pops, I can't leave you alone for a minute," she joked once the woman had gone to fetch their breakfast. But secretly she was glad to see him looking so much happier than yesterday.

"So, have you given any thought to what you'd like to do with it?" Wendell asked.

"With what?"

"The store?"

"Oh, no, not really." One thing was for certain, though: now she'd learned what an intrinsic part it played in her own personal history, the thought of selling it to a stranger felt abhorrent and like an act of betrayal to her mother. She thought of Yitzhak and what he'd said about liking the fact that the café constantly reminded him of his uncle and what he went through. "I think I'd like to keep it, though." She studied Wendell's face for his reaction. To her relief, he smiled.

"I think that's what she would have wanted. She did send the deeds to the place with you after all."

Jeanne imagined Laurence tucking the deeds to the store inside her blanket before sending her off with the priest to be rescued from the forest. Jeanne's life must have really been in danger for Laurence to have been able to send her away without her . . . unless of course, Laurence had already died. But how would the priest have gotten the key and the store deeds? Yet again her head ached from the weight of so many unanswered questions.

The waitress returned to their table with a basket of pastries and a pot of coffee.

"Thanks, honey," Wendell said before offering the basket to Jeanne.

"Must have been a trip for you seeing that priest again," she said tentatively as she took a croissant. She didn't want to cause Wendell any more distress, but by the same token she desperately needed to make sense of the latest developments.

"Sure was." Wendell nodded as he poured them both cups of coffee.

"Did he say anything to you about what had happened to Laurence when he gave me to you in the forest?"

Wendell put the pot down and shook his head. "No. There was no time for talking, and besides, he couldn't speak any English and I couldn't speak French."

"So what happened?"

Wendell took a drink of his coffee and cleared his throat. "I landed the plane and my co-pilot opened the rear cockpit so whoever we were collecting could climb on board; we were expecting it to be an agent. This guy—the priest—appeared from the trees holding something, but he didn't get on the plane. At first we thought it was some kind of trap, but then I heard him calling Laurence's name."

"Then what happened?" The scene was so vivid in Jeanne's mind it was as if the restaurant had morphed into the forest. She could practically taste the cool night air and smell the earth and trees.

"I got out of the plane and went over to him, and that's when I saw you for the very first time." He smiled at her across the table.

"But how did you know it was me? That I was yours?"

"I knew Laurence was pregnant with you, and the guy kept saying, 'Laurence *enfant*,' then he pointed to you and said 'Jeanne, Jeanne.'" He sighed. "It was the happiest moment of my life, and the worst."

"How do you mean?"

"Seeing you for the first time but not knowing what had happened to your mom, and having to leave without her. It was torture."

"How did you know she was having your baby? Sorry, do you mind me asking all these questions?"

He shook his head. "Of course not. Well, it was a few months after she'd hidden me in the room above the store . . ."

Jeanne settled back in her chair and listened attentively as Wendell's words brought Laurence back to life.

34

LAURENCE—DECEMBER 1942

"Happy Christmas!" Madame Bonheur cries, raising her glass of watered-down wine.

"Happy Christmas!" Charlotte, Odette and I all echo, clinking our glasses together.

We're sitting around my desk, which I've moved into the center of the store and turned into a makeshift dining table.

"I'm going to treasure every morsel of this meal," I announce before taking a tiny mouthful of roast chicken and letting my taste buds revel in the delicious oregano seasoning.

"Yes, thank you, Charlotte." Madame Bonheur nods heartily in agreement.

"Don't thank me, thank Hetty," Charlotte replies, with a look of guilt.

"Thank you, Hetty," I murmur, trying not to think of the beloved chicken who was sacrificed to feed us this Christmas. But as I take a mouthful of carrot, my stomach churns. I put my knife and fork down and close my eyes, willing the wave of nausea to pass.

"Are you all right, Laurence?" Odette asks. At least I think it was Odette; the nausea is so strong it's making everything sound fuzzy.

"I think I'm going to be . . ." I lurch to my feet and race into the kitchen, where I'm sick in the sink.

"My God," I hear Madame Bonheur mutter. "Perhaps her stomach isn't used to so much food any more."

"But she only just started eating," Charlotte replies. A couple of moments later, she's standing behind me rubbing my back. "I can't believe you've got an upset stomach again," she says.

"I know, and on Christmas Day too," I moan.

"Do you think you ought to see a doctor?"

"No!" I exclaim, a little too vigorously.

"I was only suggesting. What if it's something serious?"

That's exactly what I'm worried about, I think to myself. *And life is more than serious enough right now, without adding to it.*

Charlotte fetches me a cup of water. I take a couple of tentative sips and slowly the feeling of nausea passes.

"I'm sure it isn't anything bad," I say.

Charlotte looks unconvinced.

After dinner, we exchange gifts. Odette has made us all hats. Mine is a beautiful beret made from silky smooth green velvet.

"I made it from my favorite dress," she says with a wistful smile as I put it on.

"Oh no!" I gasp, instantly feeling guilty.

"It's OK. It's not as if I was going to have a reason to wear it any time soon, and besides, the beret really suits you."

The others nod in agreement and Madame Bonheur produces one of her famous vanilla cakes for us to share, Charlotte gives us each a jar of apple preserves and, of course, I gift them all with poems, typed on my final pieces of prescription paper. Then I light a fire with some sticks I gathered from the forest. It won't last for long, but I felt it was important to have some kind of fire at Christmas.

"I hope this is our last Christmas under the Germans," Odette says.

"Me too," I agree, although now the Germans are occupying all of France, I can't help feeling that's doubtful.

I stare into the flames and wonder how Wendell is spending Christmas. I wonder if he's thinking of me. If he's still alive . . . I quickly push the thought from my mind. *He is still alive because he is your destiny,* I remind myself, as I've been doing any time I feel doubt or fear, and thankfully it works. Ever since our precious time together, I've felt different. My old resolve has returned with a vengeance and thankfully it's rubbed off on the other members of our book club too as I've been able to encourage them to remain hopeful.

"To liberty!" I cry, raising my glass.

"To liberty," they reply.

In January 1943, I return to Paris. A bitter wind is whistling up the Seine, bringing with it flurries of snow so cold the flakes sting my cheeks. When I get to Michel's booth, it's shuttered closed. Trying not to panic, I reassure myself that he has probably gone to get something to eat; after all, who'd want to be outside on a day as cold as this? And if he has gone for something to eat, I can guess exactly where he will be.

This time when I walk into Café de Flore on my own I don't feel at all self-conscious. Raul's death and my experience with Wendell have changed me irrevocably. Both have forced me to grow, like a butterfly bursting from its cocoon, and I no longer feel like the naïve caterpillar. The stove in the middle of the café is burning away, providing a welcome warmth, and as always, the place is full of people and humming with conversation.

I scan the long tables for any sign of Michel's polka dot bow tie or bright auburn hair.

"Laurence!"

I turn to see Pierre standing behind me. His hair and wispy beard are longer than ever and he's wearing a shabby gray suit beneath a sheepskin jacket.

"Good day," I reply. "I couldn't find Michel down at the river so I thought he might be here."

"Come." Pierre leads me over to a table in the corner and orders two *petit noirs* from a waitress in a roll-collar sweater and short flared skirt.

"Is he all right?" I ask, tucking my case beneath the table.

"He had to go away for a while."

"Oh." My heart sinks and I fight the urge to ask why. "But he's all right?" I ask again.

"Yes, but he wanted me to give you something. Will you wait here while I go and get it?"

"Of course." I settle back in my seat and drink in the chatter and energy of the other people. I'm heartened to see that even the bleakest of winters hasn't dampened the Café de Flore spirit.

Just as the waitress arrives at the table with our coffees, Pierre returns, his normally pale cheeks flushed from the cold. As soon we're alone again, he takes a book from his inside coat pocket and passes it to me beneath the table. Keeping it in my lap, I study the bold white print on the scarlet cover:

The Moon Is Down

A Novel

BY

JOHN STEINBECK

I flick the thin book open and glance at the text.

"It's in English. The other members of my book club won't be able to read it."

"We don't want them to read it, at least not yet," Pierre replies. "Only you."

"Why?"

He leans across the table and lowers his voice. "Steinbeck wrote this novel for people living under German occupation, so you must be very careful. Les Éditions de Minuit are thinking of publishing a French edition. We would be interested in what you think of it."

"Me?"

He nods and takes a sip of his coffee.

"But why?"

"The book has caused some controversy in America. The critics there are saying that Steinbeck's been too soft on the Nazis. I want to know if you feel this is true—or if you think the members of your book club would like it. Would it make a good book for the French Resistance?"

My heart swells with pride at being trusted with such a task. "Thank you. I would love to read it." I slip the book into the lining of my case.

Pierre takes a pack of cigarettes from his pocket and offers them to me. I shake my head.

"You are no longer smoking for the Resistance?" he asks with a smile.

"No. Just the smell makes me sick these days. I think I'm better off fighting the Germans through books."

He chuckles. "Yes, I agree." He stands up and shakes my hand. "Let me know through your contact when you've read the book and when you will be back in Paris and then we'll talk about it some more."

"I will. And thank you again."

"You're welcome." He lights his cigarette and heads for the door.

As a waft of smoke catches my nose, nausea rises inside of me. I take a sip of my coffee, but, if anything, it only makes me feel worse and I feel a strange fluttering in my stomach. For a horrible moment I think I'm going to be sick in the middle of Café de Flore, which would not be at all good for my new-found confidence.

I pick up my case and hurry outside. The cold air instantly makes me feel better and I set off along Boulevard Saint-Germain. A woman is walking toward me pushing a perambulator. As they walk past, I glance down and catch a glimpse of a baby, wrapped tightly in a blanket against the cold. Normally I would smile at such a sweet image but not today. Today, all I can think is that the baby in the perambulator is some kind of premonition. *Could it be that . . . ? No . . . no, surely it can't.* As I walk along the boulevard, Paris fades into a blur and in spite of the cold I feel a hot wave of panic coursing through me. *Surely I can't be pregnant.*

Later that night back at home, I desperately try to focus on my new book, but my eyes scan the words blindly and all I can hear are my own panicked thoughts, growing louder and louder. I can't be pregnant. By the time I met Wendell I hadn't had a period for months due to the starvation diet the Germans have put us on. But what if I am? What will I do? What would I tell people? How on earth would I explain my predicament? Round and round my anxious thoughts spiral and then I feel another flutter deep inside of me. It's different to anything I've ever experienced before so I know it can't be indigestion.

I quickly count back the time in my head. If I am pregnant I'm about four and a half months gone. I put my hands on my stomach. Is it my imagination or can I feel a slight bump? I'd grown so thin last year, my stomach had actually started to curve inwards, but now there's definitely a protrusion. But it's only slight, I try to reassure myself. I can't be pregnant. And so it goes, round and round on my merry-go-round of fear, blinding me to Steinbeck's words.

For the next month, I live in a state of denial, trying to avoid looking at my body—and trying to ignore the undoubtable changes that are happening. The stronger flutterings deep inside me, the tenderness of my growing breasts. The irony doesn't escape me when I think of all the times I've longed for a bigger chest and now I'm doing all I can to disguise it!

At the end of February, I return to Paris for a meeting with Pierre. When I finally managed to concentrate on Steinbeck's words, I really enjoyed the novel. Like the German officer in *The Silence of the Sea,* the depiction of the occupying officers—or the conquerors as Steinbeck refers to them—is pretty sympathetic, but as with the Vercors book, I feel this makes the story all the more powerful and relatable.

I find Pierre alone at a table by the stove in Café de Flore, unsurprisingly hunched over a book.

"Good day," I say, taking off my coat. I've purposely worn a baggy sweater over my baggiest dress.

"Good day. Is everything OK?"

"Yes, yes, very good. And how is Michel?"

"He is OK. Still in hiding." He closes his book, and I see that it is an old paperback edition of *Le Médecin de campagne* by Balzac. "So, did you read *The Moon is Down?* What did you think?"

"I loved it. It was uncanny how Steinbeck—an American—managed to capture what life is like under occupation."

Pierre nods. "The sign of a truly gifted and empathetic writer."

"Indeed. And I found certain passages very inspiring."

"Such as?"

"I loved his notion that even a little man in a little town contains a spark that can burst into flame. It made me believe that, as a little woman in a little town, I am able to make a difference." As I tell Pierre all about the strange comfort I got from the parallels between the novel and my own life in the Valley, I forget all thoughts of pregnancy and become fully immersed in the world of the book. "And at the end when the conquerors start going crazy from fear and their nerves wearing thin," I say in conclusion, "it made me see how we can win here in France too. That even though things might look hopeless, all we need to do is keep strong and keep resisting and one day the flypaper shall conquer the flies!"

"Indeed." Pierre nods heartily. "The herd men who blindly follow one leader might have won the battle, but it is the free men—and women—who always win a war."

"I loved that bit!" I exclaim. "It gave me so much hope. I think my book club would love it too. I think all of France—well, apart from the treacherous collaborators of course—would love it."

Pierre smiles warmly. "This is excellent. I shall pass on your feedback."

"So, do you think there will be a clandestine French edition?" My skin prickles with excitement at the thought.

He nods. "Rumor has it the Swiss will be producing a French edition this year, but I can't imagine they will remain true to the original; they're too concerned with keeping the Germans happy so they don't invade. I think we will need to produce our own, unabridged edition, here on the Left Bank."

I beam at him across the table, then feel a flutter inside me so strong it feels more like a kick. Instantly, my smile fades.

"Are you all right?"

"Yes. Yes, absolutely."

"Good." He glances around the café before leaning closer. "There is to be a pickup in the Valley this week."

"A pickup?"

"Yes. We need to get someone to safety in Britain. They will be coming to your store in the next day or so."

"OK."

"You are to hide them until you hear this message." He opens his copy of *Le Médecin de campagne* and points to a sentence written in pencil at the top of the page: *Dr. Benassis lives in Dauphine.* "Have you memorized it?"

I nod. "How will I know the person I'm supposed to hide?"

"They will ask you for a copy of this book."

"OK." A shiver runs up my spine and all of my worries are gone. I have another job for the Resistance. And it will be a pickup, presumably by a pilot from Britain. Dare I dream that it might be Wendell?

35

LAURENCE—APRIL 1943

For the next couple of days, my heart skips a beat every time the bell above the store door jangles. And this, combined with the physical changes I'm no longer able to ignore, is enough to send me into a frenzy.

On the second day after meeting Pierre, just as dusk is falling, I'm about to close for the evening when I see a figure hurrying toward the store, her head down. Her cloche hat is pulled down and the collar on her coat is raised to her jaw. As she browses the store, I go and sit behind my desk. Perhaps it is yet another false alarm. Then the woman comes over to me.

"Excuse me, do you have a copy of Balzac's *Le Médecin de campagne?*"

It's not just hearing the title that makes my pulse quicken. Her voice is familiar too. I stare up at her. "Juliette?"

She nods. Her face is a lot thinner and more careworn than it was when I first met her, collecting her from the forest on my first assignment for the Resistance.

"It is so good to see you! Quick, go through to the back." I hurry over to the door and peer outside to make sure no one is looking. Then I lock the door, turn the sign to closed and close the blackout blinds. "Come." I usher her upstairs and into the bedroom. "Are you all right?"

She stands by the bed, visibly trembling. Her anxiety is infectious and my stomach churns.

"Please—sit down." I gesture at the bed.

She sits down and rests her head in her hands. "I'm so tired," she murmurs.

"Can I get you something to eat, or drink?"

"I . . . I thought I was going to die."

"What happened?"

"The Germans are after me. They intercepted my radio transmissions. They want to kill me." Her voice rises.

"How did you get here?" I ask.

"Train."

My mind starts racing. What if she has been followed? I go over to the window and peer through a gap in the blind. All appears to be normal. A group of soldiers are patrolling on the other side of the square. Others are heading inside the hotel for their evening meal. No one appears to be watching the store. But darkness is gathering in the doorways and the corners. Could someone be out there lurking in the shadows? I shiver and turn back to her.

"Is there any chance you could have been followed?"

"I don't think so."

Once again I'm filled with a feeling of utter isolation. I don't know what to do and there's no one I can turn to. But then I think of Wendell and the mysterious fluttering, kicking being inside of me and a powerful wave of wonder washes through me, sweeping my fear and denial away. *Our child is growing inside of me.* I can't fall apart now; they both need me to be strong.

"I'm going to get you something to eat," I say, crouching in front of her and taking hold of her hands. They're icy cold. "Here." I pull back the blankets and gesture at her to get into the bed. "Warm yourself. Do you remember our cover story from before?"

"That I am your cousin?"

"Yes. If anyone comes to the store this is what we must tell them."

She nods and I'm heartened to see that her trembling has lessened. Perhaps my show of strength is infectious. If only it were genuine.

I go downstairs and check the backyard. It's empty and the boulangerie is closed. To my relief, I see a loaf of bread hidden amongst my herbs. This act of kindness from Madame Bonheur fortifies me. *I'm not alone,* I remind myself. I take the bread into the kitchen, put the kettle on the stove and go through to the store, where, once again, I peer through the blind to make sure no one is lurking.

When I return to the bedroom, I find Juliette huddled beneath the blankets like a frightened child, only her eyes visible. I wonder what she has been through since we last met to make her look so haunted. I perch on the side of the bed and pass her a cup of coffee.

"Thank you," she whispers before taking a sip.

I hand her a piece of bread and the remaining half of the boiled egg I had for breakfast. Again she murmurs her thanks before setting about the food ravenously.

When she's finished, she leans back on the pillow. "I'm sorry for earlier, for being so weak."

"You weren't being weak, you were being human," I reply indignantly.

She gives me a feeble smile before reaching inside her bra and taking out an old folded piece of paper. "I still have the prescription you gave me. It has brought me so much comfort and strength."

"That's wonderful!"

"If only I could have lived up to the words," she says sadly. "I fear my soul has been far from unconquerable."

"Nonsense," I say firmly. "You're here, aren't you? You have evaded capture and soon you will be back in Britain." Oh if only I were as brave as I sound!

"Will I?" She looks at me hopefully.

"Of course. And it could be as soon as tonight. I need to get my radio so we can listen for the messages."

Retrieving the radio from its hiding place beneath the floorboard is even more weighted with fear tonight, knowing that I'm harboring a fugitive from the Nazis. Every sound in the square sends terror pulsing through me. When I hear the message crackling over the airwaves, I'm overcome with relief.

It's only when we reach the relative safety of the forest and the fearful chatter in my mind starts to abate that I allow myself to think of Wendell. Could he be the pilot coming to rescue Juliette? Will I get a chance to see him? I hardly dare entertain the thought. And besides, if I did see him what would I say? Would I feel compelled to tell him my secret—our secret—that I am pregnant with his child? As if on cue, I feel a flutter deep inside of me and I feel a renewed sense of determination. I can't afford to worry about Wendell now. I need to keep my baby safe and keep Juliette from getting killed. I press on deeper into the forest.

When we reach the clearing, Juliette turns to me and takes my hand. "Thank you so much for everything you've done for me."

"It's nothing, truly." I hand her a spare flashlight and explain what to do when the plane arrives. Then I make my way to the opposite end of the clearing, a strange kind of excitement brewing inside of me. As I hear the distant engine's hum, my excitement grows. *Please, please, let it be Wendell,* I silently will. The humming grows louder and I raise my stick, ready to give the Morse code signal. As soon as I see the flashing light from the plane, I return it and Juliette lights her stick as instructed. The plane begins its rapid descent and bounces down in the center of the clearing. *Please, please, please, let it be him.* As it judders to a halt, I run over and watch, breathless, as the cockpit opens.

"Good evening," a man's voice calls in a clipped British accent.

It isn't him. The disappointment practically floors me.

"Hello," I mutter back, and I have to turn away to hide the annoying tears now filling my eyes.

I hear Juliette running over and exchanging greetings with the pilot. I hear her softly calling goodbye to me. I wipe at my eyes, but the tears keep coming, much to my embarrassment and frustration. I hear footsteps approaching. It must be Juliette coming to say farewell. I feel a hand on my shoulder.

"Laurence?" My body freezes at the sound of an American voice saying my name. *His* voice.

"Wendell!" I gasp, spinning round. "I thought you hadn't come."

"Are you kidding me? And lose the chance of seeing you?" He pulls me to him and hugs me tightly, then just as quickly steps back and frowns at my stomach.

"Hurry up, Jensen," the British pilot calls.

"I'm pregnant!" I blurt out.

"What?"

"I'm having your baby," I whisper.

"Holy cow!" He looks shell-shocked, but then, to my huge relief, he hugs me to him.

"Nobody knows yet," I whisper. "I've been so scared, not knowing what to do."

"Don't be scared." He kisses me, then laughs incredulously. "We're having a baby!"

"You . . . you don't mind?" I stammer.

"Of course I don't. I can't think of anyone I'd rather have a child with. I mean, the situation's kind of lousy"—he gestures around us—"but you—us—this . . ." He gently places his hand on my stomach. "This is wonderful." Even in the darkness I can see that he's grinning from ear to ear. The relief I feel almost causes my legs to buckle and for the first time since I realized I'm going to be a mother I'm filled with joy and wonder rather than fear.

"Jensen!" the British pilot calls more urgently.

"OK, Bunny, I'm coming." He grips my hands. "Listen to me. I love you. I haven't stopped thinking about you. And when this is all over, I'm coming to get you. *Both* of you. I told you we were destined to meet, I told you that deer was an omen," he murmurs before wrapping his arms round me and kissing me deeply.

The kiss is over in the blink of an eye and before I know it, he's running back to the plane and racing up the ladder into the rear cockpit. There's one last wave and then the cockpit closes and the plane turns round, bumping along the ground. As it rises into the sky and out of view, a sharp breeze whistles through the trees, chilling me to the core, and I feel more alone than ever.

Don't be so pathetic, I tell myself sternly. *Tonight has been a good night. Juliette is safe and you've seen Wendell. Wendell knows about the baby! And he's happy about it.* As if it too is aware of this happy development, our baby nudges me gently in the ribs.

For the next few weeks, I continue going through the motions of my normal routine whilst becoming increasingly panicked. One by one, the outfits in my wardrobe become too tight to wear until all I'm left with is an old floral housecoat of Maman's and a baggy cardigan, which mercifully hangs loose around my growing bump. But as March turns to April and the weather grows warmer, I know that the days of hiding my body are numbered. I can't continue keeping my secret to myself, but how can I explain how I've become pregnant? It was one thing telling Wendell my secret but quite another telling my fellow townsfolk who have never seen or heard of me being involved with anyone other than Luc. In my more desperate moments, when I imagine having to tell Père Rambert my news, I even contemplate announcing that I've been the subject of a miraculous virginal conception, just like Mary.

The only time I feel any peace is in the evenings, when I lie in bed and feel my baby moving inside me. The thought that Wendell and I have somehow managed to create a new life in the midst of so much horror seems like a true miracle, but the thought of having to protect that new life also fills me with fear.

After one particularly sleepless night, I come down into the backyard in my nightgown and gaze up at the fading stars, the stone slabs refreshingly cool beneath my bare feet. It's that mysterious moment just before dawn and an almost full moon hangs low in the sky. I wonder if Wendell flew a mission tonight, and if he got back safely. *You must always get back safely,* I try telling him, as if the fading stars can somehow transmit the message for me. As if on cue, I feel a kick just beneath my ribs. *You have to stay safe for both of us.*

There's a sudden sound behind me and I turn, startled, to see the back door of the boulangerie opening. Before I'm able to escape back inside, Madame Bonheur appears silhouetted in the doorway.

"Laurence!" she cries softly. "What on earth are you doing out here?"

Keeping my back to her so she won't see the bump in my nightdress, I bend over my herb pots, pretending to tend to them. "I couldn't sleep, so I thought I'd come out for some fresh air."

"I see," she says dubiously.

"What are you doing here so early?"

"I couldn't sleep either, so I thought I'd get a head start on the day's baking. Shall we have a cup of tea?"

"That would be lovely. I'll just go in and get my cardigan, I'm feeling a little chilly."

"I'm not surprised," she replies, but to my dismay, instead of going back inside, I hear her stepping out into the yard. "Here . . ."

I have no choice but to turn around and pray that it's too dark for her to see. She's holding a baguette out to me. "Thank you." As I take the bread, I don't dare make eye contact with her.

"Right, I shall get the kettle on and . . ." She gasps. "Laurence, what is the meaning of this?"

"What?" I continue looking at the floor, just like I did when I was a child and she caught me with my hand in the sugar barrel.

"Your stomach. Why is it so . . . big?"

My mouth goes dry and my heart starts to pound. What can I say to her?

Madame Bonheur takes a step closer. My gaze remains glued to the floor. "Are you . . . are you pregnant?" she whispers.

Finally hearing someone ask the question brings a sudden feeling of release. I raise my gaze to meet hers and nod.

"Ooh la la!" Her mouth gapes open in shock. "But how? Who?"

"I can't tell you."

"Why on earth not?"

"He's no one you know. He's not from here."

She looks at me blankly for a moment, then begins to nod knowingly. "Is he one of your friends in Paris?"

"Yes!" I'm so grateful to have a story that won't get anyone killed, the word bursts from my mouth.

"I see. So is he going to marry you?"

"What? Oh—uh—no. He doesn't know yet."

"Why on earth not?"

"I haven't been able to see him."

She frowns at me.

"He had to go away for a while," I add, clutching desperately for some kind of feasible explanation.

"Not to Germany?"

Once again Madame Bonheur has unwittingly given me a cover story by referring to the new act implemented in February demanding that all French men born between 1920 and 1922 had to register to work in Germany.

"Yes, I'm afraid so." I hang my head and pray for forgiveness for my dishonesty. Hopefully God will understand that it's necessary to lie if you're doing it to keep someone safe.

"Oh you poor dear thing!" Madame Bonheur scoops me into an embrace and it feels so good to finally have shared my burden that my legs feel weak with relief. "Does anyone know?"

I shake my head.

"But you've seen a doctor?"

Again I shake my head. "I didn't want people talking."

"My God, I can't believe you've been going through this all on your own, and without your dear *maman* to guide you."

I bite my lip to stop myself from welling up. The prospect of becoming a mother has brought the loss of Maman back with a vengeance. I've tried pushing the painful thoughts from my mind but then she comes to me in my dreams and I wake up hollow with grief.

"Do not worry," she says firmly, "I shall be her replacement."

"Really?"

"Yes. You are no longer alone, do you understand?"

"Oh, thank you!" I hug her tightly.

She gives me a shy smile. "It is nothing. You are like a daughter to me, Laurence, it's the least I can do. Now go and get that cardigan and let's have a cup of tea and talk things through."

. . .

The relief I feel at telling Madame Bonheur about my predicament is short-lived as speaking about my situation out loud only
makes it more real—and more daunting. How on earth am I going
to take care of a baby? How am I going to *have* the baby? What
kind of life will it have, being born under the German occupation? It all feels so overwhelming.

"Don't be afraid," Madame Bonheur says, pouring me a second cup of tea. "You have us to support you now."

"Us?" I echo weakly.

"Yes, your friends. We shall be your family." She gives a wry
laugh. "After everything we've been through already, we *are* your
family."

My eyes swim with tears and she places her hand on mine.
Just at that moment, the baby starts kicking and I move her hand
to my stomach.

"Oh Laurence!" she exclaims, and now her eyes are shiny
with tears. "It is a miracle!"

"Really?" I look at her hopefully.

"Of course. It is a new life."

"But what about . . ." I break off, my fears once again circling
like cawing crows.

She looks at me questioningly.

"What about what it will be born into?"

"It will be born into love," she replies firmly. "And yes, it
might be hard at first, without the father here to support you. But,
God willing, this war will be over soon, and then you will all be
together."

I think of Wendell across the Channel in England. Could
I dare to dream that one day, all three of us might be together?
The first stanza from the poem "Dreams" by Langston Hughes
starts typing itself in my mind. I need to hold fast to this
dream, to get through the next few months, to get through the
rest of this awful war, to stop my life from becoming a broken-
winged bird.

"Thank you," I whisper, and I feel my baby—our baby—move inside of me, as if encouraging me.

Our next book club meeting is the following evening in The Book Dispensary. I'd asked the others to come to the store as I've been trying to avoid going out in public if at all possible due to the changes in my physique. Charlotte is the first to arrive and straight away I know something is different.

"Oh Laurence!" she exclaims, throwing her arms around me.

I instinctively pull back, but it's too late, she has me in a vise-like like grip.

"Madame Bonheur told me not to say anything until we're all here, but I can't help it, I have too many things I need to say, all dying to get out!"

"What about?" I ask, my heart thudding.

"About you—and the baby," she whispers, even though the store is closed and it's just the two of us.

"You know?"

She nods. "Why didn't you tell me you had a lover in Paris?" She clasps her hands together. "Oh, just saying those words sounds so romantic."

"I...uh...we hadn't been together all that long," I stammer. *It's not a lie,* I tell myself, trying to assuage my guilt at being deceitful to my closest friend.

"That only makes it all the more poignant." Charlotte sighs. "Madame Bonheur says that he's been sent to work in Germany under the Service du Travail Obligatoire."

I nod, unable to lie to her out loud.

"It is so unjust. Haven't those toads stolen enough from our country without stealing our young men too?"

Again I nod.

"But it will be OK. He will be OK. And, in the meantime,

we shall take care of you." Her words wrap themselves around me like a warm hug.

There's a knock on the door and I open it to find Odette standing there. She looks straight at my stomach. Clearly Madame Bonheur has told her too.

"Good evening," she says as she comes into the store. "How is everyone?"

Clearly Odette is able to contain herself rather more than Charlotte. But before I'm able to reply, Madame Bonheur knocks on the back door. As I hurry through to the kitchen to let her in, I hear Charlotte and Odette start talking in hushed tones.

"You told them!" I exclaim as I open the back door.

"Of course I did," Madame Bonheur replies brusquely before bustling into the kitchen. "How else are they going to help you if they know nothing?"

"Fair enough," I mutter to myself as I follow her back into the store.

"From now on, we are your family," Madame Bonheur says. She looks at the others. "Did you bring the things?"

"What things?" I ask, sitting in one of the armchairs.

Charlotte produces a jar of milk and a piece of cheese from her basket and Odette takes a slice of meat from her bag.

"But I can't take your food," I protest.

"Nonsense," Madame Bonheur replies. "I know you like to say that we need stories more than we need food, but for the time being, for you and the baby, this is no longer true."

As the others nod in agreement, it brings me to tears. "I'm sorry." I sniff. "I seem to be crying at everything these days."

"Of course you are," Madame Bonheur replies. "You're pregnant." She reaches into her own bag and pulls out a couple of summer dresses. "I thought you might be needing these," she says. "You are such a tiny thing that even pregnant you're still smaller than me, so they will definitely fit."

"I don't know what to say," I reply. "I don't know how to thank you."

"You don't need to thank us!" Charlotte exclaims. "All of this time you've been keeping us going with your book prescriptions—now it is our turn to take care of you—and the baby." She glances at my stomach.

I look at them all smiling down at me and I wonder how I ever felt alone before. Somehow, through the magic of books, I've created my very own family.

36

LAURENCE—APRIL 1943

The day after our book club meeting, Madame Bonheur escorts me to the town physician, a ferret-faced man with beady eyes and round glasses, named Roussel. Thankfully, Madame Bonheur insists on doing all of the talking.

"The father has been sent to work in Germany, which is why they haven't been able to marry," she informs him straight away and I nod along meekly, warming to my role as the tragically abandoned mother-to-be.

"I see," the doctor replies, peering over his glasses at me. Then he gets me to lie down and feels my stomach and listens to my heartbeat. "Do you have any idea when the child was conceived?"

An image of Wendell and I entangled in my bed flashes into my mind and my cheeks burn. "Yes, uh, September last year."

"I see. So it will be due in . . ." He pauses for a moment to make the calculation. "June." He frowns. "I would expect you to be larger by now, but all appears to be healthy."

Madame Bonheur gives a sarcastic snort. "Is it any wonder she's so small when the Germans are starving us half to death?"

"Yes, well, that is definitely a concern," he agrees.

I think of my baby starving inside of me and feel wracked with guilt.

Once again, Madame Bonheur seems to read my mind. "Don't worry, my dear, we will make sure you have enough to eat."

"Thank you." I nod weakly.

Once I've seen the doctor, I decide that the time is right to let the rest of the town know, so I give Madame Bonheur permission to tell Violeta the next time she comes to the boulangerie. The thought of the town busybody knowing my secret fills me with dread, but it is definitely the most effective way of letting everyone know. Or "like placing an advertisement on the town noticeboard," as Madame Bonheur put it. But before Violeta finds out, there's one other person I have to tell.

"Bless me, Father, for I have sinned," I say as I kneel inside the confessional.

"Laurence, how are you?" the Père replies warmly. It has been several weeks since I've seen him.

"I have something to tell you," I whisper, very thankful that we can't actually see each other.

"What is it?"

"I . . . I'm pregnant."

There's a long silence.

Please say something, I silently pray, my eyes tightly closed. *But please don't be angry with me.*

"Did someone force themselves on you? Was it one of the soldiers?" he asks in a tight, angry voice I've never heard him use before.

"No!" I exclaim, then lower my voice again. "No, it was consensual." I have the horrible feeling that in the Père's eyes this will somehow make things worse, make him think less of me.

"Was it the pilot?" he whispers.

My face burns. "N-no," I stammer, aware that, yet again, I am lying to a priest in a confessional. Surely there is going to be a *very* special place in hell for me. But I have to keep my story straight and I have to protect him. "It was a friend of mine in Paris."

There's another achingly long silence.

"And is this *friend* going to be taking responsibility?"

"He . . . he's been sent to Germany, under the Work Law."

"I see." Is it my imagination or does he sound as if he doesn't quite believe me?

"And when is this baby due?"

"In June."

"June," he gasps, "but that's only two months away."

"I know." I gulp at the thought.

"Does anyone else know?"

"Madame Bonheur and Charlotte and Odette. Oh and Dr. Roussel."

"That's good. And how about the network?" he whispers.

"They don't know—and I don't want them to."

"But—"

"Please."

"Surely you can't carry on working for them. It is too dangerous for the baby."

"Life under the Germans is too dangerous for the baby," I hiss.

"Are you sure?"

"Yes. Please, I have to do this for the sake of my child, and, don't worry, I'll be sensible. I won't take any foolish risks."

"Very well," he agrees, but the reluctance in his voice is obvious.

Père Rambert prays for me and the baby and then we emerge into the church. Sunshine is streaming in colored shafts through the stained-glass windows, creating mosaics of colored light on the stone floor.

The Père looks at me and shakes his head. "There is certainly never a dull moment with you around, Laurence." He places one of his strong hands on my shoulder. "If you need anything, anything at all . . ."

"Thank you."

When I go back outside, I'm so lost in my thoughts I don't notice Gerhard approaching.

"Good day, Laurence. How are you?" he asks, falling into step beside me.

"Very well thank you. And you?"

"I'm well. I wanted to let you know that I'll be leaving tomorrow."

"Leaving?" I stare at him.

"Yes. I'm being sent to Poland." He leans closer and lowers his voice. "And I have a gift for you, to say thank you for all the books you've provided me with these past couple of years."

Out of the corner of my vision, I see Violeta walking past, heading for the boulangerie.

"Oh, really, there's no need. I was just doing my job."

"No, I want to. I shall bring it by later."

"If you insist. Thank you."

I turn to unlock the door to the store and see Violeta in the queue outside the boulangerie frowning at me.

Let her think what she wants, I tell myself as I go inside. *In a few minutes she will know all about the baby and my fictional lover from Paris and she'll have enough gossip material for an entire month.*

For the rest of the morning, all is quiet in the store, but then, after lunch, the customers start arriving. Well, it's not strictly true to call them customers. None of them buy anything; they all seem more intent on looking at me than any of the books. Another thing they have in common is that they are all friends of Violeta. The woman herself leaves it until late afternoon before making an appearance. I'm just rearranging the children's section when the bell above the door heralds her entrance.

"Good day, Laurence," she says, eyeing me up and down, until her gaze comes to rest upon my stomach. "I understand you have some news."

"Do I?" I carry on shelving the books.

"Yes. Madame Bonheur has told me that you are with child."

"I am, yes."

"Oh dear. Oh dear, dear, dear."

My hackles rise. "I actually think that it's wonderful news."

She purses her lips. "Despite being conceived out of wedlock?"

"My baby's father and I were unable to get married due to the war."

"Yes, and who is this mysterious father anyway?"

"He lives in Paris."

"Really?"

She stares at me as if she can see straight through my lie.

"Yes." I look away, my face flushing.

"I find it strange that none of us have seen hide nor hair of this mystery man here in the Valley."

As if I'd introduce him to you! I think to myself, so indignant at her attitude that I almost forget that my Parisian lover is actually a work of fiction.

"And now, apparently, he is in Germany?" she continues.

"That's right." *Why did she say "apparently"? Why is she not believing the story?*

The bell above the door jingles, but any relief I feel vanishes the second I see Gerhard come in. He clicks his heels together in greeting to Violeta, then turns to me.

"I have your gift."

"Tsk!" Violeta tuts and glares at me. "Well, good luck is all I

can say. You're going to need it, bringing a baby into this world."
And with that she turns on her heel and leaves.

I go back to my desk and sit down, shaken.

"You . . . you're having a baby?" Gerhard stammers.

I nod.

"I didn't realize that . . ." He breaks off and his face turns a
little pink. "Congratulations." He smiles warmly.

"Thank you," I mutter. My encounter with Violeta has left
me feeling like a burst balloon.

"Here." He comes over to my desk and places a paper bag in
front of me. "I thought maybe you could use it." He nods at my
typewriter.

I look inside the bag and see a sheaf of paper about two inches
thick. "Thank you!" I gasp, unable to hide my gratitude.

He smiles again, but it seems tinged with sadness. "Do you
think . . ." He clears his throat. "Do you think that if we'd met
under other circumstances, we might have been friends?"

I want to answer no, to tell him that I could never be friends
with someone capable of being part of the Nazi regime and the
crimes they've committed. But then I think of the officers in
Steinbeck's novel and *The Silence of the Sea*. I think of Gerhard
being unable to shoot Abram and kissing the other soldier so tenderly, and my anger fades to sorrow. "I don't know," I reply.

"I would like to hope so. After all, we have kept each other's
secrets like true friends do."

"What do you mean?" My heart begins to pound.

His faces flushes and he looks away. "I know that you saw
me—that night in the forest."

"Oh—I . . ." I break off, fear coursing through me. If he knows
that I saw him, that means he saw me.

"Thank you for not telling anyone."

I nod, unable to think of what to say, my mind too busy
trying to catch up with this latest development. He didn't tell

anyone that he saw me in the forest in the middle of the night either. He kept my secret too.

" 'The truth is rarely pure and never simple,' " he says with a sad smile.

"Oscar Wilde?" I say, recognizing the quote.

He nods and extends his hand across the table to me. "*Adieu,* Laurence."

And suddenly it is as if I am inside the pages of the Vercors novel—with Gerhard the German officer and I the niece.

"*Adieu,* Gerhard," I reply softly, my eyes swimming with tears.

37

LAURENCE—MAY 1943

Over the next few days, as Violeta's tongue spreads the news of my pregnancy faster than a telegram, the enormity of what has happened hits me like a train. Now I no longer have to hide my secret from others, I'm unable to hide from it myself. In a month's time, there will be a brand new human in my life. A tiny, vulnerable human, completely dependent upon me. Although from the amount of kicking and wriggling going on inside me, I'm hopeful she will be a spirited child. I've become convinced that I'm pregnant with a girl. Every time I talk to my baby, I see a girl. And my hunch was confirmed by Madame Bonheur when she got me to lie down and dangled a ring on a piece of thread over my stomach—apparently a sure-fire way of identifying the sex of a baby. As soon as the ring started spinning in a circle, she shrieked, "Oh, Laurence, you are having a daughter!" Apparently, if the ring had moved from side to side it would have signaled a son. I'm not sure I believe in this hocus-pocus but it was nice to have my own instinct re-affirmed.

I'm picturing my daughter tucked up inside of me as I make my way across the square to visit Père Rambert. Now that I'm pregnant—and out of wedlock too—I have the perfect cover story for visiting him in search of spiritual guidance. Just as I reach the steps leading up to the church door, I hear the click of heels on cobbles rapidly approaching. I turn and see Gigi running toward me, in a beautifully fitted black dress, looking red-faced and flustered.

"Is it true?" she demands as soon as she reaches me. I assume she must be talking about the baby and I'm about to say yes, when she continues. "Is it true that you're pregnant and Gerhard is the father?"

"What?" I stare at her, my pulse quickening.

"Is it?" she says again, her face etched with fury.

"Of course not."

She looks down at my stomach, now clearly protruding beneath one of Madame Bonheur's old dresses.

"I mean to say, I am pregnant, but he is most definitely not the father."

"I don't believe you," she spits.

My shock starts turning to anger. "Why would you think I would have a child with him? Why would you think I'd let a Nazi anywhere near me?"

She purses her perfectly painted lips. "I've seen you together, having your cozy chats about books."

"I talk about books with half the town. I own a bookstore for goodness' sake!"

"Why has he been sent away then?" She stares at me triumphantly, as if she's just revealed her winning card.

"I have no idea."

"Liar!" she shrieks and I become aware of people passing by slowing to stare at us. "I'm not the only person to have noticed it, you know."

"And I bet I can guess who the other person is." I think of Violeta spreading her poisonous theory to Gigi and Gigi lapping it up eagerly and my hands tighten into fists.

The rumble of an engine breaks our silence and a large

German truck trundles into the square and parks outside the town hall. I watch, fear rising, as soldiers start jumping down from the back.

"Who is the father then?" Gigi continues, clearly unaffected by the presence of the soldiers. The fact that she can remain so cool in the face of their oppression makes me furious.

"It is none of your business," I spit back. "But I can assure you, you're the only one here who would willingly lie down with the enemy."

"How dare you!" She raises her hand, as if about to slap me.

Every one of my muscles tenses, as if my body has turned into a protective suit of armor around my baby. "You hit me and you'll be sorry," I hiss.

I see a flicker of shock and possibly even fear in her eyes. She lowers her hand. "I wouldn't waste my energy."

I take a step closer to her. "And if I find out you've been spreading false rumors about me, you'll be even sorrier."

She steps back. "I wouldn't waste my breath."

As Gigi turns and marches over to the café, the soldiers from the truck swarm like vermin through the square, calling to each other in German. I watch as they hammer on the doors of some of the houses, and as the doors open, they barge inside. A chill runs down my spine as I hear the word "*Juif*" being yelled. Old Mr. Bernstein, who had been the town jeweler until the statute was introduced forbidding him to trade, is jostled from his rooms above his shuttered store and out into the square, holding a small suitcase. The soldiers march him over to the truck and shove him onto the back.

I want to run over, grab one of their guns, demand they let him go, but how can I? What chance would I have against so many? I look around the square, desperate for someone who might try to stop this atrocity. But those who are looking from the queues outside the butcher's and the boulangerie are expressionless and moving back against the walls, as if wanting to disappear in case the soldiers might grab them too. Then I see a sight that makes me sick to my stomach. Mordecai and his mother are being bundled from their house and he's crying. As they're frogmarched to the truck, I hurry over.

"Mordecai," I call.

"They won't let me take Blue," he sobs.

"His toy rabbit," his mother explains, her face crumpled with distress. "He still needs it to sleep, but they didn't give us time to find it."

The soldiers gesture at her to get on the lorry, then hoist Mordecai up behind her.

I gulp down my fear and force myself to smile at the boy. "I have a gift for you," I say to him. "And I'm sure it will help you to fall asleep. I'll go and get it." My legs feel like jelly, but somehow I manage to run to the store and I open the drawer of my desk and take out the copy of *Grimms' Fairy Tales*. Clutching the book to my chest, I race back to the truck. More people have been loaded onto the back now, like cattle, all of them wearing the vile yellow stars marked *JUIF*. I see Mordecai and his mother sitting on one side of the truck, their eyes wide with fear. "Here," I say, holding the book out to him.

One of the soldiers barks something at me in German and gestures at me to move away.

"Please, it's only a book," I say. *You uncaring bastard!* I add silently.

Thankfully, at that moment, there's some kind of fracas on the other side of the square and the soldier runs over to deal with it.

"This is the book I read to you, do you remember?" I say to Mordecai. "The one with Little Red Riding Hood."

He smiles weakly as he takes the book from me.

"Do you remember how you worked out the real ending to the story?"

He nods.

"You must think of it any time you feel afraid, do you hear?" It takes everything I've got to maintain my calm and smiling exterior. "And perhaps you could tell the story to your mother too?"

"I will." He nods proudly, before glancing around the truck. "Where are we going?"

"I don't know." The last time I saw Pierre he told me that the Nazis had been sending Jewish people out of France to some kind of internment camps. I feel a lump forming in my throat, but I gulp it down. "Do you remember what I told you about the North Star?"

He nods.

"You have to trust that it will help you find your way back home."

"OK." He nods again, then snuggles into his mother and opens his book.

"Thank you," she mouths to me, over the top of his head.

"*Bon courage,*" I whisper back.

As I turn and trudge away, I feel my own child move inside me. I let myself back into the store and I collapse down onto one of the armchairs and begin to wail.

Over the next couple of days, Madame Bonheur engages in a medal-worthy battle of the gossips, countering Violeta's poisonous story that Gerhard might be the father of my baby, with the equally fictitious account that he is actually a Parisian bookseller, who has been sent against his will to work in Germany. Judging by the warm reception I get from most of my fellow townsfolk, Madame Bonheur has emerged the victor. Not that I care all that much. After seeing Mordecai and his mother and the other Jewish residents of the town carted off like cattle to God knows where, a numbness has descended upon me, broken only by waves of fear at what might become of my own child being born into such a world.

As before, I lose myself in imaginary stories about Wendell for comfort. But this time, instead of us fighting the Germans in our planes, I picture him swooping down to save me and our child and whisking us off to the relative safety of Britain and I replay his parting words to me that night in the clearing over and over in my head. *And when this is all over, I'm coming to get you. Both of you.*

Then, one afternoon in late May, just as I'm contemplating closing the store early, the bell jangles and a man walks in. He's wearing a suit and large round wire glasses, giving him the appearance of a wise owl.

"Good day," he greets me briskly. "I've come to return this book." He places a copy of *The Stranger* by Albert Camus in front of me.

"Oh. OK." In spite of the fact that I've never seen this man before, let alone sold him a copy of this book, I can't help feeling a frisson of delight. Camus' latest novel miraculously wasn't banned by the Nazis when it came out last year, but due to the paper shortage, only a few thousand copies were printed. It's as if he has placed a gold bar in front of me.

"There is an air-drop planned for tonight," the man whispers. "Usual place. Come alone. Look inside." He taps the cover of the book, but before I can say anything, he turns and leaves.

I flick through the book, my heart pounding, until finally I find a sentence about a woman wearing a pair of the protagonist's pajamas with the sleeves rolled up that has been faintly underlined. My skin tingles. It's been a while since I've received a message from the network and my gloom lifts. I briefly contemplate whether traipsing through the forest while eight months pregnant is altogether wise, but I push aside my doubts. After everything that has happened lately, my desire to help France win liberty is stronger than ever, and besides, going to collect a drop-off will provide some kind of link with Wendell again, however tenuous, as there's always the off-chance he might be flying the plane.

That night, I take my radio from its hiding place and place it on the bed. The baby is really lively tonight, perhaps sensing my nervous excitement, and I shift around trying to get comfortable, while I wait for the messages. At first, I think that it's going to be a no-go as message after message is read and none of them relate to the underlined sentence in *The Stranger*, but just as I'm about to give up hope, I hear the clipped voice of the announcer saying, "Margaret is wearing Albert's pajamas with the sleeves rolled up." It's on!

Making my way to the clearing feels more treacherous than ever now that I'm pregnant. The stubbly ground of the forest, which has never troubled me before, now seems full of hazards just waiting to trip me. Thankfully, by walking at a snail's pace, I make it to my destination in one piece. I position myself behind the same tree Wendell and I waited behind the night he was rescued and I think of the way he held me and told me that he loved me. But before I can lose myself in my reverie, I hear a twig crack behind me and have to bite my tongue to stop from yelping. The baby, who had been sleeping, jolts awake and gives me a sharp kick in the ribs. I place my hand on my stomach to try to calm us both.

"Hello?" a man's voice whispers.

I slowly turn and see a stranger standing there. He's tall and thin with raggedy clothes and a shock of dark hair sticking out from under his cap.

"Jeanne?" he asks.

"Yes. Who are you?"

"I'm David. I've been sent to help with the collection."

"I see."

"Brutus sent me."

Hearing Pierre's code name, I relax a little and I hear the hum of a plane approaching.

David takes a bicycle light from his jacket pocket and we both stand and wait until the plane appears over the trees. It's larger than the kind Wendell was in and it's flying at a higher altitude. A light on the plane blinks the Morse code signal and David uses his flashlight to signal back. The plane circles, then there's a soft whooshing sound and I see a parachute drifting down a little short of the clearing.

"Damn it," David curses quietly. "It has come down in the trees."

"Let's go and find it," I whisper back.

It's hard for me to keep up with David's long stride, but somehow I manage, silently apologizing to my baby for such a bumpy ride. We find the parachute draped in a tree, a wooden crate dangling from its strings. Thankfully, David starts shinnying his way up the trunk without even asking for my assistance. I watch, holding my breath, as slowly but surely, he untangles the chute and lowers the box to the ground.

"We are to bury the box," he tells me, as he jumps back down. It's only at this point that he notices I'm pregnant. "Oh," he says, looking pointedly at my bump.

"What?" I ask defiantly.

"Nothing . . . I . . . uh, how about you fold this." He hands me the voluminous chute. "And I'll get my spade."

"Sure." I fold the silky material smaller and smaller. In a couple of minutes, David returns with a shovel and starts digging a hole by the roots of a pine tree. Once I've finished, I look at the box, wondering what's inside. I think of Steinbeck's *The Moon is Down*, and the dynamite being dropped to the occupied people. Could it be that the British and Americans have sent us some more explosives? The thought makes me both apprehensive and excited.

Finally, David has dug a hole big enough to hide the box

and the parachute and I help him refill the top with earth and cover it with leaves and twigs. Then he takes a switchblade from his pocket and carves a tiny etching into the trunk of the tree.

"So that we'll be able to find it," he explains.

As I stand up, I feel a sharp twinge in my side like a stitch.

"We must go," David says. He holds his hand out to shake mine. "Thank you, Jeanne." He looks again at my bump. "*Bon courage.*"

"And to you," I mutter, the pain in my side becoming more intense.

David disappears off into the forest, as if swallowed by the trees, and I fight the urge to call after him, asking him not to leave. I lean on a tree and take a breath and feel something inside of me burst like a balloon. A warm liquid starts gushing down the inside of my legs.

38

JEANNE—1993

Charlotte arrived at the hotel at ten o'clock, smartly dressed in a lilac dress and matching silk scarf. She was accompanied by a woman who appeared to be around sixty, wearing a bright turquoise kaftan, gold gladiator-style sandals and a string of wooden beads.

"Hi, I'm Claudette," the woman said, smiling at Jeanne and Wendell. "Charlotte invited me to come with her today, to translate. I knew Laurence when I was a little girl."

"You did?" Jeanne stared at her hopefully. Perhaps she would be able to help with some of the jigsaw pieces still missing. After Wendell had opened up to her over breakfast, the story of her parents' relationship had become a whole lot clearer, and the love they'd shared was deeply moving. But the events surrounding Laurence's death still remained a mystery.

Charlotte said something in French.

"She wants to know if you're ready to go into the store," Claudette translated.

"Absolutely." Jeanne and Wendell exchanged glances. She really hoped he wouldn't make it obvious that they'd already been inside.

The four of them made their way across the square and Charlotte unlocked the padlock on the boarding over the door. Wendell helped her pull the board back, revealing the actual door of the store, a faded sign saying *FERME* still hanging in the middle. There was something so sad about this sight, Jeanne needed to take a breath. She felt Wendell gripping her elbow and she wasn't sure if he was giving support or needing it. Both, she guessed.

As they opened the door and let the light in, dust motes danced in the air. Jeanne glanced to her right and saw a mannequin, the kind you'd get in a clothes store, lying on its side in a bay window next to an old chair. Charlotte caught her gaze and started talking.

"She says that your *maman* used to have a lot of fun with that mannequin," Claudette explained. "She'd always have it reading books in the window." She laughed. "I remember it too, as a child. One day, when she held a story time for us kids, she arranged an assortment of toys around the mannequin, to look as if they too were being told a story."

Hearing these details about Laurence made Jeanne feel warm inside. It was good to know that her mom was fun and kind as well as brave. She went further into the store and looked around at the empty shelves. "Do you know what happened to the books?"

Claudette asked Charlotte and Charlotte's face fell.

"The Germans burned them," Claudette replied.

Jeanne felt a stab of anger and looked at the smashed-up typewriter on the desk. No doubt the Germans had been responsible for that too.

She went and sat on the chair behind the desk and noticed three drawers on the side. She pulled them open one by one. The only thing left inside was a pile of small sheets of paper. She took one of them out and ran her fingers over it, imagining her mom's fingers touching it all those years ago. Charlotte said something and clasped her hands to her chest.

"She says you look just like Laurence sitting there," Claudette translated. "Apparently she used to write prescriptions for her customers on that paper—things for them to read to make them feel better. When Charlotte's husband was killed in the war, she prescribed her a poem that really helped her."

Jeanne heard Charlotte say the words "Farewell" and "Anne Brontë." It sounded familiar, but she couldn't think why. Before she could give it any more thought, she noticed a figure standing outside the store, staring in. It was the strange old woman from yesterday, the one who'd left the flowers. Her mouth was gaping open, as if in shock, and her bright red lipstick was smeared all over her chin. Charlotte noticed her too and went over to the door and muttered something in French. The woman hurried off across the square, careering slightly, as if she was drunk.

"Who is that?" Jeanne asked Claudette. "I saw her leaving flowers outside the store yesterday. Did she know my mom?"

Claudette translated and, to Jeanne's surprise, Charlotte's face creased into a frown and she began speaking angrily.

"Apparently she and your mother were childhood friends—but then the war happened."

"What does that mean?" Jeanne looked at Wendell and he shrugged.

"Not everyone in town—or in France for that matter—was against the Germans," Claudette explained. "Some collaborated."

Charlotte muttered something else.

Claudette sighed. "Some, like this woman, were traitors. They had affairs with German soldiers. It meant that they had a much easier time of it during the war, but after . . ." She shuddered.

"What happened to them?" Jeanne asked.

"They were accused of *collaboration horizontale,*" Claudette replied.

"Horizontal collaboration," Jeanne echoed. She didn't need to speak French to figure out what that meant.

"Even though I was just a young girl, I'll never forget what they did to her—and others like her," Claudette continued.

Jeanne looked at her questioningly.

"Their heads were shaved and they were stripped of their clothes and made to parade through the town half naked. It's hard to imagine now, but she was a successful actress before the war, and such a beauty. But she never recovered."

Jeanne stared out after the woman as she shuffled her way across the square. She knew she ought to feel contempt for someone who had slept with a Nazi, but the woman cut such a pathetic figure, it was impossible to feel anything but pity. And surely the fact that she left flowers outside her mom's shop meant she felt genuine remorse for what she'd done. If only Laurence had lived to see it.

39

LAURENCE—MAY 1943

All I can think, as I slowly stumble my way back through the forest, is that I mustn't let my baby die, I have to get us both to safety. I don't even care if I'm caught out after curfew by the Germans. Surely they'd never suspect a pregnant woman in labor of doing anything clandestine. I could tell them that I'd been feeling some discomfort from the baby and decided to try to walk off the pain. The worst they could accuse me of is stupidity. After the initial sharp twinge, the stitch-like pains seem to be coming every fifteen minutes. Every time one strikes, I lean on a tree and breathe slowly and deeply until it passes, then I hurry on my way, taking advantage of the break.

"You are going to be all right," I whisper to my baby, but also to reassure myself. She isn't supposed to be born for another month yet. Will she be all right, arriving so early? I scan the trees, longing to see the white deer, to have some kind of lucky omen to cling to. But to no avail. "We'll soon be home," I whisper to my bump. But once I'm home what should I do? I hear the first tentative cheeps from the birds beginning to wake. "This is good," I mutter out loud. "Madame Bonheur will soon be at the boulangerie. Oh, my darling baby, you will love Madame Bonheur," I continue to chatter, almost giddy now with anxiety.

After what feels like an eternity, I arrive back in town and this time I risk going along the main road to save time. As I reach the square, I see that the sky to the east has lightened from black to dark blue. *Please be there, Madame Bonheur!* Using the walls of the shops to support me, I make my way to my store, but rather than go inside, I continue to the boulangerie next door. The blackout blinds are drawn, but I try to peer through a crack for a tell-tale chink of light. I knock on the door, but there's no answer. Another contraction grips me like a vise. I knock again and again, but there's no response.

With panic rising inside of me, I go back to my store and try to unlock the door. My hand is trembling so much, it takes three attempts. Finally I make it inside and stagger through to the kitchen and open the back door. The back door of the boulangerie is shut and locked. I hammer on it anyway, then I go back into the kitchen, leaving the back door open, and sit on one of the chairs. Another contraction grips me and I close my eyes tight and breathe my way through the pain. "Don't worry, little one, we're going to be OK," I squeak, trying to push down my growing panic.

Finally, I hear the back door of the boulangerie creak open.

"Madame Bonheur," I yell with a force I didn't know I possessed.

"Laurence?" The sound of her voice in that moment is sweeter to my ears than any dawn chorus.

"Come quick," I gasp.

She appears in the doorway and takes one look at me and flings her hands in the air. "My God, is she coming?"

I nod.

"Right, I need blankets, towels and water," she says, suddenly snapping into a vision of calm authority.

"Upstairs," I gasp.

"Are you able to come up?" she asks.

"I'll try," I reply. "My contractions are coming fast now though."

"Here." She offers me her arm and I link mine through it. Feeling the warmth of her body next to mine instantly calms me, and slowly but surely we make our way upstairs.

Madame Bonheur fetches towels from the bathroom and lays one of them on the bed. Then she gestures at me to lie on top of it, propping some pillows behind me.

"I'll just get some water," she says.

As I listen to her drawing water in the bathroom, another contraction comes over me and this time I have the strongest sensation to push.

"I—I think it's ready to come out," I gasp, trying to wriggle free from my underwear.

"Don't push, not yet," Madame Bonheur says, hurrying back into the room. Then she crouches before me at the end of the bed. Any embarrassment I might have felt at this is soon dispelled by another overwhelming urge to push.

"The head is crowning!" Madame Bonheur cries.

"What does that mean?" I shriek, alarmed that something might be wrong.

"It means that it's almost time, but you must wait."

"But I want to push," I cry. No wonder my hero Saint Jeanne stayed a maid. I too would have preferred to face the might of the English army over this.

"Just wait for another contraction," she replies firmly.

"How do you know what I should or shouldn't do? You're not a midwife. You're not even a mother!" Regrettably, the fear and pain I'm in seems to have stripped me of all decorum.

"No, but I saw my mother give birth to both my sisters, and trust me, it is an experience I will never forget," she replies, taking hold of my hand. "Squeeze on my hand if it helps."

I squeeze tightly as another contraction courses through me.

Madame Bonheur takes a look at the baby, then soaks one of the towels in the water and folds it into a wad. "Now you may push," she says, putting the wet towel between my legs. The cool of the water instantly soothes the searing pain. I push with all my might, summoning a strength that feels beyond human. I feel the baby's head slip out of me and instantly the pain eases.

"One more push," Madame Bonheur says.

I push again and then, finally, it's over. I close my eyes, gasping for breath, too stunned from what's just happened to say or do anything. Then I hear a tiny cry, like a kitten mewling.

"My baby!" I gasp, opening my eyes. I see Madame Bonheur dab at something with a towel, then she holds my baby aloft.

"Your beautiful daughter," she declares with a beaming smile. "I knew it! The ring never lies."

"Is she all right? She's so early. She's so tiny," I gasp.

"She's perfect." Madame Bonheur carefully places the baby on top of me, her tiny head resting on my chest and covers us both with a blanket.

I look down at my daughter's face, her exquisite button-like nose, her rosy cheeks and her damp fair hair. "She has hair just like her father's," I whisper. And I think back to that night eight months ago, when Wendell held me in this very same bed. When we made love so powerfully, I felt the earth beneath us move. The thought that such a beautiful moment should have led to this—this tiny, perfect human being—is the most magical feeling. Even in the midst of so much horror and fear, we were able to create something wonderful.

"What will you call her?" Madame Bonheur asks, stroking my hair.

I look up at her and smile. "Her name is Jeanne."

40

JEANNE—1993

As Jeanne made her way across the square, a huge full moon shone down, frosting the rooftops in a silvery light. Earlier that evening when she and Wendell had been having dinner on the hotel terrace, he'd looked up at the sky and said, "It's a bomber's moon tonight." When she asked what he meant, he explained that the full moons had been the best time for pilots as it helped them with visibility during the blackouts. Once again, Jeanne had been struck by the contrast between who she'd always imagined her Pops to be and who he really was. Over the years, she'd become so frustrated by the way he'd acquiesce to Lorilee's every wish. She'd seen him as too compliant, weak almost. How wrong she'd been. Wendell had been brave enough to fly right into the heart of enemy territory, risking capture and death at the hands of the Nazis. He'd had a passionate love affair with a member of the French Resistance, which he'd never truly recovered from. Laurence might have died, but Wendell's love for her hadn't, that was now apparent. No wonder Lorilee had been so cold with Jeanne; she'd been a constant reminder that if Laurence hadn't died, Lorilee and

Wendell would never have been together. As Jeanne let herself into the store, she actually found herself feeling sorry for Lorilee, and this in turn helped soften the pain and frustration that had been gnawing away at her all these years.

She took out the flashlight she'd borrowed from the hotel and turned it on. When she and Wendell had retired to their rooms for the night, she'd been too full of nervous energy to sleep and she'd felt the store calling to her, the same way she'd felt her mother calling to her in her dream the night before.

She made her way up the steep narrow steps and into the bedroom. As she shone the light around, she imagined her parents hiding in that very same room. How must they have felt, with the German soldiers just outside? She looked at the old dresser in the corner and she pictured Laurence all those years ago, gazing into the dusty mirror.

Earlier that day, Charlotte had told her, via Claudette, that she'd been born in this room. As she gazed at the bed frame, a shiver ran up her spine. This was where she'd drawn her very first breath. A tear spilled from her eye and trickled down her cheek. After a lifetime of not really feeling like she belonged, finally, in a musty room in France, she felt a sense of rootedness, of coming home. It was the strangest thing.

She took a last look around the room, then went back downstairs. Not wanting to leave yet, she sat in one of the old armchairs by the fireplace, trying to ignore the smell of damp emanating from the fabric. She took the two copies of *For Whom the Bell Tolls* from her purse, opened the French edition and shone the light on the yellowing pages. As she began leafing through, she noticed some sections had been highlighted in pencil and her pulse quickened. Laurence must have underlined these sentences, but why?

She opened the American edition and turned to the same chapter and started counting the paragraphs to try to identify the underlined section. It was from a scene where the Robert Jordan character and Maria make love and he talks about the earth moving out from under them. Why would her mom have underlined it? Was it because it reminded her of Wendell? Even though it was slightly uncomfortable to think of her parents in that way, it also made Jeanne feel warm inside, thinking that she might have been the product of such an intense love.

She leafed through more pages until she came to another underlined section. After a bit of detective work, she figured out it was the part where Jordan realizes that he probably won't have a lifetime with Maria because of the war so he ought to make up with intensity what they were going to lose in terms of time. As Jeanne read the words, she felt more tears forming. Had Laurence highlighted this section because this was how she felt about Wendell? Had she known deep down that they wouldn't have a lifetime together? The thought sent a chill right through her.

She kept on flicking through the pages until she found another underlined section near the end, this one underlined in ink rather than pencil. Jeanne read the American edition. It was a scene where Robert Jordan says goodbye to Maria and urges her to go on without him, telling her that wherever she goes, he will be with her in spirit. Had Laurence highlighted this because she was thinking of Wendell, and possibly even Jeanne? Had she known she was going to die? Had she taken solace in the notion that she could live on in Wendell and Jeanne?

The questions burning away at Jeanne became unbearable. She had to get to the bottom of how her mom had died and why the Nazis had wanted to kill Jeanne when she was just a baby. She leafed through the final pages of the book. There were no more highlighted sections, but, tucked inside the back cover, she found a folded piece of paper. She carefully unfolded it and shone the light on the faded typing. It was a letter, addressed to Wendell, and written in English. Jeanne looked at the bottom of the page and her heart rate quickened. It was from Laurence. It was written by her mother. Hands trembling, she began to read.

41

LAURENCE—AUGUST 1943

The next two months are the happiest of my life. Jeanne's birth has provided me and my fellow book club members with the tiniest beacon of hope. Charlotte is particularly enamored of her and comes to visit us as often as possible, always bringing gifts of milk and cheese, to help with my own milk production. One hot summer's day, as we sit in the relative cool of my kitchen, Charlotte nestles Jeanne to her and kisses her thatch of blonde hair.

"Is Jeanne's father . . . does he have fair hair?" she asks shyly.

I nod. At the thought of Wendell, I'm struck by a longing so strong it hurts. I would give anything to be able to see him again, to be able to show him his daughter.

"What's he like?" Charlotte asks. "You never talk about him. I hope it isn't too painful. I know you must be so worried about him being a virtual prisoner in Germany."

"He's wonderful," I reply. "Kind and funny—and so brave."

"How so?" she asks.

I bite my lip, aware that I've said too much. "He just is."

She nods and looks back at Jeanne. "Well, what a beautiful gift he will have waiting for him once he comes back home.

You'd just better not desert me and move to Paris," she adds jokily.

If only she knew.

I think back to the last time I saw Wendell, that night in the clearing and how he told me that as soon as the war was over he'd be coming to get me and our baby. An image forms in my mind of Wendell, Jeanne and I standing in front of an American-style house, complete with porch and white picket fence. The image is too bittersweet to bear.

One day at the beginning of August, I decide to write each of my book club members a poetry prescription to say thank you for all the help they've given me with the baby. I leave Jeanne asleep in the cool of the kitchen in the portable crib Odette made from an old olive crate lined with blankets and sit down at my desk. As I feed some paper into the typewriter for the first time since giving birth, a wave of contentment washes through me. I'd been so anxious about Jeanne's arrival, so fearful that I wouldn't know how to be a mother, but never have I felt the sentiment of my favorite quote from Jeanne of Arc as strongly as when I look at my daughter. It turns out that I was born for motherhood and rather than making me afraid, the love I feel for Jeanne is so fierce it makes me feel like a lioness. If only Wendell was with us to share in this love.

I hear the voice of Langston Hughes drifting up from his hiding place beneath the floorboard, urging me to hold fast to my dreams. One day, we will all be together. One day France will be free. In order to strengthen my faith in this outcome, I decide to write to Wendell about his daughter before typing up my poetry prescriptions. Even though I have no way of sending the letter to him, I'm hoping it will help us feel connected in some way. The words flow out of me, the clickety-clack of the typewriter filling the store like the sweetest music.

My dear Wendell,

I'm not exactly sure why I'm writing this. I mean, I have no way of mailing it to you! I'm just so full to the brim with love and words and excitement and I have to find an outlet. You and I have a daughter! She is the most beautiful, joyful baby and now she is here my commitment to free France is even greater than before. Every time I look at her, I think of you and our love and it emboldens me to keep fighting.

I have named her Jeanne after my hero, Jeanne of Arc and she has your fair hair and blue eyes. Having to explain my mystery pregnancy was a challenge, but I managed to come up with a convincing cover story. Oh how I long for the day when we're free to speak the truth again, free to read the truth again.

I miss you so much, but every time I read *For Whom the Bell Tolls*, I think of you and our love. I just pray that, unlike Robert and Maria, we get our seventy years together. I dream of the day the three of us are together, the day you come to get us, just as you promised that night in the clearing. Clinging to this dream gets me through each day.

All of my love,

Laurence

Once I've finished, I fold the letter, lock the door and put it in my hiding place beneath the floorboard, inside my copy of

For Whom the Bell Tolls. Even though I've no way of getting it to Wendell, just the act of speaking to him on paper has made me feel a lot better. And who knows, maybe one day when we're free I'll be able to show it to him.

I'm just about to type out my first prescription when the bell above the door rings. I glance up and see a tall, thin man with his hat pulled down and jacket collar pulled up.

"Good day," he says softly, glancing around the store anxiously, as if checking for other people. Even though I don't recognize him, there's something strangely familiar about his voice. For a moment I'm unable to make the connection, then I leap to my feet.

"Michel! Is that you?" I gasp. There's no sign of his auburn hair protruding from beneath his hat. There's no sign of his trademark bow tie either; instead he's wearing a black turtleneck.

He nods and smiles. "Although my name is now Fulbert." He gives a weary sigh. "If only I could have been renamed Oscar or Gustave after one of my literary heroes."

"Oh Michel!" I hurry over to him and touch his arm just to make sure I'm not dreaming. "Where have you been? I was so worried when Pierre said you had to go away."

"A traitorous rat wrote a letter denouncing me to the Nazis."

"No!"

"Thankfully, I received a tip-off from a police officer I went to school with. He warned me that they were about to come and arrest me."

I shake my head in disgust at the thought of the French police doing the Nazis' dirty work.

"I was able to escape to some comrades living in a village east of Paris, where I was given my new identity." He takes off his hat to reveal his shorn head.

"Baldness suits you," I lie, trying to lift his spirits.

"No it does not. It makes me look like a talking egg." He gives another sigh, then his expression lifts as he looks around. "So, finally I get to see your store."

"What do you think?" I ask, hoping desperately that he will like it.

"I love it." He walks over to the hearth and has a good look around. "It's everything a bookstore should be. Cozy, inviting and full to the brim with books."

"Well, it wouldn't exist if it hadn't been for your inspiration and encouragement."

His face breaks into a smile and for a fleeting moment it's as if the old carefree Michel is standing in front of me. "Ah, that fills my weary heart with joy. Thank you." He randomly pulls a book from the shelf. "Just in case someone comes in, you can pretend you are helping me," he explains.

"Of course. So why are you here?" I keep an eye on the door.

"Pierre asked me to come. We have another book for you to read."

Instantly, my skin tingles. "A Resistance book?"

"Yes, another from Les Editions de Minuit." He pulls a thin pamphlet-style book from a hole in the lining of his jacket as if performing some kind of magic trick. He then places the slim volume inside the book he's holding and gestures at me to come and look.

"*The Black Notebook*," I whisper, reading the title.

"Yes, it is an essay from a very well-known French writer."

I look at the author's name at the top of the creamy cover. "Forez?"

"That is his *nom de Resistance*. He has had to go into hiding after writing this. You will see why once you've read it. We would like you to distribute copies around the town."

"Of course."

"Here." He shuts the book with the copy of *The Black Notebook* still tucked inside and hands it to me. "Hopefully we will be getting some more copies to you soon. They're having to be printed at great risk and in secret on mimeographs in people's cellars, and what with the Germans implementing more travel restrictions, distribution is proving difficult."

"I understand." I glance at my typewriter, an idea forming in my mind. "Perhaps I could create some leaflets containing passages from the book."

"That's an excellent idea." He puts his hat back on and pulls up his collar. "Right, I'd better go. I got a lift here in the back of dairy truck. The driver will be waiting for me."

I feel a tug of sorrow that he should have to leave so soon. Oh for the days when we could chat about books for hours on end without a care in the world. It feels like another lifetime ago. *All the more reason for you to do anything you can to defeat the Germans,* a voice inside of me retorts.

I give Michel a quick hug and I'm comforted to catch a waft of his familiar aroma of pipe smoke.

"*Bon courage,*" we whisper to each other at exactly the same time and we both laugh.

"Until we are reunited on the Left Bank," he declares.

"I dream of that day constantly," I reply.

"Me too."

We look at each other for a moment as if trying to prolong our farewell and then he turns to go. As he walks out of the door, I have a sudden and unexpected memory of the last time Luc walked through that very same door and a shiver runs up my spine.

It isn't the last time I will see him, I tell myself, but it feels as if a cloud has passed over the sun. It's only when I hear Jeanne begin to whimper in the kitchen that it dawns on me that I didn't even tell Michel that I now have a daughter. I lock the door, hide the book and hurry through to the kitchen.

. . .

That night, I read *The Black Notebook* tucked up in bed with Jeanne feeding at my breast. The essay is a stinging attack on Pétain and all the French people who decided to side with our enemy. The author—the mysterious Forez—urges the reader not to see war as an opportunity to escape responsibility, or even worse, make a pact with the enemy, but to keep resisting until we are victorious. I drink in the words as eagerly as Jeanne drinks my milk and I recall Steinbeck's rallying cry in *The Moon is Down*: that free men might lose a battle, but they will always win a war.

Jeanne finishes feeding and gives a contented burp. I laugh and plant a kiss on top of her head, and a memory comes back to me, of her father planting a kiss on my head in this very same bed. *"Was the German officer able to do this to the niece?"* His words echo around the room.

"I can't wait for you to meet your papa," I whisper as I cradle Jeanne to me. "And I won't rest until I've helped make that happen."

The next day, I keep the blinds down and the store shut and I type leaflet after leaflet while Jeanne gurgles happily on a blanket on the floor beside me. I keep going until my typewriter ribbon has run out of ink. It's only then that the enormity of the next stage of my plan hits me. Now I will have to deliver the leaflets. This immediately poses the question, what will I do with the baby? I can hardly ask anyone else to mind her in the middle of the night, and there's no way I'm going to leave her on her own.

"What shall I do, darling girl?" I ask, kneeling down and waving the Nénette doll in front of her.

She kicks her legs in the air and lets out a giggle.

"Did you just laugh?" I stare at her in amazement, willing her to do it again. "What shall I do, darling girl?" I say in a silly high-pitched voice, wiggling the doll from side to side. This time her laugh is so hearty, it makes me chuckle too. "Oh, Jeanne, you laughed!" My joy is soured slightly by the thought that it's another milestone her father hasn't been able to see.

I pick her up and hug her to me, inhaling the sweet scent of her warm scalp. And then I have an idea that simultaneously fills me with excitement and fear. What if I took her with me? I could hide the leaflets under the mattress in her carriage. And if I got caught out after curfew, I could tell the soldiers that she wouldn't stop crying and I was driven to take her for a walk in my desperation to get her to settle. Surely they wouldn't suspect a desperate mother? I'm not sure if my idea is genius or ridiculous, so I decide to think on it awhile.

"Do you want to go and see your grandpa?" I ask, holding her up. Jeanne gurgles merrily in response. Père Rambert has become Jeanne's honorary grandpa, in my mind at least. Although, on our frequent visits, he seems as enamored of her as she does of him.

Outside, the sky has clouded over, bringing with it a sticky humidity. Jeanne is only wearing her nappy and a loose cotton dress that Odette made her from an old stripy pillow case, but I as I hold her, I can feel that her back is sticky with sweat.

"Don't worry, my sweet," I murmur, "it will be nice and cool in the church."

Just as I'm crossing the square, I see Violeta heading my way. She gives me one of her hawk-like stares, then looks at Jeanne and almost imperceptibly shakes her head. It's too hot to be bothered by her stupidity, so I ignore her and hurry on my way.

I find Père Rambert knelt in prayer at the front of the church, eyes closed and clutching his rosary beads. I try not to disturb him, but Jeanne lets out a delighted shriek.

"Aha!" The Père opens his eyes and his smile chases the stress from his face. "How's my favorite girl?"

"I'm very well thanks," I joke.

He shakes his head in mock despair as he gets to his feet.

"She laughed for the first time today," I tell him excitedly.

"The sweet innocence of children," he says with a sigh. He looks so sad, I have to fight the urge to hug him.

"Hopefully soon we shall all have something to laugh about," I say. "When France is finally free again."

"Hmm." Clearly the Père doesn't share my optimism, but I have to hold on to my dream of freedom for the sake of my sanity. "I was wondering," he continues, stroking Jeanne's peach-soft cheek with the tip of his finger, "have you given any thought to having Jeanne baptized?"

"Oh, but I thought . . ." I break off, embarrassed. "I'd assumed that because her father and I aren't married . . ."

"That is hardly the fault of the child."

"Or the parents," I quickly add.

"Yes, quite. Well, I would be honored to baptize her if you wish."

"Really?" My heart fills with gratitude. It feels so good to have the Père's acceptance. "Thank you."

"You will need to choose who you would like for her godparents."

The thought of Jeanne having another set of guardians in these turbulent times is certainly appealing. "I will. Thank you."

He shakes his head. "No need to thank me. In these times, it is more important than ever that she becomes a member of God's family."

I return to the store determined to deliver the leaflets. It was horrible to see the Père so doubtful about the French winning freedom. I have to do whatever I can to help make it happen, however grave the risk.

42

LAURENCE—AUGUST 1943

One thing I'd forgotten when coming up with my cunning plan was the squeaking noise the carriage's springs make as it bounces over the cobbles. The only way I can get it to be quiet is to walk painfully slowly. Thankfully, Jeanne remains completely silent, gazing up at the starry sky, clearly in awe at her first ever night-time adventure.

"It'll be all right, little one," I whisper down to her. "I've done this before and I didn't get caught." Thinking back to the night I delivered the leaflets about *Mein Kampf,* I'm again struck by how much has happened in the past three years. I never would have guessed back then that I would spend the war resisting through books. And I certainly never would have imagined that I'd become a mother!

I push the carriage down the hill to the poorer part of town not inhabited by any Germans. Each time I get to a house where I'm going to post a leaflet, I stop, pretend I'm checking on the baby and slip one out from beneath the mattress. Then I check the coast is clear before quickly pushing the leaflet beneath the door and continuing on my way. Jeanne remains "as good as gold," to quote Charles Dickens, and slowly but surely we make our way through the labyrinth of winding cobbled streets.

It's only when all the leaflets are gone and I'm pushing the carriage back up the hill that I hear the distant purr of a car's engine.

"Shit!" I curse, quickly pushing the carriage into the alleyway between the butcher's and Odette's hat shop. The engine's purr grows louder and louder and then disaster strikes. As if she can sense my fear, Jeanne starts crying.

"Hush," I whisper, quickly picking her up and holding her to my chest. But it doesn't work and her cries continue to pierce the silence. I take the Nénette doll from my pocket and offer it to her, hoping it will act as some kind of pacifier. Jeanne grabs it in her tiny fist but continues to scream.

The car sweeps past and I pray that whoever's inside has the windows closed, but in this heat that's highly unlikely. I hear the sigh of the car's brakes and the engine cuts out—making Jeanne's cries seem even louder. As I hear the sound of a car door opening, my heart almost stops beating.

There are no leaflets left in the carriage, you are just out walking to try to get your baby to stop crying, I tell myself before putting Jeanne back in the carriage and wheeling her onto the street. I see a soldier silhouetted beside the car, staring at us. Jeanne keeps crying.

"I'm so sorry, Officer," I say in a pathetically simpering voice. "I couldn't get her to stop crying, so I thought I'd take her for a walk."

He looks at me blankly, clearly unable to understand French. I mimic Jeanne crying and point to the carriage, then mime going to sleep.

"Ah," he says with a knowing nod. "Now you home," he adds in broken French.

"Yes, yes," I reply in German and hurry off toward the square, hardly daring to breathe.

Somehow, in spite of my trembling fingers, I manage to get the store door unlocked and the carriage inside. "Oh Jeanne!" I gasp as I hug her to me. "We did it!"

As if sensing my relief, she quietens down and nestles into me, and I see that she's still clutching Nénette tightly. Once again that doll has been our lucky charm.

I'm so full of adrenaline, I barely sleep at all during the couple of hours before it's time to get up. As I go down into the backyard, I think of people all over town waking to find my leaflet with its quotes against collaborators and praising the dignity of the resistance. If the Germans find out about it, will the soldier who saw me suspect that I had anything to do with it? Hopefully a flustered *maman* with a screaming baby would be such an unlikely suspect the thought wouldn't even occur to him.

As I step out into the yard, I hear Madame Bonheur clattering about in the back of the boulangerie and breathe in the delicious smell of fresh bread baking.

"Good day," I call, poking my head through the door.

"Laurence!" she cries, her face flushed from the heat and her hair streaked with flour. She hurries over and hands me a brown paper bag containing two fresh baguettes. Ever since I've had Jeanne, she's been giving me twice what she used to.

"Thank you so much. Are you sure you can still spare this much?"

She tuts and frowns at me. "Don't be ridiculous. As if I would let you and our precious angel go hungry!"

I laugh and kiss her on the cheek. "Thank you, thank you! And there's something I'd like to ask you."

"Yes?"

"Père Rambert asked me yesterday if I'd like to have Jeanne baptized."

"Oh, how wonderful," she exclaims, clasping her hands to her heart.

"And I was wondering—would you do me the honor of being Jeanne's godmother?"

"Oh Laurence." She bursts into tears. "Yes, of course! The honor would be mine."

Later that afternoon, I take Jeanne for a walk in her carriage to see Charlotte on the farm. Thankfully, there are no signs of her German "guests" when I get there. I find Charlotte in the kitchen peeling some carrots. As soon as she sees us, she makes a beeline for Jeanne, whisking her out of her carriage and cooing at her.

"Oh Laurence, this child is such a miracle. Every time I see her, she chases my fears and gloom away."

"Well, I'm very glad you feel that way because I was wondering…"

Asking Charlotte if she will be one of Jeanne's godmothers provokes an almost identical reaction to Madame Bonheur's and her eyes fill with tears. "I'm so happy," she keeps saying, over and over.

"I've asked Madame Bonheur if she will be a godmother too, and I'm going to ask Odette," I tell her. "After all, we are a book club family."

"And Jeanne is our book club baby," she murmurs, kissing both her cheeks.

"Yes," I laugh and as if joining in, Jeanne lets out a giggle.

"She laughed!" Charlotte cries and seeing her joy almost compensates for the fact that Wendell has missed this milestone. Jeanne might not have a father in her life yet, but at least she has four devoted mothers.

I set off for home with a heart full of gratitude, and a carriage full of apples and cheese hidden beneath the mattress. I've just reached the point where the dirt track to the farm meets the road into town when I see Louis, the butcher's boy, racing toward me, looking panic-stricken.

"What is it? What's wrong?" I ask.

"You have to hide, now!" he cries. "And hide the baby."

A feeling of nausea sweeps through me. "Why?"

"The Germans—they've just taken every woman and child they could find hostage."

"What? But why?"

"I don't know. They've locked them all in the church. I need to get home to warn my mother."

"Of course."

I watch him go, momentarily paralyzed with fear. Then I look down at Jeanne, gurgling away merrily in her carriage. The thought of those brutes taking her hostage turns my blood to ice. I spring into action and race back down the track to the farm.

"Charlotte, something terrible has happened!" I cry as I burst through the door.

The blood drains from her face as I tell her what Louis told me.

"But why would they take people hostage, what's happened?" she cries.

"I don't know," I reply, but an awful dread starts growing inside of me. Could it be something to do with the leaflets? I need to find out. "Can I leave Jeanne with you?"

"Where are you going?"

"I need to find out what's happened."

Charlotte looks horrified. "But what if they take you hostage too?"

"They won't," I say, far more boldly than I feel. I take Jeanne from the carriage and kiss each of her peach-soft cheeks. "Goodbye, little one, I'll see you soon." I hold her out to Charlotte and she looks so reluctant that for a moment I think she's actually going to refuse to take her. "Please," I plead.

"OK. But I'm going to take her to hide in the hay barn in the bottom field until you return."

"Thank you."

Charlotte takes the baby and I hug both of them close.

"Don't worry, I'll see you soon."

I'm not sure if it's my growing dread that I might be to blame for the hostage-taking, but all the way back to the square, it feels increasingly humid and difficult to breathe. Even if it isn't to do with my leaflets, the fact that the Germans have taken women and children hostage is a terrible development. What if Madame Bonheur and Odette are among their captives?

I go the long way round and approach the square by the narrow back street running behind my store. I climb over the wall and my heart sinks as there is no sound from the boulangerie and the back door is closed. But when I try the door, I find it unlocked, and Madame Bonheur weeping in the corner.

"You're safe!" I gasp.

"Oh Laurence, I thought they'd got you too," she exclaims, wiping her eyes. She looks behind me. "Where's Jeanne?"

"Charlotte has her, down at the farm. They're hiding in the barn at the bottom of the property."

"Oh thank God! Those bastards have half the town's children held hostage in the church. They stormed the school and took them from their classes."

"No!"

"They've taken most of the women they could find too. Oh Laurence, they have Odette."

"What?" I lean on the flour barrel to steady myself.

"They only spared me because they need me to make their bread." Madame Bonheur tuts angrily. "I'll poison their bread if they touch those poor babies!"

"Why have they done this?" I ask, my skin breaking out in a cold, clammy sweat.

"It's over some leaflet urging people to resist. A leaflet!"

If it wasn't for the flour barrel, I'm sure I would have collapsed to the floor.

"Apparently it was delivered to some houses in town last night. They're saying they'll kill the hostages if the person behind it doesn't come forward, but it could have been someone from out of town. Rumor has it, there are many Resistance members living in the forest now." She grabs my hands. "Oh Laurence, what if they don't come forward. What if they ..."

The thought of the Germans murdering children because of something I did makes me want to retch. And then I think of Jeanne. What if the Germans staying there discover her when they return to the farm? I long to confide in Madame Bonheur, to tell her what I've done, but I can't as that would mean endangering her life too. "I have to do something in the store," I say instead.

"OK, but then you must come straight back here, so I can keep you safe."

"Of course." I'm barely able to squeak the words out.

Somehow I make it into the yard and I unlock the back door. And somehow I climb the stairs to my bedroom. And somehow I pick up my Jeanne of Arc pendant from the dresser and go back downstairs. "Please, Saint Jeanne," I whisper, "fill me with your strength." I hide the pendant beneath the floorboard in the poetry nook, take a deep breath and walk over to the door.

43

JEANNE—1993

As Jeanne watched Wendell read the letter, his face visibly paled and his brow furrowed. She hoped she'd done the right thing by showing it to him. She hoped it wouldn't upset him and that he, like her, would find comfort in the love woven through Laurence's words. Finally he finished and put the faded paper down on the restaurant table.

"God dammit," he muttered wiping his eyes.

"Oh, Pops, I'm sorry, I didn't mean to upset you."

"I should have taken her with me," he cried, his raised voice causing the diners at the next table to look over. "That night in the clearing when she told me she was pregnant, I should have made her get on the plane with me." He banged his hand on the table, causing the cutlery to jump. "It's my fault she died."

"No!" Jeanne exclaimed. "You weren't to know, and besides, how do you know she would have come with you? From everything I've heard about Laurence, she doesn't sound like the kind of person who would have deserted her friends in the Resistance while the war was still on."

"Maybe you're right." He sighed. "That's why I always held out hope all these years—even though deep down I knew she had to be dead. I just didn't want to face up to the fact that I left her here."

"You didn't leave her. You promised to come back for her. You read the letter, you're not responsible for her death, you gave her hope to cling to." She reached across the table and took hold of his hands. "I love you, Pops."

"Aw, shucks, what are you trying to do to me?" he joked as his eyes filled with fresh tears. "I love you too, very much."

Jeanne took his copy of *For Whom the Bell Tolls* from her bag and passed it to him. "I also found some underlined sections in her copy of the Hemingway book. I've underlined them in your copy so you can read them. I think she highlighted them because they made her think of you."

He smiled at her and shook his head. "See, I told you you were a great detective."

"Yeah well, there's one more mystery I still need to solve." Jeanne took a sip of her coffee.

"What's that?"

"How she died. I think we both need to know, if we're ever going to get any closure."

He nodded apprehensively. "I guess so."

As Yitzhak pulled up outside the retirement home, he turned to Jeanne, his expression grim. "Are you sure you want to do this?"

Jeanne stared at him intently. "Do you know something you're not telling me?"

"Not exactly."

"What's that supposed to mean?"

"Nothing," he said quickly, opening the car door.

As Jeanne got out of the car, her senses were on high alert. He did know something, she was sure of it. She just had to hope that the priest was more awake this time and willing to talk.

When they got into the reception, she let Yitzhak do the talking and was relieved to see the woman behind the desk nod yes.

This time she led them along a corridor lined with rooms. Most of the doors were open and Jeanne could see the elderly occupants inside, some of them in bed, some of them sitting up in armchairs. The woman took them to a room at the end of the corridor with the door closed. She knocked and Jeanne heard a man calling, "*Oui?*" from inside. They went in and Jeanne saw Père Rambert sitting in a chair by the window reading a book, a vase of wild flowers on the table beside him. He looked a lot sprightlier than he had done on their previous visit and as soon as he saw Jeanne, his face lit up and he started to speak.

"He says he thought he might have dreamed you before," Yitzhak explained.

Jeanne laughed and shook her head and the priest gestured at them to come join him. He was much more alert than the other day, but would he want to answer Jeanne's questions? She sat on a chair beside his and he smiled and shook his head and said something.

"He cannot get over how much you look like your mother," Yitzhak translated.

Jeanne took a breath and gently placed her hand on top of the priest's. "Please will you tell him that I need to know what happened to my mother? I need to know how she died. And why the Nazis wanted to kill me."

Jeanne kept her gaze on Père Rambert as Yitzhak began talking to him in French. The smile faded from the old man's face, but, to her relief, he nodded and began to speak.

44

LAURENCE—AUGUST 1943

"Attention!" a German voice barks through a megaphone as I step outside into the square. Banks of gray cloud have massed overhead, trapping the cloying heat to the ground like an iron lid.

I stand in the doorway of the store and look at the soldier with the megaphone standing on the steps in front of the church.

"Last night, this leaflet was distributed to houses around the town," he continues, holding up a piece of paper. "Unless the author of this leaflet comes forward before midnight tonight, we shall be forced to begin taking reprisals," the soldier says, with a coldness that makes me long for the days when Gerhard translated their hate-filled missives.

You won't be forced *to take reprisals,* I want to yell. *You won't be* forced *to kill women and children, you will choose to, you bastards!* There's a sudden movement by the entrance of the church and more soldiers appear, bundling a group of startled-looking children outside. A group of women follow behind. I see Odette instantly. And then, to my surprise, I see Gigi. So the Nazis are even prepared to sacrifice one of their collaborators. I wonder what she thinks of our conquerors now.

"Midnight tonight," the soldier repeats. "Or we will start killing hostages."

One of the little girls starts to cry and I realize that it's Violeta's niece, Claudette. I put my hand in my pocket and wrap my fingers around Maman's Nénette doll and somehow I take a step forward. And another. And another. It's as if my body is being controlled by a force outside of me, like a puppet on a string.

"Laurence!" I hear Madame Bonheur hiss from behind me.

The chatter from the onlookers fades and a silence as thick as the humidity gathers as all eyes turn to me.

As I approach the church, two of the soldiers reach for their revolvers. I think of Jeanne of Arc, leading her men into battle against the English, and I keep walking, my grip on Maman's doll tightening.

"Let them go," I say, my voice quivering.

"Halt!" the soldier with the megaphone yells.

I keep walking. *I am not afraid, I was born to do this.*

"Let them go," I say again.

"Laurence, no." I hear Père Rambert's voice and I look up to see him standing behind the hostages at the entrance of the church.

I am not afraid. I was born to do this.

"I am the one you're looking for," I say and gasps ripple around the square. "I am the one who wrote and distributed the leaflet."

There's a moment's stunned silence, then suddenly a flash of murky green gray uniforms and soldiers appear either side of me, grabbing my arms.

"You?" the soldier with the megaphone says, looking me up and down scornfully.

"Yes." I think of Jeanne hiding with Charlotte at the farm

and my heart splinters at the thought of what is likely to happen next. But then I think of the mothers of all the children taken hostage. " 'All of man's dignity lies in resisting with all of his heart and all of his mind,' " I shout, quoting one of the sentences from *The Black Notebook* I'd used in the leaflet.

Something cracks against the side of my face, sending me flying to the ground and horrified gasps ripple around the square.

"Take her to be questioned," the soldier with the megaphone barks.

"Release the hostages," I call in spite of my aching mouth as the soldiers bundle me toward the town hall. As we go past the church, my gaze locks with Odette's. "Release them!" I cry again, and again I receive a blow to my head. By the time we reach the steps of the town hall, I'm barely conscious.

I'm bundled to a small room in the basement of the town hall, which I'm guessing used to be a storage cupboard. The room is bare apart from two chairs. I sit on one and hold my aching head, praying that the hostages have been released. What if the Germans go back on their word and kill us all? What if they kill Jeanne? To stop myself thinking such terrifying thoughts, I start reciting some of my favorite quotes over and over in my head and one by one I feel my favorite authors, Flaubert, Éluard, Hemingway, Hughes, Steinbeck, gathering around me like a protective shield. *Just like Jeanne of Arc's shield*, I think semi-deliriously. As Rilke appears and I try to let everything happen to me—even imminent interrogation by the Nazis—I once more feel connected to Luc. This is how he must have felt when he sought solace in the poem. "Beauty and terror, beauty and terror," I chant under my breath. And then finally, the door opens and a soldier walks in. To my surprise, I see that it is the same soldier from last night, the one who caught me out with Jeanne.

"Again hello," he says in broken French.

I nod and look down into my lap.

Another soldier comes in behind him and stands by the door.

The first soldier says something in German and the soldier by the door translates.

"So, you are claiming responsibility for this?" He waves one of the leaflets at me.

"Yes," I mutter.

"And who else were you working with?"

"Nobody. I made them and distributed them by myself."

I'm going to die; the enormity of the situation hits me, while the soldier in front of me says something in German. *I'm never going to see Jeanne again, or Wendell. They're going to kill me. I am not afraid . . . Let everything . . . beauty and terror . . . terror . . . I was . . . I was born to do this . . .*

"So while you were out walking your baby last night you were delivering the leaflets?" the other soldier translates.

At the mention of Jeanne, my heart skips a beat. "Yes," I mutter, looking down.

There's a sudden movement and the soldier slaps me across the face so hard I fall off the chair.

I am not afraid . . .

"So where is your daughter now?" the soldier by the door asks.

"I don't know," I reply, the metallic taste of blood filling my mouth.

He translates my words and the other soldier kicks me in the stomach.

As my body jolts from the force of his kicks, my vision starts fading in and out.

Finally he stops and starts barking more questions, which come echoing down at me in French.

"Who are you working with?"

"Who else here is in the Resistance?"

"Who has your child?"

As I lie on the floor in a fetal position, I think of the end of *The Moon is Down* by John Steinbeck, when the mayor has been taken hostage and is about to be shot. I think of how his death inspired other people in town to join the Resistance—other sparks, all joining together to form a flame. And I try to imagine that the burning pain now consuming my body is part of the fire that will one day free France.

After what feels like forever, they leave, slamming and locking the door behind them. I huddle in the corner on the floor and hug my knees to me. My eyes are so swollen I can barely see.

"Oh Jeanne, what have I done? Oh my darling daughter, I'm so sorry," I sob.

She'll be all right, I try to convince myself. *Madame Bonheur knows where she's hiding. She will go to Charlotte and make sure that she's safe. Please, please, please let it be so.*

I take Maman's doll from my pocket and hold her to my heart.

After an indeterminate amount of time, I hear footsteps in the corridor outside and my stomach clenches. *What if they've found Jeanne? What if they threaten to kill her in front of me?* The door flies open and the light comes on, causing me to shield my eyes.

"Oh, Laurence!" At the sound of Père Rambert's voice, I almost pass out from relief. "What have they done to you?"

I blink up at him through swollen eyes and see a different solider standing behind him in the doorway.

"Did they . . . Are the hostages free?" I rasp, my mouth so dry I can barely speak.

"Yes," the Père replies before turning to the solider. "Can you get her some water, please?"

To my surprise, the soldier nods and leaves. I hear the click of the key turning in the lock behind him.

The Père pulls me up and into his arms. "Jeanne is safe," he whispers in my ear. "But they are saying they will kill you if she isn't handed over to them."

My legs buckle, but he holds me up.

"But surely they're going to kill me anyway?"

"I think they want to use her to get you to denounce your fellow members of the Resistance."

"Never!" I gasp. "You must keep her safe, and please"—I look up at him with tear-filled eyes—"get her to her father."

"He is the pilot?" Trust the Père to have known all along.

"Yes," I whisper. "He's an American stationed in Britain and his name is Wendell. He knows about her." The thought that the Père might somehow be able to get Jeanne to Wendell is almost too much to hope for. Then I think of my beloved store. "The Book Dispensary—I want Jeanne to have it. The deeds are in a tin in the kitchen pantry. Madame Bonheur has a spare key to the back door."

"Don't worry, I will do everything I can," he whispers back.

The door opens and the solider comes in, holding a tin cup.

The Père picks up one of the chairs and sits me on it before taking the cup and holding it to my lips. "I am here to pray for you," he says loudly and I realize that he must be talking for the benefit of the soldier.

"When are they planning to kill me?" I whisper, as he feeds me some more water.

"Tomorrow at dawn."

It is the strangest sensation, being told that your life is about to end, just like a book. "Jeanne," I sob.

The Père places one of his strong hands upon my shoulder. "Jesus is with you," he says before starting to pray. I think of all the times I've heard him pray during my life, all of the times I'd been impatient for it to end, so that I could get back to whatever adventure I'd been having or planning, but now I will every one of his words to stretch like elastic, on and on forever. But after a while the soldier comes over and mutters something to him.

"I have to go now," the Père says. "But I will be here for you—in the morning."

I nod. In spite of the water, my mouth is suddenly too dry to speak.

The Père crouches down beside me. "Remember what I told you before," he whispers in my ear. "Don't let them get in here." He gently touches the side of my head.

Then they are gone and I am left in the dark with nothing but my thoughts.

Somehow, in spite of my terror, the Père's words have a calming effect upon me and I spend the night trying to block the Germans from my mind by turning it into a movie screen on which to watch memory after memory of all the people who have meant the very most to me. I picture Michel and I talking about books on the bank of the Seine. I picture Madame Bonheur calling me the sugar snatcher when she'd catch me with my hand in the barrel as a child. I picture Luc and Genevieve and I running through the forest, the sun on our skin and the wind in our hair, back in the days when battles were something we did for fun. I relive the night Luc gave me the Jeanne of Arc pendant and I think of that pendant in its hiding place beneath the floorboard. I pray that when the war is over Wendell comes back to the store and he remembers my hiding place. This thought is too painful, so I conjure the memory of Charlotte, Odette, Madame Bonheur, Raul and I all chanting the poem "Liberty" together in the forest. Then I see Wendell dropping copies of the poem from his plane like confetti.

Tears stream down my face. Was it all for nothing? What if France is never free?

Éluard's words come back to me, like the soundtrack to my mind's movie. *Liberty. Liberty. Liberty.*

Deep in the middle of the night, my breasts start aching as they fill with milk for Jeanne. *Who will feed her now? Will she starve?*

Stop it, don't think such things. The Père said she is safe. He said he will do everything to get her to Wendell. Maybe Wendell will come and rescue her. Maybe the Resistance will arrange something. I picture the Père taking Jeanne deep into the forest and Wendell landing his plane in the clearing, and the Père handing him our tiny miracle. *Please, please, please, God, make it happen.* As I hug my arms around myself, I feel damp patches on my dress where my milk has leaked. *Oh Jeanne, I'm so sorry.*

And then finally I hear footsteps outside and the door is unlocked. Two soldiers march in and pull me up. The enormity of what is about to happen almost floors me, but, once again, the Père's words of wisdom save me. And I realize that this is my last chance to do something for France, for the Resistance, for my dignity, as the mystery writer Forez urged in his essay. And so, in spite of my pain, I force myself to stand tall, head high and walk unaided toward my destiny.

Outside, the clouds from yesterday have finally cleared and the sky is streaked with the most incredible shades of pink, violet and amber. *Feel the beauty as well as the terror,* I hear Rilke urging me. *Find the poetry in every particle,* Flaubert joins in.

As we walk out onto the steps of the town hall, one of the soldiers offers me a sack to put over my head.

"No!" I say firmly. I want those cowards to have to look at my face when they murder me. *I am not afraid. I was born to do this.*

I see the Père, waiting in his robes at the bottom of the steps, his Bible in his hands. And beyond him, I see more people gathered in the square, standing in total silence. The only sound is that of the birds singing their dawn chorus, and again I hear Rilke urging me to drink in the beauty.

As I reach the bottom of the steps, I smell something smoldering.

"Laurence," the Père greets me solemnly, his face ashen and his jaw shaded with stubble.

"Père," I say, my voice breaking.

He takes my arm and one of the soldiers protests.

"Let me walk her," he booms and, to my surprise, the soldiers back off slightly.

As we start making our way to the memorial, the people who have gathered in the square part, forming an aisle for us to walk along. I glance up and see Leon the blacksmith mouthing something at me. The next person does the same and the next and the next. It's only when I'm halfway to the memorial that I realize they are all silently mouthing the word "liberty." Tears fill my eyes as once more I'm somehow able to find the beauty as well as the terror. Could my death be like the mayor's death in *The Moon is Down*? Will it ignite sparks of resistance in my fellow townsfolk that will turn into a flame?

And then I see Violeta, clutching a white handkerchief. But the word she mouths to me isn't "liberty," it's "sorry." I nod in acceptance of her apology and then, at the end of the aisle, at the foot of the memorial, I see Madame Bonheur, Odette and Charlotte. The sight of them almost causes my spirit to break, but I see the way they are gazing at me, so steadfast, the same way I urged Charlotte to look at Raul the day he was killed, and I meet their gaze and I choose to smile. I choose to love them instead of fear death.

Then a soldier shoves the Père to one side, and they bundle me up the memorial steps. One of the soldiers offers me a chair to sit on, but I shake my head and force myself to stand tall.

I look out across the square to my store and I see a smoldering pile on the pavement outside. So that's where the smell was coming from. The Germans have burned my books.

A sudden breeze whips through the square, sending sparks from the pile flying into the air. I imagine that every spark is the soul of a book and I realize that no matter how many books they burn or people they kill, the Nazis will never win. Because they will never be able to kill the spirit of the free. We will keep on loving and writing and imagining a better world and they can never stop us. Just as the mayor says in *The Moon is Down,* the herd men cannot kill the mayor because the mayor is a concept thought up by the free, and it will live on, long after he's been shot. Just as all of my book prescriptions will live on in the hearts and minds of the readers I've given them to. Just as Robert Jordan in *For Whom the Bell Tolls* lived on in Maria. Just as I will live on, in Wendell and in our daughter. She is my hope now. I picture my bright yellow canary taking flight from my soul and soaring through the sky until it finds a new home in hers.

As the soldiers form a line in front of me and cock their rifles, I stand straight and, with all of my might, and all of my heart, and all of my love, I shout the word, "Liberty!"

EPILOGUE

JEANNE—1993

Jeanne gazed around the store at the books lining the shelves. Sourcing books from the 1930s and 40s and before had been a labor of love, involving many trips to Paris, but slowly and surely, and with Charlotte and Claudette's guidance, she'd filled the store. She'd also managed to find an identical typewriter to the one belonging to Laurence, which now had pride of place on the desk. On the wall above the fireplace there was a framed copy of one of Laurence's famous literary prescriptions—a poem called "Hope" by Emily Dickinson that Laurence had prescribed for the woman who'd owned the bakery next door, a woman named Madame Bonheur. Charlotte had found the poem in Madame Bonheur's belongings after she died and kept it as a memento of their time together during the war. She'd given it to Jeanne as a keepsake from the woman who helped bring her into the world—apparently Madame Bonheur had been Laurence's impromptu midwife when she'd gone into labor early. Jeanne felt a strange fluttering in her chest whenever she looked at it. The poem was pretty awesome too—so comforting. She'd had the idea of turning the store into a living memorial to the French Resistance one night when she and

Yitzhak shared a bottle of wine in the café and he told her about the time he'd visited Anne Frank's house in Amsterdam and the profound effect it had had upon him. Having learned the truth about her mother's death from Père Rambert and the full extent of her bravery, Jeanne had felt compelled to do something to memorialize her. Laurence had saved over a hundred lives the day she gave herself up to free the hostages, and the fact that she'd refused to give up Jeanne too made it all the more poignant.

Once Jeanne had told Claudette that she'd found out how her mother had died, the truth came spilling out of her. She told her how terrified she'd been being kept prisoner in the church with the other children and women. How certain she'd been that she was going to die. And how she'd never forget the sight of Laurence walking across the square, demanding that the soldiers release them.

Although it had been deeply distressing to learn the truth about her mother's death, it had also filled Jeanne with pride. And it had completely obliterated the self-pity she'd been feeling about her enforced retirement and the dread at her fiftieth birthday. She owed it to Laurence to live the rest of her life to the fullest.

The door of the store opened, causing the bell above it to jingle, and Yitzhak came in, holding a takeout cup.

"I thought you might be in need of some fuel," he joked.

"Ah, you know me so well." Jeanne took the cup eagerly. Over the past few months, Yitzhak had helped her refurbish the store, repainting the walls and restoring the floorboards and installing a wood-burning stove in the fireplace. As they'd worked long into the nights together, they'd developed a deepening friendship, rooted in their shared past.

"Are you ready to get the VIP from the airport?" Yitzhak asked with a grin.

"I sure am." Whilst Jeanne had remained in France, Wendell

had returned to the States a few months ago, but he and Danny were flying back for the official store opening, which was taking place that weekend. And Wendell wasn't the only VIP who would be in attendance; Charlotte and her cousin Odette, Père Rambert and Claudette would be there too. Jeanne had also managed to press an invitation into Gigi's hands the last time she'd come to place flowers outside the store. Gigi had scuttled off without saying a word but Jeanne really hoped she'd come; she had a feeling it might help heal some old wounds, and not just Gigi's.

As Jeanne followed Yitzhak outside, she wondered if there'd ever come a time when she wouldn't feel a chill when she looked at the memorial, thinking of how her mom had been killed. But as Yitzhak had said to her so many times before, they owed it to Laurence and Abram to remember what happened to them, however painful it might be, for the sake of love and the sake of liberty.

Jeanne took a step back and looked up at the freshly painted storefront. She'd thought long and hard before changing the name of the store, but she knew she would never be able to dispense books in the same way her mother had; she wasn't nearly as well read. She hoped Laurence would approve of the new name, though. She smiled up at the blue, white and red letters shining in the sun. *La Librairie Liberté.* The Liberty Book Store.

A LETTER FROM SIOBHAN

Dear Reader,

Thank you so much for choosing to read *The Paris Network*. If you enjoyed it, and want to keep up to date with all my latest releases, just sign up at the following link. Your email address will never be shared and you can unsubscribe at any time.

siobhancurham.com

When I first began work on this novel, I wanted to write about a character who owned a bookstore that was used as a "letterbox" by the French Resistance during the war. I'd first come across bookstores being used as letterboxes when I was researching for my first Second World War novel, *An American in Paris*. As a lover of books and bookstores, the idea that they could be used to pass secret messages of vital importance during a war intrigued me. But as soon as I started my research for *The Paris Network,* I disappeared down a rabbit hole and was amazed to discover just what an important role books had played in the war. I knew that the Nazis had banned and even burned certain books, but I had no idea that an underground publishing industry had been set up in response in France during the German occupation. As someone who's worked in the book industry, both as an author and an editor for the past twenty years, the notion that the act of writing, publishing or even reading a book could carry a potential death sentence sent shivers down my spine. I'm also a huge fan of book clubs—not least because so many book clubs have embraced my historical fiction over the past year!—so I was intrigued by the concept of a book club that had to meet in utmost secret because the titles on their reading list were punishable by death.

And so *The Paris Network* was born—a celebration of the power of the written word and the bravery of all those who fight for freedom. Although the town where it is set is fictional, everything that happens in the story is rooted in historical fact. As always, I've tried to weave the most fascinating facts I uncovered into the plot—such as Hitler banning an unabridged version of *Mein Kampf* in France, the fire on Wendell's plane and the air force dropping poems as well as bombs! Writing this novel and having to get beneath the skin of the people who were courageous enough to risk everything for the written word and liberty made my passion for books run even deeper than before. I hope that reading it does the same for you.

Siobhan

siobhancurham.com

 facebook.com/Siobhan-Curham-Author

twitter.com/SiobhanCurham

instagram.com/SiobhanCurhamAuthor

THE RESISTANCE BOOK CLUB
READING LIST

"Go to the Limits of Your Longing" (poem)—Rainer Maria Rilke

"Farewell" (poem)—Anne Brontë

"Hope" (poem)—Emily Dickinson

All Quiet on the Western Front (novel)—Erich Maria Remarque

Souvenirs sur l'affaire—Léon Blum

Saint Joan (play)—George Bernard Shaw

For Whom the Bell Tolls (novel)—Ernest Hemingway

"Invictus" (poem)—William Ernest Henley

*The Silence of the Sea** (novel)—Vercors (the pseudonym for French writer Jean Bruller)

*Poetry and Truth** (poetry collection)—Paul Éluard

"Liberté"* (poem)—Paul Éluard

*The Moon is Down** (novel)—John Steinbeck

*The Black Notebook** (essay)—Forez (the pseudonym for French writer François Mauriac)

*These titles were published secretly and at great risk by the underground publisher Les Editions de Minuit, founded by the French writers Jean Bruller and Pierre de Lescure as a way of getting around Nazi censorship. Copies were printed covertly on mimeographs in people's homes or cellars and they were distributed from person to person. Printing them was punishable by death and the proceeds from the French edition of *The Moon is Down* by John Steinbeck went to the families of the brave printers who were captured and killed by the Nazis.

READING GROUP GUIDE

Discussion Questions

1. If you were living in France during the Second World War, do you think you would have been brave enough to meet as a Resistance book club, reading titles that were banned? Why or why not?

2. Were you surprised by any of the books that were banned by the Nazis? Have you read any of the banned books featured in *The Paris Network?* Has the novel encouraged you to read any of the banned books or poems?

3. Laurence often uses poems as her prescriptions to make her customers feel better. If you had to prescribe a poem to someone who was struggling in some way, what would it be? How do you think it would help?

4. Do you think it's ever right to ban a book? If so, under what circumstances?

5. Although *The Paris Network* is a work of fiction, the things that happen in the plot were rooted in historical fact. Were

there any historical details in the novel that surprised you? What were they and why?

6. What did you think of the 1993 storyline? Do you like historical novels that feature a more modern-day storyline or would you prefer the story to remain in the historic time period? How do you think the two timelines change the reading experience?

7. Do you think Wendell is right to blame himself for what happens to Laurence? Do you think she would have left with him if he'd asked her the last time they saw each other in the forest?

8. Although Jeanne never met Laurence, she was still able to learn/gain a lot from her. What would you say was the most important gift Laurence gave to her daughter?

9. Like many veterans of World War II Wendell never talked about his experiences in the air force until Lorilee died, almost fifty years after the war ended. Was he right to bury it all and not tell Jeanne the truth about her mother?

10. Do you think Laurence was right to risk distributing the leaflet at the end of the book, given that she was now a mother? Why or why not?

11. Has reading *The Paris Network* made you see books and their importance in a different light? If so, how?

Author Q&A

Q: What made you decide to center the novel around a bookstore?

A: When I first began work on *The Paris Network*, I wanted to write about a character who owned a bookstore that was used as a "letterbox" by the French Resistance during the war. I'd first come across bookstores being used as letterboxes when I was researching for my first World War II novel, *An American in Paris*. As a lover of books and bookstores, the idea that they could be used to pass secret messages of vital importance during a war intrigued me.

Q: Were there any surprises in writing this novel?

A: As soon as I started my research for *The Paris Network* I was amazed to discover just what an important role books had played in the war. I knew that the Nazis had banned and even burned certain books, but I had no idea that an underground publishing industry had been set up in France in response during the German occupation. As someone who's worked in the book industry, both as an author and an editor for the past twenty years, the notion that the act of writing, publishing, or even reading a book could carry a potential death sentence sent shivers down my spine. I'm also a huge fan of book clubs—so I was intrigued by the concept of a book club that had to meet in utmost secret because the titles on their reading list were punishable by death.

Q: Why did you decide to have two storylines?

A: I think having a more modern-day storyline can work well as a device in a World War II novel as a way of uncovering the historical storyline. But in *The Paris Network* I wanted to explore the way in which so many war veterans, like Wendell, never talked about their experiences. The notion of these unsung heroes returning to their normal lives whilst carrying their trauma inside of them saddened me, and I wanted to give Wendell and his daughter Jeanne an opportunity for healing and closure.

Q: How much of the novel is fictional and how much is rooted in fact?

A: Although the town where *The Paris Network* is set is fictional, everything that happens in the story is rooted in historical fact. As always, I've tried to weave the most fascinating facts I uncovered into the plot—such as Hitler banning an unabridged version of *Mein Kampf* in France, the fire on Wendell's plane, and the air force dropping poems instead of bombs! Writing this novel and having to get beneath the skin of the people who were courageous enough to risk everything for the written word and liberty made my passion for books run even deeper than before.

Creative Acts of Resistance

Did you know that during World War II the British Royal Air Force dropped poems on Occupied France as well as bombs? I had no idea that this had happened until I started my research for *The Paris Network*. Up until then I was familiar with the more traditional acts of resistance that went on during the war—things like blowing up railway lines, sending coded messages, and spying on the Germans—but in writing *The Paris Network* I uncovered some amazingly creative acts of resistance.

The Royal Air Force dropped tens of thousands of copies of the poem "Liberté" by the French poet Paul Éluard all over France in order to strengthen the French spirit of resistance. In the poem Éluard imagines writing the word "liberty" in many different places, and it's a powerful rallying call for freedom. I loved the idea of a poem being used in this way and really enjoyed imagining what it must have felt like to see poems raining down from the sky for *The Paris Network*.

I was also blown away by the discovery that writers like John Steinbeck wrote novels during the war to encourage people to resist. Steinbeck's novel *The Moon Is Down* is about the occupation of a small (unnamed) town in Europe, and it looks at the effects on both the occupied population and the occupying forces. Foreign editions of the novel were published secretly in many occupied countries across Europe during the war, including France, Norway, Holland, Italy, and Sweden.

I was really moved by the book's ending when the town's

mayor refuses to stop his fellow townspeople from taking part in acts of resistance, even though he knows this will lead to his execution. He realizes that although *he* can be killed, the concept of having a mayor, and the freedom and democracy that represents, can never die. As I read those words, I imagined people across occupied Europe being inspired to perform similar acts of courage and resistance, and it sent a shiver down my spine.

Steinbeck's novel was published in France by the clandestine publishing house Les Éditions de Minuit, which was created with the sole purpose of producing literature that would support the Resistance. Every book they published in secret contained the following statement on the second page: "*In France there are writers who refuse to take orders.*"

One of the most well-known books to be published by Les Éditions de Minuit was *Le Silence de la Mer* (*The Silence of the Sea*), which was written by the French writer Jean Bruller under the pen name Vercors. The novel tells the story of a French man and his niece who are made to house a German officer during the occupation and resist simply by refusing to speak to him. I loved this idea because it showed ordinary French people that there's always something you can do to fight back, however small or inconsequential it might seem.

Another simple yet powerful creative act of resistance I discovered during my research was defacing German posters. I was particularly impressed with the creativity the Resistance demonstrated with the German no smoking signs, which read: RAUCHEN VERBOTEN! The Resistance realized that by simply striking out some of the letters, the poster could be changed to say RACE VERTE! meaning "the green race"—mocking the Germans for their obsession with race *and* their muddy-green color of their uniforms.

I always try to throw a spotlight on lesser-known historical facts in my World War II novels, so it was a real thrill to be able to share these creative acts of resistance with readers of *The Paris Network*.

ACKNOWLEDGMENTS

HUGE thanks to my lovely new editor at Bookouture, Kelsie Marsden, for your invaluable insights and advice. It was a joy to work with you on this book. And it's a joy to work with the whole team at Bookouture, I'm so grateful to be part of such a dynamic and supportive publishing family. Special thanks to Sarah Hardy, Kim Nash, Noelle Holten, Ruth Tross, Alex Crow, Alex Holmes and Alba Proko, to name but a few. Much love and thanks as always to Jane Willis at United Agents for everything you do to support me in my writing career. I'm also hugely indebted to all of the people who took the time to review my first two historical novels, *An American in Paris* and *Beyond This Broken Sky* on their blogs, Goodreads, NetGalley and Amazon. Reviews and recommendations make such a positive difference; I'm so grateful for your support and everything you do to help the book industry thrive.

I'm also hugely grateful to the following people for being so supportive of me and my writing. First and foremost, to my dad, Michael Curham—if you hadn't threatened to break both my legs if I didn't follow my writing dream, none of this would have happened! I'm eternally grateful for your support, not to mention your slightly menacing sense of humor. Huge thanks also to my mum, Anne Cumming, for instilling a love of reading into me at a very early age. I hope you enjoy this tribute to the power of the written word! Thanks to my lovely sisters, Alice and Bea, my brilliant brother, Luke, and brother-in-law, Dan, my niece and fellow writer, Katie Bird, nephew extraordinaire,

John, and of course, my wonderful son, Jack, and Maria. Sending shedloads of gratitude to my American family across the pond—Sam Delaney, Charles Delaney, Lacey Jennen, Gina and David Ervin, Amy Fawcett, Carolyn Miller and Lauren Hardin, to name but a few—thank you so much for all of your cheerleading for my books, I really appreciate it.

And MASSIVE thanks to the following people for all of your love and support: Kayhan Etebar, Tina McKenzie, Sara Starbuck, Linda Lloyd, Sammie and Edi Venn, Pearl Bates, Stuart Berry, Charlotte Baldwin, Steve O'Toole, Lexie Bebbington, Marie Hermet, Mara Bergman, Thea Bennett, Suzanne Burgess, Jennie Gould and Sass Pankhurst. Big love to Lara, Lesley and John Strick, Pete Barber, "Captain" Iain Scarlett, Anita DV, Gill July, Gillian Davies, Claire Gee-Gee, Linda Newman, Graham Stewart, Shirley Smith and the rest of the Nower Hill Facebook crew. Huge thanks also to the following wonderful writers I'm lucky enough to know: Nathan Parker, Abe Gibson, Stephanie Lam, Victoria Connelly, Michelle Porter, Liz Brooks, Miriam Thundercliffe, Dave Moonwood, Rachel Swabey, Jim Clammer, Ade Bott, Meriel Rose, Jan Silverman, Patricia Jacobs, Mike Davidson, Mavis Pachter, Phil Lawder, Gabriela Harding, Barbara Towell, Mike Deller, Pete "Esso" Haynes, Lorna Read and Louise George. And thank you to all of the members of my Writing Adventure community on Facebook—here's to more great writing adventures to come!